THE PRIVATEER

By the same author in PAN Books

MISS PYM DISPOSES
BRAT FARRAR
THE SINGING SANDS
TO LOVE AND BE WISE
A SHILLING FOR CANDLES
THE MAN IN THE QUEUE

THE PRIVATEER

JOSEPHINE TEY

UNABRIDGED

PAN BOOKS LTD : LONDON

First published 1952 by Peter Davies Ltd.
This edition published 1967 by Pan Books Ltd.,
33 Tothill Street, London, S.W.1

2nd Printing 1967

PRINTED AND BOUND IN ENGLAND BY
HAZELL WATSON AND VINEY LTD
AYLESBURY, BUCKS

1

BELOW THE VERANDA in the noon sunlight stood a cluster of slaves and bond-servants, bright and noisy as macaws.

In other climes light is a negative thing: a mere absence of darkness. But in the islands when the fronds of the palm-trees move in the wind the light runs in and out among them like a live thing. So now when the restless island wind played with the kerchiefs and the petticoats the light, too, danced and ran, and the crowd moved continuously, like a field of flowers in the sun.

Only one among them did not move: the young man with the black hair who was leaning against the jacaranda tree. He looked equable but absent-minded.

A house-slave staggered on to the veranda carrying the estate-book. They greeted him with jests and laughter, and he stuck his tongue out at them. He put the book down on the table and fled from their mockery. Then the factor came, and waited by the table, and some of the chatter and shrieking died away. Their interest narrowed on the book. They all knew the book. Indeed, to some of them it represented all the identity they had ever had. And today the book was of acute importance.

Then their master walked on to the veranda, and the crowd hushed to stillness in the dancing wind and the light. After him came his son, to stand behind his father's shoulder.

The factor sat down at the table and opened the book, and the tired, middle-aged man stepped forward a little so that they might see him the better, and began to speak to them.

They listened to him, but only with their ears. They knew already all what he had to say. The drought. The blighted canes. The lack of work for them. The lack of food. The lack of money to buy any, to keep them alive until next season. They knew it already. They had lived with the drought and alongside the dead canes and the blasted cocoa trees. They had come there this morning to be given their freedom. That was all that interested them.

There was a written paper for each of them, he said, that would show to all that they were free men and not runaways, and they must keep the paper and show it to any who asked.

Then the factor called the first name.

'John Alison.'

A Negro capered like a figure on the end of a string.

'Field hand. Slave.'

'You may go,' said his master, and the black took the magic piece of paper from the factor and bounded laughing back to the throng.

'Michael Duchesne.'

The Frenchman came forward; a small, gnarled man.

'Field hand. Bondsman. Engaged for seven years; has served five.'

'You may go.'

'Ah Ling.'

The Chinese bowed.

'Field hand. Slave.'

'You may go.'

'Elias Brown.'

The mulatto came smiling.

'Field hand. Slave.'

'You may go.'

'Maria Perez.'

The Indian half-breed swung her full skirts in a curtsey.

'Sorter. Slave.'

'You may go.'

'William Chapman.'

The huge jailbird shouldered his way out of the crowd.

'Field hand. Slave.'

'You may go.'

'Candlemas.'

The Indian came doubtfully.

'Field hand. Slave.'

'You may go.'

'Henry Morgan.'

The young man detached himself from the tree.

'Field hand. Of late, clerk in the estate office. Bondsman. Engaged for four years and has served two.'

'You may go.'

The young man took his discharge and was turning away when the youth came from behind his father and said: 'Wait! It was you who caught my pony the day he bolted. Wasn't it?'

'That was I.'

'Here!' said the youth, and flung a coin. It was a gold coin, and it lay in the dust while the young man eyed it. And everyone else eyed the young man.

'Does a Welshman refuse good money?' asked the youth.

'No. But a Morgan cannot pick it up.'

'It seems to be deadlock.'

'Not quite. You could make it a loan.'

'Very well,' said the youth, amused. 'A loan it is.'

'Pick it up,' said the young man to the slave who was standing nearest; and the slave did meekly as he was bid and handed over the coin.

The young man bowed to his benefactor. 'At the usual rate of interest, sir,' he said, and turned away.

'Jan Martin,' summoned the factor.

But the young man did not wait to see. He went back to his tree, picked up the bundle that was lying there ready, and walked away without a backward glance.

'Harr-ee!' cried a girl, breaking from the press and running after him. 'Harr-ee!'

She came to the edge of the terrace as he came level with her on the path below.

'Good-bye, Chloe,' he said, without stopping.

'But, Harr-ee! You are not going now this minute, are you? You staying for the festa, for the dance, for the celebration? Surely! You are not going before tonight!'

But he went steadily away.

'Harr-ee!'

'Good-bye,' he called, without turning his head.

She stood on the terrace pouting, and watched him grow small down the long avenue to the lane.

When she could no longer see him she went back to her fellows.

And Henry Morgan walked away into the landscape with a bundle of clothes, and a gold coin, and his freedom.

He knew better what to do with the coin than what to do with his freedom. Having had more intimate acquaintance with the estate's finances than is the lot of most servants, he had known weeks ago that this must come, and he had lain awake of nights on his bed on the office floor pondering his future.

That he slept in peace in the office quiet, and not among the snores, stenches, and quarrelling in the bunkhouse was typical of Henry Morgan. When he had first asked the factor's permission to spread his pallet there of nights, the factor had said tartly that his office was neither a hospital nor a flop-house. Henry accepted the prohibition with the proper disappointment and began to make mistakes in his arithmetic. He continued to make mistakes in his arithmetic, and when the maddened factor asked what had come over that alert and accurate brain of his, he had explained that sleepless nights in the bunkhouse forbade that his brain should ever be either alert or accurate. After that Henry slept on the office floor. And until three or four weeks ago had slept unmoving till cockcrow.

But of late he had lain awake thinking about his freedom. And today, walking away to his future, he still did not know what he was going to do with it.

It was much too hot to be walking with any degree of pleasure, even in the shade, but at least he had an immediate purpose. He was going to keep on walking until he came to the sea. The sea was the symbol of his freedom. The sea was freedom made tangible and manifest.

And he amused himself by picturing how it would look. In what mood would he find it? Pale and translucent? Or patterned purple and green by the shoals? Or leaping all over into little white tufts like a baby's cockscomb? Or oily and dark, indigo-blue, with a sullen swell?

It was in its taffeta mood. Palest blue taffeta, of the very best quality. He stretched himself out in the shade and looked at it.

Bland and innocent, it lay at his feet, curling at the edges into a foam demure as lace.

The sea. He gave a great sigh and his eyelids drooped. The sea. He was alone and free, and the world was his for the taking. What did it matter that he was two years short of the sum he had counted on? He had never been quite sure, in any case, what he was going to do with the money. What most people did with money in Barbados was to buy land. Fine, rich, virgin land that would pay a man back a hundred-fold – when there was no drought. But not he. It was from land that he had run away. He had had some idea of buying a place in one of the foot companies that defended Barbados against the importunities of Spain. That had seemed an appropriate occupation for the nephew of two distinguished soldiers and the descendant of more. Now that was no longer possible, but he was something short of heart-broken. It had been only an idea. The world was full of ideas, running over with opportunity. He could no longer buy his future, but there was nothing to hinder his making it.

He lay supine in the shade, so relaxed that he could feel the earth pushing up against him. The leaves whispered above him, the insects sang past him in endless pursuit of unimaginable business, the surf made a soft susurration in his ears. Free. He was free. There was nothing a man could not do if he was young and free.

For an hour he lay there unmoving and dreamed; but no longer. Leisure palled. Leisure was never a love of Henry Morgan's. Moreover, when you are young you grow hungry, and when you are free you do not have to eat food out of the communal trough any more. Good food waited for him in Bridgetown. He would go and get it. He would sit like a lord at a table covered with a fair white cloth and pick and choose from a dozen dainties while menials hovered round to anticipate his wishes. A pair of denim breeches and a frieze coat were perhaps not the best introduction to the finest places in Bridgetown, but he had money to pay for what he wanted. He might lack the sum that would set him up as commander of a company, but he had, thank God, enough to buy himself the best meal west of the Azores.

This more practical dream lasted him to the outskirts of Bridgetown, where his youth and his hunger betrayed him. It was late afternoon: dinner-time; and from all around him in the frowsy suburb there rose the succulent smells of cooking. His boy's stomach yearned and his teeth were awash. Ignoring the unswept porch and the fish-heads in the dust, he stopped at a workmen's eating-house and wolfed an enormous bowlful of fish stew, hot and spiced and various. It might not be the best meal west of the Azores, but no meal had ever tasted better.

He topped it off with the usual rum, and sat, gorged and amiable, playing with the black babies who rolled at his feet in the dust. They were very beautiful, the babies; fat and merry. One had found a drooping scarlet flower and had stuck it behind his ear in imitation of the local bloods. His innocently rakish eye, together with the coquettish bloom, enchanted Henry, and he laughed aloud. Which had the effect of recalling him to his own purposes. He reminded himself that enchanting black babies grew up to be stupid and unreliable adults of uncontrolled imagination and invincible laziness, and having by this sternness detached himself from their infant wiles, he took his bundle and sauntered on into the town.

The thatch and rain-stained plaster gave place to stone and tiles, and pleasant arcades against the heat. He lingered by the shop-windows, planning a wardrobe for himself. He hung over the seawall, counting the ships in harbour and analysing their rig. The sea had stopped being taffeta and was now a burning shield of silver, so fierce and colourless that the ships lacked reflection and stood as if stranded on it.

'Looking for me, John-ny?' a woman said, laying her elbows on the wall alongside him.

'No,' he said, and moved on.

Along the harbour front were the taverns and eating-houses. The more popular hummed and clattered, and hot gusts that were as strong of human sweat as of food came reeking from their open doors. From one a sailor was pitched drunk into the gutter. He sat up, shaken and bewildered, and presently began to laugh tipsily to himself. 'Change of scene. Change of scene,' he said to Morgan as he passed. 'Vastly puzzling.' The quieter places were not yet full – or perhaps were never full. Henry passed them all in review – he was in no hurry to eat now, but he had a thirst – and chose the Dolphin, one of the older and less garish places with a garden at the back of it. After the brilliance of the harbour the interior was so dark that he was for a moment at a loss. He put out his hand and felt a chair-back. So it was the kind of place that had chairs. He had no idea that such elegance existed in Bridgetown. The chair was empty, and he sat down on it against the wall.

A voice in the dimness asked his wants and, remembering his former promises to himself, he said: 'I want some imported wine. Have you claret?'

'We have claret,' said the voice, 'but I doubt if you'd like it.'

'Why? Has it not carried?'

'Claret's a wine for the quality.'

There was a moment's pause. He could see the man now, and realized that it was not at all dark in the room. The front part of the building was used, it seemed, for those who wanted merely to drink and talk. Three arches divided it from the rear portion, which was furnished with dining-tables and was open to the garden.

'Bring me the wine,' he said, 'and let me be the judge of quality.'

The quietness of the reprimand daunted the waiter, and he went away hostile but obedient. He came back and set the wine down with a gesture that was as near insult as he could make it.

Henry had silver in his pocket, but his Celt vanity, pricked by the man's sneer, was too much for him. He dropped his gold piece with a fine casual movement on to the table, so that it rolled a little and spun before settling. The waiter checked his dawning expression of surprise and went to get change.

Henry was childishly delighted – until he saw his change.

'Claret's expensive,' said the waiter, enjoying him.

'I gave you a gold piece.'

'You gave me a Spanish "eight".'

'A gold piece,' Henry said through his teeth.

'I don't think that's very likely, now, is it?' said the man, with a diabolic air of reasonableness, and Henry, with contracted heart, realized that on appearances it was indeed unlikely. Who would take his word against the waiter's? – the word of a man in workman's clothes who claimed to have paid for a flagon of wine with a gold piece?

'The gentleman gave you a gold piece, cock,' said a gentle Cockney voice on his right.

The waiter favoured the man at the next table with a baleful glare.

'And who —' he began.

'Me and my friends don't like mistakes,' said the little elderly man in the same reflective croon, and the waiter looked suddenly doubtful.

'A conspiracy, is it?' he said, and began to retreat. 'Or should I say a cons-*pyracy*?' With which fling he gave the proper change, retired to the doorway, and stood there glowering.

'Thank you,' Henry said to his neighbour. 'I am much obliged to you, sir.'

'It's nothing, nothing,' said the little man. 'Your good health.'

The wine tasted thin and harsh after the island rum, but it was cool from the cellar, and Henry was glad of it. The place was pleasant, and the customers had the air of habitués. No one had taken any notice of the altercation with the serving-man; perhaps they had not overheard it.

From beyond the archway he met the glance of a man who was dining there with a friend. The man did not look away when their eyes met, and Henry wondered whether it was that the man found him interesting or whether he found him so insignificant as to represent merely a blank space.

He became aware that his companion was talking to him.

'You belong to the island, young man?'

Henry said that he had been employed in Barbados, but was now planning a different future.

'What name do you go by?'

'My own.'

'Well, well, don't jump down my throat, boy. I go by the name of Bartholomew Kindness, and Kindness was my father's name and Bartholomew is what I was baptised.'

'I had not meant — My name is Henry Morgan.'

'From old England,' Bartholomew said, approving.

'Wales,' said the conscientious Morgan.

'And what, if you won't jump down my throat, are you planning for the future?'

Henry said that he had not yet decided, but that if Bartholomew had no immediate plans for this evening and had not yet dined he would be very glad to be his host.

For one horrible moment, while Bartholomew hesitated, Henry was afraid that Bartholomew was doubting his ability to afford it and was going to refuse out of sheer good heart.

But Bartholomew's heart was bigger even than that. 'Thank you,' he said. 'I should be greatly honoured.'

Before he could sound Bartholomew about his own affairs, Mad Meg came in from the street, and made her mechanical round of the tables. That part of her dirty white locks which did not stand on end hung down to her sharp chin, and from their ambush her pale old eyes looked forth, bright and glowing as coals. 'Ribbons and laces,' she said, 'ribbons and laces,' exhibiting from her crone's fingers the same tattered merchandise that served her year in, year out.

The proprietor noticed her with resignation, and the waiter with fury and loathing. Neither was prepared to risk her curses. No Brahminee bull was ever safer in Hind than Mad Meg in Bridgetown.

She paused to stare at Morgan, aware perhaps that here was a new face. A little embarrassed by her withdrawn regard and by the attention that her interest was bringing upon him, he bade her good-afternoon.

'Black hair and blue eyes,' she said. And then, irrelevantly: 'It's green, green, in Kildare.'

'I'm not Irish, mother,' he said; but she seemed unaware of him.

'Tell his fortune, Meg,' someone said; and the others joined him. 'Tell the young man's future, Meg,' they said. 'He'll cross your hand with silver.'

'With gold I've no doubt,' said the waiter sourly.

But she moved on with her resumed chant: 'Ribbons and laces, ribbons and laces . . .' and then, as one changing to the second motif of a composition: 'Woe! Woe! Woe to the evildoers; the fornicators, the lechers, the deceivers, the double-dealers, the ones without conscience or courtesy —'

She broke off, debating with herself. And then, as if suddenly reminded of business elsewhere, she turned and came back down the room to the doorway. But as she came level with the newcomer she caught sight of him again and paused. In some recess of her mind she connected that face with the telling of fortune.

'You'll write your name in water,' she said. And while he stared, held by the unhuman eyes beyond the tangle of hair, and dismayed by her unhappy promise, she repeated: 'You'll write your name in water for all the world to read.'

And she went, rapt and urgent, out into the hot world beyond the door.

'Is that a good fortune or a bad?' Henry said, into the vacuum that personality leaves in its wake.

'It's a fine conspicuous one, anyhow,' Bartholomew said.

'It would be no comfort for failure to know that it was conspicuous.'

'Not you! I could have told you'd be a success in life without telling fortunes. One glance is all I need. You have a nose that's broad at the point. It's a sure sign of being able to look after Number One, a nose broad at the point.'

Henry tried very hard not to stare at Bartholomew's nose, which was so broad at the tip as to be practically all point. The little man was neat and respectable, but hardly an advertisement for his theory.

'No, not my kind of "broad",' Bartholomew said, quite without rancour. 'The kind that starts bony and has a blob on the end. It's my hobby: faces. See that man facing us through the archway? That's a clever one, that is. You'd have to start very early to get the better of that one or he'd make you feel unpunctual.'

'Do you know who he is?' Henry asked, catching again the absent glance of the man on himself.

'No, I don't know this place well. Come here now and then on business, that's all. We supply meat to ships, me and my partners. I like the islands, but I'd give a lot to see Bristol docks this minute. Even Bristol docks in the rain. I was born in London, but I married a Bristol girl. When I've made my little pile, me and my old woman's going to retire to a cottage in the Mendips.'

Henry said that he was lucky to have a home waiting for him.

'Oh, it ain't built yet, the cottage. But we've picked out the place for it. In a green valley where the moors begin half-way up the sides.'

And suddenly Henry saw Llanrhymny.

That, too, was 'a green valley where the moors begin half-way up'. He saw it small, and clear, and far away, like something in the wrong end of a telescope.

Llanrhymny.

'I expect a young gentleman like you is handy with a pen,' he heard Bartholomew say, and turned to him surprised at this apparent change of subject.

'Fairly. Why do you ask?'

'Well, you see, I can read, but I never learned penmanship, and my old woman, she misses hearing from me, and – well —'

'You want me to write a letter for you, is that it?'

'Oh, not a letter. A few lines would do to say that I'm keeping fine. If it wouldn't be imposing on you.'

'I owe you much more than that,' Henry said. 'Let us dine first, shall we, and then write the letter.'

'Well – about that dinner — Tell me, do you like sucking pig? Roast sucking pig?'

'Of course. Who doesn't?'

'Well, I was going to suggest that you come back with me to our hunting camp, back up the coast a bit, and eat hearty of the best meat in the Caribbean.'

Henry, whose appetite for the Bridgetown flesh-pots was not what it had been before the episode of the gold coin, considered a combination of roast pig, a hunting camp on the coast, and Bartholomew Kindness almost too much luck for his first night of freedom. He required a pen and ink from the Dolphin's proprietor, and wrote the letter there and then, so that it might go to England with the *Mary Ryde*, which was sailing for Plymouth in the morning. And in the intervals of Bartholomew's inspiration he watched the man beyond the archway. Henry, whose taste had a Celt flamboyance, thought his clothes a little subdued, but admired the fineness of his linen and his ruffle's candidness. The man had been joined by his son – a young man so like him that the relationship could be in no doubt – and his clever, worldly face had so softened that he looked like a different person. This was remarked with astonishment by a Henry unprepared for the idea that a father might love his son. Nor could he imagine himself sitting down and chatting happily with his father's friends, on equal terms, as this young man was doing. 'If my father had been a Royalist instead of a damned Puritan, it might have been like that,' he thought.

'Your very loving husband, Bartholomew Kindness,' finished Bartholomew, released from the pains of composition. 'And now we'll 'ave another drink.'

They had their drink, and gathering up Henry's bundle and the large sack of purchases that was the result of Bartholomew's day in town, they made their way out of the Dolphin. As they left, Henry saw that the party beyond the archway was also leaving, and he pulled Bartholomew's sleeve to detain him, so that the party from the dining-room passed out first.

'Who is that?' Henry asked the loafer outside who had touched his hat to the man.

'That's Sir Thomas Modyford,' the man said. 'Got one of the biggest estates in the island. Be Governor one day, if the Commonwealth lasts.'

'A *Cromwell* man!' Henry said.

'Isn't it going to last?' Bartholomew asked with interest.

'Nothing lasts,' said the man, but his eyes were on Henry. Henry's disappointment was too acute to be anything but genuine.

'Been everything in his time, they say,' he added, risking a mild indiscretion, and went back to his tooth-picking.

'A weathercock!' Henry said disgusted, as they walked away.

'No, no,' said Bartholomew. 'A sail-trimmer.'

'What is the difference?'

'Oh, all the difference in the world. All the difference in the world. A weathercock is a poor helpless thing that's twirled round and round by every breeze that blows. No brains, no sense, no say. But a sail-trimmer – ah, a sail-trimmer is an artist. Sees a change of wind before it comes, chooses his course, makes the wind work for him instead of drowning him, coaxes a little rag of sail to take him into harbour instead of making a distress signal of it.'

'Are you a sailor?' Henry asked.

'Yes, I'm a sailor. So that's Modyford. I told you he was a clever one. It's thanks to Modyford, they say, that the island ever declared for the Protector at all.' Henry snorted. 'Which is no small achievement for a man that fought for King Charles.'

'Fought on the Royalist side?' asked Henry, arrested.

'So they say. I told you he was an expert sail-trimmer. Now we'll go down here and collect my equipage.'

2

BARTHOLOMEW'S 'EQUIPAGE' proved to be one small donkey with neither saddle nor bridle. A rope had been arranged not very expertly in place of the absent bridle; it looked like the work of someone who knew more about ropes than about bridles.

'This is Ananias,' said Bartholomew, and hoisted himself across the donkey's bare back.

'Why Ananias, poor brute?' asked Henry.

'Well, I did call it Anna, until I found out my mistake. So I just tacked a bit on.' He slung the sack of purchases in front of him. 'Now give me your bundle and I'll put it on top.' Then, to the donkey: 'Gee up!'

But the donkey stood still.

'He doesn't understand English,' Bartholomew explained. 'I don't know his nationality.'

'You don't need any parley-vous,' Henry said. 'Just dig your heels in his ribs.'

Bartholomew did as he was bid, with gratifying results.

'You know as much about horse-flesh as I know about sails,' he said, as they moved on their way out of town. 'Owned one of your own, perhaps.'

'Yes, I had one of my own.'

'What made you leave that nice house of yours? Seeking your fortune?'

'How do you know what kind of home I had?'

'It takes more than a few square yards of denim to cover up breeding, my boy. Found your Welsh valley too narrow?'

'That's about it.' He considered the mild-looking little man riding by his side, and said: 'I would never have said that you were a sailor.'

'Well, you see, by nature I'm not one for a wild life. But tar's the undoing of me.'

'Tar?'

'The minute I smell tar I come unsettled like.' He looked back at the shipping in the harbour, and added. 'But wait till I get that cottage in the Mendips. They'll have to pulley-hauley me to get me back from there.'

They walked in a companionable silence along the dusty road.

'Think there's going to be a change at home?' Bartholomew asked presently.

'There was no sign of one when I left. Why do you ask?'

'That's the third time lately I've heard a remark about there being an end in sight to this new-fangled way of running the country.'

'The islands are always full of rumours. And what would they know about it, anyhow, four thousand miles away?'

'Ah, but that's just where you do get to know first about things like that. It's the chap who's standing outside that hears the note of the hive. The bees themselves are buzzing far too loud to pay any attention. Don't think that the Caribbean won't hear the change in the bees' buzzing when it comes!'

He rode on for a little, cogitating.

'Stands to reason it wouldn't last, anyhow,' he said. 'Folk don't want anyone just like themselves ruling them, do they?'

He was silent for another half-mile.

'You want more than a gift of the gab to rule England. No one ever loved a Parliament. It was bound not to last.'

'What do you think they'll do? If it comes to pieces, I mean.'

'Bring the boy over to take his place, I suppose.'

'How can they, if the Army is still the Protector's? It's the best army in the world, God blast it!'

'Huh!' said Bartholomew. 'Ten armies won't stop them if they've made up their minds about something.'

The high road turned inland and left them with only a track along the coast. But the track was shaded, and the rains that had come too late to save the cane and the cocoa made the undergrowth green and sweet-smelling. For another hour they followed the track, veering with the coast until all sight of Bridgetown had long disappeared and they had the world to themselves. Here and there a fence marked the limit of some planter's domain, and now and then a plank flung over a freshet showed that civilization lurked in the background. But for the most part it was a virgin world, full of the evening chatter of birds and the flight of wild animals from their approach.

At a gate in a wood fence, Bartholomew dismounted and removed the sack of purchases from the donkey. Whereupon the beast, with relief in every line of him, made joyfully for the gate.

'Hey! Wait a minute! My rope!' said Bartholomew, and removed the bridle. Then, opening the gate, he smacked the animal on the rump and said: 'Good-bye, Ananias. Glad to have met you.'

'Isn't he yours?' asked Henry.

'Oh, no,' said Bartholomew, carefully fastening the gate. 'I just borrowed him.'

He humped the sack over his shoulder and went on up the path. And Henry, picking up his much smaller bundle, forbore to offer to carry the larger one. To be no longer young, with all the world in front of you, must be bad enough, without having it brought forcibly to your notice.

Now the forest came down to the water, and the going was less easy. He had begun to wonder how far it still was to that dinner of wild pig, when the silence was broken by the high, hostile yelling of a dog, and in a moment it appeared on the edge of the slope ahead of them, and stood there shrieking their approach to all creation.

'Shut up, Killick!' Bartholomew called.

A tall man with the face of an unfrocked priest came to the edge and watched them as they toiled upwards.

'Evening, Chris,' Bartholomew said, panting.

'Who's he?' asked the man, leaning his head at Henry.

'Friend of mine. Did me a good turn. Name's Harry Morgan. Here! Take this for me.' He slid the sack from his back and held it out, and the man took it meekly. Which surprised Henry a little.

They moved together over the crest, and Henry found that the edge on which the man and dog had stood was the lip of a wide saucer of clearing in the forest, and over the floor of the saucer was spread the evening activity of a hunting camp. A man was pegging out freshly-skinned hides to dry, another was jointing meat. On a clear fire just below, a meal was being cooked; and on a second smoky one on the other side of the clearing choice strips of meat were being dried into boucan. Two men were cleaning guns, and one was washing blood from his shirt.

By the cooking-fire a second dog was standing, uncertain. Chris walked up to it and began to kick it with a businesslike detachment. Henry knew why he was kicking it. Because it had not warned them, like the other, of approaching visitors.

'Let him be,' Bartholomew said; and, again surprisingly, the man obeyed. 'I think he's getting a little deaf, but he still has the best nose a hound ever had.'

The man picked up a wooden bucket and held it out to Henry. 'If you've come to supper, Harry Morgan, best make yourself useful. Water's beyond, there.' And he tilted his head to the farther rim of the clearing.

Henry took the bucket and walked through the camp, receiving nods or stares, according to a man's mood or inclination. He climbed the opposite lip of the saucer and found that it was the high bank of a stream; a bank so high and sudden that no sound of water came over it into the camp. Indeed, he found when he made his way down to the stream to fill the bucket that he was out of sight and sound of human activity. The camp on its high hollow shelf of land might not exist.

And then he saw the longboat.

It was drawn up from the beach under the sheltering branches.

So the men disjointing pig so busily up there did not belong to the island. That caused a great many new thoughts to race through his mind while he filled his bucket. Something the Dolphin's serving-man had said came back to him. Something he had not understood at the time. A play on the word conspiracy.

He walked the few yards down to the beach, but the sea was empty. Limpid and quiet in the evening light. They had come from some other island, not from any ship.

He hauled the water up the steep bank and brought it to the fire. Some of the flayed and disembowelled pig carcases laid out ready for transportation looked a little too large and fat for wild ones, but it was none of his business. If honest traders in meat did a little poaching as side-line to their hunting, that, in the Caribbean, was a very small iniquity.

The smell of the cooking pork made him faint with ecstasy, and for a share of it he would have looked with indulgence on more spectacular sins than cattle-stealing.

When the men gathered round for supper, each with his wooden porringer or pewter plate, Bartholomew distributed the articles they had commissioned him to buy. Except that he also distributed their change, or announced deficits, he might have been a benevolent uncle doling out gifts.

'Bluey, your jew's-harp. Tugnet, your pomade, and keep it for your girl's benefit; it smells like a brothel. Timsy, your candy, and you owe me two pence on it.'

When a man stretched forward to spear a piece of meat before his turn, Bartholomew smacked him sharply on the wrist and said: 'Manners!' like a nursery governess, and the man desisted. It was difficult to know why they should obey him, and still more difficult, in the absoluteness of their freemasonry, to know who the actual leader was. There were eleven of them, Henry counted; and they were all white except for a mulatto and a man who looked like some sort of Indian from Campeche way.

'Know anything of sea business?' the man called Chris asked him as they ate.

'I came out from England before the mast,' Henry said.

'That's hardly a degree in seamanship.'

'Passed his entrance examination, though,' someone said, and they laughed a little and the atmosphere grew easier.

They argued in a desultory way among themselves where they should sell their meat. It would be easier to get to one place because the trades would blow them almost straight there, but they would get a better price in the second. The pig melted in the mouth, and they ate until there was nothing left but bones. The rum was heavy and crude and potent. One by one they lay back replete. The dogs, gorged on the offal, came to the fire and sank their muzzles on their paws. Bluey took out his jew's-harp and began to play softly. The mulatto sang the words to himself. It was all sufficiently Arcadian, and Henry was glad that he was going to sleep in the forest instead of on the office floor. He wondered if they would invite him to join them when they left in the morning. He had no idea whether he was going to say yes or no if they gave him the choice, but it did not matter. This was tonight, and tomorrow was another day. Tonight he was free, excellently fed, and beautifully rummed up; and he wouldn't call the King his cousin.

'Ssh!' said Chris of a sudden, sitting up and listening.

In the instant silence they all heard it. A familiar sound, it was. The long, smooth sound of an anchor cable rolling off the windlass.

The mulatto dived for the dogs before they could move, and hushed them.

'Stay!' he said to the obedient creatures, and joined the rush to the stream edge of the hollow. Lying there on the reverse slope they looked down the funnel of land to the sea. There was indeed a ship there. She had arrived, after the surprising manner of ships, from nowhere, and now stood large and immediate in the very middle of the picture. Already she had begun to lower a boat.

'Stopped for fresh water,' Chris said. 'They seem to know the coast very well!'

'Seen the flag?' someone said.

'Yes. Spanish.'

'I like their nerve, anyhow,' another said. 'They refuse *us* the courtesy of wood and water.'

'Ah, well, we won't have to hump that meat round the Caribbean, after all. Our customers have come to our doorstep.'

'Victual a Spaniard!' said Henry.

'Why not?' they said. 'A Spanish coin rings just as clear on a counter as any English one.'

'But that very ship may blow an unoffending English one out of the water six hours from now.'

'Not her,' they said. 'She's in too much of a hurry to get back to Spain, for one thing. And for another, six hours from now she'll be just where she is. When the wind drops like this of an evening, it won't come up again before dawn.'

'Becalmed?' said Henry. 'Then why don't we take her?'

'Take her?' they said. 'Have you had a good look at her?'

'Yes. Why?'

'Take a ten-gun ship with eleven men and some sporting guns?'

'Twelve men. And that is not the correct odds.'

'All right, we do have some muskets. How much does that shorten the odds?'

'The odds have nothing to do with muskets. It's a case of a dozen brains against let us say forty men who haven't even thought about the subject.'

'Brains!' they laughed, the only power they had ever used being force.

'How would you go about it, Brains?' asked one, spinning out the joke.

'I haven't thought about it – but I can tell you one way.' And he told them.

They listened in silence, their eyes turning from him to the ship's boat and back again until presently their eyes were on him alone.

'Even a small grapnel would make a noise like the crack of doom,' said one in a slow Dorset voice when he had finished.

'Pad it,' said Henry, noting with a lift of excitement in his chest that the questioning of a detail implied a respect for the plan itself.

'With what?'

'Moss. Creepers. Anything. You can pad it so much that it bounces like a baby's wool ball, but it will still stay a grapnel and do what it is meant to do.'

Their delight in contrivance, always acute in men who live precariously, snared them into interest.

'Yes, and Chakka can do the throwing,' someone said. Chakka was the Indian. 'Chakka can make a rope fall round a marline-spike stuck in the sand thirty yards away.'

'Are we going to lose our market just to have our throats cut on board?' asked a dissenter.

'As for marketing,' Henry said, 'I don't suppose she is going home to Spain empty.'

And at that reminder interest flared to something like eagerness. They knew the kind of cargo that ships carried from the mainland to Spain. And if she was bound home as far west as Barbados, then she almost certainly came from the South American coast. And South America meant gold, and silver, and pearls. South America was the fabled El Dorado.

Their interest went back to the boat that was being now rowed ashore, but they made no movement to go down to meet it. Instead they went over to the sea side of the camp and watched it come, through the tangle of creepers that screened them from the shore below. Through the still air they could hear the men in the boat laughing and talking as they rowed. They were glad to be setting foot on land for a little.

'I can't remember whether we are at war with Spain at the moment or not,' Bartholomew said meditatively, making his first contribution to the discussion.

'There is no peace beyond the Line,' supplied Chris, quoting a well-known tag.

'It's a holy war, anyhow,' said one. 'The Protector has said that who fights Spain fights the Inquisition and does God's work.'

'I've no mind to be strung up just to gratify Cromwell,' said the dissenter.

'A minute ago you were going to have your throat cut,' they said. 'Make up your mind!'

'I know a couple of ears that I'd like to hang pearls in,' said the man who had commissioned Bartholomew to buy the pomade.

'I know a couple of Spanish necks I'd like to screw,' said the Dorset man.

'Pipe down!' said Bartholomew as the boat grounded and the men leaped ashore.

They humped three empty casks on to the beach and rolled them up to the pools of fresh water in the gully. A youth dropped a small toy dog on to the sand and began to play with it. He had brought a ball, and he would throw it and then rush after it, accompanied by the dog, and they would roll together in the sand, each madder than the other with joy of living. The camp watched this pastime with mild contempt.

'Call that a dog!' said the mulatto, and went back to the fire where the two hunting dogs were standing in unwilling bondage to their training, whimpering with excitement and quivering all over. He soothed them and made them lie down with whispered promises and reassuring caresses, and then came back to watch what was happening below.

The Spaniards had discovered the longboat and had resolved themselves into a small doubtful cluster, looking up at the unrevealing density of the forest. One of them called something, and was hushed for his pains. They apparently decided that, whatever the longboat might be drawn up there for, it had no immediate significance. But they did not linger, as they had patently been prepared to do before finding the boat. The holiday air disappeared, and they worked quietly at filling their casks and gathering driftwood. The silly little dog, unprepared for the change in the atmosphere, got in their way and was cursed.

'Call that a dog!' said the mulatto again.

'See that there fellow with the black ringlets,' whispered the Dorset man. 'He were one of the crew of the *Santa Marta* that time I were aboard her after they sunk the *Marie Galante* off the Mosquito coast. Fresh water, indeed!' He watched the shining water being shot into the casks. 'No water at all they gave us, and no food neither, the bastards.'

Henry, lying silent, noticed that there was no further suggestion of trade. Even the dissenter was no longer vocal. They watched the ship's crew roll the barrels down the beach and up the planks into the boat, and made no motion either to stop them or to go down and do business with them. Indeed, their only personal reaction to the Spaniards' departure was to criticise their boatwork.

'What a lot of lubbers!' they said, watching the Spaniards' way with an oar. 'What a lot of tailors!'

When the boat had reached the ship's side and the water was being hauled on board they lost interest and remembered that there was still some rum. They drifted one by one back to the fire.

'If their nostrils hadn't been so bunged up with salt they'd have smelt us for sure,' Bluey said, sniffing the smoke from the boucan-drying as he turned away from the clean sea air.

Henry said nothing, waiting for his idea to ferment in their minds of its own accord. They discussed the ship in general terms at first: her tonnage, her rig, her probable cargo. Wood, they thought. Fine woods from the west South American forests.

'Why couldn't Chakka just rope the man in the stern?' Tugnet said. 'Just rope him and pull his throat shut?'

'Too risky,' said Chris. 'If he failed we'd have them all on us.'

And with this contribution from Chris the subject passed from the academic to the practical. The proposition that they take the ship had been accepted.

'It'll have to be in the first watch, if we try it,' Bartholomew said. 'The moon comes up after midnight, and they'd spot us as soon as we left the shore.'

They lay round the fire as dusk closed in, discussing ways and means, and every now and then referring to Henry about a point. 'What do you think, Brains?' 'How does that look to you, Brains?' It had been his idea, and they were playing fair by him. He was no longer a cipher in the camp; he was, on the contrary, a potential leader. Bluey went down to the longboat and came back with a small grapnel, and the Indian gathered moss to pad it. They slung a canvas on the coast side of the fire so that no hint of a hostile presence should move the Spaniards to double a guard that night. Watching the faces as they bent to admire the Indian's handiwork on the grapnel, Henry considered his allies. They were not what he would have chosen, perhaps, but if the faces were unintelligent, in some cases stupid, in some cases callous, at least none of them was mean. There was a lack of calculation about them that saved them from being evil, or even bad. That same lack of calculation made them what they were, of course; hand-to-mouth spenders of all they made, world's vagabonds and permanent tramps. Only Bartholomew, of them all, had a kind of dignity. And he now knew why. He knew, too, why he was looked up to in this gathering of odds and ends. Bartholomew was a sail-maker. Bartholomew had a trade; he was an expert in one particular line; able to make a living and take his place anywhere. It was because of that fact that, even in the presence of a more probable leader like the man Chris, they deferred to Bartholomew Kindness.

When the dark came they pulled the longboat carefully down over the sand and floated her. An hour before midnight the tide would turn, and they would let the tide float them out to the ship as far as it served them. Then they came back to the camp and cleaned and primed their weapons until it was time.

'Brains has no pistol, Bart,' someone said. And there was a long discussion as to whose pistol he should take. Not because any one of them grudged parting with his own, but because they were determined that he should have the best.

'It doesn't matter much,' Henry said. 'I'm not planning to kill anyone.'

'If I had my way we'd kill the whole boiling of them,' Timsy said.

'Anyone can kill a man,' Henry said contemptuously. 'It needs only a little piece of lead and a thumb in working order.'

'Brains doesn't need to kill,' Chris said. 'He gets his own way without.'

'And the ransom besides,' Henry added.

'Ransom?' they said.

'For the men I've kept alive,' he said; and so cancelled the effect of Chris's half-sneer.

They went down to the beach when the time came with the idea firmly in their minds that there were cleverer ways to their ends than by killing. Which – as Brains had shown – was simple, and satisfying, but extravagant.

As they pushed off into the quiet water, Henry pulled off his shoes and left them in the bottom of the boat. He sat in the bows ready, and beside him was the Indian, Chakka, with the grapnel. They had tried the effect of the padding on a floor of planks collected from various parts of the camp, and had laughed to see how their cleverness was rewarded. The grapnel fell always head down, of course, and they padded the head with moss until it was resilient as a 'baby's wool ball', as Henry had promised.

The night hung round them like velvet, and the black water bore them gently out towards the invisible ship. She had swung with the tide and lay bows to shore, so that to reach her stern they had to pass her broadside on. She had no riding-lights, but when they came nearer they saw that a dim glow came up from an open hatch on deck, and a lantern hung at the entrance to the fo'c'sle. When they came so close that her bulk was silhouetted against the sky they could see that the guards the Spaniards had set at dusk were still there. One in the bows, one in the stern, and one at the ladder in the waist.

This was the crucial moment. One cough or sneeze, one incautious movement, and any one or all of these men would give tongue, and up from her bowels would come men by the dozen and the water would be jumping all round them in a hail of bullets.

But the slow, breathless moments passed, and now they were safe under her counter, and fending themselves off her rudder with their hands. One by one in the darkness they let out the pent breath that had suffocated them and relaxed. They sat there listening to the movements of the man above, and to the subdued sound of talk in the cabin somewhere. Forward of the cabin it was quiet, and it seemed that, glad of the knowledge that they would, for this night at least, not be disturbed in their rest to work ship, the fo'c'sle was asleep.

Henry stood up on his stocking soles in the bows, and pushed off until he was standing directly below the ship's rail, the Indian ready behind him.

'Now!' he whispered to Chris, and Chris flung the stone.

It dropped into the sea on the port quarter, and the man above moved away from his post to investigate. While the noise of his boots was still loud in the stillness, Chakka flung the grapnel. It fell on deck with a thud that stopped their hearts. To their heated imaginations it sounded like a meteor landing. But Henry had no time to consider the consequences. Chakka drew tight the rope, and the hook slid quietly from the deck and caught sweetly and silently in the rail. And Henry was swarming up the rope and stepping over the broad wooden rail before he had time to think. He crouched there in the darkness.

The man took a long time over his inspection. He walked forward and talked to the man in the waist, glad perhaps of an excuse to break the monotony of his watch. But presently he came back, humming to himself, and, still humming, came to stand a couple of yards from the waiting Henry. Henry could see him distinctly against the lightening sky. He was standing with his back to him.

His right hand with the kerchief wrapped round it went over the man's mouth and his left with the knife in it pressed into the man's back.

'Be quiet!' he said.

He felt his knife go through the man's leather coat, and a mad longing filled him to kill the man. Excitement boiled in him and sought an outlet; a climax.

It was something older than either law or Christianity that stopped him. Superstition. There must be no blood on this setting-out of his.

The man stopped his instinctive struggle as soon as he felt the knife-point against his skin. Henry dragged him back a step or two to the rail and tugged the rope where it hung from the grapnel; and in a moment Chris and Bluey joined him, materialising over the rail as darker shadows in the darkness. They bound and gagged the man that Henry was holding, and passed him to the custody of the next man up.

Henry walked boldly forward to the man at the waist, and cut short the man's greeting to a supposed comrade with a pistol shoved into his stomach. The man cried out instinctively, but it was a small bitten-off cry, and they bound and gagged him without hindrance.

The bored guard in the bows came strolling aft to find what interested his comrade. Henry pushed the others into the darkness and waited alongside the silent and helpless Spaniard. As the newcomer stopped to gossip, Bluey, not waiting for Henry, flung an iron arm round the man's throat so that not even a bitten-off cry escaped from his outraged gullet. Henry shoved a rag into his gaping mouth, and Bluey drew his arms behind him and tied his hands to his ankles. The two captives were left in charge of the Dorset man, and Henry moved aft to that glow of light from the cabin.

The poop dropped to the deck in two shallow descents, and in the middle of the small half-deck was a partly-open hatch. As Henry bent his head to look down into the interior he felt a sudden chill on the back of his neck, and thought at first that it was the result of his excitement. Then he realized that it was the first breath of an off-shore wind.

In the cabin five men were sitting round the table playing cards, and two more watched from seats at their side. A man in the forward corner was stringing a fiddle, and two were asleep in bunks. There might be more men asleep on bunks on the side that he could not see. The captain was a podgy man, and he played bad-temperedly. On his right sat a man of the same age, but elegant in dress and figure. He had the air of a guest; a passenger. On the passenger's right, lying on a velvet cushion, was a small bundle of silk that Henry recognised as the toy dog. Its head was buried under its paws and its nose in the cushion. All the prowlers in the world might be gathering within a few feet of it without disturbing by a heart-beat its silken slumbers. As the mulatto had remarked: 'Call that a dog!'

Judging by the volume of excited breathing behind him that the majority of his following were now on board, Henry pressed a hand on Chris's shoulder to make him stay where he was, and moved round to the cabin entrance, which was on the forward side and led down a few steps from the main deck. So rapt were the men in the cabin on their game, and so unsuspicious of this quiet midnight on a deserted coast, that Henry stood for a moment on the last step considering them at his leisure, before the Captain, who was facing him, looked up and saw him.

The Captain's eyes bulged.

'Keep still,' said Henry, standing with his pistol levelled. 'My friends above are watching you with interest.'

The Captain understood him because he shot an agonised glance up at the faces in the reflected glow.

'Don't shoot, don't shoot!' he said in French. 'No one will move. Don't shoot!' his choice of tongue being an instinctive tribute to the French, who had made their island of Tortuga the headquarters of piracy in the Caribbean.

But his passenger was of different stuff. With a sideways glance at the shaking Captain, he bowed to Henry and said: 'You have come too late for supper, but the madeira is good, monsieur Sansouliers.'

Even a conqueror does not feel at his best in his stocking soles; and Henry was a very young and new conqueror, and a Celt to boot. The flick stung him.

'You are no more effective than your dog, Señor,' he said in his island Spanish. The animal was now standing up on its cushion and uttering small shrill yelps, and it looked self-important and silly. And then, raising his voice a little, he said: 'Bluey! Come down here,' and Bluey detached himself from the gathering above and appeared beside him on the steps.

'This gentleman is going to lend me his shoes,' Henry said. 'Will you assist him to remove them?'

Bluey was delighted.

'With your honour's permission,' he said, bowing with a flourish, and having removed the shoes, brought them to Henry and held them for him with a burlesque of servitude.

'There you are, Harry boy!' he said. 'And the nicest pieces of shoe-leather I ever did see. Might as well have a pair for myself while I'm about it. What about yours, Cap'n?'

'Presently, presently,' said Henry. 'You can line them up in a row and choose at your ease when the ship's ours. Is Timsy there? Timsy, you stay with me and Bluey. Bart, you take the rest for'ard and deal with the crew.'

He had chosen Timsy to stay with him because if anyone in the gathering was likely to start a massacre it was Timsy.

Intoxicated at having the after-guard in their hands so easily, they discarded caution with a whoop. Bart snatched the lantern from where it hung and they went roaring into the fo'c'sle like a tidal wave.

'Rise and shine, my hearties, rise and shine!' shouted Chris, as if he were routing out his own crew; and tore along the narrow alley-way of the noisome catacomb, slapping rumps, tweaking toes, and pulling hair.

Some of the men packed in tiered layers on the filthy shelves were drunk; more were sodden with sleep and half-poisoned by their own exhalations. Only three were alert enough to combat an enemy on the threshold of waking. Two reached under their canvas-bag pillows for pistols; but one pistol misfired and the other disappeared under a one-man avalanche which was Tugnet. The third man to be quick-minded was the boy who had played with the dog on the beach. He came at Bart with a knife.

'No, son, no,' said Bart in his kind-uncle tones, hitting the boy's raised arm across the biceps with the side of his open palm. This is an exceedingly painful thing to have happen to one. The boy yelled, and the knife flew from his hand and grazed the mulatto's forehead. The mulatto dropped the club he was carrying and came at the boy with his open hands. The man whose pistol had misfired used the butt of it on the mulatto's head. And in another second the fo'c'sle was a writhing mass of fighting humanity.

Bart lost the lantern in the mêlée, and when he had recovered it and held it aloft to survey the result he found the boy sitting on the mulatto's head.

'Well, well,' he said, 'so you can take care of yourself, after all, son!' and he looked round to see how the others had fared. No one was dead, it seemed; not even one of the Spaniards, although several were looking the worse for wear. In the recovered light the invaders drew off and stood covering their captives.

'Tie them up, boys,' Bart said. 'And you,' he added to the boy, 'you get off that brown man. He's the best man with dogs this side of Cape Verde.'

'Dogs?' said the boy, getting up and looking with interest at the bleeding mulatto. 'Ah, pardon, pardon.'

'Speaks English like a native,' mocked Tugnet.

'Pretty smart altogether for a Spaniard,' Bart said, mopping the mulatto's head.

'I Portuguese,' said the boy.

'Well now! Practically an ally!' they laughed.

'I Manuelo Sequerra.'

'Maybe, Manny; but you're going to be tied up like the rest,' they said.

He submitted with good humour to their binding, and apologised to the mulatto for the 'accident' to his forehead.

'It was this gentleman that I try to kill,' he said, indicating Bart in explanation.

There were fewer men in the fo'c'sle than they had expected, and they were bound in matter-of-fact fashion in the persuasive presence of half a dozen pistols. Once trouble seemed to be on the point of breaking out again when one of the drunk Spaniards spat in the face of the man who was tying him up. But the man merely hit him across the face with the back of his hand and went on with his knots. Their triumph was so great that their good humour was invincible.

'She's ours!' exulted Bluey, as they met in the cabin again. 'She's ours!'

The ship's officers, together with their passenger, had been shut into the tiny after-cabin. This led out of the cabin proper, and was an ideal prison, in that its only windows were two small ones high up, overlooking the half-deck.

'Now we see what she is carrying,' they said, but Henry said no; first they must tidy up ashore. Fetch the fresh meat and the dogs. The off-shore wind would take them out now, without waiting for dawn.

There was some argument as to who should go, but they were

still large with delight, and the impartial dice did the rest. They accepted Henry's ruling about using the wind. They had stopped calling him Brains from the moment when he had climbed that rope to the ship's stern.

Those who were left explored the ship as children rejoice in a new toy. They found that she was Dutch-built; a fact which explained much that had puzzled them when they had discussed her round the fire. More especially her light, low poop, almost level with the waist, and her lack of burdening ornament. She had been built by a people whose harbours were small and shallow; and she had been built for trade, and therefore for speed in a competitive business. That she was Dutch-built explained, too, the comparative smallness of her crew. The Dutch designed ships that could be sailed satisfactorily with two-thirds of the normal crew for the tonnage.

Whatever her original name had been, she was at the moment the *Gloria*, but Henry planned to change that at the earliest possible moment.

'Tomorrow we'll sling a man over the side, and we'll call her – *Fortune*.'

Gradually a new, less welcome, thought seeped into their exuberance. They had inspected her cargo (wood, as they had anticipated) and admired her armoury. They had even routed down below the water-line to reckon what gunpowder stores she had. But so far they had come on no strong-room. They mentioned the lack to each other, casually at first, and then urgently. When the longboat came back they were still searching for it.

'Bring the Captain here,' Henry said, when they had ransacked the cabin without result.

They unlocked the after-cabin and dragged the Captain out. But the Captain had either been coached by his passenger or had recovered his nerve. He pretended not to know what they said.

Chris produced a knife and opened it with a flick of his wrist. He thrust it within an inch or two of the Captain's throat, and moved it in half-turns so that the light from the hanging lantern glinted on it.

'I'll teach him English,' he said.

'You and your knives!' Henry said, contemptuously. 'Bluey,

fetch the steward here. I never knew a steward yet that didn't know more about his master's business than the master knew himself.'

Bluey came back to say that the steward wasn't one of the men in the fo'c'sle. He slept in the galley, it seemed. But they had all seen the galley and there was no one there. When a terrified and half-suffocated steward was at last dragged from the flour-bin in the galley they greeted him with appreciative laughter and treated him as a hero. Who would have thought, they said, that the man to beat them would be a steward?

The unhappy wretch, finally unnerved by laughter that he did not understand, made no bones about telling them where the strong-room was. It was in the little dark after-cabin that the prisoners were occupying. He showed them where it was, and told them where the Captain kept the key. And they all gathered round to learn what their fortune was.

There was neither gold nor silver. But there were pearls.

Rivers of pearls. Cascades of them.

The iron box was opened on the cabin table when the key had been turned again on the prisoners, and the share-out began. And went on, and on. Round and round went Bart's hand, dropping pearls one by one on the twelve small heaps; and the twelve small heaps ceased to be very small, and grew to be heaps of a size that made their eyes first shining and then blank with sheer incredulity.

'Eight odd,' said Bartholomew at last. 'Four of you's going to be unlucky.'

'Unlucky!' Bluey said, staring at his heap. 'What's an odd pearl! Give it to Chakka.'

'Throw mine overboard,' Tugnet said, running his fingers through his heap.

'If you're all satisfied,' Henry said, 'we'll free the middle watch and put them to the business of taking her out to sea.'

That led to a discussion as to where they should sail.

And by the time they had actually sailed it had led to something like open warfare. Henry wanted to sail the ship straight to port and have her declared a prize by an English Admiralty Court.

'Have her disallowed, you mean,' they said. 'And all of us flung into jail, as likely as not!'

'Even if they allow it,' they said, 'they'll want their percentage. By the time they've passed all their quirks and pretences on you, what is there for a poor seaman?'

Their distrust of the law was all-pervading.

This dismayed Henry; but what shook him to the soles of his new Spanish shoes was their plan for the future of the ship. They planned to sell her, if that proved easy; and if not, to sink her.

'Sink her!' said Henry, hardly believing his ears. 'But with a ship like this our fortune is made. We are set up for life.'

'What would we do with her?' they asked.

'Get letters-of-marque, and use her as a privateer. Or, failing that, trade with her. There are cargoes for the asking all over the Caribbean, and fortunes for the taking.'

'What! Work a ship in all weathers when we could be living like lords in Port Royal!' they said.

'Fortune! What's a fortune to us!' they said. 'We've *got* a fortune.'

'We're only living for the day when we can be done with ships!' they said. 'What would *we* want with a ship?'

And from that nothing Henry said could move them.

So at last he said: 'Very well. I'll trade you my share of the pearls for the ship.'

At first they thought he was joking. Then they thought he was mad. Then they remembered that he had once been called Brains, and began to wonder how they were being cheated.

'It's too big a share, the ship,' they grumbled, with a fine inconsequence.

Henry pointed out that they had been planning to sink her.

'No,' they said. 'We were going to sell her.'

'Very well. I'm offering you a fortune in pearls for her. Try to sell her – in Tortuga, I suppose – and you may find no bidders. There's my bid, there on the table.'

He emptied the little leather sack of pearls on to the table under their eyes; and, watching their faces, knew that he had a ship and was penniless.

But his heart was filled with glory.

He went on deck, and left them to their celebration. In less than an hour they were all roaring drunk.

Sometime before dawn, prowling round the deck and listening to the riot below, he came on Bartholomew sitting all alone on the fo'c'sle head polishing a pistol.

'Bartholomew! Can it be that someone is sober?'

'Ay, I'm sober.'

'I congratulate you.'

'You needn't. I'd like to be drunk as well as the next man, but my stomach won't let me. A real trial my stomach is to me.' And then, with sudden venom: 'And the way that bastard is handling the wheel takes my appetite away.'

'Can you sail her?'

'I would sail her between Silla and Caribbees and not as much as scrape her paint.'

'Get aft, then, and take the wheel.'

Henry stayed there for a little, listening to the rush and creak of a ship dipping to the sea and thinking of his future, but presently he went aft to join Bartholomew, and they stayed there together in unspoken communion above the rioting ship.

'Whose ears are you going to hang your pearls in, Bart?' he asked.

'Nobody's ears. I'd as soon push them down their throats. All the trouble in this world started when women came into it – bar my old woman, of course.' It was clear that Bartholomew was out of temper.

'For a man who has just come into a fortune, you would seem to have a jaundiced outlook on life,' Henry said, wondering whether that cottage in the Mendips was looking suddenly less desirable now that it was possible of realisation. 'Does nothing give you pleasure tonight?'

'Yes,' said Bartholomew, indicating the spread of canvas above them in the night. 'That does.'

After a pause, Henry said: 'Will you sail with me, Bart?'

'I'll sail with you – Cap'n.'

3

A MAN MAY own a ship, but unless he is captain of a crew he goes where the ship goes. And not one of the men from that camp in the forest would go anywhere near a British possession as long as they had anything to do with the ship they had taken. They would go to Tortuga, they said. From that bleak and wind-swept little island off the north coast of Hispaniola they could get passage anywhere. It was a sort of clearing-house for the whole Caribbean; and, for those who needed it, an unfailing source of employment, lawful and otherwise. To the sheltering wing of the French and the gratifying tolerance of Tortuga they would go; far from Admiralty courts and the stinking English conscience and the curiosity of the official mind.

So north away from Barbados sailed the *Fortune*, beating up through the islands into the north-east trade, day after blue-green day. Her Spanish crew worked the ship, and the victors lay about the deck in attitudes of ostentatious idleness. They ate, slept, and gambled; and were monumentally bored. The stores of pearls changed hands continuously. By early afternoon they were drunk. By night they were either moribund or quarrelsome.

It was Chris, that man with the face of an unfrocked priest, who kept them in order; and that was because Chris could drink immense quantities of neat rum without succumbing and because they were afraid of him. Even Timsy, who when drunk was a maniac, kept in some recess of his crazy mind a recognition of the lethal quality in Chris, and would stop in his tracks and whimper as the long, thin man got to his feet to correct him. When at last peace reigned because everyone else was insensible, Chris would pour a final mugful for himself and would fall asleep only one degree short of flash point.

Only one man on board the *Fortune* had a harder head than Chris. And that was Henry Morgan.

'You do not drink, Señor?' Don Christoval de Rasperu askey him, as the 'passenger' was having his daily outing and thed were walking round the deck together.

Henry said that, on the contrary, he drank a great deal. But it went missing somewhere between his throat and his stomach. Which was a sad thing for more reasons than the obvious one. It snared one into drinking more than was good for one in the tropics.

'It is sad,' said Don Christoval, looking at the large, slack form of Tugnet lying unconscious in the evening shadow below the break of the poop, 'it is sad to be given this precious gift of life and to find nothing better to do with it than seek ever for temporary death. Life embarrasses them, it would seem. They run away from it. They do their best to give it back.'

Don Christoval de Rasperu had been sent from Spain to inspect and report upon the colonies on the South American seaboard, and Henry regarded him with the tender interest of a man for his latest investment. Spain might or might not be willing to ransom the crew of the *Gloria*, but for the excellent Don Christoval de Rasperu they would pay willingly and high. It was important that Don Christoval stay whole and healthy. Don Christoval therefore got the choice times of the day for his enlargement from the after-cabin, and if sometimes he forgot to go back when his appointed time was up, no one was officious enough to call his attention to the lapse. Unless it was the Captain. Who, having got over his initial fright, and being now fairly certain that neither death nor torture lay in the offing, lived in a state of fret and fume that was melting the flesh from his bones even more effectively than the heat of the after-cabin. To be a prisoner on his own ship was bitter, but to take second place to a passenger was gall and wormwood. The only person who did his best to make Don Christoval's life a misery on board the *Fortune* was his fellow-captive and countryman, the late Captain of the *Gloria*.

The Spaniard with the dark ringlets was kicked daily by the Dorset man for his bad taste in having once made one of the *Santa Marta's* crew; but that little matter of principle having been attended to, he was left in peace. Indeed, he sometimes fell heir to the dregs in the Dorset man's mug because they shared an experience that was not common to anyone else on board.

The mate of the *Gloria* was freed altogether, so that he might run the crew and attend to the navigation; and Henry became his pupil in the matter of chart and compass. Don Christoval, who was a mathematician, would make a third at these sessions; and he and the mate would compare and argue this still new science, Don Christoval full of theories and the mate stubborn with practice; and Henry listened and learned.

This was his first real voyaging among the islands that he came to know so well – the magic, small, anonymous islands of the Caribbean. In endless permutations of innocence they stood about the empty seas fresh, it seemed, from creation's dawn. The little bays with sand so white, so virgin, that it was one with the breaking wave; the reefs with their single rank of crazy palms, like some divine awkward squad. To a practical sailor-mind they represented shelter or a lee shore, as the case might be; fresh water, food, and refreshment of body; landfall or bearing. But long after they were commonplace he would pause in the ploy of the moment to stand astare, mazed with their beauty.

And the *Fortune* was their equal in the mind of every man who sailed in her. She had been careened in America, and she handled like a dinghy. She would come about 'like a lady going back for her prayer-book', as Bartholomew said. And her speed in a following wind was such that her victors, used all their lives to the sheer dead weight that crusted the products of English and Spanish ships, could hardly believe it. It took only a week for boredom to drive the conquerors to the ship's service, and they polished, spliced, caulked, cleaned, and painted with a proprietary pride; half-surreptitiously at first, as if it were beneath their new dignity as millionaires, then openly when no one remarked on their activities. Bart contrived a Union flag out of the store in her sail locker, and it was under the proper colours that she sailed into the roads at Tortuga.

She came nosing her way through the reefs round Tortuga on a day when the wind was blowing the tops off the cobalt seas, so that the whole dark-blue ocean was shot with rainbow as the sunlight caught the spindrift. On the innermost reef, cruelly bright and clear in the pitiless light, was the remains of a ship, and they crowded to the side to look as the *Fortune* picked up her skirts and sidled past.

'That looks to me like Jack Morris's ship,' Bluey said, watching the waves spout up from her broken bows. 'I mind them dolphins as I mind my girl's eyes.'

'Your girl got eyes?' they mocked, Bluey being no beauty.

'The *Dolphin*, she was called, 'cause of them there dolphins at her bows. Or t'other way about. But that's Jack Morris's ship. Take my oath on that.'

They looked at her with the slight embarrassment of sailors in the presence of a wreck. Bart, standing by Morgan, said: 'She looks sort of ashamed, don't she? As if she was naked and we shouldn't be looking.'

But they kept on looking, fascinated.

'She can't have been long there, or they'd have broken her up,' Chris said. The seas, he meant. The seas combed over her tilted stem and rocketed into the air.

'Well, praise be to Christ and all His angels, I don't never have to go to sea again,' Tugnet said, turning away. And that was the verdict of them all. They went below for their little handkerchief bundles and their fortunes of pearls, and when the *Fortune* anchored off the port they rowed themselves ashore. They did not want any of the problematical ransom for the Spaniards, they said. They had more riches now than they would ever spend if they had nine lives, and they wanted no more.

'I'll miss Bluey's jew's-harp,' Bart said, leaning over the side, watching the boat pull away. Their farewell to him had been of the briefest; not because he had chosen to stay behind (in the weeks at sea it had become obvious that Bart was Morgan's ally, and they had accepted the fact without remark and without rancour) but because casualness was their way.

Henry wanted to say: 'How long do you think it will be before they are penniless?' but he did not know how much Bart himself had left of that heap of pearls. Bart had gambled like the rest, and it was understood that he had been unlucky; but to what extent Henry did not know. It warmed his heart, and would warm it as long as he lived, that Bart, with his fortune intact in his pocket, had elected nevertheless to sail with him.

'Well, what now?' asked Bart, at last; having watched the *Fortune's* boat pull ashore, and having reviewed the ships in harbour.

The Spaniards, with the exception of the mate, who was standing at their elbow, were locked up below. They were alone with their captives and the ship.

'There will be a bumboat along presently, trying to sell us stuff, I don't doubt. I'll go ashore with it and see if I can muster a skeleton crew to take us as far as Jamaica. It can't be more than two hundred miles from here, and the "trade" behind us all the way.'

But the day wore on to noon, and then to afternoon, and no boat came out to greet them or to hawk their wares. They freed the cook and set him to cooking dinner for all on board, and dinner was almost ready before a sail came shooting over the water in their direction.

'Too small and fast for a bumboat,' Bart said, watching the light craft come. 'Perhaps they're going to arrest us.'

The same thought had crossed Morgan's mind, and he was therefore very scornful of Bart's silly idea. What would they arrest a ship flying an English flag for?

'Yes, mighty fast and official-looking to be just paying a social call,' Bart said, glowering at the approaching boat.

The boat lowered her sail and swept round to the ladder on the lee side with an effortless piece of timing that spoke louder of seamanship than of pen-and-ink.

'*Not* so official,' Bart said, in a more hopeful tone.

There were three men in the boat, and they came up the ladder with no sign that any one of them had ever held a pen in his life. The first over the side was not very much older than Morgan; a spare, self-contained young man in good clothes that looked as if they had been made for him but were nevertheless not the clothes he habitually wore. Seaman ashore, said the clothes.

The man looked from Bart to Henry and then said to Henry: 'Captain Morgan?'

And with the magic word 'Captain', Henry's belief in his luck came back full and strong. He never forgot that Jack Morris was the first man to give him the title.

'My name is John Morris. Old John Morris's son, if you ever knew my father.'

'It's your ship —' Henry began involuntarily.

'Yes, it's my ship out on the reef yonder. And several good men besides. I don't beat about with words, Captain Morgan, so I'll tell you straight out that I heard you were looking for a crew. The *Dolphin's* crew are looking for a passage out of this hell-hole, and we'd be very glad to sail with you if you're bound for a British possession. Or anywhere, for that matter of it. This is my mate, Bernard Speirdyck, and his nephew, Cornelius Carstens.'

The stocky, blond man bowed in a jerky continental fashion, and the boy with the thatch of taffy-coloured hair smiled.

Henry, aware that his clothes were the best he could do with judicious confiscations from the Spaniards' wardrobes and that he had never in his life commanded as much as a yawl at sea, was a little overcome. He wanted to blurt out: 'You mean you'd sail under the command of a tyro like me?' But his unfailing vanity shook him to rights. 'You're not only captain of this vessel, you're the owner,' his vanity reminded him. 'You're the owner of one of the fastest craft of her size anywhere in the world today, with a clean bottom and well found, and you're a very desirable person to be acquainted with.'

So to John Morris he said that dinner was ready and they were about to sit down and they would be honoured if Captain Morris and his friends would join them. It would be sea fare, since they had not yet replenished, and not as good as Captain Morris would get ashore, but if he did not mind salt pork they would be glad of his company.

'Mind!' said Jack Morris. 'You don't seem to understand, Captain. We are on our beam-ends. We are on the rocks even more hopelessly than the poor *Dolphin* out there.'

And Henry, who if the positions had been reversed would

never have confessed to any such state, loved him for his frankness. As they went below it occurred to him that dolphins brought him luck. A Dolphin in Bridgetown brought him the *Fortune*, and now a Dolphin in Tortuga was providing him with a crew. He must remember dolphins when he was in need of luck.

Over the enormous meal of meat and strong drink that they thought suitable for a tropic afternoon, Henry explained that he was looking for an English authority to take custody of his prisoners and eventually accept ransom for them on his behalf. Where was the nearest English official? Jamaica, presumably?

'Here,' said Morris, and began to laugh.

'In Tortuga!'

'He must meet our Elias, mustn't he, Barney!'

'But Tortuga's French!'

'Not just at the moment. The Spaniards threw them out not long ago. But when we took Jamaica from the Spaniards they fled out of Tortuga in a panic to defend San Domingo against becoming a second Jamaica. And in walked Elias Watts with wife and family. He's living up at the castle; with his wife and brats and a battery of four guns, one of them workable. Making a success of it, too. Very popular, our Elias is. The French will be back in no time, of course, but until then Elias is the official governor.'

Elias Watts, however typical a piece of English colonial history, did not seem to Henry a very safe deposit for his prisoners. He still wanted to go to Jamaica, where he would find English officials of a more permanent type; officials who would not only accept his prisoners and give him his due share of their subsequent ransom, but would also supply him with letters of marque as a privateer.

'They are not very fond of privateers in Yamaica yoost now,' Speirdyck said. 'Every time a privateer slap Spain in the face, Spain come and slap Yamaica. The planters they do not like that.'

'Ay,' said Morris. 'They yell for help and say the Spaniards are treating the seas like their own, and then when we do account for a few Spanish privateers they yell because Spain is offended and comes and burns a village or two. They can't have it both ways.'

'These planters,' the Cornelius boy said, pausing in his swift, silent consumption of food to speak for the first time, 'they care for nothing but their crops. They do not care what Spain does to poor sailors or how many innocent men are rotting in Spanish prisons. For them it has never been a holy war.'

'I know someone who would think it a holy war,' Morgan said suddenly. And then, a little dashed: 'But he is away off in Barbados.'

'What's Barbados!' said Morris, whose world was the sea. 'Just a biscuit toss. I could find my way there blindfold, any time out of the hurricane season. If it's letters of marque you want, let's go to Barbados and get them. Who is your man in Barbados? Goodson?'

'Is that the Governor? No, there's a man who is just going to be Governor. A good Cromwell man,' said Henry, trying to keep his lip from curling. 'The great under-propper of the Roman Babylon, Cromwell says Spain is. I think Sir Thomas Modyford will be prepared to fight the Lord's battles to the extent of letters of marque. His estates in Barbados are not as handy to Spain as the Jamaican ones are, so he can serve the Lord, and Cromwell, and himself at the same time. There's just one thing. The *Fortune* will have to be victualled to take us back there, and I haven't a penny until I get the ransom for the prisoners.'

Bart looked up from his plate and said: 'If five pearls are any good to you, Harry, they're yours.'

'Five?' said Harry, involuntarily.

'Yes,' Bart said, shamefaced. 'That's all.'

'Bart, I'm ashamed of you. Who was the lucky one?'

'Not any one of them specially,' Bart said. 'They just went little by little. I'm still better off than I was before,' he added; and then, looking up at Henry: 'Much better off.'

Because Henry for once had no words ready, Morris said: 'Five pearls wouldn't get us far, but you can turn your prisoners over to Elias and get credit in the town for them. I hear you have an important one. On security like that Tortuga will supply you with anything you like to ask for.'

'I see my late colleagues have been talking.'

'Fluently.'

'I think when we have dined, Captain Morris, you and I had better go ashore and have a talk with your Elias.'

And so it came about that Don Christoval de Rasperu found himself being welcomed on the most infamous and disreputable of all the Caribbean islands by a worthy British matron of the most domestic type: a kind little woman who fussed over him, wiped her son's running nose, and lamented the shortage of gunpowder all in the same breath. Her husband accepted the custody of the crew on condition that he might put them to 'honourable employment' until such time as ransom was forthcoming for them. Tortuga swarmed with men of all nationalities, but not one of them would do what his lady called 'a hand's turn' on the island. They were prepared to be blown up, drowned, maimed, starved, and overworked at sea, but at the sight of a spade or a hoe they blenched. As long as the Spaniards were prepared to work for their keep, Elias was prepared to be responsible for them. For their health, that was. For any escapes from the island he could by no means hold himself responsible. He had no space to imprison nearly forty men, even if any of the Castle locks had keys. And with the sea at their doors escape was an ever-present possibility. But he would try to make their stay so pleasant that a normal return to Spain in due course would appear to them more desirable than turning themselves adrift on an unfriendly ocean.

The two sea-captains shared family dinner at the Castle, which was enlivened by the sneezes of one child and the proud recitation of the nine-times by another, admired Elias's highly ornamental battery, took a friendly farewell of an amused Don Christoval, and went down to the port to profit from the unbridled boastings of Chris, Tugnet, Bluey and company.

And so next day, the third since the *Fortune's* arrival at Tortuga, a two-way traffic was being conducted over the ship's side. Boats brought stores in quantity and took away prisoners in batches. The prisoners shook hands all round before they left.

They had had a wonderful time, they inferred. Short of a permanent pension, give them a cruise as prisoners of the English any day.

Only two made a scene. One was the boy who had played with the dog on the beach at Barbados, and the other was the ship's cook. The boy said that he, Manuel Sequerra, was a Portuguese, that he had done nothing against the English, and that in any case he wanted to sail with the Captain Morgan, who was his *beau ideal* of what a commanding officer should be. Toni, the cook, said that he was a Neapolitan, and as such had nothing to do with these insane wars that everyone was always indulging in; a stove, he inferred, was of all things the most international; it was inconceivable that he, Antonio Toscanelli, a Neapolitan and an artist, should be left to rot on Tortuga.

Since they were still short-handed on the *Fortune*, and since one of the men drowned on the reef had been the *Dolphin's* cook, neither Manuel's tears nor Toni's dramatics were necessary. Henry was very glad to have them. Toni was a very bad cook, but he was cleaner than most, and drank hardly at all.

On the night before they sailed, very late in the evening, the mulatto arrived at the bottom of the ladder, having spent his last poor coins in hiring a boat to take him out. Indeed, he had not had quite enough, and the boatman was loud in his demands for the balance from the *Fortune*; the mulatto had promised that the few odd pence would be paid when he arrived at the ship, he said. The mulatto was in tears. They had sold the dogs to a man who was going to Cuba, and the man had no need of him. He was lost without the dogs. He had also lost every pearl that he had ever possessed, but that seemed hardly to concern him. He could think of nothing but the parting with the dogs that had been his life. If Captain Morgan also had no use for him, then indeed his life was at an end.

'Manuel!' shouted Morgan.

'Captain! Sir! I come! I come!' Manuel came plummeting to the deck with a swoop that gave the unnautical Henry heart-failure.

'Kringle here has lost his friends the dogs, Manuel. He is —'

'Amigo!' said Manuel, throwing his arm round the mulatto

and not waiting for further explanation. 'And your heart is torn open and you are as if you had no skin. Come! I know. Come, and we will talk!' And he led the weeping man away forward without a backward glance.

'We didn't need that mulatto,' Bart said, watching them go.

'I wouldn't turn a dog away tonight,' Morgan said.

So the *Fortune* when she sailed with the tide in the morning, for the first time under her new name, was a happy ship. She had no pressed men on board and no prisoners. She was, on the contrary, the symbol of fortune and freedom to all on board. To Henry, who had taken her, and who had preferred her to riches. To Jack Morris, and his crew, whom she rescued from the beach. To Bart, who was Mr Kindness again and a person of importance in the world of the sea. To Toni, who was back in his own galley. To Manuel, who was sailing with his hero. And to a greatly comforted mulatto, who had strong hopes of taming a rat before they reached Barbados.

Bernard Speirdyck, being a Hollander, took personal credit for the *Fortune's* good points, and at each evidence of adaptability would say: 'Ah, yoost look at her, yoost look at her! A Hollander down to her bilges.' He called them 'biltches'. And Cornelius, when reproved by his uncle for some shortcoming, would retire to the fo'c'sle and imitate him. 'Ah, yoost look at him, yoost look at him! A Hollander down to the biltches!'

Jack Morris made good his boast of being able to sail to Barbados blindfold, and the *Fortune* dropped anchor outside Bridgetown long before the mulatto had tamed his rat. Indeed, it was a little too soon for Henry, who had secret qualms about the coming interview with Modyford. He kept remembering the elegant clothes and cool, expensive air of the man who had dined that day at the Dolphin, and wondering what such a man would think of his borrowed Spanish finery. Which, since he had no ready money, were all the clothes he still possessed. He longed to borrow that very fine bottle-green suit of Jack's, but could not bring himself to suggest it. He would have to go ashore in his Spanish things.

Bridgetown looked very neat and civilized in its green setting after Tortuga; and its familiarity after so many strange scenes made it seem oddly like home. And Henry, being rowed ashore, took comfort in the thought that Spanish clothes, however outlandish and open to misconstruction, were an undoubted improvement on denim breeches and a frieze coat. It was a thing to marvel at that only the other day he had trudged into this town carrying a kerchief bundle that might have belonged to Bluey or Tugnet. His affection for Bridgetown increased every time he remembered it. When Elias Watts had asked him where, in this new unstable world, a letter would find him, he had said: 'The Dolphin at Bridgetown will always find me.' The Dolphin had seen the beginning of his luck; it should witness the progress of it. Every now and then he would come back and trail his latest successes through the dark, cool room on the harbour front where he had spun his first gold piece.

'Meet me at the Dolphin,' he said now to Jack Morris, who had come ashore with him, 'and we'll drink to the letter-of-marque.'

Morris had come ashore entrusted with one of Bart's five pearls and instructions that he should buy drink for the whole crew with it. The crew had been promised time ashore as soon as the *Fortune* was proved acceptable to the authorities, but they had said: 'Pad round Bridgetown with nothing in our pockets! Not us!' And when the third mate had said couldn't Mr Kindness treat them to the pearl's worth just as well on shore, Bart had said dryly: 'It's drink I'm treating them to.'

It amused Morgan to find that the same loafer was still leaning at the door of the Dolphin and still picking his teeth with a fish-bone. He stopped and said: 'Well, is he Governor yet?'

'Who?' asked the man.

'Sir Thomas.'

'Modyford? Oh, aye, he's Governor. What made you ask?'

'You prophesied that he would be very soon.'

'Prophesied to who?'

'To me.'

'Never saw you before in my life,' said the man.

Upon which Henry laughed and said: 'See how easy it is to

leave denim behind, Jack!' and walked away, still laughing, to call on the Governor.

Henry had imagined himself walking into a room and talking man to man across a table with the man who had sat across the room from him that afternoon at the Dolphin. But it turned out to be not at all like that. At the official residence of the Governor a secretary interviewed him and asked him to state his business, informed him that the Governor's day was nearly over and that in half an hour or so he would be leaving for his home in the country, and that the press of affairs was very great.

Henry said that he, Henry Morgan, was one of those affairs, and the secretary left him to wait in a little hot room, where his heart grew less joyful and his head less confident. When at last the pen-and-ink man came back and said: 'Captain Morgan, please,' irritation, plain itching irritation, had taken the place of that fine flourish with which he had parted from Jack Morris.

And irritation was no quantity to take to an interview with Thomas Modyford.

Sir Thomas was very polite, and apologised for keeping his visitor waiting. He looked tired but not unfriendly. The apology did something to soothe Henry's ruffled vanity, and he in turn had the grace to regret in suitable words his belated arrival; and then, the amenities having been observed, he stated his errand.

'The *Fortune*?' said Sir Thomas. 'That is the newcomer, out in the roads.'

They were right about this man, Henry thought. Bart was right in his face-reading: you would have to start very early to get the better of Sir Thomas, or he would make you feel unpunctual. The ship had been there not more than an hour and the Governor had had 'press of affairs' all the afternoon, but he knew about the arrival.

He also knew what the arrival looked like. It looked, he said, very like a ship called the *Gloria* that the Spaniards were much worried about. The *Gloria* had disappeared off the coast of Barbados, and pressing inquiries had been addressed to the authorities about her.

'She *is* the *Gloria*,' Henry said. 'We took her, up the coast a little from here.'

'Unprovoked?' asked Modyford.

'No,' said Henry; 'they provoked us past bearing.'

'What had they done?'

'There wasn't a man of them who hadn't been born in Spain.'

'So you took her on principle. Or was it that you perhaps wanted a better ship than your own? What, by the way, did you take her in?'

'Our stocking soles.'

'What!' said Sir Thomas, startled out of his urbanity.

'Our stocking soles, I said, sir.'

'Yes, but with what ship?'

'We did not have a ship. We were hunting boar in the forest, and the ship put in for water. We liked the look of her and we didn't like the flag she was wearing, so we went out in our long-boat after dark and seized her.'

'We?' said the Governor faintly. 'How many?'

'Ten white men, one mulatto, and one Indian.'

Sir Thomas sat disgesting this for a little. 'Would it be indiscreet of me to inquire what became of the Spanish crew?' he asked at last.

'It would be very natural, sir. They are on Tortuga, waiting to be ransomed.'

'All of them?'

'When we sailed from Tortuga they were all there. I don't know how many are there now. The castle has no keys, and Mr Elias Watts has plans for them that I don't think they are going to like.'

'Plans?'

'Spade-and-hoe plans, sir.'

'Ah. Torture. That will be another black mark against us in Spanish archives. Am I to understand, then, that there were no – casualties?'

'Only some blood-letting.'

'And this Señor de Rasperu? This Don Christoval?'

'I victualled the ship with him.'

'What!' said the Governor for the second time.

'I exchanged him for some meal and salt beef.'

'You mean that he is safe on Tortuga?'

'I'll take my oath that he is, sir. The dealers are not going to let him out of their sight until they have their hands on that ransom.'

'Is he in prison there?'

'No, sir, oh no. He is teaching little Oliver his eleven-times.'

'Oliver!'

'Oliver Watts.'

A shadow of suspicion was perceptible in Sir Thomas's grey eye. But he said smoothly: 'I am glad to hear that the gentleman is living comfortably *en famille* with the Governor.'

'Well – *en famille*,' said Henry; and the shadow in Sir Thomas's grey eye deepened almost to a smile.

'So you want me to give you a letter-of-marque?' He paused and looked benevolently at Henry. 'I think, do you know, that as an example of impudence that defeats even your taking of the *Gloria*.' And as Henry looked startled: 'You must be aware, young man, that letters-of-marque are given only to men of reputation; to masters of vessels who are well known to us and answerable for their actions. An English commission is not merely handed out to anyone who asks for it.'

'I am not "anyone"!' Henry wanted to say. But instead he said: 'I have taken a ship from my country's enemies without the loss of a life, and I have handed over my prisoners for ransom. What more do you want?'

'I should want, in the first instance, to know more about *you*. How did you come to be hunting boar in Barbados, for instance?'

Now if I tell him I'm a freed bondsman, thought Henry, he'll never accept me. 'Is there anything of ill-repute in hunting boar?'

'No. But a great many ill-reputed persons do so. I never saw you before this afternoon —'

'But —' began Henry, and stopped. Then, after all, he had been for Sir Thomas only a blank space: a place on which to rest his glance.

'But?'

'Nothing, sir.'

'I had never seen you before and know nothing about you. I have, indeed, only your word for it that Don Christoval is instructing the young in the mysteries of the multiplication table and not being digested by sharks. You must have some background, my friend, before I could be responsible for giving you a commission.'

'I thought the war against Spain was a holy war!'

'It has been so far,' Modyford said with a dryness that was lost on the angry Morgan.

'How immaculate must one be to take part in a holy war? I have never heard that the Crusaders were asked for testimonials or guarantees before they went to fight in Palestine.'

'No,' Modyford said with a half-smile. 'The Crusades might have proved a greater success if they had. I admire your exploit, young man, and I would give you official recognition if it were within my power. But I have a great responsibility vested in me, and I cannot abuse it. If I can help you unofficially, of course, I shall be glad to do so. You want to dispose of the cargo, perhaps. What is it, by the way?'

'Wood,' said Henry, almost unable to get the monosyllable out.

'Wood for dyeing? Logwood?'

'No. If it had been logwood I could have sold it in Tortuga. Wood for building.'

'Oh. Not so good. But perhaps I could find a purchaser for you.'

'I should not dream of putting Your Excellency to that inconvenience.'

'I am not planning to confiscate the ship when you bring her in, if that is what is in your mind.'

'That is very generous of Your Excellency,' said Henry through his teeth.

Modyford cast him a glance that was almost pitying, but Henry did not see it. Even if he had been aware of it, it is doubtful if he would have pleaded where he had requested and been refused. He was sick with disappointment and aching with hurt pride.

'I am sorry not to be able to be of official help to you,' Sir Thomas said.

'And I am sorry to have taken up Your Excellency's valuable

time,' said Henry with a sarcasm he was too young and too angry to make light enough to be effective.

He went out in a blind anger, and stood in the dusty road until the mist cleared from in front of his eyes and his breath came more easily. Then he walked slowly back to the Dolphin. The Dolphin that had been going to witness all those progressive triumphs of his.

Jack Morris was sitting where Bartholomew had sat on that afternoon a few weeks ago, and Henry slumped into the seat by his side without looking at him, and reached for the mug on the table. He finished what was in the mug and called on the serving-man for more.

'No?' said Morris, into the silence that followed.

'I made a mistake,' Henry said.

'What kind of mistake?'

'I did not go to school with his son.'

The equable Morris let this pass in silence and waited until Henry had had the drink he had sent for.

Then he said: 'So *that* was his excuse.'

'That was his *reason*.'

'Oh, no, it wasn't.'

'What do you know about it!'

'I don't know what his excuse was – except what I can guess – but about his reason for saying no I know a great deal, and believe me, Harry Morgan, it had nothing whatever to do with you. The excellent Governor is teetering on the edge of a chasm, and he isn't going to take any step that may overbalance him. Was he civil, by the way?'

Henry tried to think back beyond the blackness of his defeat, and confessed that yes, he supposed Modyford had been civil.

'Well, that is something to his credit.'

'What chasm?'

'You said you came to Modyford because he was a good Cromwell man and would consider war against Spain a holy war.'

'Yes.'

'Well, it isn't going to do him any good any more to be a good Cromwell man.'

'Why?'

'Because Cromwell's dead. He's been dead for months.'

'No!' said Henry, all his personal failure and fury vanishing in the wonder of this news.

'The town's got over their excitement because they've known for a week, but they're waiting with their breath held for the next news. The gossip is all that young Charles will be king. And the person who is holding his breath tightest is your friend the Governor. The holy war is at an end, and he doesn't want to take any part in anything that has become unfashionable. He wouldn't give his best friend a letter-of-marque against Spain this week.'

'So *that* was it!' Henry's shrivelled 'conceit of himself' swelled and unfolded into healthy bloom again. 'It wasn't —'

He began to bask. And then, looking back at Modyford from his recovered security: 'The damned sail-trimmer!' he said.

4

NOW THAT HE was no longer a snubbed nobody, and could look down with cheerful superiority on a sail-trimming Governor, the world was once more Henry's. But if it was still a world full of opportunity, the opportunities were hardly as insistent as they had been.

What were they to do now?

'There's always trade, I suppose,' Henry said, a little dashed at this unexciting way to fortune.

'Not in this part of the world,' Morris pointed out. 'The Spaniards don't allow it. They don't even allow us the freedom of watering our ships, God blast them! The trade's all Spain's. Unless you were planning a ferry service between Barbados and Jamaica.'

Henry did not bother to answer that.

'You could sail her home, of course.'

'I'm not ready to go home,' said Henry shortly.

'You could sell her there for a good sum. They're short of ships,' said Morris, who had long ago come privately to the conclusion that Henry, who was so obviously neither criminal nor born pauper, had run away from England to avoid a debtor's prison.

'I'm not ready to go home.' Henry looked in some surprise at him and said: 'Would you and the crew go home in her?'

'No. My life is here.'

'So is mine,' said Henry, 'so let's hear no more of England. You don't think,' he added, the mention of England reminding him, 'that they're going to make peace with Spain at home, do you?'

'I think it's highly likely.'

'But they can't!' said Henry.

'Why worry?' said Morris, amused at Morgan's heat. 'It means only some ink on a paper; and perhaps more comfortable sleep for the gentlemen at home. They can't change Spanish habits with a scrape of the pen. It will make no difference to us.'

'It will make no difference to what they do to us, you mean. It will make a very big difference to what we can do to them.'

'For a little. It won't last, you know. The Spaniards always overdo things. In no time at all they'll do something that even the gentlemen at home can't overlook, and then it will be once more legitimate to what Barney calls "slap Spanish faces".'

'There are times when I could throttle you, Jack. You talk as if you were going to live for four hundred years and time was nothing to you.'

'Things always turn up,' Morris said, with a sailor's easy philosophy, and looked at the descendant of soldiers with something like affection. 'Drink up, and look on the bright side.' He summoned the serving-man. 'We have a ship, and that's something. I know a great many good men knocking about the Caribbean who'd give their right arm for that.'

'We also have a cargo,' said Henry, not too happily.

'Did your Governor show any signs of wanting to confiscate it?'

'No. He offered to help us get a buyer.'

'He did! That was vastly obliging of him, upon my word.'

'I would dump the whole lot in the sea sooner than let him get a percentage of it.' What he really meant was 'sooner than let him help me.'

'Perhaps he didn't want a percentage.'

'I never came across an official yet that didn't.'

'You didn't discuss it with him, then.'

'No,' said Henry. 'He was too busy explaining to me what an undesirable piece of flotsam I was. Did you buy the rum for Bart?'

'Yes. They've sent it down to the ferry steps, and we'll take it out with us. About the cargo: I know a little man here that used to be a carpenter in the Navy. Was chips on a frigate, and lost both his legs when a gun blew up. He makes furniture for all those new people coming out. Planters and what not. Perhaps he would take some of the wood off our hands.'

So they went to look for Mr Boobyer, and found him on the farthest edge of the town on the inland side, out of sight and sound of the sea, and half buried in exotic greenery. They followed the sound of a saw and the smell of cut wood up a little alley, and there was the ex-Navy man, looking oddly like a piece of Plymouth dropped down in the tropics.

'Well, well, Jack Morris!' he said, laying the saw carefully down and sweeping the sawdust off a bench with a fine hospitable gesture. 'You fetched up on a lee shore again?'

'Not exactly,' Morris said, and presented Henry.

'Captain!' commented Mr Boobyer. 'You haven't been wasting time, young man. Is it true what I hear about the *Dolphin*, Jack?'

'Yes. She's on the reefs outside Tortuga.'

'Too bad. Too bad. Fog, was it?'

'No. Hurricane.'

'Ah, a man's mad to go to sea when he could stay on shore. Look at me. Nothing to do all day but work with the sweet wood. Can't even smell the sea from here. Cosy as a weevil in a biscuit.'

Henry complimented him on the chair that he was making.

'Ah,' agreed Mr Boobyer. 'Nice, that is. That's for the Governor. A set of six it is. Governor's a Devon man, like me. Knows a good bit of work when he sees it.'

'What will happen if they string him up?' Morris asked.

'What for?' asked Mr Boobyer, startled.

'Treason. Or even regicide, perhaps. The Royalists are coming back, it seems.'

'Ah, Governor's a Devon man. He'll come out on top. *You* see. Any come, it has nothing to do with me. Anyone in the island will be glad to get this set of chairs. You don't get wood like that every day. No, nor workmanship, neither.'

'Find it difficult to get wood?' Morris asked, and broached their proposition.

At first Mr Boobyer was not interested. What would he do with a whole ship-load of wood?

'Not a whole load,' Henry said. 'We'll keep some as ballast.'

'Ah,' agreed Mr Boobyer. 'At least it won't sink you.'

But it was not until he had heard the tale of the *Fortune* that he really considered the deal. When Henry and Jack Morris between them had made clear to him how the *Gloria* became the *Fortune* and how the *Fortune* by being crewless had rescued the marooned crew of the *Dolphin* from boredom and semi-starvation on Tortuga, he began to wheeze, then he began to heave, then he sat down on the bench beside him and mopped his eyes, and it was clear that Mr Boobyer was laughing.

'Well!' he said, when speech was possible to him. 'If that don't beat cock-fighting!'

Then, when he had heaved and wheezed and mopped his eyes a little more, he said: 'Now about this wood.'

And it seemed that although he would need only a small amount himself, he would undertake to sell the rest for shipbuilding. He would pay them for his share now, and pay them the rest as he sold the wood.

'And I know what's troubling you, so you needn't tell me,' he said, with a sly glance at their faces. 'You're afraid to bring the *Fortune* in. Afraid they'll disallow and confiscate her. Ain't you? Well, you don't have to bring her in a fathom. You drop the logs overside and let the tide bring them in, and my boys'll rope and chain them on the beach till I want them. How's that?'

'Mr Boobyer, you put away your saw and come down to the Dolphin with us,' Henry said.

'I don't have to stump as far as the Dolphin for good liquor,' Mr Boobyer said, and produced a bottle. Then he climbed into the loft above his workroom as neatly as if he had a pair of feet instead of two wooden pegs, and brought down the price of the wood in good English currency. Henry could have embraced him.

'If they get rid of Modyford,' he said, as they went back to the harbour, 'they could do worse than appoint your Mr Boobyer as Governor. He doesn't waste any energy balancing himself on a fence.'

They felt very rich as they walked into the hot town again, and Henry lingered in front of the shops as he had lingered on that other visit, planning wardrobes for himself. But where on that previous occasion it had been an academic delight, it was now a very present form of torture. He need not wear his Spanish clothes any longer; he had money in his pocket, and he could walk in and buy the best the island had to offer. But the *Fortune* needed the money. He was poorer personally in the matter of money today than he had been that day weeks ago with a gold coin in his pocket.

But in all other ways infinitely richer, he reminded himself. So what did it matter that he must wear his Spanish clothes a little longer?

He would be at sea tomorrow, and there would be no cool grey eyes there to look him over and judge him by his garments.

'Anyhow,' he said aloud, 'they would take too long to make them.'

And Jack Morris, who had understood every unspoken word of this self-communion, and who had known all his life what it was to have the ship come first, finally rendered his allegiance.

Henry's method of compensation was to over-pay the ferryman who took them out to the *Fortune*. In what way this should comfort him for not being able to buy himself clothes, he could not have said. If he could not be elegant, he could be large.

The crew were gathered round the ladder watching them come, and it endeared them to Henry that their interest seemed to be first for the future of the *Fortune*, and only secondly for the barrel.

'What did they say, Captain?' they shouted, hanging over the side.

'Are we privateers?'

'What luck, sir?'

'Did they make you a knight, Captain?'

When they heard that they had no official standing, there was a loud groan, frank opinion of the Governor, and franker suggestion of what they would do to him and what he could do to himself.

'He may not be Governor much longer,' Henry said; and found that the news about the changes at home, after the erratic manner of rumour, had, even in harbour, passed them by.

The news of Cromwell's death shattered their unanimity.

'Well,' said a man named Wish, in a Sussex drawl, 'the old bastard'll be havin' a deal of explainin' to do at this moment.'

'Oliver Cromwell was the greatest man who ever lived!' a Lincolnshire man called Benrose said.

'He was a damned murderer and a king-killer,' said a third.

'Oh, go roll your barrel,' said Morris.

And they rolled the cask away for'ard, the fight growing louder and wordier at every step.

'There will be murder,' said Morgan, 'if that is how they feel about it sober.'

'Oh, no,' Morris said comfortably; 'there's seven Royalists to every Cromwell man.'

'I've never asked you how you feel about it, Jack?'

'About them beheading the King? I suppose I was too young to care much, and too much out of England for it to concern me very close.' And as they went down to the cabin he added amiably: 'But I hate their damned Puritan faces.'

Toni put a meal in front of them, and hastened away to make sure of his share of the barrel. They ate largely, but in silence.

'There's always piracy,' Morris said at last.

Henry did not even bother to smile.

After another silence Henry said: 'Perhaps if I had played my cards better he might have listened. If I had been cooler. He might have given you the letter-of-marque, if I had only thought of it.'

'He wouldn't give his own brother a letter-of-marque today.'

'He might have risked it for a Morris. Someone of reputation in the islands.'

'He isn't going to put his name to any commission against Spain only to find that a treaty with Spain was signed a month ago. You never had a hope with Modyford.'

Henry scraped his plate and pushed it away from him. He sat back in his chair, pushed his long legs out under the table, and lay there glooming down his nose at the debris.

'Of course,' he said suddenly in the quiet tones of one to whom a great revelation is being vouchsafed, 'there is nothing to hinder me from defending myself.'

Morris thought this over, and smiled.

'Trailing your coat, is that it?'

'Yes. Trailing my coat. You don't need any commissions and letters-of-marque to resist capture.'

'No, but you need a deal of luck.'

'I have all the luck in the world. And brains besides. And a whole stock of ball and powder that was loaded for the voyage from America to Spain and has never been touched. How many of your men were gunners?'

'Twelve. And three more could probably serve them at a pinch.'

'And we have the fastest ship in the Caribbean and the handiest. You can turn her on a groat. I can't think why I ever bothered to ask the damned Governor for his piddling commission.'

'It does make things easier afterwards,' Morris said, amused. 'They don't always believe you when you explain how you came to sink a ship.'

'I'm not planning to sink one just yet. We'll look them over till we find a good new ship for you, first of all.'

At this Morris sat back and laughed.

'What amuses you?' asked Henry.

'The breadth of your ideas. It isn't every man who designs to go "eenie, meenie, minie, moe" round the Caribbean till he finds the ship he wants to appropriate.'

'Laugh as much as you please. But I promise you that one month from now we shall have a ship for you. And not any old scow, either. Something you will be proud to sail.'

But as it turned out it was more than three months before Jack Morris took over the *City of Seville*. This was not because Henry had failed to make good his boast, but because the first ship they took was so badly mauled by a final and redundant *feu-de-joie* fired by that admirer of zeal, Walter Benrose from Lincolnshire, that she sank before they could board her; and all the *Fortune* got out of the engagement was the necessity of feeding thirty-seven rescued survivors for five days until they could be dumped ashore on an island. In the two months that separated this episode from the meeting with the *City of Seville* the life of Mr Benrose was hardly worth living. And his political friends among the crew, pinning on to the Puritans their referred resentment of Walter, went over *en bloc* with a fine flourish of illogicality to the Royalist cause.

The hunting-ground for privateers was, of course, off the mainland of America; and it was there the *Fortune* headed as soon as she had rid herself of her wooden burden and taken on board what stores were urgently needed. She proceeded to saunter up and down from Cartagena to Campeche and back again, but except for the vessel sunk by the too-zealous Walter, the only ships she met were either English privateers, with whom she paused to exchange news, or Spanish men-of-war carrying tiers of guns and a crew the size of a town's population, to whom they showed a clean pair of heels. And then one day, watering near an Indian village on the coast of Mexico, they were told by the inhabitants, to whom any enemy of Spain was automatically a friend, that a small Spanish warship was lying at Vera Cruz and was due to sail home before the beginning of the hurricane season. Any time in the next fortnight, they thought, she would be sailing.

She came up over the horizon on a thundery morning five days later: a brigantine carrying eighteen guns. The *Fortune* loitered under half her sail across the empty sea, and watched her hopefully. The Spaniard changed course like a terrier sighting a rabbit and came bearing down on her. The *Fortune* waited until she was sure that the English flag was plain and visible to them, and then, crowding on sail with every sign of panic, she fled before them. Towing, incidentally, a quarter ton of sea-anchor, to prevent her from falling over the farther horizon before the Spaniard caught up with her. As they began to close the distance she picked up her sea-anchor and with her recovered speed crossed to the windward side of the Spaniard's bows, so that the *Seville* had to come up on her port side and the *Fortune* had the wind.

'What do you make the range?' asked Henry of Morris, watching the *Seville* draw level with them. 'Are we inside it?'

'Good God, we could shake hands with them!' said Morris. 'Draw off a little or she'll blow us out of the water at that range.'

'She has to be tempted,' said Henry.

'She can be tempted just as well just inside extreme range; which was what we planned,' Morris said, watching in agony.

In action their positions were strangely reversed: Henry being as detached as if he were not personally concerned at all, Morris in a fever of foreboding.

'Do you think they are not even going to challenge us?' Henry asked with interest. 'And we an innocent English ship with our gun-ports closed and our minds on our business.'

'All that matters to those bastards over there is that we are English and defenceless and there are no witnesses.'

'We ought to sink them,' Henry said virtuously. 'Do you really want this ship, Jack?'

'Here it comes,' Morris said, his eyes on the nine gun-mouths studding the *Seville's* starboard side. 'Dear Christ, I wish I had lived a better life.'

The broadside rocked their eardrums and reverberated on the heavy air. One ball carried away part of the rail on the port quarter, one sent a shower of splinters down on to the main deck from the mast, one tore a hole in the fore-sail, one went through the shrouds of the fore-mast and left them fluttering like a hoist of signal flags, and the rest sang over the heads of the crew and fell into the water beyond.

They had not only been inside range: they had been so well within range that the Spaniard had overshot them.

Their plan had been to close in immediately they had cajoled the Spaniards into emptying their guns on that side, but the *Fortune's* lightness and speed frustrated them. She swept ahead of the *Seville*, leaving her own broadside undelivered.

'Let her go,' Henry said, 'and bring her about. We have twenty minutes before they are ready again.'

'But she'll be turning yoost now to fire the side that is still unused,' Bernard said.

'Yes, but we'll be back before she's round. She has never seen the *Fortune* turning on a groat.'

And back came the *Fortune* with her gun-ports open and swept at point-blank range down the helpless starboard side of the *Seville*. She had only five guns a-side, and instead of firing them as a broadside, she fired them individually, each at a target arranged beforehand. The five targets were gun-ports, and she hit four out of the five. The men on deck, at easy musket-shot, picked off the few men not engaged below with the guns. And then, as she bore away a little, willy-nilly, from the turning ship the *Fortune* witnessed an amazing sight. On to the deck from both forward and after-hatches poured the men from the *Seville's* gundeck.

'What is it?' asked the *Fortune's* crew anxiously. 'Is she going to blow up?' They were much too close for that to be a pleasant prospect.

'No,' Henry said. 'It can't be that, or they would be throwing themselves into the water. They seem to be holding a protest meeting.'

'Always great talkers, the Spaniards,' said Bart, sucking a splinter wound.

'Well, let's use our other broadside before they recover,' Morris suggested.

But as they came up with her again they saw that the crew had overrun the poop and were waving bits of cloth in sign of surrender.

'It's a mutiny,' they said on the *Fortune*.

And while they watched, wondering, the Spaniard's colour crept down from the masthead.

'What *is* this?' asked the *Fortune's* crew, suspicious of this easy victory.

'Do you want a boat, Captain?' asked Kinnel, the bo'sun.

'No; all things considered, we'll lay her alongside.'

So in the long oily swell and the subsiding wash of their contending the ships came together, and Henry, leaving Bernard in charge, stepped with Morris over the *Seville's* rail to take possession; and to have the mystery of their behaviour explained to him.

They had a runaway gun.

One of the *Fortune's* shots through the gunports had broken the retaining cable. This would have been bad enough in the regular swell of a sea, but in the broken water of their combined wakes the unpredictability of the free gun's maniac chargings about the gun-deck had broken their nerve. No gunnery could, in any case, take place while the blind hippopotamus plungings went on. They had seen one of their number killed and one crushed by the runaway, and they had fled to safety and to surrender before the *Fortune* should begin to batter them at her own sweet will.

'Why didn't you sail her away?' asked Henry.

'Away from that?' they said, with hand-wavings at the *Fortune*. 'One might as well try to run away from a wasp.'

But Henry, looking at the unmaimed ship, still marvelled; and Jack Morris said: 'God save me from ever being at the mercy of a crew like that.'

Their precipitancy was a little explained when it was made clear that three of the four men killed by musket-shot on the deck had been officers. The crew had come pouring up from the nightmare below to find no directing mind waiting for them. They had come from a small particular chaos to a larger, more general one, and their panic had swelled in sympathy.

'Well?' called Bernard Speirdyck, from his temporary command on the *Fortune's* quarter-deck. 'What frightens them?'

'They have a runaway gun. My congratulations to the *Fortune's* gunners.'

'Send us over the captain of her, Captain,' shouted Cornelius, 'the crew want to hang him.'

'They can't. They've already killed him. My congratulations to the *Fortune's* musketeers.'

They cheered at this, but someone called: 'Send him over anyway. We'll hang him as he is.'

On board the *Seville* the only dead apart from the three officers were the man killed by the gun and a man who had been pierced through the throat by a wood splinter. The man hurt by the runaway was now having his leg amputated by the surgeon. He had been dragged up on deck by one of the more self-possessed of his fleeing colleagues and was lying by the main hatch, where the surgeon, with that indifference to his surroundings which has come to be a characteristic of his profession, was laying out his knives and saws and needle-and-thread on a napkin. Henry, who had witnessed death in many forms on his voyage out from home – from fever, from accident, from delerium due to alcohol – had not so far seen any surgery performed, and he went down to the main deck to look.

The leg had been crushed to pulp above the ankle and was a mere oozing mess, but the man did not appear to be in any pain. He looked dazed and indifferent. A friend was engaged in filling him up with rum as an anæsthetic, and Henry could not tell whether his dazed condition was the result of anæsthesia or of his injury.

'He's about ready,' the colleague said in his own tongue to the surgeon, whereupon his friends held him while the surgeon sawed briskly through tibia and fibula and expertly sewed up the flaps of flesh. The man made no movement of protest, and the surgeon might have been trying a sock on him for all the effect it seemed to have on him. Henry, on the other hand, was acutely conscious of the sultry air that pressed all round him; air so heavy that the sweet sickly blood smell hung on it and lingered in his nostrils. What was worst was the sight of the foot in its green shoe lying discarded on deck. One of the bystanders was also fascinated by this detached part of his comrade. He picked up the shoe, shook the bloody piece of meat from it, and walked away with the shoe.

This finished the more squeamish Englishman. He went to the side and was very sick.

The whole of the *Seville's* crew had been summoned on deck, and Henry addressed them from the break of the poop in his island Spanish.

'You have surrendered without conditions after an unprovoked attack on an unoffending ship. You did not give us a chance to surrender; you proceeded to murder and sink us without so much as challenging us. It would be no more than justice to drop you over the side and leave you to the sharks. But England does not make war that way. Your three remaining senior officers will come with us to answer for the conduct before an English court. My mate here will choose from among you a crew to work the ship to port. The rest of you will be turned loose in your own boats with the necessary sails and oars and you will, I have no doubt, make the coast without difficulty.'

Morris, whose Spanish was much more fluent than Henry's, took consultation with the Spanish bos'n, who had confidently expected to be either tortured or killed outright, and was therefore in his first flush of gratitude and relief; and with his help picked out from the crew the most valuable and dependable members.

In less than an hour the sheep had been separated from the goats, and the rest were put over the side together with provisions, water, and the invalid. The invalid had passed from his coma-like indifference to something that looked like plain fighting drunk. He had discovered that his shoe had been filched, and was filled with fury and indignation. To pacify him search had been instituted, the enterprising one found, and restitution made; and the invalid went over the side clasping the useless shoe in triumph to his breast.

Morris took over the *Seville* with young Cornelius Carstens as mate, leaving the experienced Bernard to be mate of the *Fortune* and general sea-adviser to Henry; and the two ships made for shelter and provisioning among the South Cays of Cuba. In their search for a ship they had left this run for shelter much too late, and there were moments when it seemed that they would never see those delectable islands, those 'gardens of the Queen,' at all. The sullen late-July days would break suddenly into shrieking tempest, in the black heart of which they would struggle with halliards that seemed to have an evil and furious life of their own; or they would be beaten to the deck by a solid weight of rain that was like the emptying of buckets. It was not rain at all, as the term is understood. The skies just turned to water and fell down, And wringing the wet out of their clothes in the sodden fo'c'sle or going aloft to bend a new sail in place of the few sad ribbons that a hurricane had left on the yard, or eating cold tack because the galley fires had been drowned, they did not fail to point out to their master gunner that but for his zeal they would at this moment be snugly at ease in the south of Cuba.

But to the delectable islands they came in the end, considerably battered and much poorer in canvas, and in that gossip-shop of the Caribbean met their kind and exchanged news. Charles was indeed king, it seemed; and it was very pleasant, as one privateer's captain told Henry, to be able to drink that toast again. No man could be expected to drink with any emotion to something called a Protector, could they? he said. What grown man wanted a Protector! But there was also much talk of how soon they might be out of work. Would Charles be all for peace with Spain? And would he understand that, whatever they arranged in Europe, there was 'no peace beyond the Line!'

'I put my faith in the City of London,' laughed an old captain they met at Isle of Pines. 'The new king – God bless him – may want this or that, but in the end he depends on the City of London. And the City of London is devoted to the English cause in the West Indies. The City of London – God save it – will not desert us.'

It was now, viewing for the first time at close quarters his brethren in 'the sweet trade of privateering', that Henry realized how lucky he had been in falling heir to a crew like Jack Morris's. Morris, being a seaman bred and the son of his father, had his pick of the seafaring fraternity. He had no need for pressed men or jailbirds to get his ship to sea; indeed, seamen had been known to offer bribes to men sailing on a Morris ship in an endeavour to take their place and be sure of a well-found ship and a good master.

Very few masters of ships in the Caribbean were so fortunate. Even Joe Bradley, who brought his ship into Isle of Pines a few days after the *Fortune* had reached shelter, reported that a man had been blown from the topsail-yard, and added: 'A runaway plantation hand. No manner of use at sea. A deported London pickpocket.'

Morris recruited a second crew to sail the *Seville*, and the original crew stayed with Morgan. And during those months in the South Cays while they patched and hammered, and provisioned themselves from the ample game ashore, Henry came to know his crew very well, and they in their turn became proprietary about Henry Morgan. The tale of the *Gloria* and her sea-change into the *Fortune* had gone round the privateers' rendezvous at Pine Island, and men made excuses to call on the *Fortune* so as to meet this brilliant recruit to the trade. They were a mixed lot, sheltering there till it was sailing weather again: French, Dutch, English and Portuguese. At any moment a war at home might make it possible for them to take out letters-of-marque against each other, and if that happened they would sink each other conscientiously but without rancour. The only rancour they had was for Spain: elegant, civilized, eternally barbaric Spain.

Here and there among the ships there was one that was looked on askance; whose crew was coldly received ashore. These were the cannibals: the men who ate their own kind: the men who had stepped over the borders between privateering and piracy. As a rule they were shabby in appearance and bearing, for piracy was a hand-to-mouth affair, dependent on an uncertain market. A successful privateer brought his prize proudly into port, had the ship condemned and its cargo valued, and having paid his dues, pocketed the proceeds. But the pirate was in the position of the thief who must depend on the generosity of a fence. His ill-gotten riches had to be turned into a suit of sails or tubs of salt beef in some disreputable backwater, and the ship-chandler with whom he dealt had all a fence's power.

So the privateers drew the ample skirts of their coats away from those sad and seamy brethren of theirs, and made good company with their own kind. When there was no ship to visit, the crew busied themselves each according to his kind. Bart spent his days among his cloths, so that the *Fortune* should be both beautiful and strong when she went to sea again. The mulatto went on shore and came back with a dog; an odd-looking hound which he called Goodbye; no one knew why. Manuel went hunting, and continually brought trophies of the chase to lay metaphorically at Henry's feet, so that the little after-cabin where he lived became horrible with horns, tail-feathers, teeth, wings, tusks, and tails, which the soft-hearted Henry was too long-suffering to throw overboard. Bernard Speirdyck went native and had the *Fortune* scrubbed with sand and soda from end to end ('You damned housewife, it smells like a laundry!' said Morgan) and in his off-time went prospecting on other ships to see if he might like to buy them. Bernard was a merchant at heart, and war with him was only a means to an end. Some day, when he had had his share of a big prize, he was going to buy a ship, settle down in Jamaica (which according to Bernard was the coming metropolis of the New World), and run cargoes between that and the other British possessions in the Indies.

But in all the months they were in the South Cays no word came to them as to the future of privateering. It was the Navy who told them that all privateers had been recalled; six months later, down off the Mexican coast again, when they ran into some of Admiral Mings' squadron.

'This will not be of any interest to you, of course,' said the Navy, 'since you are without doubt a scientific expedition studying the incidence, habitat, and breeding habits of mermaids.'

'How did you know?' they said.

'We meet so many of you,' said the Navy.

Incidentally, they said, they had heard that Jamaica was a good place to take prizes to for condemning. They had a new Governor and the place was booming. The Governor was fresh out from home. A man called Morgan. Colonel Morgan, as far as they remembered.

'Colonel *what* Morgan?' asked Henry.

Edward, they thought. Yes, almost certainly Edward.

And they sailed away about their lawful occasions leaving Henry dazed by his luck.

'My *uncle*!' he said to Morris. 'Just consider what it means, Jack! We don't have to sit in a hot little waiting-room with our hat in our hands any more. We walk straight in. I'm the Governor's nephew. Good old Uncle Edward! I've never liked him so well!'

'Did you like him, then?' Jack asked, taking this piece of luck as equably as he took most turns of the wheel.

'He was the one I did like; the Royalist one. The other was one of Cromwell's best generals, God rot him; with a face like a fiddle and a voice like a corncrake. Uncle Edward was quite different; a kind little man, always amused. He fought for the King, and when it was all over he went back to the Continent. He had soldiered for years on the Continent and married a German woman. And now, I suppose, he has come back with the new King, and been rewarded with Jamaica. Dear, good, kind, laughing, little Uncle Edward. How good it will be to see him again!'

'Do we go now?'

'Oh, not yet, not yet. We are not going to hear the news about the privateers' recall for some months yet. We'll take home another Spaniard for Uncle Edward.'

5

THE HARBOUR AT Port Royal lay like a great round mirror under the benevolent sky, and on its surface a score of ships turned with a lazy acquiescence to greet the incoming tide. The town on its spit of land was repeated in the still water, candy-pink and mint-green, like a sweetmeat. Port Royal in Jamaica had the reputation of being the most riotous town in the islands, with a drinking-den for every five of its inhabitants, but in the limpid light it looked fresh and innocent and pretty. The inhabitants, in any case, did not largely frequent the much-quoted drinking-dens; the inhabitants were enlisted merely for statistics' sake. The pleasures of the town were for sailors ashore, and when no ships lay in the wide lagoon between the town and the mainland, Port Royal lay quiet and parochial under the sun, almost as innocent as it looked.

In the comparative coolness of the cabin in his ship *Endeavour* Captain Mansfield sat drinking madeira and being gloomy about his prospects.

'I am getting old, Exmeling, that's what it is,' he said, slumping his square body farther down in his chair. He cocked an eye at the younger man and waited for the expected denial.

'You are as young as ever you were, Captain,' Exmeling said. 'The times are inauspicious, that is all. One cannot control the conjunction of the planets.' He had a voice like honey running from a jar, and a curious trick of lingering on his consonants so that the drawl irritated like a bone stuck in one's throat.

'The planets don't alter my powers of persuasion, do they ? No either I'm getting old, Exmeling, or the English are losing their grip. Five separate times I have talked to that donkey of a Governor. "Look," I said, "it is a gift for England. Two or three ships, a handful of men, and the place is yours." But he is nothing but a lace cravat and a piece of ribbon, that Governor. "It is not a constitutional proceeding," says he. What is a colonial Governor for if not to shut his weather eye to the constitution! As beautiful a plan as anyone had since Noah made the Ark, and no one with the guts to help me to carry it out.'

'You'll do it yet, Captain,' Exmeling comforted, and raised his glass. 'Your good fortune, Captain!'

'Always drink to your host with your glass two-thirds empty,' the old man said.

'Why so ?'

'He notices how low it is.' He shot a glance at Exmeling to observe how discomfited he might be, and said: 'Well, well, I have no doubt it will be wasted on you, but if you give me that bottle that's standing on the board below the port there, I'll give you something that tastes like sunshine in your throat.' He watched the square of sunlight steal from the floor to the table as the ship swung. 'Mansfield may be getting stiff in the joints, but he has never spoilt his palate with the luck of the barrel. Always I knew what I was drinking – even when I was drunk.'

The silence arrested him, and he lifted his head to look across at Exmeling, who was standing by the board with the bottle in his hand.

'Well ?' he said.

Exmeling did not stir or answer. He was standing looking out on the harbour, staring.

'Exmeling!'

'I know I'm not drunk,' Exmeling said, to himself rather than to Mansfield. 'Two glasses. That is all I had.'

Between exasperation and curiosity, Mansfield got up to see what was holding Exmeling's interest.

'Holy Saint Michael!' he said, after a moment.

'Do you see it too?'

'Three prizes! *Three* of them.'

He turned and with marvellous agility ran up the ladder to the deck. Clustered at the side and in the ratlines were some of his crew, chattering like monkeys as they watched the ships come in.

'Who is that?' demanded Mansfield. 'Who is that with three prizes?'

'I saw that low-pooped ketch when I was in the South Cays with Bradley. It's Captain Morgan's ship.'

'Captain Morgan?' said Mansfield. 'Who is he?'

'New to the business, they say.'

'New! With three Spaniards in tow?'

'They say he catches them with a fishing-rod,' someone said.

'No, he whistles and they come,' said another.

'He whistled a bit too lively for Number Three,' someone pointed out. Number Three had her fore-topmast shot away.

'I don't think Two liked the tune much either,' the first man said.

Mansfield precipitated himself down the ladder to the cabin again, calling for his servant. 'Jacob! Jacob! Jacob, I say; where are you! Blast your black hide, can't you hear me!' and seeing that Jacob was there: 'My best coat, Jacob. And a clean shirt. And the red silk sash. Exmeling! Order a boat alongside in half an hour. I am going calling on Captain Morgan.'

The *Fortune* was not prepared for visitors so early, and Morgan himself was busy with the choosing of an anchorage for his little fleet, so scant notice was taken of the boats that came out from the shore to satisfy their curiosity. Mansfield's boat was at the bottom of the ladder before any notice was taken of it. The man at the top, impressed by the visitor's clothes, made no attempt to dissuade him, and Mansfield scrambled up the ship's side like a ten-year-old and arrived, a little breathless, but able to say: 'Captain Mansfield to see Captain Morgan.'

'He's there, Captain,' said the impressed *Fortune* man: Mansfield was a name to be reverenced from the Bahamas to the American mainland; and he tilted his head to the group on the main deck, aft. The group was a scattered one, still in their working clothes and not prepared for social demands; and Morgan was standing behind the nearer men, still in his old Spanish coat, faded now to a mud colour and not over-clean.

Mansfield walked towards the group, who had turned to watch him come; looking at them in turn and then looking on to the next. He walked straight past the nearer men and went on to Morgan.

'Captain Morgan,' he said, and bowed.

'How did you know that I was Morgan?'

'But of course you are he. It needs only to look. Have I not commanded men all my days? My name is Mansfield.'

'The Mansfield who went to Campeche?' exclaimed Henry, wishing immediately that he had on his new coat.

'Yes,' said Mansfield, laughing a little. 'And I tell you this for your good, young man. Keep away from Campeche. I came home without a *real*. But who am I,' he added with a wave of his hand at the prizes dropping anchor beyond, 'to advise such as you?'

'I am greatly honoured and touched by your visit, Captain Mansfield. Will you come below and have a drink with me? Speirdyck here, my mate, can take over on deck.'

'Speirdyck?' said Mansfield, looking at the mate. 'A Hollander? Good-day to you, Mr Speirdyck. My wife was a Hollander, and thcy tell me that I still speak better Dutch than English. Which reminds me that my wife's cousin, Exmeling, is sitting in the boat at the bottom of your ladder and he will assuredly die of curiosity before we have finished all we have to say to each other unless he is rescued. You have a little drink to spare for him too?'

'He has one of those long, thin noses, Exmeling,' Mansfield went on, as Speirdyck went to summon Exmeling and Morgan led him below. 'The kind of nose that is always poking into others' affairs and – and —'

'And not liking what it sees there,' finished Morgan, and Mansfield laughed.

'And not, as you put it, liking what it sees there. But he is a very good surgeon, Henrik. His real name is Smeeks, by the way. He enjoys surgery.'

He saw Henry shudder, and laughed again.

'Why Exmeling, then?' asked Morgan.

'He aspires to be an author, if you can believe it. Yes. He is for ever busy with pen and ink writing down imaginary horrors of the sea. It would seem that the horrors under his knife are not sufficient for him. And Smeeks, it appears, is not a very good name to be famous with. He is not altogether bad, little Henrik. He was for a time with the Dutch East India Company and has been to Batavia. I do not believe one little tenth of all he says happened to him there in gales and open boats – he is not very good in a boat – but he is not without experience. He came out to Tortuga with the "French West India", but they went ffft! and so he had to be bondsman to a physician.'

'A great many good men have been bondsmen,' Morgan said

The old man's quick ears heard the undertone, and without looking at Morgan he said easily: 'Yes, oh, yes. It is not to little Henrik's discredit that he has had to serve his time. Any apprentice does as much.'

And he presented 'little Henrik', when he arrived, with due courtesy. Henrik was dark for a Hollander, black-haired and red-cheeked, with shiny eyes and – as his cousin by marriage had pointed out – a very sharp nose. The soft, drawling voice was oddly inappropriate. It had a ventriloquial quality; as if one were watching a wooden image going through the motions of speech while the voice was supplied from some other and greatly different source.

When wine was set before them, Mansfield said: 'I have come to see you, Captain Morgan, for my soul's good.'

'I am no shriver, sir.'

'I have come to be comforted, not shriven. It does my soul good to meet someone young and English —'

'Welsh, Captain.'

'So! Young and Welsh, who has the root of the matter in him.

Tell me, my young Captain, how did you attach those three prizes to your not very war-like ship?'

'The bleating of the kid excites the tiger, sir.'

'Hah! Tempted to their undoing, hah?'

'Manoeuvred into an unhappy position, let us say.'

'Ah, my dear young Captain, how I wish that I was young again. What you and I could have done together. We could have taken the whole of America for England. And now what is there to do? Nothing! Nothing but be good boys and sit on the beach making collections of sea-shells for real sailormen to take home to their women. They suggest that I lead an expedition against Curaçao, but —'

'Curaçao!' said Morgan, astounded.

'Oh, yes. They have gone to war with Holland at home. Had you not heard? They are all bubbling over with fury at each other, it seems. But what has that to do with us out here? Out here the Hollanders are our friends. We fight Spain together. We speak alike. We think alike. We feel alike about ships. We do not torture prisoners when we take them; no, we give them something hot from the galley, God help us! We are almost one people, the Dutch and the English (and may I speak for the Welsh too, perhaps?), and it is manifestly absurd to expect us to care about their little war at home. And supremely absurd for the Governor, who ought to know better, to ask me to attack Curaçao.'

'The Governor!'

'Yes, the Governor. And I had such a nice little plan for him. Something that needs to be done and would be of enormous advantage to England, and would cost very little money and practically no lives at all, and what does he do? Nothing! He rebukes me. He will not listen to me.'

'Perhaps he will listen to me,' said Henry.

'To you?'

'He happens to be my uncle.'

'*Your uncle*! Saint Michael! is not that a miracle? And you are going ashore to see him now? And you will put my little plan to him – after due interval for rejoicing and rememberings and what not, of course – you will put my little plan to him?'

'If you tell me what the little plan is, Captain.'

Mansfield's eye swept round the cabin for the chart-rack. He got up, and after a little search brought a map to the table. He spread it out with his short, square hands and patted it as a man lingers over a favourite possession. Then his stubby forefinger came to rest in the middle of the wide expanse of blue that was the unoccupied ocean. Here, among the cartographer's decoration of curling dolphins, was a small, lonely island, the only considerable piece of earth between the great half-circle of the Islands and the American mainland.

'Here,' he said, presenting it as one responsible for its existence, 'is Santa Catalina. It is a nice little island, quite fertile and good to be lived on. And it was the English who made it like that. It was the English who cleared the trees and planted the fields. Planted the corn and the sweet potatoes and the tobacco. The first white men in all the world to come to the island to live there were the English. And they called it Providence. Puritans, they were; very full of conscience and hard work. But of course the Spaniards did not like that at all. The Spaniards came and flung them out, and it is now a fortified place. A garrison.' He patted the map again, lovingly. 'But it is not so fortified as all that. With five hundred men it could be taken – and garrisoned with a hundred. And this time it would not be a few Puritans growing corn. The island, I mean. It would be a pistol pointed at the heart of the Spanish mainland. There it sits, my nice little island, on all the routes across the Caribbean; on all the routes from Central America to Spain. It would be a very great nuisance to Spain not to own my nice little island any longer.'

'And this is the plan you put to my uncle, sir?'

'This is the plan, Captain Morgan, my dear young taker-of-prizes!'

'And he would not entertain the idea?'

'He would have none of it. And you know, strictly between you and me and the backstay, I understand why he says no. He is very new in his great office. He does not want to offend the little men who sit at desks at home in England and make policy and write out orders. But when you go ashore and have seen him and made your greetings and talked over old times, then perhaps you will remember about the nice little island that could be such a very great nuisance to Spain, 'm?'

Henry said that indeed he would remember. And the Captain must not judge the Governor by this sole incident. The Governor was no mere pen-and-ink man. He had done many brave things in his time.

'He fought for King Charles until the last hope was gone.'

'So I have heard, so I have heard,' agreed Mansfield. 'He is a very fine man, and I am apt to be hasty. I admit it. At my age one does not dawdle when there is much to do. I have lived a long life in the Islands – I know them the way a woman knows the carrot and parsley rows of her kitchen garden – and I have seen Spain make a bloody nonsense of all honest dealing in the Islands. And I would be very happy to see Spain put in her place before I die. Do you know Maracaibo? On the mainland? Maracaibo! Now there is a place where we could hurt them. It is the port of El Dorado, it is —' He stopped abruptly and cast them an embarrassed sidelong smile, like a child who has been too forward and indiscreet about his own affairs. 'There I am,' he said, 'talking. I have so many schemes that it itches me with annoyance every day of my life that I cannot live for five hundred years.'

Since this was an echo of Henry's own attitude to life, he looked on the old man with affection and replenished his glass.

'You have a follower, sir,' he said.

'I am gratified, Captain Morgan,' Mansfield said, lifting his glass. 'I am gratified.'

He drank, and then said: 'You have much to do, Captain, and you will be anxious to go ashore. I am grateful to you for sparing the time to entertain me and for listening to an old man so patiently.'

He waited while Morgan supplied the expected disclaimers as to his decrepitude, and then, collecting Exmeling as one collects an inanimate object, he made his way to the deck and to his boat with the alert vigour that belied his years. When Henry came to know Exmeling better he was to learn that this was the normal reaction of everyone to the existence of little Henrik. Unless someone wanted a wound dressed or a horoscope plotted, no one ever noticed that Exmeling was there. And if anyone had suggested that it would be advisable to pay court now and then to this long-nosed little scribbler who was 'not very good in a boat', Henry would have laughed aloud.

Now, when he had seen Mansfield off to his own ship, he went below to indulge in the delicious business of getting ready to call on Uncle Edward. He was still short of ready cash, and would be until his prizes had been sold after having passed the Court of Admiralty, but he had no less than three suits of clothes to choose from. All made by a London tailor, moreover. The London tailor was very badly wanted by the Law for arson, having, in the heightened exasperation of drink, set fire one night to a rival's shop. In the sober morning he had fled aboard a sloop and gone down-river with the tide to a new life altogether. He was now sail-maker on the *Seville*, having been recruited by Jack Morris with the rest of the fresh crew in the South Cays. And so Henry's new clothes, made out of cloth from the second of his prizes, were fashioned with art by a man in love with his job; a man delighted to be using a fine pair of scissors and delicate thread again.

Henry tried all the three coats on yet once more before finally deciding on the brocade. He felt in his bones that it was more suitable, perhaps, for an evening party, for an 'occasion', than for making a midday call, but he looked so well in it, and it was such beautiful stuff, and so obviously rich, that he could not pass it by for either the snuff-brown cloth or the dark-blue cord. He was debating whether it would be a little showy to wear a jewel in his hat as well as in his scarf, when the Port authorities arrived, and the debate went on in three-quarters of his mind while he dealt with the harbour people in the remaining quarter. The important thing was not what the harbour people thought of his arrival, but what Uncle Edward would think of this Morgan nephew of his; though he did notice in a gratified detachment that the Port people were very polite and respectful.

In the end practically the whole ship was called in to decide this matter of decoration, including Jack Morris, who had come over from the *Seville* to talk to Morgan before he went ashore. For it was typical of Henry, who in any matter involving action was so confident that he took no one's advice and never thought of asking it, that he should swither like a woman over a social detail. In the end he took Jack Morris's advice and went without any jewel at all, although it almost broke his heart.

'Spanish trinkets!' Jack said. 'What would a good English sailor-man want with that sort of thing?'

So he was rowed ashore, in the dull-green brocade, with his hair freshly curled and scented, and a dashing felt hat with a feather but no jewel. And he was pleasantly conscious of the interest occasioned by his arrival at the steps and of the glances that followed him as he crossed the wharf to the town. The trollops of the port leaned out of the upper windows and greeted him with open approval.

'Ah there, beautiful señor with the green coat!' they said. 'Whither away, *carissimo*? Come up and rest in the cool, *chéri*.'

And as he went on without a glance, as befitted a Governor's nephew: 'Drop in on your way back, sweetheart,' they said.

He asked a loafer where he could find the Governor, and was told 'at Kingshouse'. It was no distance at all, but Henry had sighted a notice which said: 'Equipages For Hire', and had decided on the instant that to arrive on foot would be unbefitting his new dignity, so he went to inspect the equipages. There were three of them in the little back-yard: a light chaise affair that was too frivolous and feminine for the occasion, a country conveyance with wooden benches, and a coach. The proprietor removed the protecting layers of old sail-cloth from this relic as one exhibiting a piece of the True Cross. From what vanished glories it had come to this distant island, this dusty little Caribbean back-yard, one could not tell; but it was, in spite of the scratched and faded paint and its worn green velvet lining, indubitably a coach. Henry engaged it. The proprietor, impressed by the brocade coat and by the indolence of a gentleman who would not walk or ride as far as the Governor's house, hurried himself into coachman's clothes, harnessed a pair of surprised-looking horses, and drove Henry out of the back-yard in style. The loafers of the town touched their hats automatically to the coach, and Henry felt that this was as it should be.

At Kingshouse a Negro ran down the steps to open the coach door, and Henry noticed his fine livery with approval. It was no mean establishment that was kept by the Governor of Jamaica, it seemed.

'I have come to see the Governor,' he said.

It would soon be dinner-time, and he saw the man look doubtful.

'I am Colonel Morgan's nephew,' he said. 'Captain Morgan.'

A smile split the black worried face. 'Ah, welcome, suh, welcome. The Governor will be delighted. Come in, suh, come in. You wait here one moment, suh, and I will tell his Excellency. Just one little moment, suh. The Governor, he will be so happy.'

Henry waited in the gloom of the hall, forgetful, now that he was on the threshold, of his fine coat and his stylish arrival, and aware only that after bitter years he was going to see one of his family again; here at the other side of the world.

'Come, please,' said the Negro's voice at his elbow. 'His Excellency so very pleased.'

The Uncle Edward he had known would have run out to embrace him, he thought; but reminded himself that the King's representative in Jamaica could hardly do that.

The servant opened the door of a long, cool room and said: 'Captain Morgan, your Excellency.'

Henry walked forward in a strange sudden turmoil, half eager, half afraid. How did one greet an uncle who was also the King's proxy?

But the elegant back of the man who was busy at a wall table had no resemblance to the solid rear of stocky, plump Uncle Edward. No resemblance at all.

The man was pouring wine, but now he turned and came down the room to meet Henry.

It was Modyford.

'Captain Morgan,' he said, putting out his hand and taking Henry's in a warm clasp. 'I am delighted to see you. Delighted. I had no idea that —' He paused, and then said in a concerned way: 'Are you ill, Captain Morgan?'

'No. No, I —. No, thank you, I am not ill.'

'Perhaps it is that you have only now learned of your uncle's death?'

'Yes. Yes, only now.'

'Come. Come and sit down. I have poured some wine for you. I understand very well how you feel. I have loved few men in my time as much as I loved your uncle. And he did such good work as my deputy —'

'Your deputy?'

'He was Lieutenant-Governor of the island, you know. We worked in such harmony that I cannot face the immediate prospect of having to deal with anyone less sympathetic, and have asked the Government to let the appointment lie vacant for a little. It is not a very necessary appointment, in any case; but that, of course, would not prevent someone from making themselves a highly unnecessary nuisance in it. Have we met before somewhere?'

'I came to you in Barbados to ask for a letter-of-marque against the Spaniards.'

'You are *that* boy?' Modyford rose and took a step sideways so that he could see Henry in a better light. 'But you look much older.'

'I am much older.'

'But why did you not tell me that you were the nephew of your uncle! Of your two uncles, indeed. If you did not think the Royalist one would interest me, there was always Thomas, wasn't there? Why did you not use that darling of the Commonwealth to enlist my benevolence?'

'I am not very proud of my Uncle Thomas,' Henry said. 'Besides, your Excellency had no more proof that I was a Morgan of Llanrhymny than that my prisoners were safe on Tortuga with Elias Watts.'

'Ah, yes. Very true. Your Elias, by the way, is continuing the education of his family in New England.'

'New England will suit Elias very well.'

'Tortuga, it seems, missed the domesticity of his régime. When the French took over, the buccaneers complained so bitterly of the lack of any softening society that d'Ogéron sent for a boatload of women from the houses in France, and housekeeping is now general on the island, I understand.'

'Did my uncle have his family here in Jamaica?'

'Indeed, yes. He had meant to settle here for life. He might be alive now if I had not let him lead the expedition against the Dutch in St Eustatia. But he was so very anxious to go. Soldiering was his *métier* and his passion. He died of a stroke during the landing, poor kind old man.'

'And his family?'

'He had bought an estate on the island, and they live out there. His widow and the children. The eldest daughter has married a neighbouring estate-owner. A very charming and talented young man, who is a member of the Assembly and commandant, besides, of Fort Charles. Robert Byndloss is his name. The two boys are still young: Charles is at school in England, and little Rupert lives with his mother and the two remaining girls. There were other children, as I suppose you know, but they died of fever during the voyage out. I am afraid that the family have been left in somewhat straitened circumstances, but when Charles comes out from England we shall find him a local appointment, and the girls will no doubt make good marriages. Charming women are scarce in the islands.'

With the half of his mind that was not engaged with this information Henry was thinking: 'Uncle Edward spent years in exile on the Continent, and lost his fortune, for King Charles; and he gets a deputy governorship. This man makes a good thing of the Commonwealth, and now lives secure and wealthy as Governor of Jamaica!'

He became aware that the pleasant voice had ceased and that Sir Thomas was looking at him with a half-quizzical sympathy, and he pulled himself together and got to his feet.

'It was very kind of your Excellency to receive me,' he said, 'and to give me the information I wanted about my family. I will not detain you longer.'

'But you will stay and dine with me, of course.'

'Thank you, but I am anxious to see my aunt.'

'You will have too much to do to go out there today.'

'Much to do?'

'A man who brings three prizes into port has a multitude of things to see to.'

Is there anything that this man does not know? wondered Henry.

'Nevertheless —' he began.

'You will not find it in your heart to be less generous than your King, I hope, Captain Morgan.'

'Generous?'

'In that little matter of "oblivion". You have heard of the Act that makes an honest man of me? Indemnity and oblivion are the words. Gratifyingly comprehensive – but not always capable of being put into practice. One can offer a person indemnity, but oblivion sticks its toes in and refuses the fence.' The cool grey eyes considered him. 'If I were in your place I don't know which would stick more uncomfortably in my throat: my refusal of the letter-of-marque, or my present position. Nothing I can say about the letter-of-marque would serve to endear me to you, I am afraid. But it may perhaps please you to know that I am Governor of Jamaica not because anyone at home has any great love for me, but because I know more about the islands than any man alive. Because I made a success of Barbados, and can make the same success of Jamaica. They don't like the tool in their hands, but it is a very good tool.'

'I think "tool" is an inappropriate term, your Excellency.'

'Dinner is served, your Excellency,' said the servant's voice behind them.

'I said that oblivion came hard,' Modyford said, smiling a little. 'But unless you utterly refuse to eat my salt – we will not count the wine, since you were so obviously in need of it – unless you refuse point blank to break bread with me, I hope that you will stay and dine. I am alone these days, because my wife has not yet come back from England. I sent my eldest son, John, for her; but unfortunately he sailed in the *Griffin*. And so there is further delay.'

And suddenly the hot, hard lump that had been in Henry's chest melted and something like awe took its place. He felt small and inadequate. He remembered Modyford's face as he had looked at his son that first day at the Dolphin. His face had softened, had been almost illuminated, in his son's company. And now he could say: 'And so there is further delay.' As if it were a matter of a lost rudder. The *Griffin* had been lost in the Florida channel on her way home. She had disappeared without trace, but it was freely rumoured in the islands that the Spaniards had sunk her. Indeed, Henry had met men who professed to know all the details of her battered end. And 'my eldest son John' had gone into oblivion with her, and Modyford dined alone because there was 'further delay'.

'Thank you,' said Henry, 'I shall be pleased to dine with your Excellency.'

'Good,' said Modyford quietly. 'Good.'

And he led the way into dinner, talking serenely in that dispassionate voice of his.

And presently a new thought seeped into the awe that held Henry in thrall. If the Spaniards had indeed killed Modyford's much-loved son, then the ingredient that had been lacking in Modyford's attitude to Spain was now supplied: the personal element. That might alter a great many things. Tack and sail-trim as he might, a man carried his heart about with him.

They talked for a little about the prizes, and how soon they could be sold and the proceeds divided among the needy crews. In the effort to put an end to privateering against Spain, privateers were welcomed into port and no questions were being asked. Communication being slow, it was acknowledged by both sides that a clearing-up could not be the work of a moment, and Henry was to benefit by the general amnesty.

'And your Excellency believes that the Spaniards will suffer a change of heart once our privateers are out of the way?'

'I believe that there is no prosperity for Jamaica as long as this intermittent private war goes on. The Spaniards have done horrible things, but they have been urged to them by a bitter trade rivalry.'

'There is a bitter trade rivalry with the Dutch, I understand; but they don't murder our men in cold blood, land on unprotected coasts and burn farms, or use innocent prisoners as slave labour on their fortifications until they die in their tracks. Nor do we. What is your Excellency planning to do, for instance, with all the Spanish prisoners that the privateers in harbour have brought in?'

'I am sending them to Cartagena. No, of course we do not do that. We do not even consider an alternative and then choose the kinder course. It quite simply does not occur to us to behave like that. It is a matter of temperament. Spain has lived too long in the sun. Actually and metaphorically. But I think the metaphorical sun is about to desert her.'

'You mean is about to be taken from her. The Spaniards will not give up one cocoa bean of their own accord. Have they offered to give back Santa Catalina to us in return for peace?'

Modyford paused with his glass at his lips and eyed Henry over the rim of it. 'My old friend Captain Mansfield has not been wasting time,' he observed. And Henry relaxed to a smile. It was little use to fight this man; he was always there before one.

'He came aboard the *Fortune* to welcome me when I came in this morning,' he said.

'And he said: "That idiot of a Governor will not listen to me, and I have got such a perfect plan, you just wait until I tell you about the beautiful plan for my nice little island!" The old rogue. When I offered him His Majesty's commission against the Dutch he called me a hired assassin and said that it was wonderful what some men would do for money.'

'It is a very good plan, nevertheless,' Henry said. 'No one could say that we have no right to the island of Providence.'

'No,' agreed the Governor. 'Our claim to Santa Catalina is uniquely immaculate. But it is also uniquely important to Spain to hold the island.'

'But if Spain happened by mischance to lose it, I take it that your Excellency would not be averse to presenting His Majesty with a piece of recovered territory?'

'Mischance?' said Modyford gently.

'Misunderstanding, perhaps.'

'There had better be no misunderstanding,' Modyford said, less gently.

'But you would accept the *fait accompli* if it did not involve the Government in Jamaica?'

'I should not, but I expect that his Excellency might.'

'What admirable wine your Excellency drinks,' said Henry.

6

THE WIDOW OF Edward Morgan stood in the shade of the upper veranda and watched Barley Sugar come up the drive with a letter. Barley Sugar's proper name, as witnessed to by the estate books, was Richard William Baker, but the children, fascinated by his particular shade of brown skin, had long ago changed all that, so that even his mistress, a fanatical pursuer of the proprieties, never referred to him or addressed him as anything but Barley Sugar. Barley Sugar had been sent into Port Royal at the crack of dawn with embroidery silk for matching, but it was conceivable, nay possible, nay probable, that he had come back with something else altogether. Anna Petronilla watched his meandering approach with irritation. Barley Sugar's method of progression was so haphazard, so vague, so butterfly-like that one was continually surprised that he did arrive at last at any given point.

A tear of mingled exasperation and self-pity shone in her round blue eye. It was unfair of Edward, poor Edward, to bring her out to this barbaric island and leave her in this ramshackle house in a half-made plantation among a crowd of black slaves away from her friends and her family, with no proper society for the children nor matches for the girls nor education for Rupert nor anything that could be of interest to a well-bred woman and a von Pollnitz. Edward, poor Edward, should have stayed at home and looked after his family, instead of dashing off on military expeditions at his age. How was Rupert to grow up a credit to the Pollnitz side of the family if he had no male control? This morning he had failed to turn up to the lesson about Julius Cæsar she had prepared for him, and she was very much afraid that he had run away to be a pirate, having been excited thereto by the slaves' gossip that a nephew of Edward's had turned up at Port Royal with ten prizes and had come ashore dripping with jewels, pistols, doubloons, pieces-of-eight, and similar proceeds of piracy. She hoped that it would occur to him before he went too far that the best way of meeting a pirate was to stay at home and wait for this Morgan nephew of Edward's to call. It was so like Edward, poor Edward, to have a pirate for a nephew.

'Couba,' she said to the shadows behind her, 'go down and tell Barley Sugar to hurry up.'

But there was no answer. The moment her back was turned that girl was down below chattering with the other slaves and shrieking with that maniac Negro laughter.

And then the final exasperation was presented to her. Into the distant bright picture that was framed for her by the pillars of the veranda came her daughter Elizabeth on horseback, and neither the distance nor Elizabeth's voluminous skirts could disguise the fact that she was riding astride. She was indeed riding without any saddle at all, her small feet dangling comfortably in rhythm with the mare's walk. She was, even more heinous offence, riding without a hat. Out in the full sunlight, ruining her complexion and her chances. What, oh what, had she, Anna Petronilla von Pollnitz, done to deserve a family like this? Why could they not all be like her dear Anna, her eldest, her own second image, her kind blonde calm Anna, who had married so well and so early and had a fine estate like Byndloss Place? What estate would come to Elizabeth, who behaved like a stable-boy, or to Johanna Wilhelmina, who spent all her time in front of a mirror being someone out of some play by William Shakespeare? It was unfair of Edward, poor Edward, to leave her with such problems.

Elizabeth came riding over the grass of the clearing, humming to herself, and went away round to the stables without glancing at the house. So she thinks that I am safe on my bed having my siesta, does she? thought Anna Petronilla.

'Couba,' she said, as the girl came in with the note that Barley Sugar had delivered, 'tell Miss Elizabeth that I wish to speak to her immediately.'

But by the time Elizabeth had presented herself a more immediate interest held her mind. The pirate nephew was coming to call that very afternoon. A most correct letter, it was, on admirable paper. The penmanship a little stiff, she considered, but the sentiment irreproachable. And all the part about Edward, poor Edward, so moving and so full of genuine emotion. Quite unpiratical and a little surprising.

'Elizabeth,' she said, 'your cousin Henry, your dear father's nephew, is coming to pay his respects this afternoon. Please go and put on your green with the violet ribbons, and do your hair again, and rub some cream into your hands and arms, and put a cool cloth on that unbecomingly flushed face. Why were you out without a hat, Elizabeth?'

'It flaps.'

'You will have freckles if you do not take care, and have a face like a bird's egg. That fair skin that goes with auburn hair always freckles at the least touch of sun. And *Elizabeth*, you were riding with a leg on either side like a man. Elizabeth, how could you be so indecent!'

'I don't see anything indecent about it. All women used to ride that way until some silly woman thought of sitting sideways. I expect she could not stay on the other way, if the truth were known. It is very ugly to sit sideways. The Greek women rode astride their horses.'

'It is what I should expect of them,' said Anna Petronilla. 'I absolutely forbid you to go riding again without a proper side-saddle, and I forbid you absolutely to go out without a hat in future. I hope that is clear. Now you will go and make yourself presentable to help me to entertain this cousin of yours. And do not forget the cool cloth on the face.'

'I have not yet had my siesta.'

'If you go riding in the noontime heat you must do without your siesta.'

'And I don't want to marry a pirate.'

'Marry? Who talks of marry?'

'You do, of course. You hardly ever talk of anything else. There is nothing I do from morning till night but I must not because it will spoil my chances of marriage. Well, I do not *want* to get married! I leave marriage to blobs of melted butter like Anna. And I do *not* like pirates and I do *not* want to meet my cousin Henry!'

And with a flounce of her wide skirts Elizabeth ran away to her own room at the other end of the house. The room was all her own at the moment because Johanna was staying with Anna, and she flung herself on her bed and tried to be righteous about the siesta that her mother wanted to deny her, but, being an honest creature by nature, she found this difficult. She had protested too often against the need for siesta to claim an interest in it now. And then she remembered that she had called kind Anna a blob of butter and she laughed a little into her pillow and was sorry. It was not Anna's fault that her mother was so maddening. But she continued to feel angry and ill-used and antagonistic.

Then from far away, through the wide-open shutters, came the sound of Rupert's high treble and a deeper, man's voice answering his questions. And presently the sound of a horse's hoofs came up through the afternoon stillness. The aspiring pirate had, it seemed, met a real one and was escorting him home.

Elizabeth, being in all respects a normal woman, got up instantly from her bed and peeped from behind the shutter. But she was still, of course, unrelievedly antagonistic.

'What a spectacle!' she said, looking down at her cousin. 'Wasn't there anything else he could hang on himself! What a sight!' And she went resolutely back to her couch.

'But do you think that Julius Cæsar is much of a help to a sailor?' Rupert said, as they walked up to the front steps.

'Is that what you ran away from?' Henry asked.

'Yes. I don't think, you know, that Mother understands Cæsar very well. Perhaps if I was to take your horse round to the stables you would go in first and – and make my peace with Mother?'

'I don't know that that would be a very good idea.'

'It wouldn't? Oh.'

'Not very grown-up.'

'Oh. What – what would be a grown-up thing to do?'

'I think it might be courteous to go in and apologise to your mother for running away from Julius Cæsar.'

'Oh.'

'And meanwhile I shall get a servant to take my horse round. And when I come in you will be friends again, and you can present me to your mother.'

'Yes, of course; I can present you! I was the first to know you of us all, wasn't I?'

It would be difficult to say which surprised Anna Petronilla more: the elegance of her younger son's apology to her, or the elegance of her piratical nephew by marriage. It was a somewhat over-dressed elegance, she noted, but she had herself a liking for richness and excess, and was not repelled, as her more austere daughter had been, by a suggestion of flamboyance.

And nothing could exceed the correctness of his manners, nor the sensitivity of his remembrances of Edward, poor Edward. Anna dabbed her eyes and felt that, however doubtful the credentials of this Morgan might be, it was very comforting to have a male relation in the house again. Moreover, he seemed very knowledgeable about sugar-canes; a crop which Anna Petronilla continued to find exotic and forbidding. Altogether a very intelligent young man. And handsome enough in a dark Celt fashion. She sent Couba to find Elizabeth.

'My little Johanna Wilhelmina is not here at the moment. She is over at Byndloss Place with her sister Anna. But my little Elizabeth is here, and will be anxious to meet her cousin.'

'*No!*' said little Elizabeth, banging her fist into the pillow and glaring at the brown girl. '*No*, I say! Tell my mother that I am having my siesta.'

'But, Miss Liz, how will she believe me? Never have you been known to have a siesta!'

'Go away! Go away and leave me in peace. Tell her that I have measles, tell her that I have jaundice, tell her that I am dead, but go away and tell her that I am not coming to be exhibited!'

'Are you staying long in Port Royal?' Anna Petronilla was asking her visitor.

'Some time, I expect. We are preparing an expedition against the Dutch in Curaçao.'

'The Dutch,' Anna said vaguely. 'They cut their ham very thin.' She noted a surprised look in Morgan's eye, and added, as if it explained everything: 'In Lippstadt we cut it thick in good juicy slices.'

Couba came in to say that Miss Liz was having her siesta.

The serene brow of Anna Petronilla blackened.

'You tell Miss Liz to come here this instant.'

'Ah, no,' said Henry, 'let the child have her sleep out. I can meet her later.'

'She has slept a sufficiency,' Anna said, very grim. 'Go and tell her so, Couba.' And, ignoring the girl's irresolute departure: 'You have met the Governor, perhaps? Ah, yes. He was very correct in the matter of poor Edward, very helpful. He is a fine Christian man and very well connected. He is a relation of the Duke of Albemarle. It is a very new creation, of course – the Duke is merely old George Monck – but of good standing and influential. He is a very good friend to have in this barbaric country.'

'Miss Liz,' said Couba, sidling into the bedroom, 'she say you got to come. She say this instant.'

Elizabeth sprang from the bed with such vigour that Couba involuntarily retreated a step as if about to be attacked. But it was to the little washstand that Elizabeth ran. She seized the jug, poured its contents into the basin, snatched the ribbon from her hair and shook it free, and plunged her whole head into the basin of water.

'*Now* go and tell her,' she said, standing erect with the dripping locks hanging round her. 'Tell her that I am washing my hair.'

'Oh, Miss Liz. But I say before that you are having siesta. How —'

'You have told a little lie, now you can tell a great truth,' Elizabeth said, and began to laugh.

When Couba came to say that she had not liked to say so before, but that Miss Liz was actually washing her hair, Henry, bored with Anna Petronilla, sprang to his feet and said heartily: 'Washing her hair, is she? Then suppose her cousin goes along and helps the child to dry it?'

And before Anna Petronilla could recover from her surprise sufficiently to utter a protest, he had swept Couba out in front of him and was harrying her towards the bedrooms.

'But, sir. But, mister! But, your lordship!'

'Go along, Couba. I want to see Rupert's little sister, wet hair or no wet hair. It is a long time since I have been domestic.'

He strode into the bedroom, past a Couba who was making a belated attempt to warn her young mistress, and stopped short.

Elizabeth was standing in her petticoat, having stripped off the dress that had suffered from the streams of water from her wet hair. She was binding a towel round her head, and she was looking a little cat-like and smug.

She glanced up at the astounded Morgan, and ceased on the instant to be smug. She blazed. She coruscated. Lightings flashed about her and danced from her lips. This, she supposed, was pirate manners. This, she supposed, was part of the vanity that walked about at midday hung about with brocade like a woman's bedstead.

'But —'

This, she supposed, was what was to be expected of a corrupter of youth, a cadger of family favours, a half-educated sailor hung about with ill-gotten gains, a Welshman of deplorable habits who probably could not even talk English except on a see-saw, an enjoyer of women who had forgotten that all women were not playthings whose privacy could be invaded as he pleased.

When she at last paused momentarily to draw breath he broke the fragment of silence with one word.

'Elizabeth,' he said, in wonder. As one making a discovery. Almost as one recognizing someone unexpectedly.

He turned on his heel without another word and walked away, leaving Elizabeth with her mouth open and her second wind unexpended.

He presented himself before Anna Petronilla again, and interrupted her renewed doubts about piracy and her confused recollections of the Sabine women to say:

'Madam, I have the honour to ask you for your daughter's hand in marriage.'

Anna Petronilla gaped even more deplorably than her daughter and wondered if he had been drinking and she had not noticed it until now. He certainly had an intoxicated look, now that she examined him properly; a dazed look about the eyes. Unfocused; like Edward, poor Edward, when he had fallen off his horse that day.

'She does not want to get married,' she said, because that was what happened to come to her lips.

'I think that I might be able to change her mind,' Morgan said.

'Well, well,' said Anna Petronilla, deciding to get Henry Archbould over at the very earliest moment, Henry being her standby in everything from rebellious slaves to insects in the woodwork. 'We can discuss that later, at more leisure. You will stay and dine with us, yes?'

Henry not only stayed to dine, he stayed the night.

And although he continued to look like someone who has fallen from his horse, and to talk much less than was customary for Henry Morgan, he was entirely orthodox in his behaviour. He made his apologies to his cousin and explained that he had taken it for granted that she was of Rupert's generation; and he continued to meet her stormy eyes across the haze of flies round the dinner-table candles with equanimity.

Henry Archbould, summoned in haste, was there at dinner, and found nothing alarming about the young man. Indeed, Tom Modyford was said to think very highly of him, and to have plans to use him in the development of the colony. At which Anna Petronilla took heart.

And Henry, on his next visit to Kingshouse, delighted the Governor by inquiring, in a detached and academic way of course, about the method of taking up land in Jamaica.

And since an expedition against a rival colony, more especially against a colony held by those stubborn fighters the Dutch, was a matter of long and careful preparation, there was time for all the members of the *Fortune's* crew to indulge in personal and private business according to their taste.

There was time for Henry to ride about this fertile island with which the Spaniards had done so little, to explore the virgin valleys and the sun-drenched savanna; time to know the planters a little and the Morgan family very well.

There was time for Bernard Speirdyck to send to Curaçao for his wife and to find a house in Port Royal. Mary Speirdyck arrived with two large chests, a cupboard, and a hundred bulbs; half of them lilies and half of them onions. The cupboard was painted all over with little flowers and had come out from Holland with her mother, and Mary would as soon have travelled without her petticoats as have left the cupboard behind. Mary was blonde and self-contained and there was a bloom on her like a grape. She went in and out of the little dark rooms of the port, stirring the dirt with a plump, contemptuous hand and shaking the sandy grit from her shoes. She was not very happy about leaving Dutch territory, but if Bernard said it was a good thing to do, then it was without doubt a good thing. And there was no doubt that Jamaica was green and lovely and kind after Curaçao, and perhaps now she would have a child to take the place of the two who had died on that bleak and distant island. She would also see to it that Cornelius got himself married to a respectable girl with presentable antecedents and if possible a bit of dowry. She did not know which she disapproved of more: the exorbitant rents in Port Royal or the extent of Cornelius's following.

For there was time for the maidens of Port Royal to be beglamoured by that ripe-corn hair of Cornelius's, that looked so strange against his sunburnt face. More mammas became acquainted with the waterside during the *Fortune's* weeks in port than in all the previous history of Port Royal, and the usual walk to Fort Charles and back was quite deserted.

There was time, too, for Manuel to sample every brothel from Fort Charles to Fort Rupert, and because of his childlike charm and his eye-lashes to be awarded cut rates in every one of them.

There was time for Jack Morris to take over the second of the prizes and fit her out to his heart's liking. The *Seville* was too slow and cumbersome for his taste, so he let it go in favour of the *Felipe*, which had some of the *Fortune's* handiness but greater gun-power, and which he renamed the *Dolphin.*

Henry was glad to have another *Dolphin* in the family, and spent a large part of his time teasing stores out of Authority for her. He took Jack Morris out to the Morgan place, where Jack sat with his knees pressed together and made polite conversation with Anna Petronilla, and was very bored. The land had no attractions for Jack; it was an alien element, and he was ill at ease in domestic surroundings. He did not, it is true, follow Manuel in his progress through the upper stories of the port. It was his habit to find a girl who suited him and live with her as long as he was ashore. But he had forgotten her before the anchor had come dripping out of the water and been made fast. The sea was his home.

The expedition being recruited against Curaçao was composed of as motley a crew as ever sailed the Caribbean: French, Genoese, Greeks, Levantines, Portuguese, Indians, Englishmen and Negroes. Everything in fact but Dutch. But when neighbours said, in that ageless neighbourly way, to Mary Speirdyck that it was odd that her husband should be prepared to war against his countrymen, Mary merely looked placid and friendly and assured them that Bernard without doubt knew what he was about. Joe Bradley brought his *May Flower* in with a prize in tow while they were in harbour, and was invited to join, but refused when he heard where they were bound.

'My crowd would mutiny if I asked them to fight the Dutch,' he said. 'They fight too well and there is practically no plunder.'

But at the word mutiny both Morgan and Jack Morris had dissolved into fits of insane laughter, and had taken Bradley aside and talked with him. And after that Bradley was an enthusiast for the project.

The most unexpected recruit was picked up by Henry one evening as he was leaving the harbour on his way to dinner at Kingshouse. Someone came running after him and a voice said: 'Harry! Harry Morgan!'

And there was Bluey.

Bluey's stockings hung in folds from his tattered breeches, and showed through the holes large areas of dirty calf. His toes twiddled self-consciously in the gaps of his shoes.

'Captain Morgan, sir,' he said, amending his instinctive form of address. And then, reading Morgan's glance at his clothes, he fumbled in a pocket and produced something which he exhibited on his palm. 'I still got my jew's-harp,' he said with a grin.

'Bluey!' said Henry. 'What became of that fine fortune of yours?'

'Oh, I had a wonderful time with it, but I woke up one morning and found it wasn't there any more. Money's like that, ain't it? Here one day, gone tomorrow. You want men, Captain? You want a man?'

Henry did not particularly want Bluey, and he did not need a man. But to turn away anyone who helped him take the *Gloria* was unthinkable. He handed out money for clothes, the amount being deftly calculated to provide margin for only a couple of drinks, and told him to report to Bernard Speirdyck. Bernard would not be over-pleased, but Bluey was a good enough seaman to get by.

The only other recruit who was not altogether welcome was Exmeling, who was coming as surgeon; and he was unwelcome only in the eyes of one member of the outfit: Bartholomew Kindness. The others accepted little Henrik with the usual indifference, but to Bart he was anathema. He scowled at the very mention of his name, he avoided his shadow, and he would not sit in the same room with him.

'His eyes are far too close together,' he would say when someone took him to task fcr his unreasonableness. 'A bad lot that, mark my words. A bad lot.' And then: 'Bile!' he would mutter darkly. 'Bile!'

Bart's share of prize-money had been more than enough to buy that cottage in the Mendips, but there was no word about his going back to England, and once more Henry forbore to remark. Bart was for ever in and out of the gambling-dens on the waterfront, and it was to be supposed that his luck was no better than it normally was.

Certainly he made no secret of his pleasure at the thought of going back to sea, but he was not unique in that. There was hardly a man of the four ships and the two French sloops which were going with them who was not either penniless or weary of the land. When on a blue April morning they said good-bye to Port Royal their mournful capstan song belied the lifting of their hearts. And although they waved with hearty gestures and ribald yells to the little group crowded on the fortifications at the point to watch them pass, their minds were already playing dolphin-like in the open sea.

Henry was one of the few men who looked back when the island was behind them, and this was the first time he had ever looked back at a place he was leaving. For among those green mountains, growing blue now and flat and sinking to the horizon, was a piece of land that was his very own. He had bought one of those virgin valleys. Bernard Speirdyck was not the only one to believe that 'Yamaica' was an island with a future.

'Aah, Jamaica!' Mansfield had said with scorn when Morgan had expressed his delight in it. 'I make you a present of it! The earth quakes and the place is full of husbandry. The sea is the place for a man.'

But Henry was no sailor bred. The land he had run away from was in his marrow; something fundamental in him wanted a permanence. He had spent what was left of his prize-money, after the *Fortune* had had her share, neither on gaming, although he was fond of it, nor on women, although he liked them. He had bought land. And moreover Elizabeth had ridden out with him one day to see it; accompanied in the cause of respectability by Barley Sugar, Anna Petronilla being of the opinion that a cousin might come within the prescribed degrees of chaperonage, but a cousin who had proposed marriage did not. Elizabeth had ridden out to the valley with the object of telling him in what way it was entirely the wrong place to buy, but she had ended in helping him choose the place for the 'big house', and where the slaves' quarters should be, and where the sugar-factory when there were canes to supply it. Barley Sugar had gone to sleep under a cottonwood tree, and they had walked to and fro about the quiet valley talking as friends with a common interest, so that when the moment came to awaken Barley Sugar they seemed to have known each other a long time, and they rode home in unspoken companionship. So Henry for once looked back at a place he was leaving.

Cornelius, too, looked back now and then as the land sank astern, for Mary had done her duty, and Cornelius was betrothed. Properly, with exchange of rings and exchange of meals, and dowry settlement, and all. He was going to marry the daughter of Charles Hadsell, who had been master of the *Prosperous* of London until she was taken by a Spanish man-of-war. Captain Hadsell had spent nearly two years in Spanish prisons before he had escaped from the last one in Havana, and he had seen his friends' heads carried in triumph through the streets by their murderers. But he had hopes of five thousand pounds from the Court of Admiralty as compensation for the loss of his ship. His daughter Jane was pretty and sweet and had a wonderful hand with pastry, and Cornelius was very happy.

His future father-in-law was acting as mate to Jack Morris for the trip, and Jack was not quite so happy about that. It is never very comfortable to have in one's crew a man who has owned and commanded his own ship, and Hadsell was not the man to make such a position easy. But in the first flush of satisfaction at being free of the land they were all brothers together, fo'c'sle or quarter-deck. They sang continually, they quarrelled not at all, even in the cramped quarters forward, and even those whose friends had been rich enough to send them aboard drunk permitted themselves to be soused by their mates with resigned good-humour.

They bore south-east for Curaçao, and the seas were kind and the winds accommodating, and the new sails looked very fine in the sun, and no one ever remembered that they had been cold, and wet, and tired, and sick, and maimed at sea. They were happy.

They were still happy and singing when, at four bells precisely in the forenoon watch some days later, all six captains received a polite deputation from their crews. The deputations, with remarkable accord and strangely identical phrasing, announced that they were unanimously against any attack on a Dutch colony and refused point-blank to go on with the expedition. They had no quarrel with the Dutch, and the Dutch had nothing worth plundering anyhow. They held that it would be more sensible and more to their liking to attempt the island of Santa Catalina, which was English by right and was moreover very handily at a point due W.SW. from where they were at the moment, so that the 'trade' would blow them there without any undue effort on their part.

The captains, on their several quarter-decks but united in sentiment, pointed out that Santa Catalina could provide no plunder at all, and it would be much wiser to obey the instructions of their commission and go on to Curaçao. Whereat the crews professed themselves indifferent to plunder while the honour of their country was at stake, and retired to the fo'c'sle to laugh themselves silly while the watch on deck changed course for Santa Catalina, a lonely little island four hundred miles away.

The island was more than lonely, it was forbidding, and they watched it rise from the ocean with proprietary criticism.

'Why do we want this place back?' they said. 'Let the Dons have it!'

'I've seen better spots in Iceland,' they said.

'A damned dreary lump of rock,' they said. 'Let's sink it.'

But they were amused and eager about it all. To slap Spain's face was worth the lack of some plunder.

'She's calved!' said Bluey suddenly from his place in the rigging, and they laughed.

There was indeed a 'calf' by her side. Another 'damned dreary lump of rock' stood alongside the main island on the north side.

One of the French sloops circled the place and came back to report that there were no ships there nor anywhere in sight. The excitement on land was tremendous, they said. Much galloping backwards and forwards and letting off alarm signals and what not. But no craft in the harbours.

Whereupon Mansfield led the English ships through the reefs that separated them from the island.

'I hope the old man knows what he is doing,' Jack Morris said, bringing the *Dolphin* in Mansfield's wake.

'I am the only Englishman alive who knows the channel through the reefs of Santa Catalina,' Mansfield had boasted when they had discussed their plan of campaign in Port Royal. And they knew that it was probably true: Mansfield was famous as a coaster. It was said that he could smell his way through reefs.

But Jack Morris, with a good new ship under him and that crazy wake in front of him, had his heart in his mouth. Blind faith was not a quality of Jack's at any time.

Through the clear water overside he could see the reefs, a few feet down, and inside spitting distance, and he remembered Tortuga and the stem of his first ship with the seas breaking over her as she lay submerged on the reef.

But their progress through that twisting channel, a fairway wide enough for only one ship, and that a handy one, went on without incident. Morgan followed Jack Morris, with Bernard standing stocky and placid by his side to do the sailing, and Joe Bradley came after Morgan, with the two French sloops bringing up the rear. *Endeavour*, *Dolphin*, *Fortune* and *May Flower*, they nosed their way through that seemingly endless passage between the reefs, disaster only a stone's-throw on either side. Nearly a whole circuit of the island the channel took them before they came at last into the wide, safe waters of the harbour – one of the best harbours in the Caribbean, where a navy could lie at anchor secure from enemy and weather.

'I've crossed myself so much me arm's paralytic,' Bluey said, looking at the calm expanse of water as the anchor fell away from the bows and the canvas came off her.

'You'll need your other arm to get us out of here,' they said, unsympathetic.

'Now Goodbye can go ashore,' said the mulatto, because that was all it meant to him.

It was early afternoon when they anchored, and for the rest of the day they occupied themselves in getting the boats overside and in smacking their lips over the sensation they were causing ashore.

'I wager we're the sweetest sight the Dons have seen in five years,' they said, mocking. 'Something to rest their eyes on, after so much sea.'

When the boats were safely in the water they sat about with their muskets and their pistols, cleaning them and swapping lies about their respective merits. Toni, encouraged by the stillness of his galley, gave them a meal that they voted 'shore food', which was the highest compliment in their vocabulary. If they had a grumble at all it was about the size of their rum allowance, but they had the sense to know that they would need their wits presently even more than they needed drink just now.

The dusk fell, the ships' bells sounded lazy and irrelevant in the quiet; and then the desultory sounds ceased and there was the silence of purposeful movement. One by one they slid down the ropes into the boats, dropping with that neatness that sailors share with cats into their places on the thwarts. The boats pushed off and the adventure was begun.

But Mansfield was not with them.

Mansfield was lying on his bunk in the *Endeavour* with two hot bricks in the small of his back and no words that were any use. He had lumbago. In the final half-hour, during the last keying-up instruction to his officers, he had bent to pick up a chart that had fallen to the deck and had stayed bent. They had put him to bed still bent, and still bent he lay there with his bricks and his dearth of words.

It was Morgan who took the attacking party ashore.

They had expected to be met with a volley as their boats grounded, but there was no sound. They waited until all were ashore and Morris and Bradley had joined Morgan.

'There isn't anything Modyford doesn't know,' Morgan said to Jack.

'What's Modyford got to do with this?' asked the surprised Morris.

'He said once that Spain's sun is about to desert her.'

'If you think because we're ashore whole and safe it's all over, you're not the man I took you for. The fort is bristling with guns.'

'I'm not thinking of the fort. If I were in command at Santa Catalina I would have had those fort guns down here before now and made matchwood of our masts. All the Spaniards can think of is shutting themselves up in the fort. That is no way to keep an empire.'

But the Spaniards had had even better ideas of defence.

When they had felt their way through the night to the fort at the north of the island, they challenged it.

'Quarter and a free passage to Spain to everyone who surrenders,' Morgan called.

There was no reply, but the guns on the landward side fired in concert and the air was suddenly thick with whining scraps of metal that struck sparks from rock as they hit and ricocheted away on a new note, or dropped with a soft, sucking sound into the earth.

'I always did hate bees,' Bluey said, his cheek on the ground.

'Anyone hurt?' asked Morgan; and when the question had been passed to the farther end of the line and back again it seemed that no one had been hurt.

'Very well. We stay here, Jack, and attack when it is light enough to see. Pass the word along to stand easy. They can sleep in turns if they want to. Let them choose their own sentries.'

But the nervous occupants of the fort continued to spray them at intervals with assorted metals during their three hours' wait, and they were all too busy finding small shelters to sleep.

'Another mistake,' Morgan remarked. 'There should not be any unevenness in the ground inside gun range. Don't they ever think one move ahead?'

In the half-light of dawn he challenged again, hoping to avoid the certain casualties of frontal attack. Frontal attack was against all his instincts, but in the final resort no method other than frontal attack would take the fort on Santa Catalina.

This time there was no answer to his challenge; neither verbal nor ballistic. A great silence hung over the fort. They watched it grow clear in the half-light and strained their ears to listen to that eerie silence.

A trick, they said, it's a trick.

'Well, trick or no trick,' Morgan said at length, 'we have to assault, so let us do it.'

They rose from their burrows and bankings and came at the fort with a concerted yell. But no guns spoke and no soldier moved on the ramparts; so that their loud defiance tailed away into doubt and their pace slackened as they came up to the walls. What trap was this?

Then Manuel, always at his best when other men were still rubbing the sleep from their eyes and wishing it were yet night, walked up to the gate and said with a fine flourish of mockery: 'In the name of his Majesty King Charles the Second of England and in the name of every single Portuguese I command you to surrender.' And he slapped the gate with a contemptuous hand.

And the gate swung ajar at the impact and creaked gently shut again.

While they were still thunderstruck, Manuel kicked the gate open and walked into the fort. They came pounding after him to rescue him, but there was no need for rescue. The fort was deserted.

'The bastards are still using our guns,' they said, pointing to the royal arms on the cannon.

'But where are they?' asked Bradley.

'Over there,' said Morgan, pointing over the battlements at Bluey's 'calf'. Across the tiny strait was the second island, so sheer as to be impregnable; and above it floated the flag of Spain.

'We'll blow them out of it,' Morgan said.

'We can't,' Morris pointed out. 'They're out of range.'

'Let them stay!' said Bradley. 'It will do them good to look at the English flag every morning.'

'Leave Spain on our doorstep? No! We'll give them a nearer view of the flag. Cornelius, take a message to the ships for me. Tell them —'

'The channel is too shallow for even a small ship, if that's what you intend,' Bernard said. 'You cannot use ships to bombard.'

'I don't want the ships to bombard. I am going to blow them out of there with their own guns. Tell Mansfield that I want wood. All the wood he can send me. No, wait. I'll write a letter. We have all the time in the world.'

He sat down at the commanding officer's very fine table and wrote a junior officer's report to his senior. It was thanks to Mansfield and Mansfield alone that the island was theirs, and all his Celt tact was devoted to making the old man feel that, although he had been absent at the last, he was the author of their victory. He explained, as a suggestion for Mansfield's approval, what he intended to do and inferred that he was doing only what Mansfield would have done if he had been there.

When the letter had been sent off he sat for a few moments looking round the dark little room, so safe and so comfortable.

'All night they had,' he said. 'All night. And they didn't even blow the place up behind them.'

'There's a man here with a basket of yams, Captain,' said that admirer of zeal, Mr Benrose, master gunner, appearing at his elbow. 'What shall we do with him?'

'Buy the yams, of course.'

'*Buy* them, Captain?'

'Yes, certainly. Here is the money. And tell him that we can use anything else they care to bring us.'

'Isn't that, if you'll excuse me, Captain, a bit unnecessary? Paying, I mean. We can just take them, surely.'

'Surely we can. And in half an hour every portable delicacy in the island would be well hidden; and they would have to be beaten half dead before they would tell us where. Tell him we'll buy their produce at the usual rates.' And as the disapproving Benrose was going: 'Oh, Benrose. The usual rate will be a third less than he asks, if I know the Spaniard.'

When he was alone again his thoughts went back to the Spaniards.

'They could have blown us all up,' he thought. 'It needed only one man with courage. A slow-burning train.'

And it occurred to him for the first time that their entry to the fort had been much too casual and trusting. They should at least have searched for the train that was not there. He must remember that next time.

7

MORGAN'S EDICT ABOUT paying for food was, of course, a counsel of perfection. It did not prevent men from taking produce as it pleased them in their comings and goings about the island.

'Who made this farm, anyhow?' they would say virtuously if the owner dared to protest. 'Us English.' Although the only crop that any of them had ever taken a personal interest in was chickweed for a cage-bird.

But few remonstrated. The civilian inhabitants who farmed the hot little valleys were too thankful to be alive and free to be critical of their conquerors. All they did was to see to it that as much as possible of what they had went to the fort, where it would be paid for, before it was stolen by passers-by. So every morning a long line of slaves trailed through the gate of the fort bearing on their heads the best the island had to offer, and the difficult matter of provisioning was taken care of.

'You will take us with you when you go?' the slaves would say hopefully; for it was a popular belief among the slaves of all the Spanish dominions that life as a slave in an English colony was a bed of roses. Negro, or Indian, the dream of their life was to be captured by the English.

'Don't worry, we'll take you!' the English said. 'You're the only thing of value on the island.' And Wish, the Sussex man, seeing a Negro bent almost double under a load, relieved him of part of it, saying: 'Don't strain yourself, black boy. I've got a share in you.'

Never again was Morgan to experience the family-party air of their stay on Santa Catalina. This picnic air was due partly to the fact that the captains of the four ships were friends and understood each other, partly to the lack of booty to quarrel over, partly to the amiability of the climate, partly to the fact that their only casualties had been five wounded, partly to the lack of drink and the absence of towns, but mostly it was due to the fact that they were too busy to be invaded by grievances or jealousies.

For the first few days they collected and transported timber to make the bridge of boats that Morgan needed to span the narrow strait; cutting and hewing fresh stuff when it was found that there would not be enough. Then they manhandled the guns from the fort down the slope and across the dipping bridge. The guns alternately balked and made mad rushes, after the manner of heavy, inanimate objects, and the men sweated and laughed and cursed and coaxed them with endless good-humour. They had nicknames for all the guns, after the immemorial habit of the English. 'Whoa, Bess!' they would say, 'take your time, lass!' or 'Come up, Bowlegs, you bitch!'

And as Morgan watched them his normally sombre eyes were bright with amusement.

'Damn you, Tenerife, haul!' he shouted at the huge, indolent sailor. 'It's not a stay-lace you're pulling!' And under cover of the laughter, to Jack Morris, who was standing beside him: 'I wonder when it will occur to them that the slaves might be doing this!'

'Why *don't* you mobilise the slaves for it?' Jack asked.

'And have nearly two hundred idle seamen on my hands!'

It was not until the last gun had reached sea-level and was being dragged on to the bridge that it did occur to any of them that their toil was gratuitous, and then it was to Tenerife that enlightenment came. He straightened himself in the act of laying hold and said: 'Why are *we* doing all this?' and his mates stopped to consider what he might mean. Then the sheer absurdity of the thing struck Tenerife in full force. He slapped the butt of the gun with his open palm and roared with laughter. He looked up the slope to where Morgan was standing, and something in Morgan's face caught his attention.

'You fooled us, Harry Morgan!' he yelled.

It was the first time that his crew had ever dropped the 'Captain' in favour of the affectionate familiar, and it was by way of being the accolade.

Morgan looked down at the upturned faces, half doubtful, not yet either amused or angry.

'I was merely taking thought for your property.'

'Property?' they said.

'You want the slaves in good fat condition for the auctioneer, don't you? No one will pay less for your carcases because they are a little underweight.'

'Aah!' they shouted, in one eloquent syllable announcing their perception of the sophistry, their appreciation of it, and their refusal of it. And one of them resolved the situation by calling: 'They're your slaves too, Harry. Come on and haul.'

And Morgan came down through the patting hands and the jests as if he were the hero of a victory, instead of the man who had made them labour like slaves for the last five days, and took his place among them, and together they hauled the last gun over to the island.

But the sight of that gun was too much for Don Esteban del Campo, safe but a little hungry on Bluey's 'calf'. He had watched the incredible English make their bridge and dismantle the fort, with a dreary envy of their persistence and their ingenuity. And now, when there was nothing in front of him but the prospect of sitting still and submitting to bombardment, he made his last retreat. He sent a messenger down to the bridge to say that if the conditions still included a return to Spain for all, then he would surrender; and presently the flag on the island was hauled down, and the prisoners began to file across the little strait.

'Jesus!' said the sailors, watching the endless stream of men from the tiny island, some of them farm-owners who had taken refuge in the fort, but most of them soldiers. 'Crowds and crowds of them. Crowds and crowds. And all they could do was sit on their bottoms on a rock and hold each other's hands.'

When Morgan said as much, in more diplomatic terms, to the commandant of the military detachments, the soldier, a bright young man who did not look as though defence would be his natural choice, said: 'Señor Captain, in the Spanish dominions we suffer from cousins. Sometimes it is nephews or uncles, but most often it is cousins. The English are new in America – if you will forgive the crude expression of a truth – and, with you, who captures also keeps. But Spain is already old in this new world, and the men who keep are not the ones who captured, but the cousin of someone at home who has the appointment in his gift. It will happen to England too, in time, that someone's cousin keeps the land men died to win.'

'I understand.'

'You must not blame Don Esteban. He is a charming man; much interested in horticulture and in the various species of moths. He admired very much the way the English had planted the island, more especially your fruit trees. The English have a genius for the growing of fruit trees. Perhaps it is that your sun is kindly, or perhaps it is that in your island no enemy comes every few years to cut them down.'

It was Mansfield, once more upright, who took surrender of the island, and he was gracious enough to hand back to Don Esteban the sword the Governor proffered. That, he remarked afterwards, was as far as he would go in obliging a Spaniard. The prisoners were locked up in the fort and fed on the weevily biscuits that the ships' crews, gorged on island goodness, had not needed.

'Just look at that harbour!' Mansfield gloated that evening as he stood with Morgan looking down at the lagoon. 'What a base to work from! Do you see that harbour filled with fat prizes dripping emeralds out of every port?'

'Yes, but out there,' Morgan nodded towards the horizon, 'a month or two from now I see the whole Spanish navy.'

'Yes, yes. It is time we got back. Time we arranged for a proper garrison. I thought we should have a quarrel about who is to stay, but it seems that Captain Hadsell is not very happy in his subordinate position and would be glad to have a command again, even the temporary command of Santa Catalina. And the wounded must stay until they can come home in comfort on the ship that brings the garrison. Forty men should be enough to keep my little island until the garrison arrives. It will be a long time before the news reaches Panama, and longer still before the Spanish organise themselves into doing anything about it.'

Morgan agreed about Spanish dilatoriness, and wished to himself that he did not have to leave Bart behind. Bart had had the back of his heel shaved off by a fragment of Spanish metal, and it was proving a bad wound to heal. It would be absurd to submit him to the unnecessary discomfort of the long and intolerably crowded voyage home, when he could come after them with his wound healed and in good condition a few weeks later. But he hated to sail without Bart. He had found a friend in Jack Morris, and a patron in Modyford, but the place Bartholomew Kindness held in his heart was all his own.

'How long will it be before the wound is healed?' he asked Exmeling.

'Who knows? Who knows?' said little Henrik. 'It is the wrong time of the moon for wounds to heal.'

So Harry resigned himself to parting with Bart until some favourable moon would reunite them. Bart himself made no fuss about being left, and seemed quite happy carving toy wooden animals.

And Morgan was glad in the event that he had not tried to take

Bart with them. It was a much longer voyage home; a long, weary tack against a wind like a brick wall. And, between the captive slaves and the Spanish prisoners, the ships were overcrowded to an intolerable degree. Anti-climax set in and tempers frayed. No one sang any longer. Even Bluey's jew's-harp was silent. It was hell.

But there was a sharp return to good humour and expectancy when at last the outline of Jamaica was clear on the horizon. And when they filed in in stately procession – *Endeavour, Fortune, Dolphin,* and *May Flower* – past the crowd on the battlements of Fort Charles, the enthusiasm of that crowd restored to the crews their island mood of achievement and well-being. The two French sloops had arrived nearly a fortnight before, and the whole of Port Royal had been waiting for this return. The waves of cheering that came over the water to them would have restored even the half-dead.

Yet something was to please Henry even more than the cheers. When he joined Mansfield on the *Endeavour* to accompany him ashore, he found the Captain surrounded by congratulatory citizens, and while he waited by Mansfield's side an old man plucked his sleeve and said: 'My cherry-trees, sir: are they still there? I have wondered very often about my cherry-trees.'

'Were you one of the settlers on Santa Catalina?' Morgan asked taken by surprise.

'On Providence, sir. On Providence. Oh, yes; yes. I had a very pleasant, well-watered little place there. There are several of us here in Jamaica, settlers from Providence. I have wondered very often about my cherry-trees.'

'You will be able to go back and see for yourself now,' Morgan assured him; and savoured this new, impersonal satisfaction.

'Now, my little taker of prizes, we go to meet the lightnings,' Mansfield said, when the crowd had lessened. 'And you will come with me and hold my hand. I am not very happy in the presence of that uncle of yours who is not your uncle.'

But the lightnings, when the culprits came within range of them, proved to be of the 'sheet' variety: a mere token illumination. It is not every colonial Governor who finds himself in a position to present a new piece of territory to his royal master. And when the Governor is also in the position of working his passage home, politically speaking, the opportunity is not one to be cast aside. Captain Mansfield was reprimanded for exceeding his commission, for giving offence to a nominally friendly Power, and for using Government stores and endangering English lives in an expedition of his own devising.

'We took the place without the loss of a life, English or Spanish,' Mansfield said proudly.

'The English took Jamaica without the loss of a life,' the Governor reminded him smoothly.

'And they've been worried by the danger of losing it ever since. They will have less to worry about now,' Mansfield said, indestructibly complacent. 'It needs only a hundred to garrison my little island, and the Spaniards will have no base in the middle of the Caribbean any more.'

But it seemed that nothing like a hundred men were available at the moment. The military had been disbanded in view of the coming peace and had taken, more or less willingly, to planting. A proper garrison for the island would have to come from England. Meanwhile, however, a ship bound for the coast of Nicaragua to load logwood would drop off Major Smith and a small detachment to reinforce the forty men left on Santa Catalina.

'Major Smith is a very able person, and will govern the island until such time as His Majesty appoints someone to the post.'

'I don't think Charlie Hadsell will take very kindly to being subordinate to a Major,' Mansfield said to Morgan as the Governor turned away to pour out wine for them.

But Henry was wishing that he could have seen that letter of Modyford's to the Government at home. How much had Sir Thomas identified himself with the capture of Santa Catalina?

It seemed that he must have identified himself pretty considerably with the affair, for he not only attended the auction of the slaves the following morning, but was himself a purchaser. The hundred slaves from Santa Catalina, having attained their life's lowly ambition, were upstanding, confident and smiling, and were sold for fabulous prices. Not only did they lack the bewildered air, the animal helplessness, of the boat-loads fresh from Africa; they spoke fluent Spanish and were used to a planting life. Many of them were second-generation slaves, born in captivity, and all of them had lived a healthy life in a good climate.

Sir Thomas's purchase consisted of a woman and her four children: boys between the ages of five and thirteen, and while he was making arrangements with his steward for their journey to Morant, a man dressed in the dreary garments of the self-consciously righteous tapped him on the arm and said:

'Friend, have you bought the father of these children too?'

Modyford did not like being called friend, and he disliked even more to be hammered very hard on his forearm by the rigid middle finger of a total stranger, but his good manners were fool-proof.

'No, sir, I have not,' he said.

'And do you consider that it is God's will that this woman should be parted from the dear partner of her joys and sorrows? From the man to whom, by God's grace, she has borne so many pledges of affection?'

The Governor turned to the woman and spoke to her in Spanish, and as she listened her brown face became irradiated with delight. She replied in a torrent of Spanish that was punctuated every now and then with a catch of laughter as her amusement welled up to choke her words. And as she finished she put her head back and opened her wide, magnificent mouth and let the laughter have full sway.

'What does she say?' asked the authority on God's will.

'She says that all the boys had different fathers, and that she had never been able with any certainty to state who was the father of any one of the four.'

'Deplorable, deplorable,' said the stranger, casting the woman a look of loathing and taking himself away from her polluted neighbourhood with all the speed the crowded place would allow.

'The worst of reformers,' said Sir Thomas, 'is that they make so many mistakes in the particular that they get no credit for the general.'

'Did your Excellency really need these slaves?' asked Morgan, who had himself bought his first three field-hands for Morgan's Valley. 'Gossip says you have far more than you need and that they eat you out of house and estates.'

'I could not resist that family: they gave me such pleasure to look upon. It is true, of course, that I have more than I have work for, and that being so I have taken a great liberty while you were away. I have sent some of the idle ones over to clear the land in Morgan's Valley so that it should be ready for you. They have also transported the materials for the house, and cut up wood for fencing. I hope very much that you do not think I have been interfering or officious. It seemed a pity to let my fellows grow fat and lazy when there was something useful to do on the island.'

Morgan could find no words. What Modyford had done represented almost a year's work with the few slaves he could afford.

Sir Thomas cast him a quizzical glance and said: 'I hope I have not deprived you of pleasure that you were saving up for yourself? The clearing of your own land?'

'You have done me a great kindness, sir. I do not know how to thank you.'

'I can tell you how. Come out to Morant with me this evening and spend Sunday with us. My daughter Mary keeps house for me until my wife arrives, and there will be no one there but George Needham, the young man she is going to marry.'

Even if Morgan's heart had not been overflowing with gratitude, an invitation from the King's Representative is not to be greeted with some such phrase as: 'Forgive me, but I want to see my cousin.' So Morgan rode out to Morant that evening to spend the week-end with the Governor.

But there proved to be company, after all, on Sunday.

'Dear me!' said the Governor, eyeing the two approaching riders over his eleven-o'clock glass of madeira, 'I had quite forgotten that Elizabeth was coming over today to choose the black boy I promised her.' And he put down the glass and led the slightly suspicious Morgan down the steps to meet his cousin, who was being convoyed by Barley Sugar. Henry was enormously gratified to see the rush of colour to Elizabeth's face as she caught sight of him, and no wise dashed to see the look of fury that succeeded it. No woman could suffer that physical betrayal and not be furious. But she greeted him in cousinly fashion and complimented him on the achievement of Santa Catalina, and seemed to bear him no malice for that momentary tide of colour. It appeared that she knew all about the progress at Morgan's Valley, and they discussed it together, she and Henry and the Governor, as they walked down to the steward's house to see the slaves before they were branded; and as once on that previous occasion, when they had explored the virgin valley, there was a sense of companionship between them, so that it seemed as if she and Henry had known each other since childhood.

The boys, gathered in the steward's office for Elizabeth to choose among them, consisted of the four young brothers from Santa Catalina and two Indian children who had been found starving after the Spaniards had laid waste their village near Cape Gallinas. Elizabeth considered them at her leisure, delighting in the choosing as a child might with dolls.

'Which would you have, Harry?' she asked, a little to his surprise.

'The one like Chakka,' he said, indicating the younger of the two Indian children.

'Who is Chakka?'

'A Campeche Indian who did me a good turn once.'

'Then I'll take the one like Chakka,' she said. 'It would be a pity to take one of the brothers, anyhow, wouldn't it? They make such a nice set!'

Arrangements were made for the boy to ride on Barley Sugar's saddle when they went home in the evening, and they left the steward to his little silver instrument and his spirits of wine. But a child's yell brought them back, and there was the remaining Indian boy in a panic. He had never seen a branding-iron before, and to his terror of being hurt was added the superstitious fear of magic. The almost invisible flame and the thin little silver rod were more terrifying than any known horror, and the eyes were starting out of his head.

Before anyone could do anything about it, the eldest Negro boy capered forward, pushed him scornfully to one side, and bared his chest with a swagger. The other three Negro children were making wild fun of the wretched craven, roaring with laughter and imitating his terror in unkind caricature. They had seen this process often, and knew that it did not hurt; and they had all the scorn of cosmopolitans for a country cousin.

The steward rubbed the boy's skin with sweet oil, heated the brand in the spirit-flame, and touched the boy with it, and there was the T.M. of the Governor's ownership on his chest. The boy regarded it proudly, as the retainer of a great noble might his badge, and the other Negro children fought for the honour of being next.

And suddenly Henry said: 'If your Excellency does not particularly want the Indian boy, perhaps you would let me buy him from you.'

'No, I don't want him; but are you sure that you do? I bought him only so as not to separate him from the boy from his village.'

It was on the tip of Henry's tongue to say: 'That is why I want to buy him too,' but he remembered in time that Elizabeth was still only his cousin.

'I should like very much to have him,' he said. 'How much do you want for him?'

'One English rose from Morgan's Valley to be delivered to Morant on the first day of May every year.' He cocked an eye at Henry, and added: 'If Jamaica is going to be English, the establishment of a few traditions is greatly desirable.'

He took the boy by the shoulder and moved him forward to face Henry. 'I give you to this man,' he said slowly to the boy.

The boy did not understand the words, but he understood the gesture. He looked for a long, searching moment at Morgan, and then the panic left his eyes. There was silence in the crowded little room while they watched him. They had half expected him to accept his new ownership with some sort of obeisance, slave-wise. But he accepted it in a fashion much more moving. He walked over and stood close beside Henry, side by side with him and a little in the rear; as one taking shelter under a tree. And Henry, unexpectedly touched, dropped his hand in a rallying gesture on the black straight hair.

'Well,' Modyford said, 'now that we have settled that, let us go and eat dinner.'

Dinner was the long, leisurely enormous meal that the English considered necessary for life in the tropics; and the talk was the immemorial talk of the colonial English: how Charles was doing at school and how soon he would be coming 'out' to take his place in the making of Jamaica; how little 'they' understood the needs of the new colony; how irreconcilable were the two main cliques in English Jamaica, and how odd it was that the original Commonwealth settlers should, when released from their strictness, be so much more debauched than any of their Royalist successors. Henry sat in the shadows and watched Elizabeth, and planned for the day when she should sit at the other end of his own table. He liked her fire and her directness, her almost boy-like frankness, her inability to trade on her own femininity, and he compared her unfavourably with Mary Modyford, who was all a soft glow in her lover's presence. Women had glowed for him, too, but he had not wanted to marry them; to spend his life with them; to have them as mother of his children. His cousin Elizabeth gave him not only excitement but the companionship that was dearer and much more rare. She was not woman, she was one person and unique. She was, quite simply, Elizabeth. Irreplaceable. And he must marry her at the earliest possible moment.

He noticed that she was a great favourite with the Governor, and wondered again whether Modyford had remembered quite well that Elizabeth was coming over to Morant this Sunday, and whether his invitation was merely a way of furthering his suit. This suspicion was almost confirmed when Sir Thomas said: 'I had looked forward to riding back to Port Royal with you tomorrow morning, Henry, but if you go tonight instead, you could escort your cousin part of the way home, since your roads lie together so far.'

So Henry and Elizabeth rode side by side under the trees in the cool of the evening, not hurrying, and greatly content in each other's company. And Barley Sugar rode behind and instructed the Indian boy in the English names of things.

'Dat a tree,' said Barley Sugar.

'Dattatree,' noted the boy obediently.

'I suppose dattas must be a cross between dates and bananas,'

Elizabeth commented. 'The poor little wretch must be very confused.'

'What are you going to call him?'

'I hadn't thought about it. What are you going to call yours?'

'Let us call them by two related names. You know. Castor and Pollux. Hengist and Horsa. Flotsam and Jetsam.'

'Romulus and Remus. Let us call them Romulus and Remus. I'll have Remus and save myself a syllable. Who was Chakka, Harry?'

'An Indian who could throw a rope over a given mark.'

There was silence for a moment, and then Elizabeth burst out:

'I *wish* men would not *put off* women when they ask questions! If I had been a man you would have told me all about Chakka!'

'But, Bet,' he said, using her little name for the first time, 'I would have told you if I had thought that you would be interested!'

'Yes,' she said, flaring. 'That is just what I am pointing out. "A man who could throw ropes, little girl; you wouldn't be interested." What am I supposed to be interested in? Still-room concoctions and poultices and betrothals and calvings, and embroidery and hair-washing, and —'

The mention of hair-washing, which her subconscious had thrown up for her tongue to use, suddenly reminded her. She stopped in full flight, and then, being Elizabeth, began to laugh. She laughed so that she rocked in the saddle, alight with self-mockery and the sheer absurdity of things.

Henry had a wild longing to reach over and pick her from the saddle and hold her in his arms while the laughter sobbed up from her mouth as he kissed her. Instead he put his hand on her rein, lightly, and said: 'Bet, my dearest dear, there is no one in the world I would sooner tell my stories to than you.'

'Then tell me about Chakka.'

So he told her about the Indian whose throwing of the grapnel had helped him to take the *Fortune*, and decided that when he went over to see Anna Petronilla he would once more make suit for Elizabeth; less surprisingly this time, and with more to recommend him as a suitor. Anna Petronilla would not be insensible to the added prestige that came from the retaking of Santa Catalina, nor to the practical fact of Morgan's Valley and the house that was being built there.

8

HENRY MARRIED HIS cousin three months later; and to mark the last day of his bachelor life the Governor gave a dinner for him at Kingshouse. The dinner began at four o'clock, and by seven was well under way. It was the most magnificent feast that Kingshouse had witnessed since the occupation, and the guests noticed and noted. It was so, was it, that Modyford rated his young friend Morgan; the rarest dishes and the best plate? They considered the guest of honour, and wondered whether he was going to settle down as a planter or stick to the sea. There was no antagonism in their regard, for it was an exclusive and friendly party. The only unrejoicing member was Colonel Thomas Lynch, who had been Modyford's predecessor in the Governorship; and Henry, watching Lynch's efforts at conviviality, could not make up his mind whether Modyford's inclusion of him was due to policy or to Modyford's own brand of gentle malice.

By eight o'clock they had finished eating and had begun the serious business of drinking. Rob Byndloss, the husband of kind, blob-of-butter Anna, was already a little drunk, and announced at intervals to anyone who would listen: 'No one in the world, sir, will ever make me wear a wig. Never, sir.' It having lately become known in Jamaica that it had become the fashion 'at home' to supplement one's own curls with artificial hair.

Henry Archbould, Anna Petronilla's adviser and stand-by, sat somnolent and owl-like, staring at the reflection of the candles in his wine. His only contribution to the conversation in the last hour had been to say that if it was true that women's skirts were to be worn shorter, then it was a deplorable thing. It would deprive man of one of the most delightful moments of his every-day life; the moment when a woman lifted her skirt and one saw her ankle. No marriage bed, opined Henry, nor any drab's couch afforded so exquisite a moment as that afforded by the glimpse of a forbidden ankle.

The guest of honour listened to the talk with half his mind, and with the other half thought of tomorrow, when he would marry Elizabeth in the only church on the island. St Katherine's at St Yago de la Vega had been the Spanish cathedral, and had now been restored in some measure from the ruin that the Commonwealth troops had made of it in their anti-Popish zeal. It was appropriate that they should be married in Spanish Town, and not at Port Royal, for the Morgans' first home had been there, and Edward in his will had left their little house there to be a parsonage for the new church. Indeed, kind Mr Hauser, who was going to marry them tomorrow, had relet the upper floor of the house to them so that they might have a town dwelling as well as the rather primitive delights of Morgan's Valley.

Henry found Spanish Town and its inland airs static and dead after the dancing air of the Port, always full of the sea's reflection. It was so like the Spaniards, he thought, to have an inland capital. No Englishman would think of a capital city divorced from the sea. Was defence always in their minds? Was defence a natural, instinctive thing with them, and not a sign of their degeneracy at all? Were they losing their place in the sun *because* of this innate leaning to defence, and not being defensive because they were losing their place?

That made him think again of Santa Catalina, and of Mansfield. He did not like to think of Mansfield. The old man had gone away sorrowful because the Spaniards still had great possessions and Henry would not come with him to relieve them of some more. When Henry pointed out that any captain would be proud to sail under his command, that he had his choice of captains, Mansfield had said: 'Aah, they are all mere herrings in a barrel! They can sail and they can fight, but can they think? No! They can not! But you and I, Henry, you and I. Between us we could take America from the Spaniards. Take all America from them.'

But for the moment Henry's mind was on shore. He had not

been able to think of sea business while Elizabeth was still not his. The island swarmed with single men looking for wives, and Henry, though vain, was not conceited. He rated himself no higher as a suitor than any one of the well-to-do young planters who came out to risk their future in the new colony. He had to make sure of Elizabeth before he went to sea again.

In which his reaction was curiously like his bride's.

'Do you love him, Bet?' Johanna had asked, lolling on their mutual bed and watching her sister try on a new bodice.

'I don't know whether it is love or not,' Elizabeth said, soberly. 'I do not want very much to get married, but I cannot bear the thought of his being married to anyone else. So I do not have much choice.'

Her reaction to his formal proposal had been to say: 'You know, Harry, I do not want to be married to anyone, but I like Morgan's Valley very much, and I think it is worth being married for.'

When he ventured to hope that she liked him, too, in some measure, she said: 'Oh, *yes*; of course I do!' and added: 'I like to watch you.'

With which cryptic utterance he had to be content.

But now that he had made sure of Elizabeth, and tomorrow they were being married, he had leisure to think of Mansfield, and to be sorry that he had not been more patient with the old man's babblings about Maracaibo. For three solid weeks, in season and out, Mansfield had talked Maracaibo to him. When Henry, trying to head him off, had pointed out that the French had sacked the place already, he had said: 'Aah, who ever heard of the French tidying up a job properly! And in Maracaibo there is no end to it, anyhow. The gold runs out of a man's boots there.' And later, faced with the blank wall of Henry's determination to remain on shore, he said: 'You are not thinking of turning planter, are you, Harry?'

'Not until Morgan's Valley is safe from Spain,' Henry had said, dryly.

And Mansfield had looked suddenly happier. His parting words had been: 'I shall come back for you, Harry, my little taker of prizes; and you will be sick of the dust in your nostrils, and you will come with me once more to strike at Spain where it hurts.'

He had sailed away on business of his own to the South Cays of Cuba. Joe Bradley, not caring whether he had a commission or not, had departed for the Bay of Mexico to see what he could pick up. So the only sailor at this party in Morgan's honour was Jack Morris; who was getting drunk in the same fashion as he did everything else: with a sort of neat circumspection.

It was stifling in the room. The night hung against the open windows like a curtain, velvet and opaque. The heavy air was so still that the candle-flames stood up like bright lances in their surrounding haze of insects. When, about half-past nine, a small white object sailed in a high curve through the window and dropped through the mist of flies to land with a plop on the table, only two men were sober enough to react normally to the phenomenon.

Modyford reached forward and took the paper from the table, unrolling it from the weighting stone. But Morgan, even after five hours' eating and drinking, still thought faster than the Governor. Even before Modyford's hand had gone out for the thing, Henry had pushed back his chair and made for the garden. There was a cry in the dark, and the sound of physical contest, and Henry reappeared frog-marching a scared maroon.

'Here is your serenader,' he said. 'What does the love-note say, or is it personal?'

Modyford looked up with an odd reluctance from the paper he was reading, as if as long as his eyes were on the paper he could postpone the evil ahead.

'It is personal,' he said. 'It is from Major Smith.'

'Smith! Oh. From Santa Catalina. Then why all this coyness?' Henry shook the man he was holding.

'The man is a runaway slave from Puerto Bello.'

'Oh.' Henry's grip slackened. 'And what was he doing in Santa Catalina?'

'He was never in Santa Catalina. The Spaniards took Santa Catalina nine weeks ago. The survivors are in prison in Puerto Bello.' He read from the paper. '"We fought until there was not a scrape of powder left. When the shot ran out we broke up the organ in the church, and fired away sixty of the pipes at one shot. When there was nothing left to fire we surrendered on the same conditions as we had given them. But it proved to be 'a Spanish promise'. Those of us who survive are doing blacks' work on the fortifications here. Please reward the slave if you get this."'

There was a long silence.

Henry felt for the back of his chair and sat down.

'How did you come by this?' the Governor asked the slave.

A white man working on the castle of San Jeronimo at Puerto Bello had given it to him, he said.

'And why did you not wait to be rewarded?'

He did not know what might be in the letter, he said. He supposed that it would tell about the white prisoner of the Spaniards, but it might also tell that he was a runaway slave.

Henry took out a gold piece and gave it to him, saying: 'Stay in Port Royal where we can find you.'

'If you give him that,' Modyford said, 'he'll be in jail five minutes after he presents it.'

'Yes, of course,' said Henry, taking back the gold piece and giving the man its value in silver. Only Modyford, he thought, would be able to consider a detail like that at a moment so shattering.

The maroon melted into the night, and everyone suddenly began to talk at once. But it was Jack Morris's voice that over-topped them.

'We are going back to Santa Catalina, aren't we, Harry?'

'No,' said Morgan. He looked very white in the candle-light, as if he might be going to be sick. 'No. We are going to Puerto Bello.'

There was silence again at this, while they considered it.

'Even Drake failed there,' Modyford reminded him.

'Put it out of your mind, Morgan,' Henry Archbould said. 'If Frankie couldn't do it, you can't. No one could.'

Rob Byndloss laughed a high, drunken laugh and said: 'Tell you one thing our Harry's done no man ever did before! He's made Spain hurry! Terribly shocked over Santa Catalina they must have been to come running so fast to its rescue, all through the nasty steep seas and the hurricanes. Shook Spain's liver, our Harry has!'

'How many of them were there?' Henry asked Modyford.

'Half a navy,' Modyford said, pushing the paper over to him.

While he read it, the Governor watched him with sympathy and some anxiety. The colour had not come back to Henry's face. The high cheek-bones stood out sharply, as if he had been wasted by fever, and the wide mouth had lost its curves and straightened into a line. He looked a man of forty, and an ill man at that.

The hubbub had broken out again, but Henry took no notice of it.

'It will take more ships than Santa Catalina, of course,' he said at length. 'Nine at least.'

'Put it out of your mind, Harry,' Modyford said. 'The place is notoriously impregnable. We can effect an exchange of prisoners.'

'Can we?' Morgan said. 'When we make Spain a present of all we take?'

'In any case,' a cold voice said, 'we cannot very well take action when Spain has right on her side in the present instance, can we?'

This brought even tipsy conversation to a pause.

Everyone had forgotten the presence of the Opposition in the person of Lynch.

In another second Rob Byndloss would have launched himself on the Colonel, but Morgan held him while the Governor said smoothly: 'We have all had too much spirit to think to the letter, Colonel.'

'No doubt, no doubt,' said Lynch. 'It is with regret that I must leave so delightful a meeting, but I have a long way to go, and the roads are deplorable.'

It was so like Lynch, Henry thought, to add that flick about the roads at such a time.

Archbould and two others went with him, not because they loved Lynch, but because their ways lay together and no one rode alone at night along the roads of Jamaica if they could help it.

'Do you think we could do it, Harry?' Jack asked under the confusion of leave-takings. Not doubtfully, but in hope.

'Do you know that the narrows at Puerto Bello are fortified all the way, so that any ship entering harbour is subject to crossfire at point-blank range?' someone said.

'And when you are in there is a third castle to welcome you with a broadside,' another said.

'I can think of something more daunting even than that,' Modyford said, returned from speeding his guests.

'The mosquitoes?' they asked.

'No. The cost of such an expedition. No obliging Government is going to finance it for us, obviously. Then how otherwise could it be done? The victualling alone of such a fleet would cost a fortune.'

'It is possible that we might be able to save the Exchequer any anxiety on that score,' Henry said, drawling.

Modyford looked across at him, and was relieved to see that the colour had come back to his face. His mouth had recovered its curves.

'When you look demure, Harry,' he said, 'my very soul faints within me.' And being rewarded by the shadow of a smile in Morgan's eyes: 'Well? What is your idea of a larder?'

'There are very fine herds in Cuba, I understand.'

'In the interior of Cuba.'

'I walk better than I swim.'

'If you think that I am going to give you a commission for the invasion of Cuba you are not as intelligent as I thought.'

'No, I am going to give your Excellency evidence, gathered in Cuba, of plans and enlistments for the invasion of Jamaica. *Honest* evidence.'

'Oh, Harry, Harry! Only you would have thought of undertaking one expedition to victual yourself for another. If you don't get us both hanged, you may be Governor of America one day.'

'Only I will hang,' Henry assured him. 'You will be honourably executed. Your cousin Albemarle will see to that.'

'Well, put our wretched countrymen out of your mind for a day or two at least. Tomorrow is your wedding day.'

But at the mention of the prisoners, the bleakness came back to Morgan's face.

And next day, in the dimness of the church at Spanish Town, Elizabeth looked at him once or twice, doubtfully; wondering if the mere being married to a woman could make a man's face so suddenly grim, could so steal the youth from it.

She did not hear what had happened until they were alone in the little upper room at Mr Hauser's. When he told her, she flung her arms round him in the first caress she had ever given him and hugged him to her in pity and regret. 'Oh, Harry, poor Harry!' she said, as she might to a child who had fallen downstairs.

He had expected her to say: 'But you're not going to leave me and go away off there so soon after we are married!'; not because it was particularly true to the Elizabeth he supposed she was, but because it was what he expected a woman to say. Her instant identification of herself with him moved him almost to tears.

'Bart is there,' he blurted, saying the thing he had not said even to Jack Morris.

'Poor Harry! Never mind! You'll get him back,' she said into his ear, and kissed him.

But in the morning she was brisk and practical. If Henry was going to be busy organising an expedition, these rooms in Spanish Town were not going to be of much use to them. They must find something at the Port.

'There is nothing but standing-room at Port Royal.'

'Mary Speirdyck might find us something. You will be going to see Bernard about – about Santa Catalina, won't you? Ask Mary if she could find us a couple of rooms somewhere.'

He had waited, in the cold anti-climactic light of morning, for her to revert to femininity and bring up the subject of Morgan's Valley, and the desirability of his remaining on shore to develop it. But nothing like that had happened. Her only mention of their future life together was this suggestion of finding rooms near the Port. She took his going to be the obvious and accepted thing, as a male comrade might. He looked across at her in wonder and delight, and promised to give Mary her message.

But when he had climbed the steep, cobbled alley to Mary's house and stood looking into her cool, bare living-room, he nearly forgot. For sitting at the table eating a meal was Charles Hadsell, late commandant of Santa Catalina.

'Hadsell!' he said. 'How did you get here?'

'Came in this morning in the *Alice* from Nicaragua. How are you, Captain? Married, I hear. My congratulations. Perhaps you'll do us the honour to come to my daughter's marriage? She and Cornelius here are planning to get hitched in about three weeks' time.'

'You mean you went on to Nicaragua with the ship that brought the reinforcements to the island?'

'I certainly did. I didn't fancy being junior to a soldier boy with the down still on his cheeks. Had a fine voyage. Bought myself a share of the cargo, too. Add a bit to Jane's dowry. Eh, Cornelius?'

Mary replenished his plate from the stove, and Bernard came in from the street and greeted Morgan with surprise and welcome.

'You are early abroad for a bridegroom, Captain,' he said, and set glasses for himself and Morgan on the table.

'Yes,' said Henry. 'A skeleton came to my marriage feast.'

'A skeleton?' Bernard said into the startled pause.

'Skeleton of what?' asked Hadsell.

'Santa Catalina.'

'Santa Catalina!' repeated Hadsell. 'You mean something has gone wrong on the island?'

'The Spaniards took Santa Catalina nine weeks ago, and our men are in prison in Puerto Bello.'

'No!' cried Cornelius.

His uncle let loose a flood of his native tongue and was reproved half-heartedly by Mary.

'How do you know?' asked Hadsell.

Henry told them.

Hadsell put down his knife and fork as if his appetite had of a sudden deserted him. There was the same dismayed silence in the little room as had fallen over the Governor's board the night before.

It was the boy who broke it. 'What do we do, Captain? Take the island again?'

'No,' said Henry. 'We won't have to take it back. Some day it will drop into our laps like a ripe cherry because the Spaniards will be too busy defending the mainland to have spare men and energy for an island.'

'You mean we are going to win back Santa Catalina on the mainland of America?' Cornelius said, his face alight.

'Yes.'

'Where?' asked Bernard, beginning to pour brandy.

'Puerto Bello for a start.'

Bernard's hand stopped its pouring for a moment and then went on. But Hadsell supplied the inevitable comment.

'Have you forgotten Drake?'

'No.'

'And they have fortified the place beyond recognition since Drake went there.'

'Perhaps Drake did not have any men who were prisoners on shore.'

'I knew that soldier boy should not have been given charge of an island,' Hadsell said, virtuously. Which roused Morgan.

'Major Smith defended the island very gallantly and very efficiently,' he said, in his quarter-deck voice. 'They scraped the last grains of powder from the magazine floor before they surrendered. They left the fort only after defending it to the last possible moment.'

Hadsell recognized both the snub and the comment on his own conduct, and subsided.

'Does anyone know where Joe Bradley is? We must prepare a rendezvous as soon as the gale season is over. And Mansfield. And anyone else who is not too careful of his skin. But no one but ourselves must know where we plan to sail to.'

'Don't worry,' Hadsell said. 'No one would believe it anyhow.' And his tone was not complimentary.

But Bernard had news of Joe Bradley, and Cornelius suggested new names, and so, in Mary's cool, bare room in a blazing August Jamaican noon, the first tentative ripple began of a wave that would roar across the world and come flooding up the

Chancellory steps of Europe. And in the succeeding weeks, through the damp hot days and the flickering storm, a centre of calm purpose sent its radiation through the welter that Nature made of the islands. Men riding out the bad days in the Gardens of the Queen, in the sheltering cays, men in bars and taverns and bawdy houses up and down the islands, told each other that at the end of the year Harry Morgan was sailing again. Harry Morgan was taking the *Fortune* out on some new ploy when it was sailing weather once more. He would be at Pine Island in November with the *Fortune* freshly careened, and he was looking for ships and men.

Mary found not two rooms but three in the dripping huddle of Port Royal, and Elizabeth arrived drenched on the ferry from Passage, with Couba as maid and Remus to carry her unused finery in its little leather trunk. The rooms were small and dark and the roof leaked, and the house was loud with the noise of the wind and the sea, but it was there, only a few steps for Harry to walk at the end of the crowded days, and it was there, close to the sea, for the men from the sea who had business with him. Hardly a day passed but Couba opened the door to some man standing on the threshold with his cap in his hand and an identical phrase for utterance: Captain Morgan wanted men, they said; Captain Morgan wanted men.

Henry's own original crew began to trickle back from their various destitutions. And some, indeed, from prosperities of their own. That admirer of zeal, Walter Benrose, master gunner from Lincolnshire, had bought himself a dinghy and was doing quite well as a water-man. The two dog-lovers, Manuel and the mulatto, were found to be running a very profitable little business called LOST DOGS FOUND, in which the mulatto enticed away the dog and Manuel, all eyelashes and innocent charm, returned it and claimed the reward. The mulatto had lately blotted his copybook by enticing the same dog twice in five days, and a faint breath of suspicion was beginning to mar their relations with Port Royal. They were glad to be going to sea again. Next time, Manuel said, they would think of something else. Fighting-cocks. Or find a very fast dog and offer to course it against all comers.

Even Exmeling turned up, a little vague as to what he had been doing lately. Henry was glad to have him, and remembered with a pang that there would be no Bartholomew this time to object to his presence in the ship. When asked why he had not sailed with his relative by marriage, Captain Mansfield, he said that Mansfield had told him that he was going to the South Cays merely to careen his ship, and to refit afterwards at Tortuga, perhaps, and had no need for a surgeon. He had no news of Mansfield, and neither had anyone else.

Henry invited Exmeling to drink brandy with him and presented him to Elizabeth. And it seemed that Bartholomew was not unique in his dislike of little Henrik. Elizabeth did not like him either.

'But why?' asked Henry, genuinely puzzled. 'He is a harmless creature, surely. No one ever notices that he is there.'

'You don't notice that a snake is there either,' Elizabeth pointed out. 'Do you have to take him with you?'

'I am glad to. He is a good surgeon, considering that he has had no professional training.' He remembered what Mansfield had said, and added: 'He enjoys surgery.'

'Yes,' said Elizabeth. 'I expect he does.'

Several times they rode out to Morgan's Valley to spend a night in the half-finished house and to arrange what should be done during Henry's absence. Henry had tried to persuade Jack Morris to buy a piece of land near them for 'the day when he would want to settle down'.

'For *what*?' said Jack, and laughed.

But it was Elizabeth's triumph that he did come very often to the cramped little rooms in Port Royal and seemed at home there. The constraint that normally overcame him in the presence of good women was not apparent in his relation with his friend's wife. Indeed, he came to treat her as something between a sister and a sister-in-law. He would sit at ease with them of an evening and talk quietly about ways and means, or be silent over his wine. For this, too, Henry was grateful to Elizabeth, and for this, too, he loved her.

When the time came that the *Fortune* and the *Dolphin* rode ready and waiting in harbour for their voyage to Isle of Pines,

Jack took Elizabeth out to show her over his ship, that being the kind of courtesy that he would have offered a fellow-captain whom he respected and admired. And Elizabeth, visiting her husband's ship later to say good-bye, did not fail to point out that on board the *Fortune* she was merely a poor female creature on sufferance saying farewell to her lord, while on the *Dolphin* she had been an honoured guest.

Her farewell to Henry was to say: 'I wish that I was coming with you, Harry!'

Don't forget me, come back to me, come back safe, come back soon, women were saying all over the town. But Elizabeth's only spoken wish was that she might go with him. And watching the small, upright figure being borne away across the water in the stern of the boat, Henry found himself wishing that it might indeed have been possible to take her. She had mettle enough for two men. Even with the pressure of her arms still alive on the back of his neck, he had a suspicion that her wish was at least as much for the adventure as for his companionship. She would make a wonderful lieutenant in a ploy.

'At least I shall not have to worry about the state of your clothes while you are away,' she had said when she was packing his sea-chest for him. 'Romulus will see to that.'

For the Indian boy, who took no interest at all in sea matters, was enchanted by clothes and all that pertained to them. Romulus patted a piece of cloth with exactly the same gesture that Mansfield used when he patted a map. And this minor passion of his, allied to his major passion for Henry, was like to make Henry the best-groomed captain in the Caribbean. A rent, a spot, a frayed lace, and Romulus was there with needle or sponge to make all perfect immediately. If there were no repairs to be done, Romulus was still there, of course; sitting in Henry's shadow, silent and still. Henry was the reason for his existence. He had submitted without a quiver to being branded at Henry's hands, at the same time as the new slaves for Morgan's Valley, and had won Morgan's heart by taking the terrifying moment with his eyes wide open and fixed in fathomless trust on his master's face.

It was the New Year before the *Fortune* was ready to sail,

and by that time almost two-thirds of her old crew had rejoined. The remaining third was made up not of seamen but of old-soldiers, Royalist and Commonwealth, who found planting life too hard or dull, and were glad to give their services in return for adventure and their victuals. Bernard Speirdyck, seaman to his marrow, looked askance at these, but Henry had plans for them. Bernard was, of course, sailing as mate; and Cornelius, very sedate, as befitted a Benedict, as second. And Jack Morris had not this time to put up with any disgruntled master as mate, for Charles Hadsell had fallen heir to a prize by way of temporary compensation for his own lost ship, and was now master of the frigate *Maria*. The *Maria* followed the *Fortune* and the *Dolphin* out past Fort Charles in the cool grey of a Spring dawn, bound for the South Cays, and early as it was the Point was gay with women's dresses and vivid with kerchiefs waving them a farewell.

'I had no idea we were so popular,' said Henry, much gratified.

'That is not for us,' said Cornelius who had spent the night ashore and had left his bride in bed.

'No? For whom, then?'

'For Manuel, I suspect.'

'Manuel!' Henry took a longer look at the gay fluttering on the point and realized that the colours were a little too bright to be altogether respectable. Cornelius seemed to be right. Every trollop in the port had come out to wave good-bye to Manuel.

9

FOR A FORTNIGHT the three ships clawed their way up-wind, glad if they gained a mile in the hour; and the crews had time to settle down with each other, and Henry had time to wonder how he was going to deal with any Frenchman who might be waiting for him at Isle of Pines. At home, so it was understood, the French had come to the assistance of the Dutch, and were actively fighting England. How much would this weigh with the French in the Caribbean, the French who had been so long an ally against the pretensions of Spain?

When he expressed his doubts to Bernard, the Hollander's normally wooden face melted into curves. 'Yoost look at me, Captain, yoost look at me! At home your people sink my people like it was the best fun in the world. All over the North Sea they sink them. But does it make any difference to my appetite for salt pork and yams? Does it make any difference to the fact that we like each other, you and I, Captain, and we do not like the Spaniard? No! And the French they do not like the Spaniard either. It will not matter one little piece to the French what anyone does at home. You will see.'

But Henry still thought that it might be much less easy to handle the French than it had been up to the present.

They picked up Isle of Pines on a morning of tumbled seas and glancing light, but it was late afternoon before they came on their last tack into the quiet water in the lee of the island, and saw the ships sheltering in the wide lagoon.

'Yoost look at them,' said Bernard. 'A navy, by Gar! That is John Ansell there, with the broken figurehead. And that over there with the long sprit is Tom Clarke. And that tub with the foremast stepped too far for'ard is Tom Rogers' *Gift*. She is a cow to sail, the *Gift*. And there —'

But Morgan was looking for the stubby masts that would tell him that the *Endeavour* was there. All the way north he had looked forward to seeing Mansfield; to putting his plan in the old man's lap and seeing him laugh with pleasure at its impudence and its reasonableness. Looked forward to hearing him say: 'Ah, my little taker of prizes, you have come of age, it seems. You plan like a veteran. Like Mansfield himself.'

But there was no sign of the *Endeavour*.

The only familiar sight was the *May Flower*, lying well under the lee of the land as if she had been there for some time.

Well, at least Bradley was here. Bradley might have news of Mansfield.

He found his old colleague of the Santa Catalina expedition

in the ramshackle village ashore. He was sitting on the veranda of Charley's as if he had been sitting there for months and had got embedded.

'You've been a damned long time, Harry Morgan,' he said. 'I'd nearly given you up,' he said. But he said it without feeling, and he looked pleased to see Morgan. 'Has Jack Morris still got the *Dolphin*?'

'Yes. That's him coming ashore in the boat now.'

'And who's your frigate friend?'

'Charlie Hadsell.'

'Oh,' said Joe, without enthusiasm.

'She's the *Maria*. A prize. Where is Mansfield?'

'Not here. And that's all I know. I thought *you* would give *me* news of him.

'Has *no one* news of him, then?'

'Not a soul, as far as I know.'

'That's odd,' Morgan said, troubled.

'There's nothing odd about it. Mansfield always plays a lone hand. He's probably nosing round the coast of the mainland making charts for his future purposes. He has a passion for coasting.'

Neither of them mentioned Santa Catalina. The loss of the place had been the chief talking topic of the Islands for the last six months, and there was nothing to say about it. They watched Jack's boat come to shore and his neat, spare figure come up the beach to them, and Bradley gave a running commentary on the ships in the bay for Henry's benefit. Several were 'untouchables', pirates on their own secret and unlovely business; here to refit or careen. One or two were legitimate prizes on their way to surrender to a reputable authority. A few more were birds of passage, bound out after they had obtained fresh food, wood and water. But a considerable number were privateers, or ex-privateers, looking for business.

'I see Tom Rogers is here,' Jack said, coming up and greeting Joe Bradley with pleasure. 'I never know how he manages to make that thing sail at all, but sail her he does. He can make her go two forward and one back like a lady dancing at a party. He'd be a good man to have with us.'

'What are your plans?' Bradley asked.

'I'll tell you after supper,' Henry said.

'Oh, God! do I have to stay sober?' said Joe.

The sky flared suddenly into sunset, and Charley, looking at the crowded condition of his crazy veranda, built a fire of driftwood on the beach below and carried his huge cauldron of peppery fish stew out from his kitchen to keep hot on it. His customers followed the appetising reek and were served while they sat about the blaze. As each newcomer arrived he was introduced to Morgan by either Bradley or Jack Morris, and as the swift twilight fell and the shifting light of the fire grew brighter, Morgan considered the faces of these strangers, speculating and comparing. Was this one too vain to accept orders, was that one too reckless to be trusted to carry them out, was the next one too cautious to take a legitimate risk?

Rogers he was sure of at once. Rogers was a little dark man with eyebrows so thick and so black that they looked like smudges. He was talkative and quick-tempered and volatile, but there was nothing pinchbeck about him. Rogers was the genuine article: courageous, imaginative, and dependable. Another dependable-appearing creature was the big fair man on the other side of the fire; a man with a rough-hewn square face that was ruddier than ever in the light. 'The cherry-trees will be white soon, in Kent,' he was saying. 'I'm going to give up the sea, so help me I am, now that England's a country fit for gentlemen to live in again. I'm going to get me a bit of land and an orchard and I'll never eat another fish stew as long as I live.' The Celt in Henry recognized the Saxon salt-of-the-earth and paid tribute to it. He wanted to have the Kent man with him.

When they were gorged on turtle and shell-fish they lay around drinking and swapping stories while the moon climbed into a bland sky and stared at them. Morgan was well aware that a great interest and curiosity settled on him, but that their innate good manners prevented them from open question. They knew that if he wanted to tell them of his plans he would, and that if he wanted to keep those plans to himself, question was both unmannerly and useless. He watched the weaker brethren grow a little drunk, and removed them from his consideration: not because they were drunk, but because if they had allowed themselves to become drunk, then they were not vitally interested in any plan that he might have in mind. For the same reason he dismissed those who eventually left the fire to gamble in the back room of the little eating-house. The drunken ones went back to the house when the rum gave out, to replenish the jugs, and stayed there, so that presently those round the fire were the survivors of a natural process of selection of which they were unaware. But they were aware of a mental unbuttoning, a lessened need for discretion, now that the company was less general.

It was Tom Rogers, just a little flown, who gave expression to this growing relaxation.

'You don't by any chance happen to have a use for the *Gift*, do you, Captain Morgan? I know she's the joke of the Caribbean, but I can lay her alongside as neat as a dove's tail in the time you'd take to make up juice for a second spit.'

Morgan savoured the quickened attention of the sprawled figures round the fire, and lengthened the moment for his own enjoyment.

'I don't need ships at the moment,' he said. 'I am going into the cattle business.'

'Cattle!' they said, shocked. 'Where?'

'Cuba,' said Henry, demure; and nearly laughed aloud as the lounging figures sat up as one man.

'*Cuba!*'

'Yes. It's a very fine cattle-country, I understand.'

'Oh,' they said, relaxing. 'You are going to land a poaching party to victual the *Fortune*.'

'Oh, no. It is all quite open and above-board. I am taking a thousand head of beef out of Cuba in the next few weeks.'

They sat up once more and considered this unlikely statement.

'And how will you manage to run off a thousand head under the Spaniards' noses?'

'Oh, I shall have permission, of course.'

'Permission? Whose permission!'

'The Spaniards, naturally.'

'The Spaniards! You think they will give you permission?'

'For a consideration, they will.'

'You're mad, Henry Morgan,' they said. 'Not for any money will the Spaniards oblige an Englishman to the extent of a thousand head of cattle. You can save your breath and your money.'

'I had not thought of money.'

'No? Then what was your "consideration"?'

'I think the Spaniards will give me the beef as the price of not sacking Puerto Principe.'

There was complete silence at that. A staggered silence.

'But Puerto Principe is in the very heart of Cuba,' they said. 'Thirty miles at least from the coast.'

'That is why I think it would be a good bargaining counter.'

'Why?'

'It has no defences worth mentioning.'

'Perhaps,' they said. 'But the rest of Cuba has plenty. The place bristles with fortifications.'

'Only at the Havana end. They take it for granted that Puerto Principe doesn't need any. No one, they think, would come into the heart of the country to attack it.'

'And I don't blame them,' said little Rogers in a burst. 'By God, it is so daft that it is very nearly sensible.'

'There is a further reason that makes Puerto Principe a handy thing to dicker with. The plains round the town are black with cattle. The best beef in Cuba.'

'And what will the Spaniards be doing while we are coming openly across the plain?' asked the Kent man.

'We, Captain Ansell?' said Morgan, and his heart lifted.

'If you're going to hold up a town in the centre of Cuba, you're not going to do it with a ship's crew, Captain Morgan. And if you're planning to take over a thousand head of cattle, then you're planning to victual more ships than the *Fortune*. I want to be part of whatever is forward.'

'I shall be very pleased to have your help, Captain Ansell. And as to your question, we shall do the thirty miles over the hills between a dawn and a dawn, so that we come down into the plain while the world is still asleep. We shall be in the town before they are aware of us.'

'Have you anyone who knows the interior of Cuba?' Rogers asked.

'Yes. Captain Hadsell here escaped from Havana across country, and lay in hiding on that coast for some time.'

'And how many men do you plan to use?' Ansell said.

'About four hundred if I can get them. But it can be done with less.'

The blazing logs slipped one by one, in sudden cascades of sparks, to scattered embers while they discussed the affair; and when at last, in the bright calm of midnight, they got stiffly to their feet and went their several ways to the boats, the verdict was the one that Tom Rogers had so impulsively given at first hearing: It was so daft that it was very nearly sensible.

'What about the French?' Morgan asked Rogers and Ansell as they walked down the beach together. 'There are three of them in the lagoon. Are they to be trusted these days?'

'Why not?' said Ansell. 'My family have been marrying back and forth across the Channel for hundreds of years, and I never found a war with France make any difference to our mutual plans.'

'Let them make the offer – don't you go courting them, Captain – and then they'll stay by you,' said Rogers, who was a Celt like Morgan, and therefore more devious-minded than the Kent man.

And Morgan took this to be good advice.

He held it to be even better advice next morning, when he saw a boat from the *Galliardena* being rowed across to the *Fortune*, and a tall, thin, chestnut-coloured man – chestnut hair, chestnut eyes, and chestnut skin – came on board and introduced himself as Captain Pierre Gascoone. Henry made him welcome, and as soon as sea etiquette was satisfied – that is, as soon as he had accepted a second drink and thereby paid tribute to the quality of the first – he broached the business he had come on. He and his two fellow-captains had heard much of Captain Morgan's prowess against Spain, and it was freely rumoured in the Islands that Captain Morgan was planning a new adventure in that direction. He had no wish to force any confidence, but he would like Captain Morgan to know that if he was looking for assistance, he, Pierre Gascoone, and his two colleagues, Captain Tribetor and Captain Linaux, would be glad to join any expedition that Captain Morgan might have in mind. All three of them had suffered at Spain's hands; and all three crews were very short of back-pay. Two cogent reasons for an early foray among the shipping of Spain.

'Or into Spanish territory?' Morgan said.

'Or into Spanish territory,' agreed Captain Gascoone, not batting an eyelid. 'The mainland, perhaps?'

'Presently. But the ships will have to be victualled first. And that can be done successfully only by disciplined crews. Crews that can be held in when excited.' How much, he wanted to know, could the Frenchmen depend on their crew's coming to heel when wanted?

'Like little dogs, they are,' said the Frenchman. 'I whistle, they come. I put up my hand, they lie down.'

So Morgan told him of their plan for victualling. And the chestnut-coloured eyes in the brown face danced and laughed.

'Captain Morgan,' said the Frenchman, standing by the ladder as he was taking his leave, 'always I have liked the English, but never do I like them as well as today. They have a panache that makes even my countrymen seem as flat as a yesterday's lettuce. I am delighted to have made your acquaintance, Captain Morgan, and will be delighted to be a partner in your impudences.'

So the plan was accepted, and preparations went forward. And every morning when he went on deck Henry looked round the bay to see if Mansfield had come in during the night; and every evening as the light failed his last glance was to the horizon in the hope of seeing the *Endeavour* coming up. It was unthinkable that this first step towards the avenging of Santa Catalina should be taken without the old man's presence and blessing.

But the days went by, and the plan grew tighter and neater, and still no ship brought Mansfield into shelter at Isle of Pines. Nor did any ship that put in have news of him. And in the end they sailed without him; sailed east, through the endless small islands, to the Gardens of the Queen. To port lay the great bulk of Cuba, five times the size of Jamaica, well settled, well fortified, and solidly Spanish. But the islands along its south coast were anyone's ground; an adventurer's paradise. And it was among those islands, close under the lee of Cuba, that they hid their ships before they took to the boats for their inspired impertinence.

The landing was done at night, on deserted beaches so that it should be unheralded and so that the forced march over the hills could be done for the most part in daylight, and therefore at the necessary speed to bring them down to the plain before the following dawn.

Henry had left nothing to chance, and his crew made merry over the detailed arrangements ('Is it you I give my hand to when we meet in the Grand Chain?' said Bluey to his companion on the thwart as they pulled away from the *Fortune*), but his care was justified, and one by one the boats slid up the dark sand in the appointed order at the appointed time, and the men went to cover in the order in which they would set out on the march as soon as it was light. Charlie Hadsell, being the authority on the country, led the advance party, and the rest followed on his heels; each man carrying his own ammunition and enough food for two meals. The soldiers in the *Fortune's* crew had suffered much during their weeks as seamen, both from unaccustomed tasks and too accustomed comment, but now they came into their own. The seamen, improvident as always, ate their food when the pangs of hunger prompted, and arrived at the midday halt destitute. They also arrived footsore. And the still limber soldiers laughed at them as they ate their dutifully conserved rations.

Early in the afternoon, in a small sudden valley, they came on a shack where a man and his wife were living with two children: a baby and a boy of seven. And it was here that they made their first mistake. They took the man with them for safety's sake, but left the boy.

It was Hadsell who made the second and more serious mistake. He lost his way; and, being Hadsell, refused to admit it. By the time that the error was so patent that even Hadsell could no longer support an appearance of libelled virtue, the damage had been done and they were two hours late on schedule. The dawn overtook them still struggling along bridle paths and through unexpected streams, sweating and cursing, blistered and chafed. And when they cleared the last ridge and looked down on the town it was nearly eight o'clock.

Very clear and neat and bright-coloured lay the town, all gay tiles and dazzling wash, like a child's toy. And very active indeed was the town that they were to have taken by a surprise attack in the dawn. Trumpets sang and horsemen galloped and fugitives ran from the cattle-black plains into the shelter of the city; and from the other side of the city a trickle of laden mules showed how the rich and the provident were already sending their treasure to hiding in the farther hills.

The privateers, English and French, gathered on the slope and stared. Bluey took the boots from round his neck, and hobbled to a rock. 'We wasn't expecting a reception committee,' he said, 'but if there's a pair of cloth slippers in that town ten thousand Dons won't keep me out of it.'

A whine came through the still morning air and something fell with a brisk crash through the trees below them. Then three more whines and crashes in quick succession.

'Cannon!' said Bluey. 'God love us, a battery. And me with nothing but a pair of bleeding feet and a musket.'

But Henry was looking at the smoke of the discharged cannon where it floated up from an orange-grove between them and the town.

'He's a fool, whoever he is,' he said. 'He should never have taken those guns out of the town.'

'Who is responsible for this?' the French wanted to know.

'It is too early for inquests,' Morgan said.

'But someone must be punished for the blunder.'

'The blunder, gentlemen, was to under-estimate the heart of a seven-year-old.'

'Seven-year-old what?'

'Boy.'

'You mean a child reported our coming?'

'If you doubt it, look at his father's face,' Henry said, nodding to where the Spanish settler was standing, still a prisoner. The man's face shone with glory.

'If it had been my luck to get a son like that,' Henry said, 'that is how I should look too.'

'So; and now?'

'I suggest that we send a party round behind that battery to deprive that silly fellow of his cannon and leave the road clear for us. After that, we shall send a message into the town to make an offer: we will refrain from a siege if they surrender their cattle.'

But while the battery was being rendered harmless, it became evident that siege was not in the Spaniards' minds. They believed in counter-attack. As the privateers came down *en masse* towards the town two troops of cavalry came trotting out, formed into line, broke into a canter, and came charging at the astonished invaders. The sailors, taken aback, hesitated and made as if to run for cover. But to the soldiers this was an old story, and they reacted automatically to the stimulus. They dropped to their knees, primed and loaded their clumsy muskets with unhurrying fingers, propped them with an artist's care, took a leisurely aim, and fired. The charging line wavered and broke, and fled away to either side like a river meeting a rock. The soldiers took down their muskets and began to reload while the cavalry circled backwards to re-form. The sailors, heartened by this demonstration, recovered their presence of mind and imitated the soldiers. And the cavalry, coming back, were greeted with something that was to become famous as a destroyer of far finer formations than the gallant defenders of Puerto Principe: the withering blast of steady English musketry. It was too much for them, and they did not attempt a third charge. They fled for the shelter of the town.

And on their heels came the once more confident invaders. Not as a mob, but in formation, with colours and drum. They had come to demand the surrender of a town, and they would do it decently and in due form. But the town did not wait for parley. The town began firing as soon as they were within range.

'The hasty, excitable bastards,' said the English. 'Can't they be still for a minute and listen?'

So they drew off a little, and Morgan sent in a messenger. Let the Spaniards give them two things: free entry into the town, and a guarantee that they could drive off all the cattle they needed without interference, and no harm would come to the life or private property of any of the inhabitants.

The Spaniards' answer, translated into the vernacular, proved to be: 'A likely story!' So the English, hungry and exasperated, began to fight their way into the town, street by street; snatching food from the empty houses as they went. A bedridden old man in a room on the outskirts told them that the Alcalde had been killed leading the cavalry charge, and the Bishop had taken over the volunteer infantry he had raised – seven hundred of them, according to the invalid – and was in charge of the town. He had sent all women and children to safety in the church.

Morgan blessed the Bishop for his common-sense, and discounted the seven hundred. From the size of the place, at least half of that number must be slaves and coloured men. They would be into the heart of the town by noon.

But it was nearly evening before they debouched into the main square and found the Bishop, very magnificent, waiting on the steps of the church to make formal surrender, and by that time a great many of their number were lying dead or wounded in the shadow of the silent streets. The Spanish method of house-building – the tiny grilled windows, the back-of-the-house-to-the-street – was ideal for defence, as the invaders had found. Exmeling and his assistants were busy.

Morgan, very angry at being made to fight for something he had not particularly wanted, was stiff with the Bishop. His terms, he said, had been honest ones; but his price was now, of course, higher. As well as the beef, and the salt to pickle it, he would demand a money ransom as the price of not sacking Puerto Principe.

Alas, said the Bishop, there was no money in the town.

'No,' said Morgan, 'it went out by the mule-load this morning. You will get it back by noon tomorrow. If there is not enough to make up the sum, the balance will be contributed from the private property of the citizens. Meanwhile you will order your men to provide a meal for three hundred and fifty within an hour from now, here in the main square; and you will send out food for another fifty to the French who are picketing the approaches to the town. And now, direct me to the Alcalde's house.'

The house, which stood on the square, bore evidences of a hasty gathering together of valuables, all of which were now either in church with the Alcalde's women-folk, or safe in the farther hills. But it was not for valuables that Morgan had come. It was neither silver nor jewels that he planned to take out of Puerto Principe. He found what he had come for in the Alcalde's office, a neat, cool room at the end of the courtyard. In the Alcalde's desk he found it: a list of seventy names. Above the list was the heading: Enlistments For The Projected Expedition Against Jamaica: The Puerto Principe Contingent. That this contingent of seventy had not been bubbling over with desire to go in arms against the English in Jamaica was witnessed to by the tidy-minded Alcalde, who had added after each man's name, for his own private information, the reason why the man had consented to be pressed.

This was satisfying enough, but when Henry turned over the paper and found what was attached to it, he nearly laughed aloud. The attached document was a letter from Havana, from the Governor of Cuba. The Governor congratulated the Alcalde on his success in the recruiting business, specified the numbers contributed by the other districts of the island, and detailed the plan for eventual concentration before attack. Contingents from the mainland, said the Governor, would arrive in the next few months. Those from Vera Cruz and Campeche would rendezvous at Havana, those from Puerto Bello and Cartagena at St Jago.

As Henry's eye lighted on the word Puerto Bello, the breath came out of him in a silent laugh that was praise and prayer and amusement and satisfaction all rolled into one. The road to Puerto Bello was open.

Henry slept that night in the bed of the dead Alcalde; and the only ghost that haunted his slumbers was the image of Bartholomew Kindness, working his heart out as a slave on the fortifications of Puerto Bello. In the morning he was brusque with the delaying tactics of the Bishop, who was patently hoping for rescue from the capital.

'Havana is three hundred miles away,' said Henry, 'and I have enough men to hold the roads from there for weeks.'

So the Bishop gave up, and the mules began to file back into the town, and herders were mobilised to drive the cattle down to the coast, and salt was weighed and loaded on to the mules that had brought back the treasure. But about one thing the Bishop stuck his toes in. He would not produce the boy who had brought the message warning the town of their arrival; and the never very shockable Henry was shocked to his soul when he discovered that the Bishop's refusal was due to the Bishop's belief (which he apparently shared with all his flock) that it was their intention to torture the child.

'Great God, what minds!' said Henry. And to the Bishop, who was once more reporting his inability to find the boy: 'I wanted to meet the boy because I admire him. Is that too much for a Spanish understanding? Because if I had a son I should like him to be just like that.'

The Bishop looked first surprised, then doubtful, and ultimately relieved, and the boy was at last produced. Morgan was dining with his fellow captains at the Alcalde's house when the child was brought to the house by his father. It was the fourth and last night of their stay in Puerto Principe, and the meal had an air of celebration. Tomorrow they would bundle and go, following the cattle-drive down to the sea, and they were mellow with achievement and good-fellowship. They received the astonished child with acclamation, piled cushions on a chair until they reached a convenient height, and set him among them at table.

'Do you know why we have sent for you?' Morgan asked him, in Spanish.

'My father says that it is to do me honour,' said the child. 'But that does not seem to me likely. I have been a thorn in your foot when you were in a hurry. Why should you want to do me honour?'

'Because you had courage and resource, and the English admire all who have courage and resource.'

'In *that* case,' said the child, 'may I have some of the honey-cake?'

They plied him with dainties, and toasted him in English, Welsh, and Spanish; in rum, wine and brandy; and he sat eating composedly and watching the laughing, unaccountable English making their incomprehensible gestures. By the time their mellowness had grown blurred and a little fuddled, he had fallen asleep where he sat. And Morgan, still sober, picked him up and carried him outside to his waiting father. For a moment, as he saw the limp body in the Englishman's arms, the man's eyes widened with dread.

'I am afraid he is going to be very sick tomorrow,' Morgan said. 'We have allowed him to eat everything in sight.'

And the man let his breath out again, and smiled.

'You are a good man, señor,' he said.

No one, so far, had ever called Morgan that. He handed over the child half-amused, half-embarrassed.

'Good-night,' he said. 'I envy you your son.'

And went back to spend the rest of the night at table. For they were leaving at dawn and it was not worth while to go to bed.

Before the birds wakened, the silent half-light was filled with the beat of drums summoning the men to muster in the square, and before the sun was far enough up to clear the surrounding hills they were marching out.

'I'd like to have seen what those señoras in the church looked like,' Bluey said as they left the town behind them. 'But at least I got me slippers.'

He had two pairs. The ones he was wearing, of soft Spanish leather; and a jewel-trimmed satin pair which he had filched for a girl in Port Royal.

They did the thirty miles to the sea on wings; and even the hard work waiting them on the beach was not sufficient to damp their spirits. Indeed, they faced the slaughter and dismemberment of a thousand head of cattle in a spirit of saturnalia, and for days the beach was a riot of carnage. Sweating and bloodstained they laboured, under the canopy of screaming birds: flaying, eviscerating, jointing. Jack Morris had brought up the ships at the appointed time from their hiding-place in the Cays, and they stood around waiting to be loaded. The barrels were floated ashore from them empty, and filled with the salted flesh. Higher up the beach were the slow fires where the choice bits, cut into strips, were being smoked into boucan. The wounded, who had been sent out to the ships in advance of the cattle-drive, made miraculous recoveries and found excuses for trips to the beach so that they might purloin the coveted marrow-bones.

It was in the matter of marrow-bones that the first break in good temper showed among the labouring crews. Marrow-bones were perquisites, more prized that meat or offal, and the rage of the man who found his hard-won delicacy snatched from under his nose was in direct proportion to his growing weariness and the blue haze of flies in which he worked. The wounded were harried back to the ships, but tempers did not sweeten perceptibly with their disappearance. It was the fifth day of their orgy, and the beach stank in the sun, a mile of slaughter-house, when, with the suddenness of an explosion, uncertain temper flared into riot. '*Salaud! Salaud!*' screamed a high French voice above the shrieking birds, and one part of the long beach became immediately black with men, as ants swarm to a point of interest.

Morgan, who had been standing in the shade of the first trees testing the samples of boucan brought to him, shouted: 'Stay where you are! Not a man moves a step!' and the sound of his voice stayed the men below him from their instinctive rush to the centre of trouble. They stood looking doubtfully from Morgan to the distant clamour, their butcher's knives in their hands, their ears still hearing that French challenge.

Morgan, who wanted to go at once to the scene of the fight, was held there by the necessity of controlling them; if he moved, then they would move with him. But he was saved from having to resolve the situation, for the centre of trouble was moving rapidly towards him along the shore. Indeed, it seemed that the whole east end of the beach, the French end, was advancing *en masse*. In the heart of the human mass was a small swirl which proved as they came nearer to be a man struggling in the grip of his fellows. He was fighting like a maniac, in spite of the fact that a moment's consideration would have shown him that with odds several hundreds to one against him it might be as well to go quietly.

They dragged this whirling piece of human protest up to Morgan, and yelled: 'This creature of yours has killed one of our men! He must be executed! He must be executed immediately!'

'I have no power to execute anyone,' Morgan said coolly. 'But an inquiry will be held. Whose man is he?'

He was one of the *Gift's* crew, they said. And he had stabbed a Frenchman in the back with a knife. He must be executed forthwith.

Morgan looked at the unlovely object of their animosity, and was troubled by a vague sense of familiarity. The man was caked to the eyes with dried blood but none of it seemed to be his; he had just not bothered to wash lately. From the brown-streaked face the silly, pale eyes, distended and shallow, stared with an animal fury. Surely, thought Henry, he knew those eyes?

'Why did you take a knife to the Frenchman?' he asked.

'He stole my marrow-bones! He stole the whole of my first lot, and I found him making off with the ones I had saved today! Killing's too good for him. He ought to be carved up bit by bit, like a bullock, only alive!'

Yes, the voice went with the eyes. But whose voice, and whose eyes?

The French clamour had broken out again. The man must be strung up. The sun could not be allowed to go down on a comrade unavenged, on an insult unpaid for.

'Your comrade was a thief, it appears.'

A torrent of contradictory information and comment greeted this.

But Morgan was suddenly very still. A trail of smoke from the boucan fires had provided the stimulus he needed. For a moment he was back in that camp in Barbados, with the wild pig roasting, and the boucan drying, and Bart doling out his day's purchases. And he knew now who the man was.

It was Timsy.

Timsy, who had helped him to capture the *Gloria*. Timsy, the born killer with a child's passion for candy. Timsy, who had gone overside at Tortuga with a fortune in pearls in his pocket.

'If the man has committed murder,' he said, 'he will be put in irons and sent back to stand his trial in Port Royal.'

'Aaah!' they yelled. 'You want to save him. You are cheating us. When he is back in Port Royal you will let him go.'

'On the contrary, he will almost certainly hang.'

'Then hang him how! Let us see him hanged.'

'You can go to Port Royal and see him hanged. The Law does not concern itself with the ordinary citizen's convenience.'

'Law!' they yelled. 'We want justice, not law!'

'You will get both, I hope. What you are asking at the moment is neither one nor the other. There is law in the islands, and if a man does wrong he will stand trial for it before a properly constituted court. You are all at liberty to be present at the trial and to provide witnesses against the man.' He saw out of the tail of his eye that Tom Rogers had materialised at his side. 'I am handing over the man to the custody of his own captain, and he will be sent back in the sloop that is sailing for Port Royal the day after tomorrow. I shall ask Captain Gascoone, as the senior captain among you, to arrange for witnesses to be sent at the same time to state your case.'

'And you think an English court will condemn their own man!'

'Certainly. Would not a French one do as much?' As this gave them pause, he added: 'We come of civilized races, the French and the English. Let us not descend to Spanish ideas of justice.'

Their rage had sunk to grumbling by the time Pierre Gascoone arrived, and they allowed Timsy to be pried from their clutches and handed over to his Captain, who sent him under escort to the *Gift*.

'I won't waste any tears over Timothy Hare,' Tom Rogers said, watching him go. 'He was always more trouble than he was worth. Half crazy, I think.'

But Morgan was miserable.

He sat late, that night, by the dead fire in front of his tent ashore, unable to sleep. And presently there was a stirring in the bushes and Bluey's voice said: 'Beg pardon, Captain, but can I speak to you for a moment, sir?'

'What is it, Bluey?'

'You're going to let him go, aren't you, Captain?'

'No, Bluey, I am not.'

'But Captain, it's Timsy!'

'Yes, I know. He must stand his trial, just like anyone else.'

'But they'll hang him, Captain. They'll hang him, sure's death.'

'Yes, I am afraid they will. His victim was innocent.'

'But he doesn't have to get to the Port, Captain. He could just disappear quietly over the side some night. There's plenty of islands where —'

'No, Bluey. He is going to Port Royal. He is going to be tried in public, to show all the French, and all the Islands, that English justice is what it represents itself to be.'

There was silence for a little, while Bluey was apparently trying to understand his captain's point of view. In this he failed, it would seem.

'I suppose I just don't see it your way, Captain.' And then he added unhappily: 'He thinks you're going to let him go, Captain. He won't understand. Couldn't you just talk to him and – and – well, explain things somehow to him?'

'What good would that do?'

'He wouldn't think then that you did it without caring. I mean, if you explain to him why it has to be, he won't think we've just let him die without it mattering to us one way or the other.'

'I see. I'll think about it, Bluey.'

And having thought about it, he went next evening to see Timsy, sitting in irons in the *Gift's* fo'c'sle.

'You're going to let me go, aren't you, Harry?' he said, his wide, unadult eyes searching Morgan's.

'No, Timsy; I am not.'

'But, Harry; but, Captain —'

'I came to see you for that very reason: to tell you why I can't let you go. You believe I would if it was in my power, don't you?'

'But you can, Captain. You can.'

It was hopeless from the start, of course. It was no more possible to make poor Timsy understand than it had been to make

Bluey see some reason in the course he was taking. He went away from the *Gift* with Timsy's agonised cries in his ears. 'Harry! you can't! You can't! If you send me to Port Royal they'll hang me! Harry, you don't have to. You *don't have to!*'

And when the sloop sailed with the dispatches for Modyford, the dispatches he was so proud of – the evidence that he had promised to obtain about the proposed invasion of Jamaica, and his account of the taking of Puerto Principe – it carried also one prisoner in irons on his way to trial at Port Royal.

And Henry watched it go, soberly, his schoolboy elation about Puerto Principe almost dead with him. He could not hope that his own men would understand any better than Bluey the abstractions of equity. They would believe only that he had sacrificed a fellow-countryman in order to placate the French. So he watched the little ship bear away his triumphant dispatches, and was conscious only of a bleak feeling under his ribs.

He was growing up.

10

'IT'S A GOOD THING we're five hundred miles from Port Royal,' Jack said, watching the pay-queue snake along the beach at Isle of Pines, 'or we'd never get a man of them to the mainland of America.'

The ransom from Puerto Principe had worked out at fifteen pounds a head, and to men whose only coin for months was either a luck-piece or a dud this was riches. Balked of the opportunity for immediate spending, they fell back on their second love, and gambled from morning till night. If they won they celebrated, if they lost they drowned their sorrows; and there was not one of the nine captains who did not breathe a sigh of relief when at last the anchors came up and the ships filed out on their long journey to the mainland.

Eight well-found ships followed the *Fortune* out of the roads at Isle of Pines, but the *Endeavour* was not one of them. Mansfield was still unaccounted for. And of the nine captains only three knew their destination: Morgan, Jack Morris, and Charlie Hadsell. There was to be no gossip, blown seed-like on the wind, to warn Puerto Bello behind its smug fortifications. So it was not until weeks later, down off the American coast, that Morgan faced his colleagues with the proposition that they take Puerto Bello.

It was almost summer by that time, and the ships, loitering at the rendezvous, creaked and sweltered. Canvas flapped irresolute in the hot air, and men pursued a piece of shade across the deck with an ardour they had never brought to the pursuit of women. One by one the ship's boats ferried the various captains to the conference on board the *Fortune*, and Henry set before them the best meal that Toni's galley could produce; feeling, rightly, that to stomach Puerto Bello would require some preliminary cushioning.

But, as it turned out, two-thirds of them took the dose with every sign of pleasure, with laughter and admiring oaths; only the French gagged. The French would have none of it.

'It is insane,' said the French. 'The place is notorious. It is the boast of Spain, the fortifications there. No one would survive such a foolhardy expedition.'

'But I have told you. I have no intention of trying to force the place. We take it from inland.'

'A hundred miles in small boats, and then nothing but pistols and cutlasses against a town with three fortresses!' said the French. 'No! No, indeed; we thank you, but no!'

And from that nothing would move them; not even Henry at his most persuasive. Not even the dazzling pictures he painted of the wealth of Puerto Bello, the port of the Isthmus, the funnel through which drained all the riches that Panama, the capital, had gathered from the Pacific coast of Central America, moved the practical French to any noticeable degree. It was an insane project, and they would have none of it.

And that evening he watched a third of his fleet crowd on sail to catch the heavy airs and float gracefully into the darkness and out of his ken.

'Let them go,' said Jack. 'I feel more comfortable when I

don't have to watch the ground in case I tread on someone's toes.'

But Henry was hurt.

'After Cuba, they might have trusted me,' he said, sulky and injured. And then, recovering, he flung an arm round his friend and said with sudden relish: 'But ah, how sorry they are going to be that they did not come with us.'

And sorry they were. Very sorry indeed.

The English took two hundred and fifty thousand pieces-of-eight out of Puerto Bello; together with treasure worth half as much again. For that they paid in blisters, bites, sweat, sunburn, wounds, and heat-stroke; but only eighteen of them with their lives. And in after years they were accustomed to refer to 'that time at Puerto Bello' as a kind of paradise; a whole month of ease and fat living. Indeed, the only part of the exploit that left any permanent mark on them was the boat trip. A hundred miles in open rowing-boats under a tropical sun is no pleasure jaunt, and there was not one of the four hundred who did not wince in remembering it.

Henry would have brought the ships fifty miles nearer if he could have chosen, but there was no wind to sail them. And to hang about the coast waiting for a wind was to put the mainland on its guard, and so deprive them of their trump card. So they toiled the whole hundred miles in the boats, watching the green, secret coast slip by with a maddening slowness; setting a rag of sail hopefully when the air stirred, only to take it down a few minutes later and take to the oars again. Every hour the oars weighed more, moved more clumsily in the rowlocks, and came more reluctantly out of the water. It was like rowing through treacle with a piece of mast. The colourless light, constant and pitiless, beat off the sea in their faces; and the blazing heat, constant and pitiless, beat down from the sky on their defenceless bodies. At noon, for two hours, they put in to shore and lay like dead men; indifferent to the million stinging insects as long as they were for a little in the shade and it was not their turn to man an oar. Evening came like a pardon; and night was a haven that taught them the meaning of salvation.

It was on a still midnight, half-lit by a rising new moon, that they came to shore for the last time, and left their boats behind them. In front of them was the wet green forest, and beyond the forest was the Beautiful Port of their ambition. And to lead them through the swampy woods to their goal they had the ideal guide: the maroon who had brought the message from Major Smith. The maroon nowadays led an uncertain existence as assistant to Toni (whose temperament had all the violence of the would-be artist), but there was nothing uncertain in his knowledge of the forests through which he had escaped; nor anything uncertain about his joy in being the means of retribution. He had a long account chalked up against the Spaniard.

At three o'clock in the morning, the maroon led them into a clearing and said that this was as far as they could go. They were now behind the town; and less than five hundred yards in front of them, through the screen of trees, was the inland one of the three forts: San Jeronimo. It stood by itself on a small promontory jutting into the bay and commanded the town, as the two other forts, on either side of the harbour entrance, commanded the mouth of the bay. It was a quadrangular redoubt of stone with a great wooden door on the land side. In front of the door was a flat paved terrace where a sentry was always on duty.

Morgan wanted that sentry, and the maroon offered to bring him in if a volunteer would go with him. Out of an immediate press of volunteers Morgan chose the one whose guile, grace, impudence, courage and complete ruthlessness made it likely that he would not only be able to approach the sentry without announcing his presence, but that he would bring back the man as expected. So Manuel went with the maroon, the two slim, dark figures melting into the forest without a sound; and the others, with the sailor's infinite capacity for casual slumber, curled themselves up on the hot, damp ground and relaxed. They roused themselves half an hour later to inspect the gibbering captive who stood propped between an amused Manuel and a grim maroon. Manuel had used the same technique as a very young Henry Morgan had used to silence the watchman on the *Gloria*: the padded hand over the mouth and the knife in the small of the back. The suddenness of it all had been too much for the wretched Spaniard, and only the solid grip of his captors kept him erect at all. He babbled all he knew at the first asking. The fort was under-manned: only a hundred and thirty men all told. There was ample powder and ammunition. All the guns were trained out to sea. He was due to be relieved at dawn.

They gave the shuddering creature a drink – much to his surprise – gagged him, and set his face towards the fort again; and with him went the attacking party: two hundred men who planned to take San Jeronimo with sword and pistol. With sword and pistol, and one other weapon. Henry had never forgotten the *Gloria*, and tonight he planned to repeat on a larger scale the technique that had proved so successful in capturing a ship. Round the shoulders of each member of the advance party, therefore, was coiled a rope, and to the end of each rope was bent a grapnel.

Silently, in the last of the darkness, the men moved to their appointed places; Manuel and the maroon to the sentry-walk in front of the door, the rest to surround the fort close under the walls. Then Manuel took the gag from the sentry's mouth and whispered: 'Now then, little frightened one, shout as you were told!'

It was a poor, feeble sound that came from the sentry's throat, but it was sufficient in the silence of the coming dawn to attract attention from the fort. What was biting Diego? the fort wanted to know.

Diego summoned some alto to give body to his first treble effort, and told them. An army of Englishmen were here in front of the fort and demanding admittance. They offered terms if there was no resistance.

This, as Henry had reckoned, had one immediate result. Every man who was awake in the fort, and all those roused from sleep by the scurry, ran to the battlements on the land side to look over at the suspectedly mad sentry. And as soon as this had happened, twenty grapnels whirled round the heads of the advance party and twenty ropes went snaking out and up to fall over the deserted battlements. As the hooks settled home the first men went swarming up, and stepped over the wall unmolested. So did the next lot, and the next; the whole garrison being still engaged in hurrying to the point of sensation above the main gate. In less than ten minutes there were fifty Englishmen inside the fort with no more damage to their persons than some skinned knuckles. When another thirty had joined them they left twenty to guard the tops of the rope ladders and see that the rest arrived safely, and moved in on the occupants of the fort. They moved without care, sure that they would be mistaken by the Spaniards for colleagues. Not in their wildest nightmares would the Spaniards imagine that the English would drop into their impregnable fortress like flies alighting on a cake. So the invaders moved in on the garrison like fishers with a drag-net: mopping up the stragglers as they cornered them and advancing in force to hem in the men by the parapet above the gate. These last felt, unbelieving and dazed as the poor sentry had been, the press of a knife or pistol in their backs and remained transfixed, broken prayers trickling out of their slack lips. The completely unbelievable was happening, and they had no resources to deal with it.

The grey light came as they submitted to being disarmed, and the sudden tropic dawn saw the great wooden gate being opened to receive the invaders' main force. Henry, who had gone over the wall with the assault party, received his fellow captains with an air of doing host that Charlie Hadsell for one found intolerable. But the rest were too elated to care, and too grateful to Morgan to be critical. And Henry himself had no thought to spare for Hadsell's ill-humour; he had not yet achieved the thing he had come fifteen hundred miles for.

Where, said Henry, to the still stunned Commandant, were the English prisoners?

The Commandant had never heard of any English prisoners.

'No?' said Morgan. 'Let me refresh your memory. Men from the garrison of Santa Catalina – Englishmen – were put to work on your fortifications here, against all civilized practice. Where, I ask, are these men kept?'

If there were such prisoners, said the Commandant, it must have been on one of the other fortifications that they had been employed. He knew nothing of them.

'The water defences were finished years ago. It is on San Jeronimo that the work has been done. Where are the men?'

The Commandant was a small fat man with an expressionless face, but a twitch in the flesh of his sallow cheek betrayed the agitated clenching of his teeth. The Commandant was very frightened indeed. He was also lying.

'Very well,' said Henry. 'We shall search.'

'The cellars are pestilent,' said the Commandant quickly. 'It is as well not to go near them. We had slaves there who died of plague, and we have – have closed the place up.'

The cellars proved to be cool and sweet and filled with the heady smell of wine-impregnated wood. But below the cellars, deep in the heart of the ground, were dungeons; and the reek of the dungeons came up the slippery stone stairway with a force that made even their hardened stomachs heave. Into this noisome catacomb they descended by the flare of torches, picking their way gingerly down the treacherous steps that were slimed with moisture from the trickling walls. As they went down the smell of the place almost stopped the breath in their throats, and when at last they stood in front of a barred door and savoured the stench that poured out through the grille even Bluey mopped his forehead and looked sick. It was too sudden a change from the fresh greenery of the forest.

There was an animal stirring beyond the door, but no sound of human voices.

'Is anyone there?' Henry called.

There was silence for a moment on both sides of the door: a silence so complete that even the drops that fell from the roof to the floor sounded loud and petulant.

Then beyond the door a voice cried: 'English! English!'

It sounded like the voice of a man seeing heaven opened.

Morgan flung back the bars and pushed the door open. The smell of damp straw – straw made damp by unnameable exudations and trodden into pulp with age – was suffocating, but from this obscene bed human forms were struggling up into the light of the torches. So ragged and insubstantial they were that it seemed that they wavered in the wavering light; as if they were part of the shadows.

'Bart,' said Henry, suddenly afraid. 'Bart! Are you here?'

'I'm here, Harry boy,' said Bart's mild voice a yard from his right foot. 'But don't touch me. I'm crawling.'

'Bart!' said Henry, on his knees in the filth, a great rush of relief and thankfulness pouring through him. 'Bart!'

'I knew you'd come sooner or later, Captain,' said Bart, his sunken eyes bright in the light of the flare. 'That couldn't be Bluey you've got with you, could it?'

Bluey was crying openly. 'Here!' he said, shoving his torch at the man nearest him. 'Hold that.'

He bent and picked Bart from the straw as if he were a child, and carried him up the stairs to the light and the air, the man following with the torch.

Two others had to be helped, but the remaining eight walked out of their prison like jaunty skeletons, macabre in their rags. These were all that was left of the Santa Catalina garrison. Eleven men.

'They took Major Smith and his second to Panama a year ago,' they said. 'We don't know what happened to them.'

They had no nails, most of them; or what was left of the nail was invisible in the broken finger-ends. They had been carrying stone with their bare hands. The skin of their bodies, blistered in the first unaccustomed heat, had flayed into open sores that had had no chance to heal. Their bones stuck through the polluted flesh. They were crusted with dirt.

Bart was a little heap of limp bones held together by his spirit.

'The good thing about having no flesh left on your bones,' he said, as Bluey laid him down in the clean early-morning air, 'is that the mosquitoes leave you alone.'

The crews were breakfasting in the courtyard of the castle when the survivors filed up into the light, and they rose to their feet and cheered. But the cheers died away uncertainly as they took in the state of their countrymen, and though they hurried to the prisoners with question and reassurance and succour, an odd silence fell on the bulk of the men. They made no more motion to eat, and their eyes went from the filthy and tattered skeletons to the well-fed Spaniards herded weaponless at the far end of the courtyard.

Morgan, coming up from the dungeon, walked into this odd

silence; and recognized it. Once, long ago, he had heard it in a crowded tavern; and he still remembered what those three bodies looked like, torn apart by the bare hands of a crowd that had gone berserk.

He walked through the men as they sat about on the ground, their half-finished victuals before them, and found no reassurance. They were so far beyond the moment that they did not even make way for him; they looked at him without seeing him.

He did not need in any case, to have their state of mind translated to him. There was murder in his heart too.

It needed only a pistol-shot to explode that charged silence into action, and he would have on his hands, on his head, and on his reputation a massacre of unarmed men.

Before he could consult with his captains, or suggest that they draw off some of their men as soon as might be, a voice said loudly:

'Eleven men! *Eleven!*'

It was a voice high with hysteria, and it stirred the motionless crowd like a wind. In another second they would be on their feet.

'Give the Spaniards back their swords!' shouted Henry; and that gave them pause.

They waited to see what this might mean.

'They didn't give *our* men a chance, Captain,' a voice said. 'We'll take them as they are.'

'Not while you are under my command.'

But the most heart-felt protest came from the Spaniards; they did not want their swords back. They were prisoners, unhurt, and doing very nicely. It was monstrous to make them fight now. The crews looked at their plump faces, and kicked the food-plates out of their way as they got to their feet.

'But you are three to our one!' said the Spaniards, the swords hanging limp from their palsied arms.

'Mercifully,' was all Morgan said.

So the English took their price for the skeletons who had died on the fortifications of San Jeronimo. And this was one of the things that they did not talk about afterwards.

'The Garrison consisted of one hundred and thirty men, of

whom seventy-four, including the Commandant, were killed,' said Morgan's official report.

His report of the taking of the great fort at the narrows was no more expansive, although that was an orthodox exercise of war. When they had marched through the panic-stricken town – women fleeing to the convent, men fleeing to the forest, and five hundred militia making themselves scarce in the direction of Panama – they were faced with the reduction of Fort Triana, and that they accomplished by a combined operation. The sailors swarmed up their scaling-ladders while the ex-soldiers exhibited once more their prowess in musketry and picked off the defenders as they swabbed their guns or tried to repel the climbing sailors. Before they had finally proved the irresistibility of this combination, the officer commanding the fort decided to salvage at least his dignity from what was like to be the wreck of his command, and offered to surrender on condition that he might march out his garrison with their colours flying.

This did not please either troops or sailors, but it pleased Morgan. He had never any liking for frontal assault. Life was always a wonderful thing to him; sparkling with possibilities; and to throw this unique and irreplaceable thing away offended his very soul. To die on the glacis of a barricade was never any ambition of Harry Morgan's.

By afternoon, therefore, they had two of the three fortresses in their hands; and they decided to leave the Gloria, the fort on the far side of the narrows, until tomorrow. For the rest of the day they would take over the town. Morgan sent Cornelius, in a sloop, to tell Jack Morris that by the day after tomorrow the narrows would be open and he could then bring up the ships from where they were lying at Bogota.

'I hope they won't blow the boy out of the water; but I think she's too small and too fast to be hit by gun-fire,' he said, watching the tiny craft growing small in the direction of the open sea; and forgot all about the unreduced fort until two hours later, when raised voices and pointing hands and marvelling exclamations called his attention to the opposite headland.

Above the grim bulk of the Gloria was floating the English flag.

'They've surrendered!' they said, gaping. 'They've surrendered of their own accord!'

'I hardly think,' said Morgan, 'that they had an English flag waiting to be run up. Someone has been persuading them, it seems.'

The someone proved to be Cornelius. 'We did it on the spur of the moment,' he explained afterwards. 'We moved in close and said that Fort Triana had been given honourable terms, and we were prepared to receive their surrender on the same conditions.'

So Fort Gloria surrendered to five Englishmen and a Hollander. And Puerto Bello, the impregnable, the pride of Spain, was in English hands.

Presently, of course, an attempt at rescue would come across the Isthmus from Panama, but Morgan did not wait for that to arrive. He sent out some of his best marksmen to camp themselves as comfortably as possible on either side of the first suitable defile they came to on the Panama road; and to wait there until such times as they could give the advancing rescue party a suitable reception. When that elegant gentleman, magnificent personage, and ardent devotee of Our Lady of the Immaculate Conception, Don Juan Perez de Guzman, Governor of the Province of Panama, arrived hot-foot with a small army to avenge the insult and drive the infidel back into the sea that had spawned them, an irreverent rain of infidel bullets halted him in his tracks and cooled his ardour to the point where he began to entertain the thought of ransom. Repugnant though the idea of ransom might be, it did mean that the English would go. That they had not come as the advance-guard of an invasion. That he, Don Juan Perez de Guzman, might go on living magnificent and unmolested as Governor of the Province of Panama, without having his peace, his security, and his prosperity sullied by a war. He made a camp on the farther side of the infidel-haunted defile, and began to negotiate. When he heard what the English wanted by way of ransom he thought for a moment that war could not be much worse. He refused to consider it. If he was firm the English would reduce their demands.

But it was not the English he was dealing with: it was a

Welshman. And the answer that came back from Puerto Bello, deprived of its formality and official phrasing, said: 'Just as you like, señor. We like Puerto Bello and have thoughts of staying here for good. It is the best base on the Atlantic coast.' So Don Juan sent word to the city of Panama to collect the required sum as soon as might be, that the fair soil of Spanish America should be rid of the English pestilence.

And the English settled down in the Beautiful Port to wait.

The ships came sailing in through the narrows, their crews looking with amazement at the great forts with their silent guns, and Jack, stepping ashore, said: 'I think I hear Drake laughing.'

The recovered prisoners were housed in the very fine Spanish hospital and fed and cosseted and spoiled; not least by the Spanish ladies. They had had no idea, said the Spanish ladies, that any English prisoners were being tortured in Puerto Bello, and they were horrified that their countrymen should have been guilty of such reprehensible practices, and here is some fine fresh fruit for you, poor man.

It was Morgan's boast, and one of his pet vanities, that no 'lady of quality', in which term he included that lesser class known as 'respectable females', ever suffered insult from any man of his. And it pleased him that when he offered both the ladies of quality and the respectable females safe-conduct to the Governor's camp on the other side of the pass they refused it and elected to stay in the town. Captain Morgan had very little experience of Spanish soldiery, they inferred, or he would not have suggested it.

'Besides,' said a dowager, shaking her diamond earrings at him, 'if I left my home you would loot it even more thoroughly than you have already.'

'Come, madam,' he said. 'We have levied, not looted.'

'What is the difference?' she said, tart.

'The difference is that you still have your earrings, señora.'

When they were not loading the ships with merchandise from the great store-houses where it was waiting for transport to Spain, the victorious English amused themselves after the immemorial habit of invaders: they drank, wenched, stole, made friends with the children, learned the local songs, imitated their partners in the local dances, and were initiated by their victims into the niceties of the local game. The criminal tenth indulged their propensities to the limit of their power in the first two days, and by the end of the first week were all in jail. So that an odd kind of peace settled on the captured town, a holiday air. The seventy dead in San Jeronimo were strangers to the place – merely some of the Spanish soldiery to whom the Puerto Bello ladies had referred in such contemptuous terms – and no one wept for them. The town, with its cool arcades, its blazing fruit-stalls, its fountains playing in the sun, was a paradise, and both inhabitants and invaders settled back to enjoy it: the former because they were accustomed to it, and the latter because they were not.

At the end of three weeks the ransom arrived from Panama, and with it came a letter from Don Juan Perez de Guzman. When the English left Puerto Bello, said the Governor, would they leave behind a pattern of the arms with which they had taken the town, so that Spain might have a chance of meeting them on equal terms next time?

Morgan sent him a pistol and half a dozen bullets. 'These are the weapons, Excellency,' he wrote. 'I am delighted to lend this sample to you until such time as I come to Panama to reclaim it.'

He was pleased with this leave-taking, but it was Don Juan who, after all, had the final word. A messenger came back four days later and asked to see Morgan. 'My master asks me to say that it would be waste of Captain Morgan's time to come to Panama,' he said, 'for this is all that Captain Morgan will ever take out of it.'

'This' proved to be a gold ring set with a large emerald.

'Some day,' said Henry, contemplating the ring after the messenger had gone, 'I really must think seriously of going to Panama. If he can afford something like this merely by way of a gesture, what would he not disgorge under a little pressure?'

He put the ring on his finger, and looked with delight on it.

The parting delight of the men, on the other hand, was to spend a hot and happy morning dismantling the forts at the narrows and tumbling the guns into the sea. They did it with laughter, and mocking farewell shouts as the unwieldy objects splashed like fat women, wallowing into the crystal water. But San Jeronimo they did not dismantle. They blew up San Jeronimo; business-like and without laughter.

11

ON THE MERE practical plane Henry was glad to be leaving Puerto Bello. It was now late July, with the hurricane season imminent; and Port Royal was eight hundred miles away up-wind. To lose a ship was at any time a hard thing; but to lose a ship loaded to the hatches with silks, linen, velvet, silver plate, carpets, swords, and jewelled baubles was unthinkable. So Henry watched his conquest grow small across the widening strip of water and had nothing in his heart but thankfulness. Even the men, calling ribald farewells, turned to the sea again with pleasure in their vagabond hearts. They had reached the stage when the lazy life in the sun-drenched *patios* had begun to pall, and their incurable English restlessness pricked them.

'It is good we go,' said Bernard, looking back at the dream-like loveliness. 'And it is good that the Spaniards should keep the Americas.'

'Good?' said Morgan.

'Men grow soft and weak there,' said Bernard. 'It is too much effort to think quickly, it is too much effort to stir oneself. So every day they grow more like animals. Without pride and without foresight. It is no place for white men, the Americas. It is as well to let the Spaniards keep it.'

But Henry had other ideas about that.

Bernard, of course, took an entirely personal view of the existing situation in the Caribbean, his interest being in trade and not in conquest. And now that he was about to be rich enough to buy that long-desired ship, he was willing to make a present of the rest of the world to anyone who wanted it. That Spain, unchallenged in the Americas, might object to his simple trading ambitions, was something that he did not, in his present liberal frame of mind, pause to consider.

It was Bart who had the surer instinct about the American Spanish. He sat about on deck, criticising the hang of the sails ('a fair disgrace the way that new cloth was put into that fore-sail there!') and snuffing the sea air as if it were perfume.

'They're rotten, Captain, the Spaniards,' he said. 'They've gone bad. They don't want to fight for what they have, but they want to kill anyone that takes it from them. They run up a surrender flag if you're armed, and they make a slave of you if you're not. They're bad, Captain; bad.'

And Henry, looking at the rescued prisoners, found it in his heart to regret their recovered lustiness. He would have liked to show them to Port Royal as they had been; in the full extremity of their humiliation. That was something that Port Royal would never be able to visualize for themselves.

But perhaps they would be impressed by the plain arithmetic of the thing. By the fact that the number of survivors out of a garrison of nearly a hundred was eleven men.

When they did at last reach Port Royal, however, on a day of wild squalls and stinging rain, they found that the Port's arithmetic was entirely devoted to their own exploit, and that the wonder of the conquest of Puerto Bello by less than four hundred men armed with pistols and swords had sent the whole place a little mad. Port Royal was not unused to the heroic: it had welcomed Captain Freeman after his taking of Tobasco, and Jackman home from his capture of San Francisco de Campeche, and many others from raids as daring. But none of these exploits had possessed the startling, the almost fabulous quality of the taking of Puerto Bello. The town was delirious.

'My Governorship is in the most precarious condition,' Modyford said to Henry, with his small, dry smile.

'But have you not told them about the levies? Have you not sent them the papers from Puerto Principe?'

'I was not referring to the Government. I was referring to the populace. With the smallest encouragement they would make you Governor tomorrow.'

'And kick me out the day afterwards,' said Morgan, who had

vision as well as vanity. 'They don't love us so much when we are penniless on the beach,' he added; and then, with a transition of thought: 'I see you hanged the man I sent you from Cuba.'

'Yes. The jury had no alternative. It was a knife-in-the-back affair.' He looked at Henry's withdrawn expression for a moment, and then added: 'He was a poor type: not quite human; not, perhaps, altogether sane; but he achieved more in the manner of his death than he could ever be expected to in his life.'

'You mean he died well?'

'No. Although, as it happens, he did die well. I meant that his trial and condemnation in open court by his countrymen has done more for England's reputation in the Islands than anything else in our history.'

'It didn't keep the French with us at Puerto Bello,' Henry said nastily.

This time Modyford smiled quite broadly. 'That does not surprise me,' he said, and added wickedly: 'Did you miss them?'

'No,' said Henry. 'It was perfect. A family party. Just the right size, and no strangers. There was only one thing wrong with it. Mansfield was not there. Where is he, do you know?'

The Governor made a little movement with his head that Henry took to be negation.

'Have you no news of him?' he asked.

But the movement had been one of regret.

'He's dead, Harry.'

Henry put down the glass he was drinking from, and sat without words.

'How?' he asked presently.

'He had gone to the South Cays to refit, and was attacked by a Spanish warship. The *Endeavour* was sunk.'

'You mean he went down with her?'

'No.'

'Well? Let us have it! What?'

'They took him to Havana. With the survivors of his crew.'

'And?'

'Put him to death.'

'By shooting?'

'No. They hanged him. And fifteen of his crew.'

'On what charge!'

'Piracy, I understand.'

'*Piracy!* On what evidence?'

'Oh, no evidence. I don't think that there was any question of evidence being required.'

'No? Why not?'

'Evidence is one of those tiresome conventions demanded only by a properly constituted court.'

'You mean they just strung him up?'

'I don't know. But Davila boasts that he has executed more than three hundred pirates in the last two years; and even in the Caribbean he would find it difficult to achieve such numbers if he were hampered by a small thing like evidence.' He glanced at Harry and added: 'I loved the old man; and I think that you loved him too.'

'Yes.' He wanted to say: He was the kind of father I should like to have had; but it sounded childish and a little absurd.

'I wish it were not now that you had to hear about it: on your first day home and in the middle of so much rejoicing. But life is like that. It is never unspotted glory.'

No, it was never unspotted glory. He went away from Kingshouse with Mansfield's voice in his ears: 'I shall come back for you, Harry, my little taker of prizes, and you will come with me once more to strike at Spain where it hurts.' He was glad that he had bitten back the words he had nearly shouted at the Governor: 'And are you still sending Spanish prisoners home safe and sound?' For of course, the Governor was right. It was no answer to meet the Spaniard on that level. The answer was to meet him with a fleet; to teach him manners with an army.

So Henry went soberly back to the town, only half aware of the people who stopped him, the salutes and the curtseys and the blessings, hoping that Elizabeth might by now have arrived from Morgan's Valley and that in her warmth and companionship this small personal desolation that was marring his public triumph might be dissolved. But Elizabeth was not there. Half the island was in Port Royal, being rowed round the fleet or toasting the returned heroes in the taverns, but Elizabeth was not there. And a more immediate emotion woke in Henry. All Spain was of no more consequence than a rotten apple if anything had happened to Elizabeth. The ships had been hull-up at dawn, and the news must have gone to every corner of the island before they had beaten their way into harbour. Now they had been nearly a whole day in port, and the town swarmed with planters and countrymen, but there was no Elizabeth. Foreboding fell like a blight on him. She was ill, she was dead, she was lost. Something had happened to her between Morgan's Valley and the Port.

He went down the stairs from the emptiness of the little apartment with panic on his heels, commandeered the horse of a man who was dismounting opposite the Brown Duck, and rode away into the sunlit afternoon that stretched hot and quiet beyond the noisy town. His borrowed mount, shocked by a change of routine, shied at the shadow of every moving frond, and he dug his heels in and cursed it. The world was all of a sudden black and frightful. A life without Elizabeth would be unthinkable.

He met her coming riding down the forest path, at a walking pace because of the bad going. She was riding decently side-saddle, and she was wearing a broad-brimmed straw hat tied with ribbons under her chin. That it was a slave's hat, made of coarse straw, detracted a little from its allure; but it was evident that allurement had not been in her mind.

'Harry!' she called. 'Oh, Harry! I was over at St Ann's Bay, and so I did not hear until — Oh, Harry!'

He had forgotten that she was so small and light.

'You haven't remarked on my hat,' she said presently. On the lips of any other woman this would mean 'on the hat I am wearing'. With Elizabeth it meant 'on the fact that I am wearing a hat'. 'I am wearing it for you,' she said, 'so that my skin shall not be freckled.'

'It seems to have been an afterthought,' he said, and kissed her sun-burned nose. Only Elizabeth, he thought, could manage to look delightful with a skinned patch on the bridge of her nose.

Her eyes went on towards the horse he had been riding, and she said, 'You haven't *bought* that, have you?'

This piece of practicality at so heart-full a moment was so much Elizabeth that he began to laugh, and being a little silly with relief and over-wrought after the emotions of the day, he went on laughing, so that he must needs sit down by the forest path and drag Elizabeth down with him; and they sat there laughing helplessly together because they were glad.

But as he was aiding her to remount she said: 'Did you find him, Harry?'

'Who?' said Henry; who had come a long way from his wedding night.

'Bartholomew Kindness.'

'Yes,' he said shortly; and then remembered her strictures about men 'putting off' women when they asked questions.

So as they rode back to Port Royal he told her about the dungeons of San Jeronimo, as he would have told another man, sparing her nothing. And she listened in silence, looking straight in front of her between her horse's ears.

Their entry into the town proved, unintentionally, to be in the nature of a triumphal procession. Port Royal, having eaten and drunk all the afternoon, had poured itself, no longer very sober, into the open air to enjoy the evening; and through the press of people rode the hero of the hour with his wife.

'The Captain's lady!' yelled the *Fortune's* crew, and converged as one man on this new subject for a toast. They had drunk to each other, to their ships, to the King, to the Duke of York, to the landlord's daughter, to the landlord's wife, to absent friends, to sweethearts and wives, to a short life and a merry one, and of course to Harry Morgan; and their invention was failing. Here, like a gift from heaven, was the Captain's wife; as pretty and suitable a Captain's lady as ever wore shoe-leather. They swarmed round her, clutching at her bridle and urging that she should dismount and come and be drunk to. It was Jack who saved the moment from embarrassment and turned it into a procession. He appeared at her horse's head in the unobtrusive way in which he did everything, took the bridle from the huge sailor who was hanging his weight on it, and led the frightened horse through the crowd; who closed in happily on either side and escorted their Captain and his lady to their lodgings.

'Dear Jack,' said the lady. 'How nice it is to see you again; safe and well.'

It was Jack, too, who got rid of the crowd when they arrived at the apartment. When Henry had obliged, very readily, with a speech, and the crowd began to require a speech also from the lady, Jack demanded to know if they had no bowels. Had none of them ever had a wife, and had none of them ever been parted from her for more than six months, and had they in such circumstances ever wanted to stand gossiping on the bottom step of a flight of stairs?

As the crowd let them go, with sympathetic laughter and frank felicitation, Elizabeth said: 'But *you* are coming up, Jack aren't you? Just for a little!'

But Jack would not come up. 'I'm a lot drunker than you'd think,' he said. 'I think I'll just go and complete the process. But thank you all the same.'

So they went up alone, on this night of rejoicing, to the cramped little rooms to which they had first come after their wedding nearly a year ago, and though the shouts of the town came up through the open window, they sounded distant and irrelevant.

'What is that, Henry?' Elizabeth asked, noticing for the first time the emerald on the hand that was unbuttoning her bodice; and she caught the hand away from her to look at the ring. 'What is that?'

'An invitation to Panama,' he said; and stopped her mouth from further questioning.

But Elizabeth lay awake that night looking at the great emerald where it rested below her shoulder. And she decided that she would not mention Panama again, even to find out about the ring; so that he might not be reminded even for a moment of that invitation. He was home; here, safe beside her; unharmed and triumphant. And not even by the utterance of a word would she remind him that there were still other worlds to conquer.

Which was an excellent resolution if the word that haunted

Henry had been Panama. But it was not Panama. The word that haunted Henry in the weeks to come was Maracaibo.

'Maracaibo,' said his horse's hoofs as he rode round the growing estate at Morgan's Valley and admired what Elizabeth had done in his absence. 'Maracaibo,' said the rain dripping from the eaves at night. 'Maracaibo,' said the long surf on the beaches. 'Maracaibo,' said the palm leaves clattering in the wind. 'Maracaibo,' said the racket of pails in the stable, the tinkle of hammer on anvil, the chatter of spoon against plate. Maracaibo, Maracaibo, Maracaibo.

When his mind was idle for a moment he would hear Mansfield's voice saying it. As he had said it through those weeks before his marriage when he would not listen to him.

With his conscious mind he repulsed the word; repudiated it. What had Maracaibo to do with him? He was a planter, a married man, and he was rich. He had done what he set out to do: he had avenged Santa Catalina and brought home his men; what more had he to do with a world outside Jamaica? Let the English Navy teach Spain manners henceforth; that is what the Navy was for. It was the business of Henry Morgan to stay on his new plantation and found a family. More especially to found a family. As Anna Petronilla bluntly pointed out when he went to pay his respects to her.

'A year!' she said, her wide, china-blue eyes indignant. 'And not a sign! She must embroider more, she must embroider.' And, before he could remark on this odd recipe for conception: 'How can she expect to have a child if she is for ever running hither and thither? She is out every day, in all weathers, riding round the estate like an overseer. You have no money for a factor?'

Oh, yes, Henry said; he had ample means to pay a factor now; it was just that Elizabeth happened to be interested in estate matters and found it boring to sit at home.

'A set of chairs,' said Anna Petronilla. 'Put her to a set of chairs. That is very absorbing; practically a life's work.'

They laughed together over the set of chairs, Henry and Elizabeth, and it became a catch phrase with them. 'When I begin my set of chairs.' 'The kind of woman who embroiders a set of chairs.' Henry did not mind that she had no child yet; she was still very young, and they had all their lives in front of them. Some day, of course, he would have a son: a child like that Cuban boy, upstanding and independent. But meanwhile he had Elizabeth.

He had Elizabeth and Morgan's Valley and an unassailable standing in the land of his adoption, and with all that for his pleasure it was absurd that an outlandish name should toll at the back of his mind like a bell, like a summons.

He refused to be seduced by the tolling name, and busied himself with the affairs of the island and with the colossal task of assessing and sharing out the treasure from Puerto Bello. The courts did the assessing, of course, and sharing out was a matter of strict privateer agreement and precedent. One fifteenth of all went to the King; one tenth of all to the Duke of York as Lord High Admiral; and so on down the scale to the carpenter who got an allowance for the use of his tools, and the surgeon who was paid so much for the upkeep of his medicine chest. All these admitted of no argument. But besides these unvarying percentages, there was a long list of compensations to be awarded, and a list almost as long of rewards for special bravery. It was in these lesser matters that Morgan's advice was continually being sought. Privateer custom decreed that for the loss of a leg a man was entitled to four hundred pieces-of-eight, but if Dick Buttonshaw had lost his leg by getting drunk and falling between the ship and the wharf, how much compensation, if any, was he entitled to? And if Ted Budge, Jeremy Willett and Ben Twizel all claimed to be the man who hauled down the Spanish flag on Fort Triana, to which of the three should go the recognized amount of fifty pieces?

If he was not being summoned to give his advice, he was being summoned to have Government dispatches read to him. This happened almost every time a ship put in, for if Port Royal had been stirred by the affair at Puerto Bello, its effect on the chancellories of Europe had been cataclysmic. The authorities in Madrid were still short of breath from the body-blow of Puerto Principe, when they were rocked back on their heels by the upper-cut of Puerto Bello. Their rage knew no bounds; and neither did their eloquence. The Spanish ambassador to the Court of St James's was kept busy. Why, asked the grieved and furious Spaniards, when their one wish was for friendship and peace, did the English make both peace and friendship impossible by acts of barbarism for which there was no precedent, excuse, nor adequate description?

The Court of St James's deplored the hot-headedness of privateer captains who exceeded instructions; and directed its ambassador in Madrid to ask for the release of Captain Robert Delander and his crew, who had been in prison in Seville for the last nine months, having been deported there from Havana after their ship was confiscated and sold by the Cuban authorities. It was not, said the Court of St James's gently, notably conducive to either peace or friendship to grant the captain of a dismasted ship the courtesy of a harbour, and then to confiscate the ship and send both captain and crew to prison half across the world.

Meanwhile the dispatches being hurled out with such speed and in such numbers to Port Royal said (at least in their private enclosures): 'My God, Thomas, what *have* you been up to? How do you think we are going to get you out of this? How are we going to get out of it ourselves? For the love of Heaven send us some ammunition!'

So Modyford, week and by week, sent them ammunition.

One week it would be the case of Rocky Garretson, who had just come into port in his tiny three-gun ketch, bringing with him as prize a Spanish warship of twelve guns. This great bully, said Rocky, had left a fleet of fourteen sail to harry him and to say that if he did not surrender they would 'hoist him in'. However, they were what Rocky called with delightful euphemism 'much deceived', and on examination after capture the ship proved to be His Majesty's ship *Griffin*, which had disappeared with all her crew on the way to England two years ago.

Another week it would be the affair of Captain Edward Beckford, who, hailing a friendly ship off the South Cays, was met by a volley and the sight of Spanish colours being run up. On this occasion, too, the assailants had been 'much deceived,' and the ship, which was now at Port Royal, proved to be the property of Alexander Soares, who had sailed in it from New England eighteen months ago, since when there had been no word of either ship or company.

'They may say that papers found in Puerto Principe are forgeries, my dear James,' wrote the Governor to his brother, 'but even the English cannot forge ships. Tell your Spanish correspondents that they may come here – as our guests – and inspect the ships at their leisure. They may also, you had better assure them, depart at their leisure when it seems good to them. We have no dungeons at Port Royal.'

And to his cousin Albemarle: 'There will be no sure future for Jamaica without peace, but there will be no peace while Spain sits like a great jealous hen over every egg in the Americas. I understand that the treaty you propose to ratify makes no mention of the West Indies. I take it that that means that Spain reserves the right to apply it to the West Indies or not as it may suit her. If we attack her, the treaty applies; if they attack us, the treaty will be held to apply only to European waters. It seems a puny mouse to have been brought forth with such mountainous labour. Meanwhile I reprimand the privateer captains daily, and nightly give thanks for them.'

So Morgan drank the Governor's good brandy while he was having dispatches read to him, and from his fertile mind produced more 'ammunition' for Modyford's replies.

And when he was tired of both planning and Government business, he would go down to the harbour and help Bernard Speirdyck to admire the *Mary and Jane*.

For Bernard had bought his ship.

She had been the *Isabella*: another Spanish ship which had indulged in aggression and been 'much deceived'. The Spaniards had used her for trade, and she was light and fast and roomy, and altogether the ship of his dreams. So Bernard had not only spent his last penny of privateering gains on her, but had mortgaged his future for some years ahead in his desire to be master of her. Cornelius was his partner in the enterprise, having one share to Bernard's two; and they had renamed her the *Mary and Jane*: Mary for Bernard's wife, and Jane for Cornelius's bride. They were spending the bad-weather months in re-fitting her, and when it was sailing weather again she would be ready to go out on her peaceful trading life as trim and well-found as two Hollanders bred to the sea could make her.

'Mary says if the child were coming sooner she would sail with us,' Bernard said, 'but I think better she stay and be something to come home to. A man who lives by the sea wants always something to come home to.'

'Where do you plan to trade?' Morgan asked, hanging with Bernard over the rail and admiring the line of her bows to the bowsprit.

'With the Indians on the coast to begin with. Hides, shell and log-wood.'

'I shall miss you, Barney; how I shall miss you!'

'But I shall see you often,' Bernard said, a faint surprise in his voice. 'You will come in when I am in port.'

'In? In from where?'

'From Morgan's Valley.'

And it was in that moment that Morgan knew that he was not going to stay in Jamaica. For his involuntary expression of regret at losing Barney had been made, now that he looked at it, not from the point of view of a man parting with a comrade, but with the regret of a captain parting with a good mate. 'I shall miss you, Barney,' he had said, and what he had meant was: 'I shall miss you on board the *Fortune*.'

He looked at the *Fortune*, turning to the tides far out in the bay; the ship he had taken from Spain on that calm night on the coast of Barbados; and it seemed that she curtseyed to him. And for the first time since he had heard of Mansfield's death he went home and slept with no outlandish name tolling in his mind.

Not that he gave up without a struggle. The sober, sensible, land-owning side of him was still strong. Indeed, in the next few weeks he worked so hard at being the complete planter that Modyford cocked an eye at him and said: 'You remind me, Harry, of nothing so much as a cat that wants to get out of a room and can't find an opening.'

And at that Henry gave up.

He gave what sounded like a laugh under his breath, and said: 'When I first had the felicity of meeting your Excellency in Barbados I came to the conclusion that you knew everything, and I have never had any reason to revise my opinion.'

'Well?' said Modyford. 'What is it that you want to do?'

Henry looked out at the harbour, where five of the nine ships that had taken Puerto Bello were still anchored. 'I want to take that fleet out again before it is scattered beyond recall.'

'Out? Out where?'

'Cruising,' said Henry, very bland.

'And what is to be the excuse this time?'

'The reason,' amended Henry. 'The reason is the long series of unprovoked attacks on peaceful English traders pursuing their lawful occasions in West Indian waters, and the lamentable lack of any apparent willingness on Spain's part either to put an end to such depredations or to provide compensation for lost or confiscated ships or for the widows they have made.'

The Governor received this suggested piece of dispatch in silence.

'You have the fleet,' he said after a little, 'but would you get the crews? Judging entirely from the state of the town last night, the men are not yet penniless.'

'Judging entirely from the state of the town last night,' Henry said dryly, 'it will not be long before they are.' And added with a spurt of vanity: 'In any case, the crews would come to sea with me, even with money in their pockets.'

'Would you go without a commission?'

'No,' said Henry at once. 'I have no intention of being hanged as a pirate.'

'If I give you a commission I may be hanged as a sacrifice to Spain.'

'Executed,' Henry reminded him. 'But in what a magnificent cause, your Excellency!'

At which Modyford laughed.

'Well,' he said, mock contemplative. 'I don't deny that it would be very pleasant to get the crews out of town. Port Royal is really a very charming little place when not in season.'

And Henry, taking this as capitulation, forbore to press his immediate advantage. But Morgan's Valley became in the succeeding days a sort of week-end home for unemployed captains;

and Elizabeth creamed her freckled arms, and put on her best dresses for them, and arranged meals, and made no remark. In his more nearly idle moments Henry had the grace to worry about the thing he was proposing to do to her, and to speculate a little unhappily on her possible reception of the news when he broke it to her.

But again she surprised him.

'If we are going to take in that field on the north side, Harry,' she said one evening, looking out at the virgin forest of Jamaica that bounded the clearing of Morgan's Valley, 'we shall need four more slaves at least. You had better see to buying them before you go, hadn't you?'

'Go?' he said. 'Before I go where?'

'Wherever it is that you are going.'

He found this acceptance of his intended departure admirable but disconcerting. No woman had any right, he felt, to be so Spartan. There was a decent mean in such things; a due appropriateness.

When he blurted something about her not being angry, then, that he should leave her, she said: 'I have always thought it very unbecoming wear for a man.'

'What is?' he said, at a loss.

'Apron-strings,' she said.

And, being Henry, it did not occur to him that this detachment had been achieved at the price of secret tears; nor could he know that the 'apron-strings' remark was a quotation borrowed from Johanna.

'What am I to do, Jo?' she had said. 'I have tried him with sugar-cane; and horses; and good food; and standing for the Council; and even in bed. But not one of them is any use. I know that he is planning to go to sea again.'

'But that's why you married him, Bet,' Johanna had said.

'Because he would go to sea!'

'No, goose. Because he is that kind of man. That kind of man would be no use to me at all. I like to be cherished. I want to be an old man's darling. Indeed, I am seriously thinking of marrying Henry Archbould!'

'*Mother's* beau!'

'Yes. He would be just as handy for Mother to ask advice from if he were her son-in-law. And he is just the kind of adoring man I want to have round the house. I want everything to revolve round *me* when I get married. I don't want him to have another thought in his head but me – and poor Henry has not very many thoughts altogether, so that would not be difficult to achieve. But you would not like that, Bet. You would hate a man with apron-strings tied to him.'

Elizabeth had recognized the truth of this, but it had not made the situation any easier to bear.

'I had no idea when I married,' she said miserably, 'that it would have this dreadful softening effect on one's inside.' And the tears rose in her eyes again.

Upon which Jo had hugged her and said: 'Never mind, Bet darling. Presently you will have children to love, and it will not matter one little bit to you that the silly creature must needs be off after his guns and his glory. You will grow happy and placid, like a turnip; like Anna.'

'A blob of melted butter,' Elizabeth said, remembering; and began to smile. 'That was the day that Harry first came to see us.'

She knew that Johanna was right. She would not have him any other way. And the price she must pay to have him as he was would be the parting with him whenever his daemon drove him to action.

So she was calm with Henry, and Spartan. And Henry found it admirable but disconcerting. Was it conceivable that so much equanimity could exist in alliance with love? Was it possible that she did not care about his coming absence?

He had no time to brood on this problem, even if he was minded to, for he was faced with a greater one. He had boasted that the crews would come to sea with him in whatever condition they happened to be; and that was indeed true. But it seemed that not all the captains were willing to sail with him. It had never pleased Charlie Hadsell to serve under the command of a man almost young enough to be his son, and now he was filled with the notion that what Morgan could do he, Charles Hadsell, could do also. When next he went privateering he planned to be in command, and he had already detached two of the smaller ships from their allegiance to their late commander.

The captains of these ships were both older men who, if they lacked Hadsell's jealousy, were nevertheless not sorry to take orders from one of their own generation and upbringing. Neither of them had been of any great consequence, but they had what was to Henry the supreme virtue: they were trustworthy. They had fitted into the general scheme efficiently and unobtrusively; doing their part without question and without faltering. Now he would have to fill the gap they left, and he would have to do it with untried men. There would be no leisurely review and election, as there had been before Puerto Principe. He would have to fill the gap with the best available.

He sailed, in the end, feeling that he had not done too badly. His brace of substitutes were at least well salted. Nick Gaytor had sailed for years as a privateer with a commission from the French, and his crew was still partly French. And Johnny Toplass – One-eye Johnny – had sailed for years as a privateer without bothering overmuch about a commission from anyone. Both were first-class seamen.

'I am signing this commission, Harry,' the Governor said when it came to the moment, 'on the clear understanding that if the treaty with Spain is ratified you will bring your ships into port without delay and without waiting for any summons from me.'

'Is there anything in the treaty about recognizing the English occupation of Jamaica?'

'Not so far as I am aware.'

'Then they will hardly be such fools at home as to ratify it.'

'The degree of folly to which the fools at home are prone is incalculable. I want your promise that you will offer no provocation, not even so much as trailing your coat, once the treaty is ratified.'

And Henry promised.

He had no intention of being anywhere near English sources of information for the next three months at least; and by that time Maracaibo would be behind him.

12

MARACAIBO LIES ON the north east of South America, at the coast end of a great inland sea. The inland sea is large and square, a hundred miles across; but the entrance to all this wealth of water is a narrow strait a mile or two wide and much given to silting.

To command this unwelcoming entrance, and to add the perils of gun-fire to the terrors of navigation, thc Spaniards had of course built a fort. And being confronted on a blue spring day with the astonishing sight of no less than seven English ships coming boldly out of nowhere, English ships so unabashed and unaware of their enormity that every one of them was openly flying the English flag, the fort replied with such a panic cannonade that the ships, having one by one trailed their coats under the fort's batteries and learned the position and range of every gun in the fort, drew away out of sight down the coast, leaving the fort chattering and aghast.

Out of sight beyond the green headlands, Henry arranged for attack. And since he was Henry, the attack was to be an oblique one. He had no intention of engaging the fort while trying to navigate his ships through the narrows. It was to be Puerto Bello over again, therefore; except that this time the journey in boats was to be made through the narrows, past the fort. By night.

Over the side went the boats as soon as it was dark. There would be no moon until an hour after midnight, and by that time they would be ashore beyond the fort. It was a calm night for the time of year; and more than once, feeling the soft air and smelling the green forest-smell in the blackness, Henry was reminded of the night they took the *Gloria*. He had come a long way from that exquisite piece of petty larceny.

They let the tide bear them in, as once on the Barbados coast they had let the tide bear them out, with only a dipped oar for guidance; so that no rhythmic warning should mount to the no-doubt nervous ears on the battlements. One by one the boats drew level with the fort; visible now only as a dark bulk against the sky; and one by one passed safely without being challenged. The navigation through the narrows was done by a Frenchman of Nick Gaytor's crew, who had been at Maracaibo with l'Olonois, and he did it so successfully that they made landfall at the exact spot on which they had agreed: where the beach shelved on the inland side of the fort. One by one the boats came to rest with their bows in the sand, and the men scrambled out of them and went up the beach to cover until the moon should come to light them to the fort.

It was to be Puerto Bello over again; the scaling-ropes, the challenge at the main gate to provide diversion, and the swarm over the walls. If this San Jeronimo technique failed for any reason, then Henry had decided to wait until daylight and substitute the method that had proved so successful with Fort Triana: the attack by seamen covered by the excellent musketry of Civil War veterans.

But it was not to be at all like that. Not at all like either of them.

The moon came, surprised and brightly curious, from behind the black trees on the headland, and the world turned silver and naked-looking. They picked up their weapons and moved from shadow to shadow until they were standing under the walls, the angular shadows of the fort flung across them like a cloak. The night was so still that their breathing sounded loud in the silence. They strained their ears to listen for a sentry's step on the ramparts, for a voice, for the clink of metal as a man changed position in his vigil. But the silence was absolute. The silence pressed down on their ear-drums like a tight cloth, so that it seemed to them as if they had suddenly grown deaf, and they were seized with a mad longing to make a noise that they might be reassured that they could still hear.

Then, loud and shocking, came their own challenge.

And then the silence again.

The empty silence.

Once more Morgan's voice rang out across the moonlit space, demanding the presence of the Commandant to parley.

But the fort stood silver and naked and quiet in the night; irrelevant, somehow; like an apparition.

And then Jack's voice came out of the shadows on the far side.

'Harry! Have you noticed what is odd about the place?'

'It's all odd,' said Morgan.

'No. I mean their flag. Look!'

And they looked, and saw that there was no flag there.

'They've cleared out,' they said. 'By God, they've cleared out!' And they moved away from the walls to gape.

But still they suspected a trap. And it was not until they had pushed open the great gate and taken in the empty spaces of the courtyard, and savoured the panic-mess of hasty departure in the barrack rooms and the kitchen, and appreciated the great store of undestroyed weapons, that they gave way to the realization that the place was theirs, and fell to rejoicing. They lighted every lamp in the fort, and torches beside, as if to compensate themselves for the chill doubt of those moments in the moonlight outside, and they fell on the food that had been laid out on the long tables for a garrison that had not waited to eat it.

But something in that waiting meal puzzled Henry and worried him. It was too untouched, too prepared. Surely, if it had been made ready for men who were in too much of a hurry to eat it, at least one of them would have swung a disgruntled arm as he passed and swept some of it to the floor. Something was wrong with the picture.

Poison?

No, surely not. It would take all the poison in the Americas to make any impression on a company so large.

Then what?

They had been meant to eat that meal; to fall on it exactly as they were falling on it now; eager and triumphant and oblivious and —

And suddenly Henry was back on Santa Catalina.

Back in that other deserted fort, that the Spaniards had so reprehensibly left undamaged for their use, when they might have —

'Search!' yelled Morgan above the din. 'Search!'

The terrible urgency in his voice stopped the movement and clatter on the instant.

'For what?' they said, looking stupidly at him. 'Treasure?'

'No! A match! A powder train! Search, damn you! Every God-damned one of you! *Search!*'

And he made for the stairs, snatching a torch as he went.

It would be somewhere in the cellars.

As he flung himself down the circular stone funnel he tried to think how long it was in minutes since they had first come into the fort and found it empty. Six minutes? Ten? Five? How long a fuse would it be? Not less than a ten-minute one, surely. The man who lit it hoped to get away with his life, if he could. It would not be less than ten. Had they been as much as nine minutes in the fort?

The torch hit the curving side of the stairway and faded to a mere glow. He cried aloud in his desperation, and thought quite distinctly how unfair, how inappropriate, it was that he, Henry Morgan, should die so ignominiously; should end without trace, in a great flash of gunpowder on a distant and barbarous coast. He, who had Morgan's Valley to go back to. He, who had so much in store.

All his passionate joy in living rose in him and curdled into one great concentration of fear and protest as he stumbled and fumbled his way into the cellar.

What if it was not here? What if it was here and he could not find it in time?

It was only afterwards that he was to realize that the quenching of his torch, which had seemed to him at the moment the mockery of unfeeling gods, was in fact his salvation.

In the full light of the torch he would not have seen the small blue light at the farther end of the cellar. Now he saw it; that small, secret, gloating light.

Another half-minute, he reckoned, looking down at the dead fuse under his foot. Another half-minute, not more.

He sat down on the floor and wiped the sweat from his face with shaking hands. His torch went out altogether, and he sat there in the dark; limp as a rag doll, all virtue gone out of him.

It was Jack, coming clattering down the stairs in search of him, who roused him from his stupor of relief.

Jack paused on the threshold of the dark cellar, questing with his torch.

'Harry!' he said, his voice sharp with anxiety.

'I'm here,' said Henry from the floor.

'What is it?' Jack said, coming to him. 'Are you hurt?'

'No. My stomach doesn't feel very good,' said Henry. 'I've just trodden on a snake.' And he pushed his foot towards the dead fuse.

Jack lowered the torch to look, and then lifted it to see what the cellar contained. 'Mother of God!' said Jack. And then, as the stacked tiers of gunpowder kegs drew his eye upwards: 'Sweet Mother of God! It would have blown us to Port Royal.'

'There's one comfort,' Henry said. 'There is so much, that this must be the only fuse. There can't be more powder than this in the fort.'

'There can't be more in the world,' said Jack.

'No,' agreed Henry, beginning to take a proprietary interest, now that feeling was coming back to him. 'It's a nice little nest-egg, isn't it? And a whole arsenal upstairs to prime with it. They have no moderation, the Dons, have they? A very wholesale race.'

He got to his feet and propped himself upon his still-shaking legs. 'I feel as if I were out of bed for the first time after a long illness,' he said.

'Well,' said Jack, 'you'll certainly never be nearer death's door. Let us go and eat. That is a very fine meal your wholesale Spaniards left us.'

And Henry found, as everyone does after escaped peril, that he was ravenously hungry. His body, in its reaction from imminent death, craved food, and love-making, and sleep. And since he could have neither the sleep nor the love-making, he made do with food. Food and drink.

But he saw to it that the barrels in the wine-store were not broached that night. And he set sentries and arranged for their relief every hour. Somewhere in those black forests under the fading moon were the Spanish garrison, waiting for their destruction. And when that great blaze of annihilation did not come, the Spaniards would, if they were not utter poltroons, try other methods of discomfiture.

But day came, and there was no sign from the forest. The sun rose into a clear, ardent morning with an on-shore wind that whipped the channel into scarves of white where the shoals streaked it. They ran up the Union flag as soon as the light came, and presently the ships came in, floating in calm procession past the fort and dipping their colours in salute to the flag on the fort. And for the rest of the day all seven crews were busy transferring the great store of powder, muskets, swords and ammunition from the fort to the ships. On the following morning, still without hindrance, they transferred everything else that was useful to them; more especially the contents of the larder and the wine-store.

'Do themselves well, don't they?' said Bluey, looking at the sugared fruits, and the delicately cured meat, and the kegs of brandy. 'No salt pork for the Dons!'

When the fort was stripped of all but its fixtures, they spiked the guns, took down their flag, and left the place as silent as they had found it.

'Where do you think that garrison are, Captain?' asked Kinnell, the one-time bos'n, who was now mate in Bernard's place, as they set sail for Maracaibo.

'Waiting for us at Maracaibo, I expect,' Henry said.

Although he would never say so to Kinnell, he was not very happy about the prospect. And he was even less happy an hour later, when the *Fortune* grounded gently but firmly in mid-channel. They got her off by hauling, and the smaller *Gift* scraped by her to try the channel in her stead. But even the *Gift* touched the bottom, and it became apparent that of the seven ships only the two smallest - open-decked schooners - could make the passage and come to anchor opposite Maracaibo.

'The channel does not stay the same for six months together,' said the Frenchman who had been with l'Olonois, dismayed by this set-back to his piloting; and Henry could not blame him; the Frenchman had been of incalculable help to them already.

He looked at the virgin country ashore, his mind searching it for the means of oblique attack. But he would have no guide to that country, as he had had to the backwoods of Puerto Bello, as he had had to the sea approaches of Maracaibo. He would go into it blind, pathless. He could do it with a chosen fifty, but what hope was there that the ships' crews as a whole would follow him in so toilsome and risky a ploy? They liked their risk without toil. They liked to go roaring in to attack in full face of the enemy, taking the chance they had counted on. To hack their way through primitive country for days on end, perhaps, just to lessen the risk, when they could sail comfortably to the scene of battle in their own boats, would seem to them the wildest absurdity. It would have to be the boats, and frontal attack for once.

But he would see to it that the attack was as little frontal as he could make it.

Through the channel they came in their boats, therefore, and out into the great spaces of the Lake of Maracaibo, a burnished glory under the midday sun; and the wind took them down to the town.

It lay by the water's edge, its neat wharves reflected in the sea, but behind it stretched a wide half-moon of huddled suburb, infinitely more squalid than the slave suburbs of Puerto Bello had been; and Henry, looking at that barrier between the town proper and the forest, was comforted for his lost hopes of attack from the rear. If they had come that way they would have had to fight their way through that mess of housing; and he remembered too clearly what the street-fighting in Puerto Principe had been like to want any more of it.

He had expected the garrison from the fort at the channel to be snugly settled down in the castle at Maracaibo, and as they drew in, he looked up at the redoubt with its bristling gun-mouths and waited for the reception. But the strip of water between the town and the boats went on narrowing, and still no volley greeted them. That the water-front should be empty of people was understandable, but that the fort should let them come so far unchallenged was very strange. Had they mined the beaches, and grudged the ammunition for even a token defiance?

Then Manuel's caressing voice just behind him said: 'I think it is that even Spain grows ashamed of the Spanish flag.' And

Henry, whose whole attention had been concentrated on those waiting gun-mouths, lifted his glance to the tower, and saw that the staff was bare. The fort was deserted.

'Well,' said Henry, 'it can blow up at its leisure. We are not being entertained with any powder-trains today.'

He had chosen to land on the beaches rather than in the harbour, partly because the reception would be hottest at the centre of the town and partly because the beaches gave him a wider front for simultaneous disembarking. But now that the opposition was not to come from the orthodox direction – from the castle – every man dropping over the bows to shore felt his steps weighted with question. Where was the booby trap in all this?

But they advanced up the beach, wary and step-picking, and arrived safely on the road level, and they took heart again. If it was merely that the Spaniards were waiting in the town for them, that was nothing. They had dealt with Spaniards in towns before now. They began to sing. And singing they marched into the town.

Into a silent and deserted town.

One by one they ceased to sing, defeated by the silence. Until presently the only sound was the tap of their drum as it kept time to their marching feet. Their eyes slid sideways at the blank windows, alert for ambush. But the windows stayed blank. The closed doors frowned on them and nothing moved in the shadows. A chicken pecking in the dust looked so alive, so natural, that it was a relief. They called each other's attention to it, and laughed at it as they passed. But that was the only living thing that met them in all their march from the beaches to the harbour front. They came out into the wide paved space and the unbroken sunlight and stopped breathing short. No one could ambush them here. But even here the silence lay thick and eerie. A shutter slatted back and forth in the wind, and a curtain bellied out and sank back again. No human being but themselves moved in all the dead town.

Here and there were the signs of flight: a child's shoe in the roadway, a stable door left open, a burst bag of flour left to spill itself on the street. It was panic that had emptied the town, not ambush. And some of the atmosphere of that panic still hung in the silence and inhabited the deserted houses so that a man's skin crept at his neck.

'Well,' said Henry to his crew, 'it seems that we have the choice of dwellings for our stay.' And in the bustle of choosing their billets some of the strangeness was exorcised. They went in and out of the empty houses with the curiosity of children; marvelling at this, debating the use of that, mocking at something else. Any privateer found to be keeping loot on his own behalf invariably lost his share of the general loot (any other arrangement would have meant chaos and would make privateering unprofitable for both captains and men), but a great variety of articles of no value found their way into English and French pockets before night. A dress for a doxy, a toy for a child, a crucifix for a shrine.

Henry decided to make the Mayor's house on the harbour-front his headquarters, and since it was a large place and fine, he suggested that the others should share it with him; that they should make a captains' mess of it. Bradley, Rogers and Ansell were pleased and agreed. But Nick Gaytor, the newcomer, took a long look at the pillared coolness of the Mayor's rooms, the carpets, the silk curtains, the flowers in the stone tubs in the courtyard, and said: 'Much too fine for a plain sailor-man. I'll leave you to play gentlemen, friends, and stay with my men in the priest's house.' He spat loudly on the tiles in the patio and went away; and it seemed that he took the other newcomer with him, for One-eye Johnny Toplass was found next day to be also occupying the priest's house by the church.

Henry regretted this break in their unity, but had no time to worry about it. And in any case, as Ansell pointed out with Kentish good sense, it might be a pity to be separated, but it would be worse to have Gaytor with them. What worried Henry was the bareness of the town. It had been stripped clean of all that was valuable, from the Mayor's plate to the trinkets of the Madonna in the church. Even the warehouses were empty – the warehouses of which he had hoped so much. This was El Dorado: the place where the gold stuck to the soles of a man's shoes; fabulous El Dorado. And all he had for his pains was an empty little town with the shutters flapping in the wind and the warehouses gaping and void.

That there had been organised evacuation of goods was obvious: only the domestic flight had been hurried and individual. And that being so there must be a hiding-place; probably one single hiding-place. A cave somewhere? A building in the forest?

But there was no one to tell him.

At the earliest possible moment he must get back some of the missing population.

'Why the wholesale flight?' he said to Jack in the morning, picking up the child's shoe from where it was still lying in the dust.

'You said they were wholesale,' Jack reminded him.

'Yes, but why not wait and hear our terms?'

'I expect they remember l'Olonois,' Jack said dryly.

So patrols of twenties and thirties were sent out to find some inhabitants and persuade them that this was not invasion à l'Olonoise. And presently embarrassed sailors began to herd weeping women from their inadequate retreat in the forest. Their children hung howling to their skirts, and neither mothers nor children were coherent on any subject. When asked where their husbands were, the women with one accord said that they had no husbands.

'Even l'Olonois couldn't be responsible for nearly fifty widows,' Henry said when he had reached the forty-eighth widow in two hours. And he waited hopefully for what the wider sweep might bring in.

By nightfall thirty-four of the 'widows' had been reunited with their husbands, and the husbands had been relieved of the various valuables that they had been found guarding in their various caches. But real progress came only when the slaves began to trickle back. The slaves needed no persuasion to talk. They owed no loyalty to Spain and no love for their masters; and being slaves, with little interest outside the household that numbered them as a unit, there was nothing about their masters' business that they did not know. Negro or Indian, they talked; and talked with pleasure. Here were the English: the fabled English who had walked into the heart of Cuba and walked out again unhurt, who had taken Puerto Bello and lived in it for a month; the English who hated the Spaniard as they themselves hated him; here were the wonderful English in Maracaibo, and the slaves, Negro or Indian, were glad. What did the English want to know? They had only to ask.

From the most intelligent of these – a tall, middle-aged Indian – Morgan learned all he wanted to know. The Governor, who lived in the castle, had organised the evacuation of valuables. In this he had used only the troops under his command, and no one in town knew just what he had done with the stuff. But he and his men had sailed in a ship to the fort of Gibraltar at the other end of the lake, so the townsfolk had taken it for granted that the goods were in the hold of the ship. He had taken with him such of the important men of the town as were his friends, and had left the leading 'opposition' citizens to their fate.

The Indian gave a list of those deserted rich ones, and told where they might be found, and they were duly gathered in for ransom.

And that being done, Henry prepared to go after the Governor.

The ships, stalled below the bar, were brought up to Maracaibo by the proper channel, and provisioned, and a week later he set sail for Gibraltar, nearly a hundred miles away. With him went Ansell, Bradley and Rogers, but Jack he left behind with the two newcomers. When Jack protested ('I always get the baggage-train job! I did at Puerto Principe, and again at Puerto Bello!') Henry pointed out that he must have someone he could trust in command of the captured town.

'You can trust Joe Bradley!'

'Not as I trust you.'

And with that Jack had to be content.

And away sailed Henry in search of a ship that held, crammed into its one hold, enough wealth to buy a kingdom. But when he came to Gibraltar, there was no ship there. There was a fort, certainly; a very superior and impressive-looking fort; and this time it was occupied, if they were to judge by the Spanish colours tumbling in a brisk breeze round and round the mast. But in the harbour there were only fishing-boats, and in the roads only a small ketch.

What had happened to the ship? Had they unloaded the stuff into the safety of the fort, and then sunk her?

And was it to Gibraltar that the garrison of the sea fort had fled, since it was not to Maracaibo? If so, then this fine fort with the rollicking flag was now packed with troops as well as with hypothetical treasure.

So Henry settled down to parley.

Ten gentlemen of Maracaibo, said Henry, at present living as his guests, were anxious that they should be ransomed by their friends at the earliest possible moment. Failing the ransom, he would be obliged to take them back with him to Jamaica where they would of course live in comfort until the ransom was paid. In addition to this quite personal bargain, there was the further matter of the ransom for the town of Maracaibo. For a sufficient sum he would evacuate it on a given day, leaving it in all respects as he had found it.

Two days passed in this verbal give and take, conducted on the English side by a sad member of the Maracaibo town council, and on the Spanish side by the Commandant of the fort.

'Why not the Governor?' asked Henry, when the hostage was reporting the fifth failure of his eloquence.

The Governor was not there, the hostage said.

'*Not in the fort?*'

Almost certainly not, said the hostage. It was common gossip among the troops that he was not there.

At that Henry stopped setting to partners and decided to take the fort without further delay. He would make a feint attack in force from in front, and take the place in the rear.

But the worst of an individual technique is that sooner or later one's enemy becomes acquainted with it, and anticipates it. 'Harry Morgan's way' had become a byword in the Islands; the impudent plan and the oblique attack. And every last detail of the taking of Puerto Bello had been studied with a passionate interest by the still undisturbed Spaniards along the whole coast of two continents; not least by the Commandant of Gibraltar. The Commandant did not wait for the English troops to cut off his rear; he used his rear for retreat as long as he had a rear to retreat to. So the English came into the fort from the land side to find it occupied only by a battery of gunners who were blazing away at their colleagues of the feint attack in front. The gunners desisted with the unemotional air of actors interrupted during rehearsal, and fell to polishing their pieces with a detached nonchalance. It was not necessary to search the fort to know that they were defending nothing; that their performance was a ritual, a mere taking part in a play.

Henry went back to the *Fortune* disgruntled. Another empty conquest!

But if the fort was deserted, the water-front was busy. The Indians had come to trade; and the sea round the ships was gay with boats bearing fruit and vegetables, skins, hides, and leather goods. On board the *Fortune* Henry, missing the waiting figure of Romulus at the top of the ladder, looked round for him, and saw that he was looking on at the trafficking between crew and vendors. But it was not the actual bargaining that interested him and caused that unwonted animation in his brown, carved face. His attention was on the boats lying idle while they waited their turn to come to the ship's side; he was listening to the chatter of the waiting Indians in the further boats, and his face was the secret delighted face of a child creeping up on an adult.

Henry moved over to him and said: 'Do you understand what they say, Romulus?'

But Romulus, fascinated by the talk and forgetful for the moment, now that he was in his own country, that he was a slave, made a slight, imperious gesture with his hand for silence without even turning his head to look at his adored master. This amused the master, and he waited patiently like a snubbed child, until his small slave might be ready to talk to him.

'They are my aunts,' Romulus said at length; his English being still as prentice as his way with clothes was expert.

'Uncles,' suggested Henry.

But it seemed that what Romulus really meant was something like cousins. The men were, in fact, from a tribe that had been neighbours of his own at Cape Gallinas.

'They laugh because you know not where is the ship,' said Romulus.

'The ship!' said Henry. 'And do *they* know?'

'Oh, yes. Indian know everything.'

'What have they done with the ship, the Spaniards?'

'They have taken it into the forest.'

Henry's heart sank. Some Indian chatter; half meaningless, half magic.

'How could they sail it into the forest?' he said, to please the boy.

'They sail it up the Tacuyo creek.'

'What!'

'Twenty-two mile they sail it to where is a little' – he paused for a word and then tried one – 'pool?'

'Lake?'

'Little lake in the mountains.'

'Is that where the garrison have gone? The men from the fort?' He leant his head to the fort on shore.

'Oh, no. Soldiers go to Merida, to new fort. Sit in crow's-nest like Governor.'

'Is the Governor not with the ship?'

'No, no. Governor sit in crow's-nest and spit.'

No one was more patient than Henry when he wanted information out of friend or foe, and in the end it was unravelled.

The Governor had retired with his own personal fortune to a hunting lodge which he had built in the mountains. The lodge was situated in a tiny valley – a valley so small as to be almost a crevice in the rock, and it was impregnable. The path to it, narrow and almost sheer, admitted only one man at a time, and the owner of the lodge could sit on his veranda and pick off undesired visitors at his leisure. The place had been built and provisioned not against a possible English invasion, which was one of the last events that the Governor anticipated, but against an Indian rising; a matter which in any Spanish settlement was a constant source of speculation. His insurance against Indian massacre was now proving a godsend against English invasion. He had food and ammunition for months, he had his fortune intact, and he could sit there comfortably until the English went. Sit, as Romulus said, in his crow's-nest and spit down on them.

The ship, on the other hand, was there for the taking; lying snugly up one of the creeks, and guarded only by her crew – who were no doubt busy at this moment unloading the most precious stuff and bearing it to even surer hiding in the woods.

Of the two prizes, the Governor and the treasure-ship, the ship was out of all computing the more important. But the ship represented only riches; the Governor was challenge. So Henry sent Joe Bradley to take the treasure, and he himself set out to test the story of the Governor's invulnerability.

A large proportion of the two hundred who went with him had also done that journey in rowing-boats along the coast at Puerto Bello, and in after years they were wont to argue when they met as to which was worse: the open boats in the sun, or the mountains of Maracaibo in the rain.

For it rained.

It rained all the way into the interior: solid, perpendicular rain; constant, leaden rain that fell with a loud single note like the buzzing of insects. The steady monotone got on their nerves, and their need to keep powder dry irked and fretted them. The rocks they climbed were slippery with moss, and their fear of breaking a leg and being helpless in this wild claustrophobic country damped their spirits and infected them with a caution foreign to their natures.

And when at last they arrived at the Governor's retreat and looked up at his eyrie, they found that rumour for once was true. The place was impregnable.

By that time they had been three days without hot food, and they sat down to contrive a fire while Henry sent an ambassador to the Governor. But a man holding a straight flush does not need to draw any cards. The ambassador – another member of that unhappy town council of Maracaibo – proved *persona non grata*. Indeed, the Governor had not recognized his diplomatic status at all, and he came back with two bullet-holes in his soaking hat and another in his breeches. Nor would the meagre fires that the men contrived under overhanging rocks stay alight for more than a few minutes. Nothing would burn in this great sodden wilderness.

Reluctant, Henry wrote off the Governor as a dead loss, and turned for home. At least he had verified the reports.

But the way back had altered in the most frightening fashion in forty-eight hours. Streams that had been purling brooks dimpled by the rain were now wild torrents of angry water in which a man, even at the end of a rope, was whirled away and dashed against the rocks downstream. They tied up their broken ribs and spent depressed hours searching up and down the muddy banks of every little gully for a possible fording place. When they had achieved the long, difficult business of getting every man safely over, they were faced with a tangled wading of flooded and often indistinguishable paths before reaching the next torrent-filled gully and beginning the business all over again.

Their powder was no longer dry, and they were as helpless against the enemy as they were against the elements. Indeed, it was from this fact that Henry, typically, plucked comfort from a comfortless situation.

'Now I *know* that Spain's sun is setting,' he said, as he stood on the brink of a torrent on their fourth day of homeward travail, waiting for his turn to cross. They were still two days away from civilization, and their clothes weighed them down like armour. The rain ran down Henry's black, uncurled hair and shot in separate streams from the end of each lock to his rain-black tunic. But his eyes were bright and amused. 'Fifty men with pikes could have made an end of us any time in the last seven days.'

'There is still time,' Kinnell said dryly.

But Henry went on looking superior and amused. And Henry was right. They came back into Gibraltar, into an ironically sunny afternoon that showed up their draggled state in a tactless clarity (which annoyed Henry very much more than the Governor or the floods), and in all the days of their struggling impotence not one Spanish musket had barked even a token defiance.

Joe Bradley had come back that morning with a procession of boats laden with treasure from the ship in the creek, and the sight of it banished the last regret for the Governor from Henry's mind. It was almost worthy of El Dorado.

'If you don't plan to take Merida too,' Joe said, with just a hint of criticism, 'it is time we were getting back to Maracaibo.'

So they set sail; but it took them another two days, beating up against the wind on that great inland sea, to reach Maracaibo. They came into the roads late on a thundery evening, with the sunset lighting the heavy sky to a sullen glow, and dropped anchor with a feeling of achievement. As his boat lowered sail and lost way under the breakwater, Henry looked up and saw Jack waiting for him.

'We got the ship, treasure and all!' he called.

But Jack made no answer, even by a sign. And Henry wondered whether it was that he had not heard what he said, or whether Jack, the normally imperturbable, was still hurt and sulky at being relegated to guard duties.

Puzzled, he came up the breakwater steps and prepared to greet his friend. But before he could move the few steps towards him a woman flung herself on him, clawing at his face with her nails and shrieking unintelligibly. Her weight and the suddenness of her attack pushed him back to the wharf edge, and but for Jack he would have gone over. Jack pulled him to safety, and then, turning on the woman, struck her thrice in the face with all his force. This astounded Henry far more than the woman's attack. Not only had he never seen Jack hit a woman, but he had never seen him out of control before. Now he looked half-crazy; furious and ashamed at the same time.

'Jack!' he said. 'What is the matter?'

The woman had sunk to her knees on the wharf, crying and blaspheming, and a woman from the little knot of spectators came up, timidly, as if she too might be struck, and took her away.

Henry stared from the screaming, dishevelled woman to his friend, standing in angry embarrassment looking after her.

'Did you have to hit her so hard, Jack? She is only a poor demented creature with a grudge.'

'She must learn to confine her grudge to the proper quarter. It was no fault of yours.'

'What was no fault of mine?'

'That her daughter is dead.'

'Her daughter? Is it someone's fault that the girl is dead, then?'

'Yes. Nick Gaytor's men.'

'How?'

'Rape.'

'Jack! I trusted you!'

'You didn't tell me what I was to do with two hundred men mad drunk on brandy.'

'What brandy?'

'The Governor's wine-store.'

'But there were guards on that.'

'Yes. One-eye came and said why were the castle guards always *Dolphin* men; didn't we trust them? I said you had arranged it that way; but they made an issue of it, and rather than have bad blood, I agreed to alternate the guard. Everything went normally till last night, when Nick Gaytor's men were on duty.' He paused a moment as if he found it difficult to go on. 'In the Mayor's house down in the harbour you don't hear much of the town noises. It was only in the small hours of the morning, when Wat, my bos'n, came to fetch me, that I knew what was going on. By that time the town was a roaring hell. They had dragged people from their beds and were "persuading" them to tell where they had hidden jewellery. Most of the poor wretches weren't well off enough to have any jewellery, but they were too drunk to think of a small thing like that. Some were good-natured enough and were dancing, but the drunken ones were sheer maniacs. One or two were tumbling women in the open street.'

'*Dolphins?*'

'No!' said Jack hotly. 'My men were like me, down by the harbour and asleep. I went down for them, and Wat, Ted, and I went back with a picket of thirty each and cleaned up the place. It took us three hours, and two of Nick Gaytor's men are dead.' He paused again. 'But of course there was no way of undoing —'

'Where was Gaytor?'

'Getting drunk with One-eye in the priest's house.'

'Is – the girl – the only —?'

'No. An old man they tortured died of fright. And a man whose hair they burned off is in bad shape.'

There was a long silence.

'No unspotted glory,' said Henry at length, and turned to walk up the wharf as if his feet were weighted.

Nick Gaytor was still lying drunk on the priest's bed when Henry dragged him into a sitting position and flung the contents of the water-jug over him.

'Are you sober enough to understand what is said to you?' he asked, as Gaytor's wandering eye managed to focus itself on his face.

'Harry, my friend! Welcome back, welcome back, Harry my friend!'

'Captain Morgan to you, you unmentionable scum.'

'Oh, now, Harry, is that friendly! Is that —'

'Keep your mouth shut and listen to me, or, so help me God, I'll pistol you where you sit and take my chance about it. You will collect your men as soon as they are sober enough to stand, and you will take them and yourself and your ship out of Maracaibo as fast as a wind will take you.'

'Oh, it's that way, is it? Don't think you can play the Admiral with me, Harry Morgan. I'm partner in this exped —'

'If your ship is still here at noon tomorrow I'll blow the masts out of her and leave you to get home any way you can. You're a disgrace to your country, to your profession, and to the mother that bore you, and it would give me the greatest pleasure to hang you from the yard-arm. The best I can do is to see that the rest of the fleet are free of you and your jailbird crew.'

'Aah, you make me vomit! You and your discipline and your rules and your guards and your piddling dole of drink once a day! What do you think my men came to Spanish territory for? A couple of trinkets and kiss-me-hand through a window? No! They came for the fun they couldn't get in —'

Gaytor's shirt-band gave with a loud tearing sound as Henry twisted his collar and dragged him to his feet.

'I took you on this expedition because you had the reputation of a good seaman, but all you have done is to blacken the reputation of the men unfortunate enough to sail in your company. You would turn the stomach of a Spaniard, Nick Gaytor, and it makes me sick to think that you were ever a man of mine, and sick to the soul to know that you are English, and mud for the

Spaniards to fling back at us! You are to be out of here by noon tomorrow, and every last man of yours with you.'

'If you think that I am going without my share of —'

'Listen,' said Morgan through his teeth. 'I meant what I said about wanting to kill you. I've only once before wanted to kill a man, and I stopped that time because I was superstitious. There isn't anything stopping me at this moment but my common sense and my common sense is running out very fast. You be out of Maracaibo at noon tomorrow, Gaytor.'

He released his grip from Gaytor's throat and let him drop back on to the bed.

'Come on, Jack,' he said to Morris, who had been standing in the doorway, a silent witness of the colloquy.

'My men may have their own views about that,' Gaytor said, rubbing his neck and trying an attitude. 'If they refuse to go, who is going to make them?'

'The *Fortune*, the *Dolphin*, the *May Flower*, the *Pearl*, and the *Gift*,' said Morgan, and banged the door.

But by noon the following day no ships at all could sail from Maracaibo. No English ships, that is. For the Spanish navy that had been searching for Harry Morgan for the last six months had at last found him; and in the straits were those mighty and Royal ships, the *Magdalena*, the *San Luis*, and the *Marquesa*; forty-eight guns, thirty-six guns and twenty-four guns respectively.

And lest there were not sufficient to bottle him up, the fort at the narrows was once more occupied, its spiked guns replaced, and its ammunition stores replenished.

They were trapped.

13

HENRY'S REACTION TO this apparent *impasse* was characteristic. He sent a letter to the Spanish naval commander suggesting that he might pay the ransom for Maracaibo.

'Do you expect him to?' said Jack.

'No. But the notion will entertain him for a day or two,' said Henry, and sent to Gibraltar for the empty treasure-ship.

'One more ship isn't going to make any difference against three floating forts and a land one,' Joe Bradley said.

'One spare ship is going to make all the difference,' Henry said. And when the treasure-ship arrived at Maracaibo, he looked at her lovingly and said: 'Now we are going to make this sad little tub into a proud ship of war.'

'Her gun-deck won't bear more than four guns,' said Kinnell, who had sailed her from Gibraltar. 'And if it's those heavy cannon from the castle you're thinking of, sir, the deck won't bear them at all. Not to fire them, it won't.'

'Seven guns a side, I think,' said Henry; 'and a couple of light ones on the quarter-deck. And now go and tell the men to collect all the pitch, tar, brimstone, and other inflammable stuff that they can find in the town. Dried palm leaves, thatch – anything.'

'Inflammable!' said Kinnell, and his face lighted. 'Yes, of course! Yes, certainly, Captain; at once.'

Never had troops or crews enjoyed themselves as the English at Maracaibo did for the next few days. They not only made Henry's 'sad little tub' into a ship of war, they gave her a crew. They not only broke open gun-ports and provided her with 'guns' made from the long native Indian drums, but they made dummy figures to man her, complete with hats, swords and bandoliers. And Henry was amused to notice that at least one of these effigies was meant to be a portrait. He was greatly pleased by the sardonic leer they had imparted to his mouth, and the rakish tilt of his hat. Never had a fire-ship sailed under a more dashing commander.

When the thing was finished, there was the matter of a suicide crew to man her; and in view of the wholesale nature of the volunteering, it was decided to draw lots for it. Two men to go from each of the six ships. Nick Gaytor's men, being still in disgrace, were held to be unworthy of the honour of suicide for a cause.

When the lots had been cast and the twelve heroes chosen, Henry addressed the men who crowded the market square and read them the letter he had received from the Spanish naval commander. The letter was in Spanish, but that all might understand he read it first in English and then in French.

'I have put into commission again that fort which you took from a parcel of cowards,' wrote Don Alonso del Campo y Espinosa, 'and I am here to dispute your passage out of the lake. Nevertheless, if you surrender all that you have taken – treasure, slaves, and prisoners for ransom – I shall grant you free passage and let you go back safely to your own country. If you decide to resist, I shall give no quarter to any man of you, but will make an end of you entirely.'

'Well?' said Henry, into the silence that succeeded the reading. 'It is for you to decide. Privateering is a partnership, and it is for you to say. What shall I tell the Spanish commodore?'

'Tell him —' yelled a voice from the back.

And a great storm of laughter drowned the sentence before it was finished.

When Henry came down the wharf next morning, he found that they had put the finishing touch to the ship. They had given her a flag.

'Not the Union flag,' Bart explained, 'because we didn't like the idea of burning it. So we made her a flag of her own. Pretty, ain't it?'

The gay bit of nonsense flipped and wriggled above the lethal mass below, as if trying to be free of the mast before it was too late; but Bart looked at it proudly and the men with satisfaction. It was their answer to Spain.

They had loaded her from the still great store of powder that they had taken from the sea-fort, and, with their tireless ingenuity, had devised fire-crackers in place of musketry. She was a floating menace, and they loved her.

On the last day of April, with the slaves (willing and unwilling) in one ship, the prisoners for ransom (all unwilling) in another, and the treasure in a third, they weighed anchor and set their bows towards the sea. The three great warships were at anchor across the straits, directly below the fort; but as they saw the English fleet coming they up-anchored and hoisted sail so as to be able to manoeuvre.

Breathless, the men in the following ships watched as the fireship closed the *Magdalena.* If those twelve men failed to keep the *Magdalena* stern-on they would be at the mercy of her soaring tiers of guns; and all their labour and hopes of the last week, and the lives of twelve brave men besides, would be lost in an instant. But the ship, with her light load and her handiness, followed the slowly turning warship, lessening all the while the distance between them until she was within musket shot. The puzzled Spaniards met her with a crackle of light arms, but the next moment she was alongside and grappling, and they saw her at last for what she was. Frantically they tried to fend her off with boat-hooks and pikes, but it was too late. She burst into a rose of flame, and the men on one side of her moved back from the blaze while twelve men on the other side dropped from her deck to the water. Thirty seconds later she blew apart in a great fountain of burning fragments that soared to the great ship's topmost rigging and stuck there and burned. The *Magdalena* became outlined in flame, her yards dropped from their burning ropes and canvas to burn on the already burning deck. Panic-stricken, her crew came scrambling up from below and followed the original twelve to the safety of salt water. Her mainmast fell and listed her port side almost into the water. And just as the foremast was breaking out of the deck her magazine blew up. She settled slowly and disappeared altogether.

The *San Luis's* crew, watching in horror this destruction of the flag-ship, found the *Fortune* bearing down on them, and took it to be another fire-ship. Without waiting to take a second look, they beached their ship under the guns of the fort and set fire to her. If she was going to burn, then they would do the burning, and they would do it where they could step on shore first.

But the *Marquesa's* crew was made of better stuff. The *Marquesa* took on the *Fortune*, the *Gift* and the *Dolphin*, and kept them busy for nearly an hour before striking her flag to them, and when she had surrendered they filed one after another past her battered bulk and cheered her.

Then they lowered their boats to join the boats from the ships bearing the treasure and the prisoners, which had been lowered as soon as the *Magdalena* had blown up. But it seemed that the drowning Spaniards did not want to be rescued; indeed, they resisted it with fury. And the puzzled English, dragging struggling men into the boats, said to each other: 'What is it? Do they think we keep thumb-screws on board?' They learned afterwards that it was not fear of torture that made the Spaniards prefer death to rescue, but that they had all sworn an oath not to surrender on any conditions. At the time their seeming perversity merely exasperated their rescuers.

'Aah, you silly bastard,' said Bluey, hitting a man over the head with a piece of broken thwart and hoisting the stunned creature over the gunwale with no tender hand, 'if you must go to Heaven, do it in your own time, not mine.'

It was not the Spanish dislike for safety that made them desist in the end, but the fort on shore; which, now that there was no danger of crippling a Spanish ship, began to fire with a fine impartiality on rescued and rescuers alike. So the English ships left those who still remained in the water to swim to shore or cling to wreckage in the hope that their own countrymen would rescue them, and drew back a little into the lake again. They had still, somehow, to navigate those straits in front of the fort; and since the fort had now been strengthened by the complete crew of the beached *San Luis*, it was unlikely that they could solve the problem by taking the fort.

But there were other methods.

All next day the Spaniards in the fort watched boat-loads of English being rowed ashore to the beach behind the point. Boat after boat, heavy with men, wallowed from the distant ships to the shore and came back empty; until the Spaniards marvelled that seven small ships could carry such an army.

What they could not see at that distance was that the 'empty' boats going back to the ships were carrying a full load of men lying hidden in the bottom. That no one at all was being left on shore.

'Little did I ever think I'd row *you* as a passenger,' said Bluey to the large Tenerife, lying relaxed between his feet.

Up at the fort there were no 'passengers'. Everyone spent the day dragging the guns from the sea side to cover the land approaches, in piling ammunition, and in levelling various inequalities in the ground outside the fort so as to deprive the attack when it came of any possible cover.

They reckoned that the attack would come in the half-light after sunset.

But after sunset came the turn of the tide; and on the ebb came the English ships, floating past the fort in the half-light, silent and ghostly. For the first time since he went adventuring, the little *Fortune* did not carry Henry into action or lead her consorts to their work. The English ships were led out to sea by the twenty-four-gun *Marquesa*, Spanish ship of war, with Morgan on her quarter-deck.

And it was the *Marquesa's* guns that gave the fort the mocking seven-gun salute in return for the belated and out-of-range cannonading that was all the sweating and outwitted Spaniards could manage by way of protest.

And it was in the *Marquesa* that he came back to Port Royal.

'You're not deserting the *Fortune* altogether, are you?' asked Jack, after he had been conducted round all five decks of the *Marquesa* in Port Royal harbour and they were coming ashore in the very elegant little cockleshell that had been her captain's private property. 'Twenty-four guns isn't everything.'

'I'm tired of that poky little cabin in the *Fortune*,' said Henry, who had vastly enjoyed the luxury of the *Marquesa's* living quarters. 'Besides,' he said, catching Jack's sideways glance at him. 'I love a ship that fought well.'

'She'd have fought a deal better,' said the unimpressed Morris, 'if she was a bit handier. That hulk of guns and wood-carving couldn't get out of the way of a piece of driftwood. I wouldn't have her as a gift.'

'You're not being offered her,' Henry said, good-humoured; and then, with a sudden descent to gloom: 'Anyhow, she will have to be sold.'

'That shouldn't worry you,' Jack said. 'You're a planter from now on, aren't you?'

'If I'm not arrested,' Henry said, still gloomier; and went away to Kingshouse to take his medicine.

And this time it was no jam-coated purge.

'Maracaibo!' said Sir Thomas, pacing up and down the room with a quite unwonted vigour. 'Merciful Heaven, Harry, what madness moved you to an adventure like that! When the news first came in, a matter of ten days ago, I refused to believe it. He is rash, I said; he is even mad; but so far it has been a very methodical madness. He would never institute an attack for which he could find no vestige of excuse! *Have* you an excuse, Henry Morgan?'

'Not one that would satisfy their lordships, I'm afraid. But does it matter?'

'*Matter?*'

'When we do have an excuse, and offer them evidence in the enemy's own handwriting, the Spaniards merely say we are forging. We went to Puerto Bello "to anticipate the planned attack on Jamaica". Let us say that I went to Maracaibo as reprisal for one ship's captain and fifteen men hanged without trial in Havana.'

'That would hardly be an appropriate excuse at this moment,' Modyford said.

'It is an appropriate excuse at any time, if the men are English,' Morgan said, with a bite in his tone.

'You misunderstand me. It is inappropriate at this moment to remember the misdeeds of Havana, because I have been busy patching up a local peace with the Governor. If one cannot have peace from the top down, then our only hope is to begin from the bottom up, and make our little local peace and hope that it may spread.'

'And your Excellency thinks that the Governor of Cuba will respond?' Henry asked, still dry.

'His Excellency is of that opinion,' Modyford said, still drier. 'I am expecting Bernard Speirdyck back any day now, with the Governor's answer.'

'Why Bernard?'

'When he took the *Mary and Jane* in cargo to Cuba, I gave him all the Spanish prisoners we had here, for repatriation, and a letter to the Governor. And now, God help me, I have a Spanish warship captive in the harbour, and more prisoners than we have ever had before.'

'And thirty thousand pounds,' said Henry, making an entry on the credit side.

'Which we shall no doubt have to pay in compensation,' Modyford said, refusing the bait.

'Not if the Lord High Admiral smells it first,' said Henry, unrepentant. 'The Navy is so hard up, I understand, that they have to pawn the rudder to buy rope.'

'Oh, go home to Elizabeth, you unprincipled disturber of the peace —'

'*What* peace?'

'– and don't let me see you again until I can look at you without my choler rising.'

'When will that be, does your Excellency reckon?'

'You might try coming to dinner the day after tomorrow.'

The chastened Henry went away feeling that, considering the enormity of his crime, he had got off lightly; and two days later he presented himself at Kingshouse prepared to help the Governor in the concoction of dispatches for home consumption. He had come by invitation, and to dinner; and he was surprised when the Governor kept him waiting. Was it possible that Sir Thomas was seriously angry? Was he being put in his place?

When at last he was shown into the long library that the Governor habitually used as a living-room, he had the impression that someone had just been pushed out of sight into the little parlour off it; and this surprised him even more. Lady Modyford had come back from England and was living out at Morant; which left Sir Thomas ample scope for intrigue if he had wanted it; but even at his loneliest the Governor had always had a reputation for austere self-sufficiency, and it was hardly likely that he was entertaining a surreptitious petticoat.

Morgan watched him as he poured wine for his visitor; and thought that he had never seen that fine, cool face so distracted by private emotion. What could be moving Modyford to that extent?

The Governor asked for Elizabeth, and inquired about progress at Morgan's Valley, without giving the impression of being really aware of what he was saying. He even inquired about Henry's health when he was in South America.

'You escaped the fever?'

'Yes. Four of my men died of it, and some have brought it back with them. But I have escaped so far.'

'That is good.'

He had never seen Modyford like this before.

A small sound came from the farther room, and the Governor winced as though it had been a thunder-clap.

Because he was sorry for him and anxious to relieve the unacknowledged tension, Henry broached the obvious subject for conversation: the matter of his own misdeeds. Since the commission given to him by the Governor had been granted at the request of the Council of Jamaica, he said, would it not be possible for the Council to take the beating? A council had a broad back and no individual feelings whatever – especially when they unanimously approved both of the Maracaibo expedition and of the thirty thousand pounds that were going to be spent largely in Jamaica. The Council would not mind being whipping-boy in such a good cause, surely?

'We shall not need a whipping-boy,' Modyford said.

'Not need one? Why?'

'Because we have been reprieved. And I wish with all my heart that it were not so.'

'Who has reprieved us?' Henry asked, watching the Governor get up and walk to that inner door.

'One Manoel Rivera Pardal,' the Governor said.

Since this meant nothing to Henry, he was still at a loss.

'You had better hear the story for yourself,' Modyford said, opening the door and revealing the figure that was waiting there.

It was Cornelius.

The boy's thatch of blond hair hung limp and lustreless, and his eyes were sunk in his head. He looked old and tired; at the end of his tether. He was clutching a woollen cap between his hands and twisting it in an odd, childish, not quite sane fashion.

'Come in, Cornelius,' Modyford said gently. 'Captain Morgan is here now.'

The boy came into the room, still wringing the cap, and sat down on the edge of a chair without taking his eyes from Morgan's for a moment.

'Cornelius came to me first,' Modyford said, 'because he could not find you. I told him that you were out at Morgan's Valley but that you would be here to dinner in a very short time.'

'They must pay for it, Captain,' the boy said. 'They must pay for it.'

'For what, Cornelius?'

'For the *Mary and Jane*. For Bernard. And the others.'

Henry looked up at Modyford as the significance of this came home to him.

'Is *this* our reprieve?'

'Yes.'

'Merciful God!'

Since the boy was without words, Modyford went on:

'They were quite well received in Cuba, and allowed to trade their cargo. And Bernard was given a receipt for his prisoners and a letter of thanks from the Governor for me. Then two days out on the voyage back to Jamaica they met a ship flying the English colours and sent two men in a boat to her for news. As soon as the two men were on board, the stranger fired a broadside that crippled the *Mary and Jane*, so that she had to stay and fight. They fought for three hours. By that time she was on fire fore and aft.'

'Did she sink?'

'No,' Cornelius said, although the question had been asked of Modyford. 'They boarded us and put the fires out. We could not put them out ourselves because by that time we were too few.'

'How many?'

'Nine.'

The *Mary and Jane* had had a crew of eighteen.

'Was Bernard one of the nine?'

'No.'

'How was it, Cornelius?'

'A splinter in the throat. A big splinter. As thick as my wrist.'

'And this ship. Who was she?'

'The *San Pedro y La Fama*; Captain Pardal.'

'What size?'

'Ninety-six men and twenty guns.'

'*And* a commission to wage war,' said Modyford.

'*What!*'

'To be exact, two commissions.'

'From whom?'

'One from the Queen Regent of Spain, "for five years through the whole West Indies as reprisal for Puerto Bello". And one from the Governor of Cartagena; which seems to be the *San Pedro's* home port.'

'What have they done with the *Mary and Jane*?'

'They turned the nine of us loose in our longboat, and took the *Mary and Jane* to Cartagena,' Cornelius said, still with those unwavering eyes on Morgan's. 'They have to pay for it, Captain. They have to pay for it.'

'Never fear, Cornelius. They'll pay.'

'And you'll take me with you to the paying?'

'I'll take you with me.'

His thoughts went to Mary Speirdyck as he had seen her two days ago, sitting in her spotless little room above the harbour, playing with her baby son.

'He is so like Bernard,' she had said, laughing. 'So like Bernard when Bernard is wakening up after a nap.' And she had added, soberly: 'This one will live. It is a green, kindly country, Yamaica: good to be little in. Not like Curaçao.'

How would Mary take this? This cutting in two of her life? This catastrophe on the threshold of happiness.

And who would tell her?

In the end it was Morgan who told her. And she neither wept nor blasphemed. She looked at her child in its cot, and said: 'By the time he grows up men will have found how to live without fighting.'

And Morgan went away envying her this small fragment of the future to which she could cling for salvation. For him there was only the present; and anger tore him night and day like a mortal disease.

He took the *Marquesa* as his share of the Maracaibo prize-money, and repaired and refitted her with money that should have gone to the improvement of Morgan's Valley; and when

Modyford asked what he planned to do with her, Henry said: 'I have an invitation to Panama.'

And Modyford for once made neither criticism nor protest.

On the contrary, he was lavish with Government stores; and more resigned than usual to the good-natured barbarities of the privateers-men who swarmed in Port Royal. (Their favourite ploy was to broach a barrel of wine in the street and make all who passed drink to the current toast.) It was almost as if he saw an end coming, and wanted, before that final line, whatever it might be, was drawn, to have done with half-measures, and compensations, and balances, and fence-sitting.

His only comment was made when he learned the size of the fleet that Henry proposed to take out with him.

'You won't forget that peace treaty that they are still playing with in Europe, will you, Harry? If they ratify it, you will not be able to take any fleet out.'

'Don't worry,' Henry said. 'The fleet will be ready before the ratification.'

But, as it turned out, it was a near thing.

When Henry went to say good-bye to the Governor before sailing for his rendezvous in the Cays, he knew that letters had come by the ship which had touched at Port Royal that morning, and he cast an anxious look at the papers that littered the Governor's desk. Modyford saw the glance and smiled.

'Not yet, Harry. But any day now. I have had private letters. Spain has been moved to concessions.'

'What moved her?' said Henry. 'Puerto Bello?'

'Oddly enough, yes. Or so I think. They have been hit so often and so dangerously that it begins to dawn on them that they can no longer consider themselves sole proprietors of the West. There seems to have been one good event to our mutual villainy.'

But Henry was staring at the table.

'What interests you?'

'My name.'

'You read upside-down?'

'Oh, with ease. Would it be graceless of me to ask what your correspondent says of me?'

'It is not a letter, Harry. It is a notice that was found stuck on a tree near St Ann's Bay.'

He handed over the paper, and Henry read it aloud; with some difficulty, because the ink had run and the script was foreign.

'"This, from Captain Manoel Rivera Pardal, is to the chief of privateers in Jamaica. I am he who took Captain Speirdyck and carried the prize to Cartagena, and I am now arrived on this coast and have burnt it —" *Burnt?*'

'Yes. Five of the little farms between St Ann's Bay and Dry Harbour.'

'Just the buildings?'

'No, they devastated the place. Set fire to the plantations, and took away both slaves and whites as prisoners. Old Cary and his daughter are both dead; and so are the two Lawton brothers, and Phil Burstall and his wife.'

There was a silence. Henry's glance went back to the paper, and he read slowly: '"I am come to seek Admiral Morgan, with two ships of war of twenty guns each, and I challenge him to come out and meet me that he may see the valour of Spain."'

He stood a long moment looking at the paper.

'The valour of Spain,' he said. He folded the paper and put it in his pocket. 'Since the communication is addressed to me you will not object to my keeping it. You were not going to tell me about this?'

'No.'

'Why?'

'You were leaving today. It seemed a useless – exacerbation.'

'Don't tell me about that ratification either. That would be a far worse exacerbation.'

'I shall have to send it to you in the Cays if it comes in time, Harry.'

'Then mark it: "Not to be opened".'

'I can hardly do that.'

'Then frank it: "The valour of Spain",' Henry said savagely, 'and I shall keep it to read to Don Juan Perez de Guzman in Panama.'

And he went away with a hot heart and a cold mind to meet the fleet he had summoned to the rendezvous.

It was a very pretty sight, the fleet, if a little lacking in homogeneity – the smallest volunteer being a ten-ton sloop – and this time he had seen to it that his commission made him not only leader but master of it. Never again would he be helpless against the irresponsibility of the baser sort as he had been at Maracaibo. He was by his commission sole commander of those who chose to sail with him; and his fleet accepted that condition with a readiness that was flattering. Most of them had the wit to know that the strict discipline for which Harry Morgan was notorious had had no small share in the successes which had made him famous. And all of them would have served anyhow, with no conditions at all, under a man who had taken his first ship with eleven men in their stocking soles and Puerto Bello with a handful of men and some muskets.

Even the French came back, in the person of a tall, thin chestnut-coloured man who came on board and said, with his chestnut-coloured eyes twinkling: 'I was right about the panache, Admiral. We should have trusted your flair, and followed you to Puerto Bello. Now that our peoples are friends again at home, may we perhaps follow you to Cuba?'

'And if it happened not to be the rumoured invasion of Cuba, Captain Gascoone?'

'We will follow you anywhere, Admiral. A man like you is born only once in a century.'

So the French came back; four fine frigates, a ketch and three sloops; and the seas in the lee of the Cays were thick with sail. Sometimes, looking across the anchorage at the little *Fortune*, Henry was filled with a regret that was one part sentimentalism and one part superstition. He had given the command of her to that Robert Delander for whom the English ambassador had spoken in Madrid and who had been turned loose, penniless and without compensation, in Spain; and he felt that no more appropriate transfer could have been found for her. But the regretful feeling, half love, half doubt, shot through him each time he caught sight of her, riding so lightly on the still water, so intimate, so familiar, so feminine; and the feeling annoyed him very much. How could he, Admiral of a fleet, sail in the *Fortune*, or receive visitors in that humble little cabin that

Manuel had once made hideous with trophies of the chase? It was absurd even to think of it. Her name was mere chance; just something that he had thought up himself. He might as easily have called her the *Prosperous* or the *Queen* or a score of other names. It meant nothing that her name was *Fortune* and that he had deserted her. Nothing whatever.

They spent the bad-weather months making ready, and adding to their provisions from the game on shore. But by November they were ready to sail, and Jack Morris had still not turned up at the rendezvous. And Henry was torn with anxiety. Not Jack, his mind said. Anyone but Jack.

But Jack came up over the horizon one morning in his usual leisurely, effortless fashion, in company with a twenty-gun frigate.

'Who is your recruit?' asked Henry, when he came on board.

'That bastard' said Jack 'had the impudence to try to pot me like a sitting bird when I was watering at Two Mile Cay.'

'Is she *Spanish*?'

'She was,' said Jack. 'She came prancing in and fired a whole broadside at us without so much as a hail.'

'What is her name?'

'She's the *San Pedro y La Fama*.'

There was a moment's silence.

Then Morgan said: 'Send me over the captain of her.'

'Pardal?' said Jack. 'I can't. He's dead.'

14

DON JUAN PEREZ DE GUZMAN, far away in the safe and lovely city of Panama, had not even remembered that gift of an emerald ring except as a story to tell sometimes over dinner. The elegance of the gesture had pleased him, and it had pleased him even more that he should have had the final word. For of course the affair was finished. Spain had suffered a disgrace at Puerto Bello, but he had by a fine gesture taken some of the blackness from her shame; and so he could sit back and feel at peace again. Over on the Atlantic coast the jealous mendicants who clung to the rich petticoats of Spain would no doubt continue to raid the settlements if opportunity offered; but here, on the other side of the continent, on the calm Pacific coast, there was only Spain. Nothing but Spain along the whole sweep of two continents. Spain unchallenged; rich, and settled, and secure.

So Don Juan heard the news of Maracaibo without being markedly discommoded. He noted that the hero of it was that Morgan creature again, and in a passing thought regretted that the creature was not Spanish. There was no doubt that Spain could do with an infusion of the ferocious energy and willingness to take risks which characterised the Islanders. He turned over his collection of gems, and decided to give the second-best string of pearls to the Virgin in the Cathedral, by way of averting the evil eye.

When his friend, the Governor of Cartagena, wrote to say that a great fleet of mixed English and French ships was at sea and making southward to the Isthmus, he was still undisturbed. But he did go and have a look at the little pistol and its six bullets. And he gave the Virgin the ruby bracelet that he had intended for his mistress.

The news that the fleet was actually approaching the Atlantic coast of Panama roused him to send reinforcements to Puerto Bello. And as a further insurance he presented the Virgin with one of his most prized relics: a toe-bone of St Peter.

And having done all that mortal man and faithful believer could in the matter, he left the Atlantic Coast to take care of itself. He propped his bad leg on its silk cushions, and prepared to go on enjoying his sunlit peace as much as his erysipelas would let him. Around him was all the best of two worlds: the elegances of the Old, and the beauty and fabulous wealth of the New. And he could enjoy it with no one to disturb or hinder.

When a messenger came to say that the English had made a landing on the Atlantic coast, he said: 'Well, well. They have landed before. The road from Puerto Bello to Panama can be held by a handful of men: as we found to our cost when we wanted to go the other way.'

'But they have not landed at Puerto Bello,' said the messenger. 'They have landed at Chagres.'

'That is unusually stupid of them,' said Don Juan. 'There is nothing at Chagres but a quite impregnable fort on a precipice, and a quite impenetrable forest behind it.'

'It is no doubt monumentally stupid of them, as your Excellency suggests, but it has been to a certain degree successful.'

'To what degree, may one ask?'

'They have taken the fort at Chagres.'

'Nonsense,' said Don Juan.

'Yes, your Excellency,' said the messenger, submissive.

'By what mortal agency could a fort on the top of a precipice be taken?' And as the snubbed messenger did not reply: 'Well?'

'Hand-grenades and determination, your Excellency,' said the messenger, goaded by the snubbing.

'And what are the egregious English doing now that they have the harbour at Chagres?' said the Governor, tacitly admitting the possibility.

'They are coming up the river in boats.'

'They will not get very far,' Don Juan said. 'Neither hand-grenades nor determination will provide them with water to float their boats after the recent drought.'

And this was the one thing that Don Juan was right about in all the story of the Panama campaign.

The thing he was most wrong about was the supposition that a lack of water in the river would stop the English. Even while the messenger was talking to him on the terrace above the blue Pacific, the 'egregious English' were transferring light arms, food and ammunition from the last of their lightest-draught boats to their own backs. If the river had failed them, then they would reach Panama by foot through the forest.

It was Joe Bradley who had taken the fort at Chagres, and he had died in doing it, and thirty of his men besides. It was the most spectacular achievement on the part of the English in all the story of the Americas, and it had been accomplished in the face of a Spanish resistance that was heroic beyond praise.

'Tell Harry when he comes that we opened the way for him,' Joe said when he was dying.

And Morgan, when he came into Chagres, felt that a bit of him had died with Bradley.

Morgan had stayed behind to collect Santa Catalina. If this was, as it seemed, to be his last voyaging, then it was time to see to it that Santa Catalina should be Old Providence again, and a place for Englishmen and their cherry-trees once more. He came into the harbour at Chagres thinking how pleased Mansfield would have been that his little island was English again. ('There it sits, my nice little island, on all the routes across the Caribbean'), only to learn that he had lost Bradley.

'Was there *nothing* you could have done to save him?' he said to Exmeling.

'Nothing, Captain,' Exmeling said with that oracular condescension that is so maddening to the layman.

But Morgan, too moved to be tactful, still looked doubtful; and Exmeling's too thin skin was chafed. Not for the first time.

The English were dog-tired long before they reached the point where they had to abandon their boats. Their progress up the river had not been either a lazy water-borne journey or a steady pull. It had been an endless series of portages; of transferring equipment to shore and hauling the boats through the rapids and then wearily reloading. It had been sometimes, in the later stages, a matter of lugging the boats themselves overland to the next possible navigable water. So that it was with a sense of relief that the men, soldier and sailor alike, said goodbye to the river altogether and took to the forest 'light'; with nothing but what they carried on their own backs.

It was with this equipment that they proposed to take Panama, and already the weaker spirits were vocal.

The hot, damp forest depressed them. The inability to see more than a few yards ahead. The steaming, oven atmosphere. The physical effort of shouldering loads over the pathless uneven ground. The million biting insects. The snakes. The creepers that felt like snakes. The rotten branches that looked like snakes.

And presently, worst of all, the glimpse of half-seen naked

brown bodies through the leaves, and the knowledge that they were not alone in the forest. That they were being escorted every step of the way by Spanish Indians.

Not all that marching file of nearly twelve hundred men were easily impressed, by either the forest or the invisible enemy. Tom Roger's crew, to whom had been given the honour and ardours of advance guard, hacked their way hour by hour through the virgin forest; and when their turn to be relieved came refused to give up their place. And directly behind these came surely the strangest sight ever to have been witnessed by a Central American jungle: two hundred men in the red coats of the Commonwealth army. Nothing at all – snakes, Indians, mosquitoes, creepers or steaming heat – dismayed these veterans. When every sailor in the column had discarded everything but shirt and breeches, the old New Model men were still wearing their red coats; of which they were inordinately proud. And when every sailor in the column had consumed his last crumb of food, the red coats still had their rations almost intact.

It was in this matter of food that the rot became apparent. Morgan had expected to provision his men from the country; from the small stockaded settlements that studded the river at intervals. But as they came out into each clearing by the water-side, they found the same deserted village and the same still-smoking ruins. The Spaniards had cleared out and had left nothing consumable behind them. The buildings had all been wood-built and thatched with palm, and they had burned with a satisfying ease and completeness. The hungry men prowled among the charred wreck for something that might still be eatable, and quarrelled bitterly over a handful of cindery corn or some brittle beans.

Then fever came to add its vapours to their misery. And men marched through an unreal world in which not texture, distance nor sound had any validity. On feet that felt like pillows, or on feet that seemed to have no existence at all.

The seriously ill were left in the deserted river clearings, to be fetched by canoe and taken back to Chagres, and the others who could still walk and keep direction stumbled on with the aid of their stronger fellows.

On the evening of their second day without food, they came on a cave with two sacks of meal, a few bunches of plantains, and two jars of wine; and Morgan stood over the food with a pistol while it was divided among the sick and exhausted. This saved a few more from having to be sent back by canoe, but even the fact that he had no mouthful of it himself did not endear him to the men who had discovered the cache.

'Cheer up,' said Morgan. 'Tomorrow we shall reach Venta de Cruz, and there we can eat our fill. At Venta de Cruz the forest ends and the road to Panama is open.'

But between them and Venta de Cruz lay a new hazard and a new terror. The dim light of the forest grew darker and the country closed round them, soaring above them to unseen heights; and it was apparent that their only advance must be through a gorge in front of them. This was unnerving enough to men exhausted and half-starving, but it was now that the half-seen enemy who had tagged them so long chose to attack them. A soft flight of arrows fell on the first men to enter the gorge. By sheer luck the volley had been dispatched too soon, so that the arrows fell harmlessly in front of them, and with this warning they covered with continuous musket-fire each party to go through the defile. But even so, only the hope of food, and the sheer impossibility of retracing their steps to find any, hounded them through the pass. By now the soldiers were chewing their leather belts, and the crews were eating leaves.

They came out into the light, still attended by their invisible foes, and made their way down to Venta de Cruz like homing horses; all of a sudden confident and good-tempered. The Indians, kept by the covering fire too far away for accurate aim, fell back on mocking shouts in Spanish, and the men replied in kind. Presently they would eat. Venta de Cruz was the place where goods coming by road up from Panama were loaded on to boats for passage down the river to Chagres. At Venta de Cruz would be storehouses full of food. At Venta de Cruz would be an end both to their hunger and to the struggle through virgin forest. They were jubilant.

At Venta de Cruz, in fact, were one sack of bread, and fifteen jars of Peruvian wine.

Nothing was alive in the burnt-out village and the empty warehouses but a few stray dogs.

Those lucky enough to catch the dogs killed and ate them.

The first to reach the wine drank it down on their unprepared stomachs and dropped in their tracks insensible. The unlucky dropped in their tracks anyhow, and lay there; too far beyond emotion for either cursing or tears.

In the morning they got gingerly on to their swollen feet and began their march over the cobbles of the road to Panama. It was their eighth day out from Chagres, and all that they had left was their muskets, their ammunition and the spirit that kept them going. It was fantastic that this column of dazed and unshaven scarecrows proposed to take a city.

Although they no longer had to hack their way, the forest was still round them as they hobbled over the rough mule-path, and the attendant Indians were still there. Every now and then the soft, bird's-wing sound of a chance arrow would startle a man out of his coma, or a mocking yell from the bush would set the column cursing.

They came in the evening to open country at last; the blue haze of stinging flies grew less as the wind rose, and the Indians, deprived of cover, left them alone. They bivouacked for the night in open savanna, where three stone-built shepherd's huts, empty but unburned, offered shelter for the sick. And there their final wretchedness came upon them.

It rained.

It rained as it can rain only in the tropics with the wind behind it. Like whips, like rods, like cat-o'-nine-tails. They lay on the wet earth, without cover, without hope, and almost without caring. Nothing more could happen to them.

Morgan, lying on the sodden grass and enduring his first bout of fever, was conscious only that he had been saved from disaster by the presence of those stone huts. For in the huts, along with the sickest men, was the ammunition. Whatever else had happened to them, their powder was still dry. They were still an army.

In the morning he was still light-headed enough to be full of secret plans for making the three little stone huts into a great church, as a thank-offering for his deliverance; and he had difficulty in collecting his thoughts when he addressed the men. The words would not come out of his mouth in the right order without the most careful marshalling. But the men were more interested in the matter than the style, and the matter pleased them. Today, he told them, on this ninth day of their march from the sea, they would reach the top of the slope from which they could look down on Panama. That was the ridge, in front of them, and they would reach it before noon.

They listened to him in attentive silence, their wet clothes steaming in the sun; and Bluey put into words the feeling of every man in the crowd when he said: 'Panama's the richest town in the world, they say, and all I want out of it is a beef-steak!'

Their minds were so filled with the anticipation of food that they failed to anticipate the sight of the sea. It took them unawares, and with the most surprising result. What not the thought of their survival, of the riches of Panama, nor of the food to come had done, the sight of the sea achieved. Their dead minds wakened into wild glory; wave after wave of mad cheering rolled to and fro along the ridge; and when their empty bodies would no longer cheer they stood there laughing like maniacs because there was the sea.

It was a blue and smiling sea, if distant; studded with small islands and flecked with sails. The town lay at its edge, bright and shining and washed after the storm, very clear in the morning air, like the little landscape that Italian painters liked to put by the left ear of some Madonna. In the plain between the slope and the city the light splintered on the helmets of manoeuvring cavalry, but the English had no eyes for the troops. Just below them on the green plain were droves of cattle, placidly grazing. Fine fat cattle. Beautiful cattle. Magnificent cattle.

They went down the slope singing, built their fires, and for the first time for seven days sat down to a meal. The half-raw steaks, still warm from the slaughter, slid down their throats without benefit of teeth. The fires looked gay and home-like – as the sea had looked. Their strung-up bodies relaxed, and one by one they lay back and slept; gorged and at peace.

Only Morgan did not sleep. He lay in the meagre shade and tried to keep his thoughts clear. Presently he would have to face all the appurtenances of war: artillery, cavalry and foot. He looked round at the recumbent bodies: shabby, half-naked, untidy and worn; and reckoned as far as his unruly mind would let him. Reckoned their spirit against the power of Panama. Affection rose in him as he looked at them. They had cursed him, these last few days; cursed him for bringing them on a fool's errand; there were times in the forest when some of them would have liked to kill him. But even in their sleep, he noticed, there was no supineness of spirit. Each man slept with his arms about his musket, and his ammunition to hand. Bart had even spread his coat over his as an insurance against a repetition of last night's deluge before he wakened.

Morgan's eye lingered on Bart, and a more personal worry swam up out of the whirling ends of thought that filled his head. Bart had aged greatly since his servitude on the fortifications of San Jeronimo, and Morgan had wanted him to stay behind at Chagres, but Bart would have none of it. Indeed, he had been so hurt at the suggestion that Henry had wished that he had not made it. Now, looking at Bart asleep, he wished that he had insisted. This was no work for a man who must be nearly sixty. Bart should be back on the ship, sitting in the shade with his scissors and his measuring tape and his sail-cloth.

He propped himself on his elbow and leaned over to draw the edge of the old man's coat forward so that it made a shade for his face; and as he did it the light caught the emerald on his finger, and the direction of his thoughts changed. He lay back and smiled. Worried he might be, and uncertain with fever, but he had a notion that the state of Don Juan Perez de Guzman must at this moment be a great deal more feverish than his was ever likely to be.

And in that he was right.

When the fugitives from the stockades on the river arrived in Panama with the news that the incredible English, baffled by the shallow river, were now advancing through the forest, Don Juan sent out Indian irregulars to keep the English in the forest and had himself carried to the Cathedral, where he presented the

Virgin with a diamond ring worth four thousand pieces and swore an oath to die in her defence.

When the Indians came back to say that the English caught their arrows in mid-air and shot them back (with muskets, presumably) and were now through the forest and out on the savanna, and feasting on stolen cattle, Don Juan ordered that the Virgin should be taken out of the church and carried in procession round the town, attended by the complete fraternity of St Francis, the nuns of Our Lady of Rosario, of San Domingo and of the Mercedes, and all the images of the saints and patrons belonging to all these bodies. He was once more going through his collection of jewels with a view to further insurance (with side-glances now and then at the little pistol with its six bullets) when his cavalry commander, Don Francisco de Haro, came to say that if the English were feasting on meat after their ardours in the forest they would tonight be so dead asleep that they could be surprised and butchered where they lay, and the whole matter would be ended in an hour.

Don Juan considered this a wonderful idea; and was very much disappointed next morning when his cavalry commander came back to report that Morgan had had the same idea.

'He had his men roused at two o'clock in the morning,' reported Don Francisco, frustrated but admiring. 'An Englishman who thinks is a very dangerous animal, Excellency.'

This was the final, insupportable straw. Don Juan made a complete sweep of all that he valued ('all my jewels and relics collected in my pilgrimages,' as he reported sorrowfully to Madrid) and divided them between all the other images in town. ('Hedging his bets', as Jack said later, comparing the dazzling Virgin of Don Juan's devotion with the after-thought-upon saints and madonnas.)

And then, denuded of all but faith, he prepared to honour his oath to die in defence of Our Lady of the Immaculate Conception at Panama, by taking the field at the head of his troops.

When Morgan saw the troops he could hardly believe his eyes. It was like a child's game on some nursery floor. All laid out, neat and bright and orthodox and static. Cannon in front, infantry behind, and cavalry on either flank. He had lived so long in a guerilla world that he had forgotten that war could still be waged like this.

'Ain't they pretty?' said Bluey, sucking his teeth.

And truly they were pretty. Their clothes were bright-coloured, their metal glittered, their guns gleamed, their horses shone, their banners flowered in the sun.

There was only one thing lacking in this brilliant array; as Don Juan did not fail to report to Madrid. It was the thing in which the sad-coloured thousand facing them were so rich: heart. More than fifteen hundred of them, said Don Juan, were arrant cowards and not Spanish at all; and the Spanish, on the other hand, had no faith in the arms they had to fight with. A carbine, they felt, was no match for a musket, even at odds of six to one; and anyhow they had not fired anything at all for years except some fowling-pieces in their off-time. The gunners were in even worse shape; they were frankly terrified of the temperamental monsters they were required to fire. The heretical English seemed almost friendly compared with a mass of metal that might blow up in their faces.

The heretical English were at that moment hearing their own version of the Mass, and commending their souls to their Maker. As firmly as they believed in nothing in this world they believed in the next. So they knelt on the soft savanna grass and recited their prayers, demure and trusting as children.

'I gave strict command that none should move without my order,' wrote Don Juan to Madrid; but even trained troops will not stand to be fired on from the scrub on their flank. The Spaniards had considered that scrub to be impenetrable; but the English, who had bested a dry river and a virgin forest, were in no mood to be defeated by some scrub. Jack Morris's crew sat comfortably in the dense cover of the little hill and picked off the troops below them at their leisure. This was entirely contrary to the book of rules, and Don Juan was dismayed. But Don Francisco came to his help.

'I told you the animal thinks, Excellency. We must not give him further time to think. Let me charge him with my cavalry. He has no cannon, and we shall not give him time to reload his muskets after the first volley. We can mow his troops down.'

And once again Spanish cavalry came charging to their lesson on English musketry. It was not one volley that met them. As the front rank fired, the second rank took their place; cool and deliberate, as if they were shooting for a prize. And when the second volley had been fired, the third rank had their turn. The thundering line of horse which a moment before had seemed a wave of destruction that nothing could stop broke, and withered, and died along the whole front of the English line as the surf dies against a rock.

Don Francisco, looking at his shattered squadrons as they cantered back to safety, decided that orthodox methods were too expensive. He came to Don Juan with a new suggestion.

'A herd of cattle!' said Don Juan, shocked to the soul. 'But that is a most – a most *ungentlemanly* method.'

'It is a question of living as plain men or dying as gentlemen,' said Don Francisco, tart from his lesson in musketry. 'It is for your Excellency to say.'

His Excellency decided, therefore, to abandon the book of rules and overwhelm his enemy by some effective barbarism. To wit: the close-packed and irresistible mass of a bolting herd of wild cattle.

'One must sacrifice the graces of life when necessity drives,' said Don Juan, feeling smirched by this lowly stratagem. 'At least we have the comfort of knowing that our sacrifice will be decisive. No man born of woman can stand still in front of a charging herd of cattle.'

The old New Model could.

And did.

Cavalry, snakes, Indian arrows, starvation or charging cattle, it was all one to them. They knelt and fired into the brute mass as methodically as they would meet any other attack. By numbers. On the spot.

As the front row of cattle succumbed to the volley, the beasts behind fell over them, and their combined bodies made a natural barricade that dammed the full weight of the charge. Those animals who were forced, by panic or by the impulse from behind, to surmount the struggling mass were daunted by the bright-coloured barrier that waited for them and fled along the line in search of escape. So that a black thundering river flowed harmless along the waiting English line, and the redcoats poured volleys in at their leisure. They would need meat anyhow.

This seeming miracle was too much for the Spanish army. The rear ranks began to melt away.

And in the silence that succeeded the drumming roar of the stampeding herd, Jack's fore-top-ahoy voice yelled from the scrub on the Spanish flank: 'Come on, Harry! They're breaking!'

As the English came on, 'the retreat' as Morgan said, also reporting to superiors 'became plain running'.

'They left me there with one Negro and one servant,' wrote Don Juan to Madrid, 'but I went forward alone to meet the enemy so as to comply with my promise to the Virgin to die in her defence. But my chaplain protested that this was not Christian. Twice I rebuked him, but on his protesting a third time I retired, it being a miracle of the Virgin to bring me off safe among so many thousand bullets.'

The English, sore about that herd of cattle, pursued the flying Spaniards *con amore*, but Don Juan Perez de Guzman was not one of their victims. Don Juan got away to the hills, bad leg and all, and sat there writing letters to Spain.

15

THAT NIGHT the city of Panama burned.

The proud Spaniards said that they had fired it to prevent its falling into English hands.

The unimpressed English pointed out that the panic-stricken Spaniards were in such haste to blow up the main fort that they not only killed forty of their own men, but scattered burning fragments for a mile all round, and that it was this rain of burning brands from the explosion that set the roofs on fire.

What is certain is that the English, who had looked forward to the delights of food and sleep, spent the hot, windy night in frantic effort to put out the flames. No one would pay ransom for a burned-out town. But the wind blew, and the flames roared; and the ransom went down-wind and up with the flames. When dawn came there remained only the stone heart of the town: the courts, churches, convents, hospitals, stores, and the more palatial houses. The elegant little cedar-wood houses had perished along with the palm-thatched wattle of the slaves' quarters.

The stone-built part of the town, oddly Moorish in this far Pacific setting, was intact; and when Henry installed himself among the mirrors and damasks of the Governor's house, he found the staff still there, and openly philosophical about this change of owners. The Governor, said Domenico, the black major-domo, had promised that 'no harm would come to them because he had given the house into the Virgin's charge'.

'If no harm comes to you,' said Henry, tired and caustic, 'it will be because the English are civilized.'

He looked at the great bed in the Governor's room, piled high with soft pillows and hung with thick silk that would shut out a disappointing and importunate world, and every bone in him ached to lie down on that softness and sleep; and sleep, and sleep. Making himself walk away from it and downstairs again had the quality of a physical tearing, as burned flesh sticks to the thing that has mastered it. There could be no sleep yet for a man with a city in his hands. Even before he had chosen an office from the ground-floor rooms, the stream of callers began. Senior officers complaining, junior officers wanting advice, men wanting instructions. The long tale of incident; of the unforeseen and the unallowed-for. The incipient quarrels, the arbitrations. Burial parties, pickets, guards, deputations. Billets, commissariat, reconnaissance, medical supplies, lines of communication. It went on all through the long, hot morning, and far into the afternoon.

The most urgent business was to get into commission again the one ship left in the harbour – grounded by the Spaniards – and with her help bring back the ship which had taken all the rich inhabitants out of Panama with all their portable treasure. This gratifying job (they had not expected to find any ship at all for their use) kept the seamen busy and out of mischief for the next two days, and they sweated so heroically in this good cause (as much to spite the Spaniard as to recover the treasure) that on the third day Ansell took the ship to sea.

Henry had just grown used to the thought that there would be no ransom for Panama, when Ansell came back to say that there was no hope of finding the escaped grandees or their treasure, since the ship bearing them had stood straight out to sea bound for Peru. He had, however, brought in three other refugee ships which he had found at the small islands off the coast, together with the refugees themselves, who had settled down to a normal luxurious existence in supposed safety on Tobago and the other islands in the vicinity.

'Are your prisoners still on board?' asked Morgan.

'The men were on one ship, and I've unloaded them into the customs-house on the quay. They're quite resigned to being prisoners. But the women want to go back to their homes now that they are here in Panama again. They say that you can ransom them just as easily from there.'

'Of course they can't go home,' Morgan said, impatient. 'They must go to a convent. The Rosario is half empty; they can go there.'

'I wish you'd tell them that,' Ansell said, shamefaced. 'I don't mind admitting they put the fear of God in me. I'd as soon have a mutinous crew in a ship on fire in a hurricane, as sail with that crowd of peacocks. You tell them yourself, Admiral, will you?'

'I'll tell them,' said Morgan, very grim. 'You send the men up to the Franciscans and ask the brothers to billet them in the chapel if they have no spare cells; and then bring the women ashore to the customs-house. I'll see them there when I've inspected your captured ships.'

The three captured ships, added to the one they already had, made a small fleet, and the possibilities in this so interested Henry that he had to be reminded of the existence of the women. He went to the customs-house with swift, impatient steps, prepared to be short with female preferences. The last week had sucked him almost dry: dry of vitality, of humour, and of joy in living. He had taken twelve hundred cursing and half-dead men across the Isthmus. He had fought a battle with them, and won it. He had wrestled with a burning city, and now he was saddled with the administration of a province. And he was sucked dry. His sick blood played traitor to his will, and every day or two he found himself having to deal with the world through a haze of unreality that was worse than pain. Intangible spider-web bonds that were strong as chains would hold him where he sat, so that getting up was like the tearing of cables. His thoughts stuck, or floated away beyond his control, so that the effort of forcing them into order sickened and exasperated him. Nor was night a respite. He lay in the soft cushions of the great bed, sleepless and weary, watching the hours pass. At dawn he would slip into an exhausted insensibility, and two hours later would be on his feet again to face another day of self-driving.

He strode into the customs-house in no tolerant mood, and addressed Ansell's 'peacocks' with bite and precision. This was one of his lucid days, and he made the most of it: it was luxury to have the words come neat and appropriate from his tongue without having first to arrange them in his mind. It was absurd, he told them, to suggest that they should be scattered over the town as it seemed good to them. They were there to be ransomed, and until they were ransomed they would stay where they could be found.

But we can be found in our homes, they protested.

He doubted it, said Henry. He very much doubted it. The town was open to the countryside, without barricade or fortification, as it had always been. The temptation to depart would be very great. And if they thought that he had men to spare for a separate guard on each of them, then they were wrong. It was ridiculous, he said —

And stopped there.

He heard the silence that flooded in on his broken sentence.

What had happened? Had his fever come back? What had stopped his thoughts?

He struggled with the silence, but had no power to break it.

In a dumb panic he sought for the source of his distraction, and found it. It was the Madonna by the doorway to the quay.

It was a living Madonna, for all her stillness and repose. Warm and alive, for all her calm gaze and her folded hands.

He took his eyes away and tried to think what he had been saying. Something about a guard. A guard for someone. A guard. A guard. A guard. She must be alive, because the lace on her bosom had been moving. Something about a guard. A guard for whom? It might be just the air from the quay that stirred the lace. No living woman could look like that. What was it that he had been saying?

The silence dwindled into small sound as the crowd began their chatter and their protests again.

'You will be escorted to the convent of the nuns of Rosario this evening, and food will be sent to you there,' he said. And turned on his heel and went out by the opposite door, without looking again in her direction.

He had been on the way home to dinner with his officers, but this failure in control so dismayed him that he punished himself by thinking up a new duty, and went to see Bart in hospital. Bart was very ill with fever, and was every day looking more and more as he had looked when Bluey had carried him up the steps of San Jeronimo to the daylight. He had also begun to talk again about that cottage in the Mendips: a subject on which he had not touched for a long time. The visit did nothing to strengthen or comfort Henry.

Nor did the succeeding days bring release. The need to see the woman again was paramount whatever he was doing. Her face came between him and the papers on his desk, and hung between him and the dim ceiling in the small hours. Her face was inside his closed eyelids and inside his mind.

It was easy to see her again. Interviewing prisoners held for ransom was a normal proceeding, and he had only to wait. He could have placed her first on the list, but that would have been to acknowledge to himself that an unknown woman could have the power to dictate his actions, and that was unthinkable. So he forced himself to wait until the moment when his door opened and the Franciscan friar who was acting as his secretary said that the wife of Don Vincente de Alcandete was here.

She stood as she had stood by the doorway to the quay, quiet and still. And again he was at a loss for words. It was a very young Madonna; ageless and innocent. Not woman at all. Mere essential beauty. Loveliness incarnate. Perfection made manifest.

'Your husband owns the big house on the other side of the square,' he heard himself say. 'Where is your husband?' And he waited with his breath held to hear her speak.

Her husband had gone to Peru on business, she said, and it was music.

'Since your home is in the centre of the town and surrounded on all sides by our own headquarters, it might be possible, I think, for you to live there if you cared to.'

That would be very gracious of him, said the music.

Unconsciously, Henry had expected her to say that she could not take privileges that were denied to her friends. But of course one could hardly expect a Madonna to be greatly concerned with, nor aware of, human relationships.

'Have you servants to look after you if you go home?'

Yes, she had servants.

'Then I shall give instructions that from now on you may live in your own house.'

She bowed her head a little, with no change of expression, and went away.

And in the evening of the following day he went to call on her.

She received him without surprise, and he sat for half an hour absorbing and marvelling at that serene perfection. She did not volunteer any remark, and he sat like a tongue-tied schoolboy, but the silences that fell between his questions had the same serenity as her beauty. He felt drugged, and happy for the first time for weeks.

But there was no happiness for him once he had left her. Only a feverish waiting until it would be evening again and he could go and see her.

And that became the pattern of his life in Panama.

The crowded days were full of business; decision, arbitration, contrivance. But the long, full day was merely a tunnel down which he must pass to the thing that mattered; to his hour with the wife of Don Vincente de Alcandete. To that longed-for, waited-for, satisfying, unsatisfying hour with beauty.

'What do you want of her?' he would ask himself in moments of sanity, and found no answer. He could take her at any time, but to bed with her seemed to him as shocking as it would be to bed with a saint; as unthinkable as that Bet – sleeping alone among the slaves at Morgan's Valley with a pistol on her pillow – should be forced by some stranger.

'Why are you not afraid of me?' he blurted one evening, resentful of the serenity that snared him.

She looked at him with the wide, unchanging grey eyes that had the lavender shade of the sea in a calm dawn. Of what should she be afraid? she asked. The Admiral was a great man, and gently born. He would not make war on women.

Defeated, he looked round the room, and saw the travelling-chest that he so much admired. 'I am nevertheless planning at this very moment to rob you,' he said; absurdly glad to find even this trivial way of asserting his hold over her. 'I want that chest to carry some of the loot I am taking out of your country.'

He was welcome to the chest, she said. It was one of a pair. She had brought her trousseau in them when she came from Tobago to be married.

And at the mention of her marriage he was straightway disorientated again. What was stopping him? She was a married woman, wasn't she? A human creature, feminine and desirable.

But her serenity hung between them like some unspoken taboo. And he went away, as always, half-satisfied, half-frustrated; and by now wholly miserable.

'Why the consideration for Don Vincente's wife?' Jack had asked one day.

'She is delicate,' said Henry; and hated all the world. He was being ridiculous, and the realization added the last ounce to his suffering. If the normally tolerant and silent Morris was moved to speech, then the affair was matter for common gossip.

For nine days thereafter he spent his spare hours with Don Juan's reigning mistress, a complaisant lady of extensive talents, hoping thereby to exorcise from his mind the image that haunted it. Perhaps in satiation he would find ease for his torture. He left her in a rage on the ninth evening because she had said, indifferently, between two bites of a fig, as if it were a matter of no great moment, that the wife of Don Vincente de Alcandete was the stupidest woman in the two Americas. 'She is so stupid,' she said, her interest on the fruit in her hand, 'that her nullity is positively dazzling.' And he had thrown down his table-napkin and flung out of the room and out of her house; unhealed and unassuaged.

'I am sick, that is what it is,' he would assure himself. 'It is part of my fever. It is just an illness that will pass.'

But the illness rose to a climax as the day for departure from Panama drew near, and he was forced to the knowledge that in a matter of hours he would be seeing her for the last time. He clutched at the fact that her ransom had not yet been paid, and that he might for that reason legitimately take her with him.

Take her where? said the cool Henry somewhere at the back of his sick mind. Home to Elizabeth?

No, of course he could not do that. But just to keep her with him a few days longer. To put off the moment when she would not be there any more; nor ever again.

She apologised in her gentle musical Spanish for the inconvenience that the late payment of her ransom was causing him. It would mean an extra mule in the pack-train to carry her as far as Venta de Cruz, but it would not be farther, she promised him. The ransom would catch up with her at river-head.

Three more days, perhaps, four, he reckoned; like a beggar snatching small coins spilled in the street. And he rode behind her all the way across the plain and up the cobbled track into the hills, rode behind her all the way to the Chagres river, so that his eyes should not be cheated of those minutes, so fast running out, when they could still see her.

More than a mile long that pack-train was. A hundred and seventy-five mules, loaded to the limit. For even without the lost ransom for the city and without the personal wealth of the escaped grandees, the treasure of Panama was fabulous; greater than that of Puerto Bello and Maracaibo put together. The number of men who had to share it was also, of course, more than doubled, so the final dole might not be so princely; but no one could take from them the credit of their achievement, and that would be theirs long after the last coin had been rung on a tavern table and they were once more penniless.

At Venta de Cruz they camped for ten days while the pack-loads were shipped into canoes for carriage down the now swollen river. And on the eighth day two friars came into camp bearing the ransom for Don Vincente de Alcandere's wife. They brought it in silver, in the second of her trousseau chests; and since it was late afternoon, they waited until morning to begin the journey back. And that night Henry lay awake, staring up at the low-hung stars that looked as if they could be picked out of the sky by any man energetic enough to put up a hand, and saying to himself: 'There are a million million suns, strung through space unimaginable. Suns. With worlds spinning round them. What does the beauty of one woman matter?'

But nothing could ease the constriction of loss and grieving in his breast; the desolation.

He took a public farewell of her next morning, and watched her ride away with her empty trousseau chest and her two attendant friars for just so long as the regulation few moments that politeness enjoined from a host; and then turned away to take up his life again.

He went down to Chagres with the sick, for the sake of being with Bart; leaving Jack to escort the treasure. Bart looked better, and was radiant at the thought of seeing the Atlantic again. 'None of these foreign seas for me,' he said. 'The old Caribbean's good enough.' And Henry laughed, and found comfort in the fact that Bart would, after all, sit in the shade on deck again with his scissors and his measuring tape and his sail-cloth.

But on their first night back in Chagres, Exmeling sent for him after midnight, when the victorious captains were still sitting round their supper-table celebrating; and he got up from the hot, hilarious, wine-fumed candle-light and walked through the salt darkness to the hospital tents on the shore. Exmeling met him at the entrance, where the lantern hung, and Morgan was puzzled by the odd mixture of apprehension and smugness in his expression. Long years afterwards he would see Exmeling's face as it was that night, in the lantern light, and try to analyse it. That mixture of secret satisfaction and overt fright.

'What is it?' Morgan asked. 'Is he bad again?'

'He's dying.'

'He can't be. He was getting better. You must do something.'

'There is nothing that anyone can do – Admiral. Not even you.'

'What did you say?' Morgan said sharply, thinking he had not heard the last words correctly.

'Not even Henry Morgan can do anything about what is happening in there,' Exmeling said, very smooth.

Morgan pushed past him and bent over Bart.

He looked now as he had looked that morning in Puerto Bello: a little heap of limp bones kept together by his spirit. His eyes were closed and he seemed to be asleep. But as Morgan watched, the eyes opened and recognized him.

'I looked in to say good-night, Bart,' he said.

But Bart was not deceived.

'We've 'ad some good times, Harry boy – Captain, sir.'

'We have indeed, Bart.'

Bart thought over the good times.

'Will you tell me something if I was to ask you?' he said.

'Surely.'

'*Was* it a gold piece?'

Morgan had come so far from Barbados that it took him an appreciable time to identify the reference, and to remember that dark room in which he had found Bart sitting by his side – and Modyford eating dinner beyond the archway. On that first day of his freedom; when Bart had saved him from being cheated by the serving-man and had taken him in charge and put his feet on the road to fortune. On the road to Maracaibo and Panama.

'Of course it was a gold piece!' he said, surprised. 'Didn't you *know* that it was?'

'No,' said Bart. 'I just didn't like his face.'

This apparently referred to the serving-man. He thought over the serving-man for a little, and then said: 'But I liked yours, Harry boy. I liked yours the minute I saw you.' And after a moment: 'She was right, wasn't she? She was right.'

'Who?'

'That mad woman. She said you'd write your name in water for all the world to read. . . . And I was right, too, wasn't I?

About you 'aving the right kind of nose for getting on in the world. Ah, you can't fool me about faces.'

His glance went over Morgan's shoulder to someone in the background, and he said: 'Send him away.'

Morgan looked back at Exmeling, and made a dismissing movement with his head.

'But —' began little Henrik.

'Go away,' said Morgan; and he went.

'I never liked that little bastard,' Bart said in his breath of a voice, 'and I'm not going to have him watch me go to Heaven.'

'But, Bart! That's nonsense, you know.'

'It's not. He has the wrong kind of nose.'

'I mean about your leaving us. What would I do without you, for one thing?'

Bart looked at him with such a wealth of affection and pride that Morgan's heart turned over.

'I think you'll be all right on your own from here on,' he said, as one setting down a child to walk alone.

'But there's that cottage of yours in the Mendips, Bart. You can retire now, and live like a lord in that cottage of yours.'

Bart's eyes had closed, but a small smile – a tolerant smile, as for the frailty of human nature – lighted his worn face.

'Well, it was nice to think about, anyhow,' he said.

And did not speak again.

Morgan sat by him till he died, an hour later. And he went on sitting there for a long time afterwards, the slow tears running down his cheek. In all the long road from Barbados to Panama he had wept neither for himself nor for another. But now he wept for Bart.

He went to bed in the dawn, and after sleepless weeks fell instantly into unfathomable slumber.

He was wakened in full daylight by Jack shaking him.

'Wake up, Harry, for God's sake, or do I have to throw a jug of water over you? Mother of God, Harry, I thought for a moment you were dead. Have you managed to get drunk at last?'

'No, I just went to bed late.'

'Are you awake enough to take bad news?'

'If it's about Bart, I know.'

'No. What's wrong with Bart, anyhow?'

'He's dead.'

'Oh,' said Jack indifferently; and seeing Henry's face: 'I'm sorry, of course, Harry; but just now I can't think of anything but the trouble we're in.'

Morgan sat up. If it was worse trouble than Bart's death —

'What trouble?'

'You know that chest that we packed most of the good pieces in: the Virgin's jewels?'

'Certainly I do. What about it?'

'That chest had a bit of leather missing where it had been scraped against a pannier edge or galled by a rope.'

'Well, what of it?'

'This is the day of the share-out, and I was looking through the things the treasure-party brought down-river, to get them in some kind of order. And that chest in the storehouse on the quay, Harry, is not the chest we packed the things into in Panama.'

'*Jack!* You're mad!'

'I am, very nearly,' Jack said. 'The very thought of what we may be going to see when we open that chest makes my mind reel. You get on your clothes and come down to the storehouse with me, before I'm stark raving with terror.'

He waited while Henry dressed, and in the air between them hung a further question. Something for which there were no words at all.

'It *couldn't* be!' Henry blurted, as they went down to the quay. This was the total sum of their conversation on the way; and Jack did not bother to make any reply to it.

The two sentries outside the storehouse saluted them and then resumed their chat.

'I'm away for two years, and she asks me to believe —' one was saying; and the homely tale had the poignancy of a safe, familiar country seen from a storm-tossed sea. Drowning, Henry clung to his sole rock: the hope that Jack somehow was mistaken.

They opened the chest with the only known key to it: the one in Henry's possession; and it opened easily. The contents, as far as Henry's stricken senses could perceive, seemed to be small pieces of rock wrapped in scraps of cloth.

Jack wasted no time in contemplation. He began to collect the fragments of stone and cloth and hand them to Henry. 'Put these in your pockets,' he said. 'And sit down. If you're going to faint, put it off till we're safely out of this store.'

Having emptied the chest, he began to unlash the nearer bundles.

'What are you doing?' Henry asked, wiping the cold sweat from his face with a child's unco-ordinated movements.

'That chest has to be filled with something,' Jack said, taking a handful here and a handful there of the better stuff that remained: gold-inlaid pistols, jewelled sword-hilts, crosses decked with semi-precious stones. 'Thank God there's a second lot of trinkets.' He opened the iron-banded box and seasoned his collection with a liberal sprinkling of necklaces, bracelets, and brooches. 'That looks not so bad. I hope to God no one has set his heart on that ruby bracelet of the Virgin's. They'll never believe that we haven't pocketed it.'

In twelve minutes from the time they had entered the place the substitution was complete; and Henry walked away again bowed down by more than the weight of the stones in his pockets.

'Those scraps of cloth,' said Jack. 'Did they remind you of anything?'

'Yes,' said Morgan.

They were the brown frieze of which Franciscan habits were made.

'I thought at the time they were a very worldly looking couple for friars,' Jack said.

And that was the only remark that he ever made on the subject.

For, after all, there was nothing that could profitably be said; and Jack was never a man to waste speech. In the minds of both of them was the picture of the little cavalcade riding away that morning at Venta de Cruz: the madonna, her two attendant friars, and the chest swaying and dipping on the back of the pack-mule.

It had been Jack's men on guard that night, Henry remembered; but it made no difference. Bribery was inconceivable. Even had the fierce pride of being 'Morris's men' not sufficed, no man would give up his share of such prodigious wealth for a bribe; nor could any man of the guard hope to survive the rage of his fellows when the substitution was discovered. However it had been worked, it was not by suborning. And that was the one small scrap of comfort in an intolerable situation.

They had used her to fool him.

Had she known? Had she planned it?

But no; she was too —

He had almost said it: the unutterable word that had been used so lightly by Don Juan's mistress. He pushed the word away, and thought up a more presentable one.

She had no guile. Her lovely simplicity was without sin.

She had carried back a king's ransom on her pack-mule to Panama, but she had not known about it. Most certainly she had not known.

'I shall have to stand the loss out of my share,' he said to Jack, as they walked up the harbour.

'Yes,' said Jack, accepting it. Without the philandering with Don Vincente's wife there would have been no duplicate chest for substitution. The thing must have been planned as soon as it was known that loot was to be taken out of the country in that chest.

At ten o'clock the assessors began their work, and it went on for three days. And for every moment of those three days Henry waited for someone to remember some particular trinket and make application for it. But no one did. The habit of accepting the 'lot' was so ingrained in privateering souls that choice did not normally interest them. All they cared about was the total.

Henry sat late on that first dreadful night, facing his humiliation. On the second night he sat late reckoning what each man's share would have come to had the chest been still in their possession, and calculating what he must now add to bring each share to its proper total. Sick with shame and penitence, he calculated generously; so that it cost him nearly everything he had.

And it was the final touch of wormwood in the gall when, at

the distribution on the fourth day, the men broke into open protest at the smallness of their reward.

'It is less than we got for Maracaibo!' they said. 'Less than for Puerto Bello!'

'There were only five ships at Puerto Bello, and seven at Maracaibo,' he reminded them. 'Today we have more than thirty.'

But they were in no mood to calculate coldly. 'It is not enough!' they insisted.

'Every man entitled to either compensation or special award has had the full amount,' Morgan said. 'That is a first charge on both officers and men. After that what is left is shared out in the recognized proportions; according to the scale under which you signed on. Every man of the fleet has had his due share of the total; no more and no less. Do you want the widows' share too?'

'He's right,' said the saner ones. 'Thirty-odd ships makes a deal of difference, come to think of it.'

But the others nursed their grievance and preserved it in rum; and by evening, when they were drunk, they congregated in a noisy shifting gang under the balcony of their Admiral's lodging and made open accusations. The officers had lined their pockets at their expense, they said. The officers had filched the best stuff.

The final irony was supplied by the fact that a good third of the said officers were thinking the same thing of Morgan. Morgan had skimmed the cream, they said. Even divided among more than thirty ships' crews, surely the wealth of Panama should have produced more than a wretched ninety pounds a-piece.

'Let me tell them that you haven't a penny piece,' Jack said, moved by this injustice. 'Let me tell them about the loss of the chest.'

'And have them mock me for a fool! No! Let them think me knave if they want to.'

So only a handful of captains came to the parting supper that Morgan gave that night; and these were men who knew him personally and who had served with him before.

In the small hours of the morning, Cornelius, still playing cards in a wine-shop on the harbour front because sleep did not come easily to him these days, felt a small tug on his sleeve and looked round to find Romulus standing there.

'Capitain not come home,' he said.

'I expect he's making a night of it,' Cornelius said. 'I don't blame him.'

'Better in bed. You come help.'

'You don't imagine he'd listen to me, do you?' said Cornelius, going on with his game.

But the boy plucked his sleeve again, and said: 'You come help.'

Since it was never any use trying to get a coherent story out of Romulus, Cornelius good-naturedly gave up his game and accompanied him to see what he wanted. When he stood outside the door of the dining-room and the boy motioned him in, he said: 'What *is* this? I can't go in there! They're at supper still. I can hear them talking.'

But the boy threw the door open and led him in.

Supper, it seemed, was over, after all. Of the entire party, the only ones who were not under the table were Ansell, Jack Morris and Morgan. It was Ansell who was talking. He was seeing how far he could count. At the moment he had got to five thousand four hundred and eight-two, and was making heavy weather of it. Jack was neatly asleep in his chair. Morgan was sprawled over the table in an attitude of utter abandon and defeat.

At long last Harry Morgan had managed to drink himself into insensibility.

With the help of Romulus, Cornelius hoisted the limp bulk on to his shoulder and carried it to bed. He prepared to help Romulus with the undressing, but Romulus pushed him out and shut the door on him. The dressing or undressing of Henry Morgan was his sole affair.

'I must try this again,' Henry said when he wakened in the morning and found himself in bed. 'It has always irked me to walk home after a party.'

But his hard head continued to intervene, and in the month that remained of his stay in Chagres he walked to bed on twenty-two nights out of the thirty.

16

THE FLEET BEGAN dispersing the morning after the final share-out, and a new disgruntlement sullied that parting. The peace treaty with Spain had been ratified.

'Ah, well,' said the more philosophical, 'the logwood trade is very profitable, they say. And who knows how long this peace will last, anyhow?'

The others told each other that there were still eight months before the treaty would become operative, and they might as well make the most of those months. So the ships faded away over the horizon, by twos or threes, or singly, leaving Morgan with his friends. And in that more intimate atmosphere some of the family-party air that had characterised their early adventuring came back; but what would never come back was the light-heartedness.

Soberly they sailed at last away from Chagres and the Spanish mainland; away from their unbelievable achievement. And it was in no twenty-four-gun frigate that Morgan sailed home to Port Royal; for his fine flagship was lying hopelessly aground in the Chagres river. He came home in the little *Fortune*; and it was in the familiar little stuffy cabin that he spent the long, fever-ridden days at sea. He would watch the figures as they came and went, never quite sure if they were real or not. Don Christoval de Rasperu came often, to sit at the table with his little toy dog a silken bundle on the cushion beside him, and talk about navigation and the deplorable thirst for oblivion that afflicted mankind so that they must get drunk.

'But a man wants respite from life,' Henry told him. 'A respite from thought and feeling.'

And Don Christoval would wag his elegant head and say: 'It is too precious a gift, life, to waste even a moment of it.'

Mansfield was there quite often, drinking wine, with little Henrik in the background. Henry knew that little Henrik was not real, because little Henrik had departed to England on the very morrow of getting his pay. He was going home to Holland, he had said; so he could not be in the cabin. But Bart was; and he was sure that Bart was real. He had had a dream about taking a sloop out from somewhere and burying Bart three miles out at sea where he would be comfortable and at home. But that was all nonsense, thank Heaven. Bart was here, alive and well. Poor Bart! with only five pearls left.

Kinnell and Cornelius sailed the *Fortune* home between them, and worried endlessly about the man lying in the cabin. On his good days Morgan would come on deck and be his lucid and caustic self. But in no time he would be lying in the cabin again, watching unseen creatures come and go, and occasionally conversing with them.

Kinnell grew so worried that during one of his Captain's spells below he closed the *Dolphin* and asked Morris to come over. Jack came and looked and was dismayed, but had no remedy to suggest. His very individual reaction was to think that Elizabeth must not be allowed to meet him like that without being prepared. So Jack was first back to Port Royal.

But nothing in Jack's deliberately casual account prepared Elizabeth for the reality; for the slow-moving, thin man with the sallow skin and the eyes sunk deep in the haggard face.

'Harry! My *darling*!' she said; and ordered him to bed at once.

And to her dismay he went.

'I should have gone to see the Governor,' he said, lying flat and still, with his strong hands spread out nerveless on the counterpane. 'To report. But I shall feel better tomorrow, and he will understand.'

'There is no haste,' she said. 'It is not to Sir Thomas that you will be reporting; and Colonel Lynch can wait.'

'Lynch!' he said.

'Yes. Drink this.'

'*Lynch!*'

'Yes, but don't get into a fever about it. It hasn't quickened the Modyford pulse at all, so it needn't quicken yours.'

'Dear Bet,' he said, a smile in his eyes; and drank what she gave him. 'So the chickens are coming home?'

'They're home and roosting,' she said. 'And the only really worried person is poor Colonel Lynch, who, as far as Jamaica is concerned, is in a minority of one.'

'The damned psalm-singing Puritan,' Henry said, and fell asleep.

In the sitting-room she found Jack waiting.

'Did you tell him?' he asked.

'Not yet.'

'I ought to take the *Dolphin's* crew up to Kingshouse and beat the liver and lights out of that – that —'

'That damned psalm-singing Puritan,' supplied Elizabeth.

'Yes. It's a Spaniard's trick to invite a man on board ship and then arrest him when he's your guest. An Englishman should be ashamed even to think of a method like that.'

'He was afraid,' said Elizabeth. 'He's a poor thing, and he was afraid. Afraid that – that someone would take a ship's crew and stop him.'

There was a moment of silence, and then Jack said, in a gentler tone:

'You do know, don't you, that it is only a matter of time before – before *his* turn comes?' He leaned his head towards the inner room.

'Yes,' she said. 'I think he knows it himself. He said that the chickens were coming home to roost. But he is too tired to care.' She waited a moment, as if debating with herself whether or not to put something into words; and then said: 'Is it only the fever, Jack, that has – has so sucked him dry?'

'Yes, of course,' said Jack, too hastily. And then, realizing his slip, added: 'That and the heavy burden. The responsibility. They'll tell you that Panama was taken by thirty-two ships and fifteen hundred men. But that's only a manner of speaking. It was taken by Henry Morgan.'

'Dear Jack,' she said.

'At least I didn't have to tell him about the canes,' she said. 'I was so afraid he would ask.'

'Is it very bad?'

'It couldn't be worse.'

'Cocoa too?'

'Yes, everything. Dead and brittle with the drought.'

But in the morning, when Henry heard that Modyford was a prisoner on board the navy frigate in the harbour, bound for England, that he was not even to be allowed to come ashore and say good-bye to his wife, he got up and dressed himself in the best garments that the little Port Royal apartment could produce, and went to Kingshouse. It was one of his good days, with his thoughts coming pat off his tongue in the most appropriate form; and the delighted servants, clustering round the library door and fighting for the best eavesdropping places, reported that never had the normal phrases of polite conversation managed to be so blistering.

When Colonel Lynch ventured to ask what the reward of his adventure was likely to bring to the Admiral personally, the Admiral was heard to say:

'Nothing like fifty-thousand-pounds-worth.'

Which was the sum that Lynch was understood to have lent the King in return for his Governorship.

And when the new Governor ventured to hope that the usages of civilization had been employed towards the prisoners in Panama, the Admiral said Oh yes; that the prisoners had been openly arrested, not kidnapped, and had never been held incommunicado.

Somewhere about the ninth round, when the new Governor was almost out on his feet, Henry asked that he might be allowed to visit his friend Sir Thomas Modyford on board the frigate before she sailed. But Colonel Lynch could still think. To a man who had crossed Panama and taken a capital city with a handful of men, spiriting a man off a ship would be child's play. So Henry was not given permission to see his friend.

But Sir Thomas was allowed to send letters ashore.

'My dear Harry,' he wrote, 'Spain is demanding my head, but I hear that my countrymen are going to let me off with an eye-tooth. I am hoping that this token sacrifice will be held to be a general absolution and that you will be left in peace to tend your cabbages. You are young, and you are at the beginning of things still, and you have Elizabeth. But if not, I shall look forward to seeing you in London. No time is all loss that is spent in London with a friend.

'You have rocked Spain to the foundations by the taking of Panama, and if, as I hear, it has cost you something in health, it has saved England from a long war with Spain. Or so I think. The realization that even their Pacific coast is vulnerable will do more than anything to bring Spain to the point of compromise over the Americas. Panama has been for them the writing on the wall.

'Your writing, Harry, my friend.

'God bless and keep you till we meet again.'

It was a long time before they met again. Partly because the order for Admiral Morgan's arrest was delayed, and partly because once it had come none of the new clique at Kingshouse dared to hurry the Admiral in the small matter of giving himself up. So Henry pottered round his place at Morgan's Valley; put the *Fortune* into the logwood trade with Cornelius as master, in the hope of being able to recover the loss on his wasted fields; and was dosed with noxious fluids by every doctor in the island – for he was an impatient creature and a chronic doctor-hopper – in an effort to cure his intermittent fever. When he had spun out nearly a year of this pastoral life, Captain Keene came into harbour in his ship H.M.S. *Welcome*, and Henry decided that if he must travel to England under arrest, he might as well do it with Keene, whom he liked.

Only the fact that Harry Morgan was going voluntarily kept the island from open revolt; and Lynch found himself in the odd situation of being grateful to him. Lynch had spent the last months trying, out of his great wealth, to buy himself into the island's good graces. But the island was still flooded with privateering money and impervious to bribery. Colonel Lynch's only recruit from the waterside proved to be Captain Charles Hadsell, who had turned out to be a sadly unsuccessful privateer. His attack with six ships on the town of Cumana, on the Venezuela coast, was notorious as the only failure in all the history of Jamaican privateering; and 'Cumana!' had become a Spanish taunt whenever English ears were within hearing distance. So Hadsell, who had spurned the Morgan flag in his prosperous days, was glad to creep into the opposition fold now that he was an object of scorn in his old haunts.

The whole town turned out to see the *Welcome* sail, with bands, and singing, and waving kerchiefs, and cheers. And Henry dragged himself up from the cabin so that he could stand on her quarter-deck as she sailed past the battery on the Point, and acknowledge the island's farewell to him. After that he went back to his bunk, and let Romulus pile the blankets on him and dose him with rum till his mind and senses grew blurred and he could stop either thinking or feeling.

The *Welcome* was three months at sea, in one of the worst voyages she had ever experienced, and when at last she came into calm water at Spithead, Captain Keene looked doubtfully at his passenger and wondered whether he should report on the health of the prisoner before they took him into custody.

But it seemed that there was to be no handing-over to a guard. Admiral Morgan, said instructions, was to make his own way to London, and there hold himself at His Majesty's convenience.

'The damned penny-pinching housekeepers!' said the admiral. 'They want me to pay for my own cell.'

He had also to pay for his transport to London, but it proved to be one of the most rewarding expenditures that Harry Morgan had ever made. It was summer time; the beginning of July. And before his eyes as the coach made its slow way up to London was trailed the green, wild-rose loveliness of England. He had never seen it before: this ultimate loveliness of Nature; and he sat enchanted. 'Home' to him had meant Llanrhymny; Llanrhymny with its soft West air. But when Englishmen said 'home' this was what they meant; this incredible perfection.

He tried to think of something that might challenge its incomparability: the liquid light of Caribbean seas, the flaming blossoms in the dust, the savanna grass, the jungle prodigality. But all these were lovely details in a picture; here the whole picture was composed of lovely detail; fresh and jewelled as an illuminated letter. He sat and watched it, hour after hour. England. This was what men meant when they said England.

If England put a cool hand on his fevered senses, then the

English supplied the first balm to his galled vanity. He had been a personality in Jamaica long enough to take that distinction for granted, but it had not occurred to him that his fame might have gone in front of him to the extent of making his name as much of a household word in this unknown England as it had been in the islands of his adoption. It was therefore sweet oil on his self-love, still raw from the personal failure of Panama, to hear inn-servants tell each other: 'It's Harry Morgan in the coach! Harry Morgan home from the Caribbean.'

Home, he said in his mind. And liked the sound of it, prison or no prison.

He distributed largesse to the small boys who thronged round the coach-door at his morning departures to ask how many Spaniards he had killed altogether, and pretended not to notice Romulus's jealousy of this intrusion. Romulus had exhibited a mounting distrust of this strange country and all its works – a distrust that reached a climax when they made their entry into London. They came into London on a sunny evening when the rose and buff and sepia city lay warm and beautiful beside its pale blue river, and Morgan forgot that he had ever shivered or sweated, and expanded almost visibly into well-being. He had been recommended to the Blue Boar in the Strand, but he found that he could have rooms at the Dolphin; very expensive rooms indeed, but dolphins brought him luck, so why carp at an extra guinea or two?

'We go home tomorrow?' said Romulus hopefully, as soon as they were alone together in the first-floor room overlooking the street.

'Don't you like London, Romulus?'

'We go home,' suggested Romulus firmly; and from that attitude he never wavered.

But London opened its arms to Henry before he was well awake next morning. He had spent a broken night listening to the incredible racket that was night in London: the thunder of iron-shod wheels on cobbles as late coaches bore revellers home and early carts brought produce from the country, the fights, the singing (did Englishmen never go to bed?), the intrusion of watchmen calling the hour and reporting on the weather (Merciful heaven, could the English not smell tomorrow's weather the evening before like any good seaman ?), and he had wakened tired and short-tempered and apt to remember that he was a prisoner who was being required to pay the expenses of his prison. But with the arrival of the breakfast he had sent for, there arrived, too, an elegant stripling who followed the chambermaid into the room and said gaily:

'Is your levee public, Admiral?' And as Henry turned from the window to face him: 'My cousin said that I should find you here!'

'Your cousin?' said Morgan, at a loss.

'Sir Thomas.'

'*Modyford?* Is Modyford free, then!'

'Oh, no; he is in the Tower.'

'Then how could he know that I was here?'

'He said: "If the *Welcome* arrived at Spithead four days ago, then Harry Morgan must be in London by now. And if he is in London he will be staying at the Dolphin, since he is a wildly superstitious creature with no money sense."'

The tall boy said this in Sir Thomas's own dry drawl, and Morgan looked at him with appreciation. At first sight one saw only the remarkable good looks and the fashionable clothes; but presently one noticed that the eyes in the reckless face were hazel-brown and kind.

'Then you must be —'

'Yes. I'm Albemarle. "Old George Monck's son." I expect I shall go to my grave as "old George Monck's son".'

'I doubt it,' said Morgan, considering him.

'Really?' said the boy, delighted. 'Admiral, I am your servant! I had heard that you had courage, and ingenuity, and doggedness, and generosity, and most of the other virtues. But now I perceive that you also have perspicacity. Are you going to invite me to breakfast with you?'

Morgan was about to give instructions for another cover when he noticed that a second cover had already been provided. 'I perceive that your grace is gifted with forethought. A valuable quality,' he said, and laughed a little.

'I learned from "old George Monck" to anticipate events,' the boy said, dragging up a chair. 'That is how he became Albemarle.'

'Is Sir Thomas allowed to have visitors, then?' Morgan asked as they settled down to their steak and ale.

'Oh, yes. He is living in the greatest comfort. He instructed me to ask you to call upon him as soon as you found it convenient.'

'Does one just go and knock?'

'It is customary to say that one has come to see a prisoner on matters concerning his defence. As if anyone could advise that very shrewd lawyer my cousin on any matter whatever! He admires you very greatly, Admiral. I confess that it puzzled me that Tom Modyford should so reverence a buccaneer —'

'A privateer,' put in Henry, smoothly.

'I beg your pardon. A privateer. But now that I have met you I am no longer at a loss.'

Henry was used to hero-worship, but not to seeing it in the eyes of a young Court gallant. He was warmed and a little confused by it.

'When you have seen my cousin, and attended to any pressing business,' said the boy, 'it would give me great pleasure and make me very proud if you would be my guest at supper. I promised Carlisle and Johnny Vaughan that they should meet you.' He paused and looked up from his steak with a smile in those unexpectedly gentle eyes. 'They are going to get a shock, Edward and Johnny. They think you eat babies for breakfast.'

'I *could* roughen up my manners, if it would be any obligement to you,' Henry said, a shade dry.

'Oh, pray don't. I long to see their faces when they find out what a bucc – a privateer really looks like.'

'At any moment now,' Modyford said when Henry saw him that afternoon, 'Christopher will "go for a pirate". The King will never forgive you if you seduce the boy. He is the reigning favourite.'

'I don't know that he would be much good as a privateer,' Morgan said, 'but I think that he might make a very good Governor one day.'

'So?' said Modyford, raising his eyebrows; and having considered it: 'So!' he said. And the two men whose horizons stretched to the curve of the earth sat for a space in the little dark room on Thames-side planning how to shape this material in their hands. Then Sir Thomas said:

'I hear that they have failed to find any criminal charge against you, so there will be no case to go to the courts.'

'What then?'

'They are passing the affair to the Trade and Plantations people, I understand.'

'To a Government department! What qualifications have they to try anyone!'

'It is not to be a trial. It is to be an inquiry.'

'Inquiry! I suppose that means that I stand on the mat while a pack of clerks who would not know a stay-sail from a woman's kerchief lecture me on my misdeeds!'

'It means that you will be able to state your case in public and that it will be written down. That is something. Indeed, it is an opportunity to be valued. Something that you have great need of.'

'Need?' said Morgan, puzzled by the change in Modyford's voice; the sudden – gravity, was it?

But Modyford evidently decided to shelve it, whatever it was.

'It is a gossip-ridden town, London,' he said, lightly. 'Worse than any village. And much more ill-natured. It is as well to have the truth written down. Their lordships the Commissioners for Trade and Plantations will at least do you that service.'

Morgan damned their lordships, and dismissed them from his mind; he was beginning to enjoy London. And it was not until very late that night that he discovered what Modyford had been talking about.

The supper at young Albemarle's was a success, except for his disappointment about Lord Vaughan. He had, quite unconsciously, looked forward to meeting another Welshman in this still-strange town, looked forward to getting into the mental undress which one wears in the society of a compatriot. He was also a little flattered, even now, after all his personal achievements, to be meeting someone of so much Welsh importance as Carberry's heir. But he had disliked Johnny Vaughan at sight. He hated his prim mouth, and his intellectual pretensions, and the suggestion of the spurious that hung about everything he said or did. That this belief in his synthetic quality did not have its roots in personal prejudice seemed to be proved by a thoughtless remark of Albemarle's. When they had sat over their wine for some time, the boy said: 'Let us go and visit Mother Temple.'

'No,' amended young Carlisle. 'Madame Bennet. Her girls are much prettier.'

Henry said that he was too old for brothels.

'It is a sad and boring way of spending an evening, anyhow,' Vaughan said.

At which Albemarle laughed and said lightly: 'Johnny will sneak there by himself when we are all in bed.'

So Henry deplored the Welsh blood in Vaughan and disliked him with all the heartiness of a fellow Celt. But he liked Carlisle, an amiable young cynic, and he went willingly with the three of them to a fashionable party; which was the alternative, it seemed, to Mother Temple's. He enjoyed the party less than the supper, since it seemed to him to have some of the same spurious quality that characterised his fellow-countryman. Everyone seemed bent on being a little larger than life: whether in wit, rudeness or style.

'What do you want for him?' asked a man, indicating the Indian boy who, since 'black boys' were beginning to be the rage, was allowed to walk at Morgan's heel.

'He is not for sale,' Henry said, snubbing.

'*Everything* in this town is for sale.'

'Not now.'

'Now?'

'Not since half-past six yesterday evening,' Henry said.

'Half-past six? What happened then?'

'I arrived in town.'

'I see why you conquered Panama, Admiral,' said the man, and bowed himself away.

They moved on into the inner room where the gaming-tables were.

'Let us not waste time on Madame Chance tonight,' Albemarle said. 'There are too many other charming women waiting the pleasure of your acquaintance.'

'I never pass the tables without throwing Madame Chance a guinea,' Carlisle said. 'She likes the little attention.'

So they paused to risk a guinea each.

While they waited the result of their gesture, Morgan examined the faces of the crowd round the table, thinking how little they differed in their mixture of the dissolute and the daring from his own ship's crew gambling round any barrel-top in Port Royal. His glance came to rest on a young man directly opposite, and he forgot about the crowd. He forgot about London, and Albemarle, and Carlisle, and Johnny Vaughan, and the fact that he was Admiral Henry Morgan. He was standing by a jacaranda tree in the dancing wind and the light, and before him was another crowd: a dark-skinned, gay-coloured crowd that moved like a field of flowers in the sun.

'Who is that?' he asked.

'Who is who?' Carlisle said, and followed his glance. 'Oh! Poor little Tim Driffield. For ever trying to make enough to get married on.' He laughed a little. 'His *inamorata* would marry him tomorrow and live on his pay, but she has a dragon of a mother. The result is that he loses his pay continually, and so has neither the pay nor the girl.'

Morgan picked up the little heap of gold that Madame Chance had returned for his guinea, and moved round the table. The crowd were already busy with the next decision of luck, but the young man had not moved. His pockets were evidently as drained of money as his face was of hope.

'If you will permit me, sir,' Morgan said; and set the neat, cylindrical, small tower of gold by his elbow.

The young man (and he was not so young, after all, Morgan noticed, now that he could see the lines) looked first startled, then unbelieving, and then indignant. His face flushed.

'Sir,' he said, very low and between his teeth. 'I do not understand by what pretension you feel free to offer me money —'

'By the obligation of a debtor,' said Henry, cutting him short.

'A debtor?' said the young-old Mr Driffield, no wise mollified. 'If you think, sir, that by so transparent a ruse, you may, even in the way of kindness —'

'You lent me a guinea, Mr Driffield. One day in Barbados. I promised to repay you at the usual rate of interest. I hope that the interest may bring you as much luck as the original guinea brought me. We will waive the formality of a receipt. It was a gentlemen's agreement from the beginning.'

And, very pleased with this further gesture, he allowed himself to be led away to meet the loveliest women present.

He was presented to a great many beautifully dressed females who all seemed to have the same well-supported pair of breasts and the same rolling eyes. They all said how enchanted they were to meet so distinguished a sailor, but he had the feeling that not one of them really knew who he was. The men did, though. The men knew all about him, as he could tell by the turning heads, and it was because he had begun to sun himself in the warmth of their interest that he was unprepared for the blow that was coming to him. He was back on his heels. Wide open.

He had lost the other two for the moment, and was standing by the gaming-table with Lord Vaughan, watching the play, when a middle-aged man stopped to talk to his companion. Henry liked his face, and waited happily to be introduced. And presently Vaughan said:

'Let me present my fellow-countryman, Admiral Morgan, home from Jamaica.'

The man's face lost its friendly animation on the instant. He bowed his head the fraction of an inch, nodded to Vaughan, and turned away without another word.

'Don't let that worry you,' Vaughan said. 'He is an ardent Roman Catholic.'

'A Roman Catholic? What could that possibly have to do with me?'

'I expect he can't forget those nuns.'

'*Nuns?* What nuns?'

'The ones you used as a screen for your men at Puerto Bello,' Vaughan said.

'What!'

Morgan's voice, at its full hurricane pitch, startled the chattering room.

'Come out of here,' said Vaughan, hastily; and drew the furious Morgan into the garden.

'Now let us hear about this nonsense,' said Henry. 'What am I supposed to have done at Puerto Bello?'

'I can't tell you if you are going to roar at me again.'

'You'll tell me any way I want you to, my lord, and without loss of time. What am I supposed to have done at Puerto Bello?'

'The tale is – of course I do not believe it, please do me the credit of —'

'*Will you stick to the matter in hand?*'

'The tale is that when you were unable to take the fort —'

'Which fort?'

'I don't know. Was there more than one?' asked Vaughan, giving Morgan his first acquaintance with the home-front mind.

'Never mind. Go on.'

'The tale is that when you failed to take the fort you sent nuns and priests up the scaling-ladders in front of your men, as a shield. Of course you did not expect that the Spaniards would fire on them, we quite understand that – I mean, that is understood.'

'And did the Spaniards fire?' asked Morgan, suddenly silky.

'Oh, yes. There was a – there was supposed to be a massacre. That is why Sir William was – was cross with you just now.'

'Cross,' said Henry, savouring the word. 'And you are not cross?'

'I have said: I do not credit wild tales. Everyone knows that barbarities are committed in the heat of battle —'

'Such as ordering nuns up scaling-ladders.'

'No, of course, that is an extreme case.'

'It is an extreme case of invention,' Morgan said. 'The only fort that was taken by scaling-ladders at Puerto Bello was taken by seamen under cover of army musketry, and you will do me the kindness to say so next time you hear this ridiculous story repeated. Where did you first hear of this absurdity?'

'It is one of the stories in the book, of course.'

'*Book?* What book?'

'The Dutchman's book.'

'What Dutchman?'

'Eskmellin, or whatever he calls himself.'

'Exmeling!'

'Something like that.'

'You mean that Exmeling has written a book! A book about me, about the Caribbean?'

'But I thought that you would certainly know, Admiral,' Vaughan said, uncomfortable. 'It is the rage of the town.'

'Is it, by God! You mean that all those people in there' – he waved his arm towards the lighted room behind them with its high screaming voices – 'have read this – this enormity and believe it and did not throw me out into the street?'

'But why should they? Your exploits are the pride of England —'

'Including the exploit of using nuns as a battering-ram, it appears. You will excuse me, Lord Vaughan, if I leave you now. I have been troubled by marsh fever caught in the Isthmus, and late hours —'

'But, Admiral, you must not take to heart a —'

'Allow me to bid you good-night. Perhaps you will be kind enough to give my thanks to the Duke of Albemarle for a delightful evening —'

But the boy intercepted him as he came into the hall.

'Admiral! You are not leaving us so early!'

Morgan swung round on a heel to face him.

'Does your Grace possess a copy of this obscenity, by any chance?'

'Obscenity?' said Albemarle, startled and at a loss.

'This book that my surgeon has written.'

'Oh; the Exmeling thing. Yes.' He looked faintly embarrassed. 'Yes, I do. I —'

'Would it be presumptuous of me to ask for a loan of it? I think that it is time that I found out what I really did in Puerto Bello and Panama.'

'Admiral, I know that the book must be very displeasing to you, but do not blame the town too much for their acceptance of it. They had a picture in their minds – as I had – of the buccaneer as they imagined him —'

'*I have never been a buccaneer!*'

'No, sir, I know. But the town does not make nice distinctions. And they picture to themselves a pirate – knife between the teeth and pistols in either hand – and have no knowledge of the reality. Most of them have never seen a ship bigger than a vegetable hoy from the Surrey shore. Now that they have the opportunity of meeting you they will —'

'Would it be possible for me to have that book tonight?'

'Of course, of course,' said the boy, abashed. 'If you wish it, Admiral. I shall send it round to your lodgings as soon as I reach home. I am sorry from my heart that you had to learn about the book in this uncivil fashion – I had thought that you would have known about it – and if there is anything that I can do to contradict its influence, please believe that I shall be very glad to do it.'

'Good-night,' said Morgan, and went into the night.

Into a night blacker than any he had yet experienced.

He had thought that the ultimate in suffering had been reached that night in Chagres, on that hot, damp night when he had at last managed to drink himself insensible. But even that night in Chagres had been nothing like this: this absolute in misery.

He went up to his room at the Dolphin and sat staring at the opposite wall, while Romulus moved about preparing him for bed. When a footman came with the book he said: 'Go to sleep, child. I shall not need you again tonight.' But Romulus sat down in a corner, prepared to watch with his god.

It was worse, far worse, than he had expected. There was no silliness too great for Exmeling to set down; no atrocity too hideous for Exmeling to invent. It was of a monumental absurdity: a 'pirate tale' such as seamen spin for illiterates over a tavern table in return for a drink; but it was also extremely readable, and it had the fascination of the frightful. One turned the page to find what new horror might be in store on the next. Little Henrik had found the perfect formula for selling a book.

Morgan learned something that night at the Dolphin. He learned that helpless anger is by far the most destructive of human emotions. It mauled and tore him. It consumed him like a furnace. It shook him in its clutches as a cat shakes its prey.

He did not know which he longed the more to kill: the creature who had smeared him with this filth, or the fools who had believed him.

Had they no minds? No critical faculties? Did they think that the achievements of Puerto Bello and Maracaibo and Panama were possible to an undisciplined rabble?

Could they not see the absurdity that lurked in every invention? He had burned Panama, it seemed. Did they not even pause to consider whether a man would burn the city he had crossed a continent to capture?

Did the relish with which the tortures were described not waken doubt in their presumably educated minds?

If their minds were not capable even of this simple analysis, then surely the sub-title was a sufficient guide to the credibility of anything that the book might contain. 'The Englishman Is Devil Rather than Human,' said the sub-title, addressing itself to the Hollanders at the end of a bitter war with the English.

And yet this revolting, this loathsome piece of ordure-throwing was 'the rage of the town.'

He sat with the book on the table in front of him, and watched the candle burn down. Sat and writhed.

He was still sitting there when the dawn came, staring at the cold guttered wax that had borne so fine a flame.

17

'YOU CANNOT REACH the wretched Exmeling,' Modyford said to him, 'but you can extort very substantial damages from the English publisher. After recent sales, I do not doubt Mr William Crooke's ability to pay.' He looked across at Morgan's exhausted face and was moved to further speech. 'Shall I tell you what interested me most in the Dutchman's work? His admiration for you.'

'Admiration!' said Morgan, very bitter.

'Yes. He fights desperately against it, but it overcomes him continually. He is a poor little nobody, Exmeling; the kind of man whom no one notices in a room; but he passionately wants to be a Henry Morgan. He hates you because you are all he would like to be and never will; but the admiration for what you are is stronger than he is. It seeps through his tale in spite of himself. I found it extraordinarily interesting.'

'I am glad that your Excellency was entertained.'

'Poor Harry! You feel defiled, don't you?'

'I am defiled.'

'Yes. But at least there will be vindication.'

'Did you ever know a vindication that overtook a vilification?' Morgan asked.

And Modyford had no answer. Nor had Henry expected one.

The damage to his reputation was irreparable, and they were both too intelligent not to recognizc that fact.

'When do you see the Commissioners?' Modyford asked.

'On Monday afternoon.'

'I hope you have ammunition for the contest.'

'I have three out-size pieces of artillery.'

'I am glad to hear it. What are they?'

'The Queen of Spain's commission to Manoel Rivera Pardal to wage war against the English for five years; found in Pardal's cabin in the *San Pedro y La Fama*. A commission from the Governor of Cartagena to the same effect, from the same source. And the dispatches of Don Juan Perez de Guzman, Governor of Panama, to the authorities in Madrid.'

'Don Juan's dispatches!'

'Yes. We intercepted them.'

'Will they prove useful?'

'Well, he boasts about how clever he was in burning Panama before we could get to it. That will interest their lordships, I hope.'

It interested their lordships very greatly, as it proved.

Quite the most bitter reproaches that Spain hurled at the Court of St James's were reserved for the barbarism of the pirates who burned Panama, and the touching pride of Don Juan in this same destruction was a matter of sober delight to their lordships.

But they were inquisitive on other matters, and intolerably longwinded.

Had Henry received Sir Thomas Modyford's dispatches announcing the ratification of the treaty with Spain before he left his fleet rendezvous en route to Panama?

No, Henry had not.

Did the word Commander-in-Chief, in his commission from the Council of Jamaica, refer to his fleet, or was it a military commission permitting him to make war on land?

And so on.

And so on, through many summer afternoons; with the river light wavering on the ceiling and the Spanish ambassador sitting in an attitude of polite unexpectancy at the end of the table.

The cherry-leaves in the gardens were red before their lordships decided that there was nothing they could profitably or legally do to Henry Morgan. The Spanish ambassador would have to be disappointed.

The direct result of this whitewashing was an intimation that Admiral Morgan might now present himself at the Whitehall levee, and for eight successive mornings Morgan, dressed in his best, stood among the waiting crowd in the ante-room while the King moved down the line talking to a chosen few before disappearing to the outer world and his day's occupation. On the ninth day, bored by this vain repetition, he was late, and had just reached the outer door as the King began his progress down the line. And this time Charles's black eyes did not skim over him in passing. Charles stopped in the doorway.

'Admiral Morgan,' he said. 'I hear that you have been waging peace in the Caribbean.'

Not sure whether this was reproof or jest, Morgan bowed and was silent.

'I understand that sailors hate walking, but if a short walk in the park would not bore you unbearably, I should be glad of your company.'

So Harry Morgan went out to walk with his King in the park. And it was very soon apparent that this was no affair of a moment's impulse. Charles wanted to know about Jamaica. Poor Sir Thomas Lynch was very gloomy, he said, because they could not spare ships from the navy for the defence of Jamaica, and now he had no privateers for its defence. The privateers refused to come anywhere near Jamaica, because he confiscated their ships and set them to planting; they had all gone to Tortuga in the hope of commissions from the French.

'Sooner or later privateering must come to an end, Admiral. How are we to settle the men on the land and at the same time defend the island against possible attack?'

Henry said that was simple. Make no attempt to settle the men on the land. Let them be free to go into the logwood trade, using Port Royal without let or hindrance, and they would be there for use as a fleet whenever they might be needed.

'Sir Thomas is not very happy in his Governorship, he tells me. And yet he is a worthy man.'

Morgan said that Jamaica needed more than worthiness in a Governor. It needed someone above faction.

'Someone from England, you mean.'

Yes, Morgan meant just that.

'And whom do you suggest?'

But Morgan was not to be caught in the snare. He had been so little time in England, he said, that he might be excused from answering that.

And Charles looked amused. 'You fence as expertly as you fight, Admiral,' he said; and asked if the Admiral proposed to go back to Jamaica in the near future.

Morgan said that the choice was not his, since he was unfortunate enough to have a law-suit on his hands.

'Ah, yes,' said Charles, contemplative. 'The malice of small persons. So much more destructive than war. I wish you well, Admiral.' And he went back to talking of Jamaica; its crops, its climate, its possibilities.

So Morgan, having achieved the rehabilitation for which he had come to England, had now, on his own behalf, to struggle for a far more vital rehabilitation. The autumn mists hung about the trees and lay in the ditches, and his fever came back. That green and daisy-pied England that he had seen from a coach window seemed more compact of fantasy than any figment of his present fever. He had planned, during the hours of that summer journey, to take a coach once more across this jewelled perfection, to take a coach all the way to Wales, so that he might see Llanrhymny again. Now the roads of England were mire, and Llanrhymny merely a far place with a familiar name, and he yearned daily for the hot sun and the transparent seas and the wild fecund land of his adoption. He watched Romulus grow daily more wraith-like and if possible more silent, and by the end of November the boy's daily question had the sound of a knell.

'We go home tomorrow?' Romulus would ask, day after day.

'Not tomorrow, but soon,' Morgan would say. 'Very soon, Romulus.'

And he would watch the child with foreboding. If they did not go very soon he might have to go alone.

But out of this unhappiness there flowered unexpectedly two gratifications to be a solace to him. One was the lasting friendship of the boy Albemarle. ('I had never suspected Christopher of the crusading spirit!' Charles said, surprised by the boy's ardent partisanship.) The other was the fact that his sturdiest and most instant defence came from men who had no cause to love him. Indeed, two of the captains who had been most bitter about the division of the Panama spoils wrote, one from Bristol and one from Portsmouth, to refute the charges against Morgan totally and absolutely. And there were other, even more unlikely defences.

From the court of France, to Louise Kéroualle, came a letter from a young Spanish woman married to a Frenchman, who said that she had read in a Spanish translation a book purporting to give an account of the deeds of the English Admiral Morgan in Puerto Bello, and in view of the nature of this account she thought it right to send dear Louise a letter written by her mother during the occupation of Puerto Bello by Captain Morgan's men; in the hope that it might help to save a brave man from being traduced.

'We live very peaceably and comfortably, in spite of the English occupation,' wrote the dowager to her daughter in Spain.

'Indeed, to tell the truth, the last contingent of troops from home proved much more upsetting than Captain Morgan's men – except that they did not hold us to ransom. The good sisters are very peeved because their fine altar-plate has been scheduled as part of the levy, but I still have my diamond earrings – as the wretch did not fail to point out.'

But the most unexpected defence of all was forwarded from the Trade and Plantation offices. It had apparently been written to the writer's specification by some clerk, and the faultless copper-plate contrasted oddly with the sense of what was written.

> To Whom it May Concern (said the communication)
>
> Seeing that a damned Dutchman seeks to asperse an Englishman whose boots he isn't fit to lick, even if he is a bit too big for them, the Englishman, meaning the boots, this is to state that Captain Morgan is the damnedest scourge as to hard discipline that ever disgraced the sea with soldier notions. A man has more chance of raising hell round Portsmouth of a Saturday night than he ever has with Harry Morgan in the Indies, and if the writer ever meets the said damned Dutchman he will, so help him God, do things to him that Harry Morgan never thought of. He will do things to him that the Dutchman never thought of.

Underneath the beautiful copperplate of this, in a large, painstaking pen-and-ink scrawl, was the signature: Nick Gaytor.

Morgan had builded better than he knew when he had in the end decided to let Nick Gaytor's crew have their share of Maracaibo.

This document had been addressed to the Commissioners of Trade and Plantations, and having gone round the Colonial Office and provided amusement for all the civil servants, it went on to Morgan, and thence to his solicitor, John Greene; who filed it away against that case in the King's Bench at Westminster.

But the case was, after all, settled by consent. Mr William Crooke had no leg to stand on, and had the wit to know it. He agreed to publish the next edition prefaced by a full retraction and apology, to fork out substantial damages, and to pay the costs of the man he had injured.

'I ought to have taken him for all he had,' Morgan said to Modyford, reporting the result. 'I ought to have stopped the sale of the book.'

'You have,' said Modyford. 'Don't you know anything about human nature? No one will buy a book to read about horrors if it is prefaced by the announcement that there is not a word of truth in any of them. They like to think that the horrors really happened. Do you think Lord Carlisle would be a good person to keep our Jamaican Governorship warm until Christopher is grown-up enough for it?'

'Carlisle! Yes. Yes, indeed. Would he think of it?'

'I understand that he is not too averse to the idea. There is a lady from whom he would be glad to be separated by the width of a sea or two, it seems.'

'Excellency, is there *anything* in this world that you do not know?'

'Go away and talk Jamaica enticingly to Edward Howard.'

But alack, someone else had been talking enticingly to Lord Carlisle.

'Oh, that!' Carlisle said, when Morgan broached the subject. 'Yes, I did think of it, but Johnny wants to go.'

'Johnny?'

'Johnny Vaughan. He aches, it seems, to be a Governor. And Tilda has got herself a new protector, so my need to fly the town is less urgent than it was.' He caught Morgan's expression, and said: 'Don't you want Johnny?'

That was putting it inadequately; Morgan was appalled by the thought of Vaughan in Jamaica. But he could hardly say so to Carlisle.

'He's very biddable, you know,' Carlisle went on. 'He's so afraid of being in the wrong that he will do anything to avoid it. You'll find him quite easy. Anyhow, the King has agreed, so there is nothing much one can do about it now.'

But it seemed that Charles himself thought that there was something that might be done about it.

Admiral Morgan was summoned once more to Whitehall, and this time it was not to a levee, but to an audience.

'You will no doubt have heard, Admiral Morgan, that Lord Vaughan is going out to replace Sir Thomas Lynch as Governor of Jamaica,' Charles said; and cast a glance of secret amusement at the stony countenance of his most famous sailor.

Morgan managed a bow.

'Lord Vaughan is inexperienced in the duties of Governorship and ignorant of Jamaican affairs. I think it would be advisable to give him the assistance of a Lieutenant-Governor who is experienced in administration and has some acquaintance with the island.'

It would indeed be advisable, said the unrelenting Morgan.

'I know that with a young plantation on your hands your time must be very fully occupied, Admiral; but do you think that you might find sufficient spare time to undertake the duties of Lieutenant-Governor?' asked the King, toying with the sword that was lying across the papers on his desk.

Morgan stared at the sword, fascinated.

'Your Majesty —' he managed at last; and stuck.

Into the silence Charles said: 'You'll have your work cut out with Johnny. He'll slip through your fingers like water.' And he lifted the sword from the desk.

Morgan still had no words.

'It is customary,' Charles said, 'to knight a man when he is appointed to a Governor's place. I understand that you have been suffering sadly from rheumatism in our damp river airs, Admiral, but I shall not keep you kneeling for more than a moment.'

Morgan knelt.

'And that, Sir Harry, is an end of your privateering,' Charles said, putting out a hand to help Morgan to rise.

'Is that why Your Majesty did it?' asked Morgan, finding his tongue.

'No,' laughed Charles, 'though I should have liked to say that it was. I am sending you out to administer Jamaica because you have all the qualities. Jamaica is your own parish, and you are knowledgeable about it, but your horizons are too wide to allow you to become parochial about it. You are wonderfully popular, but you have the moral courage to risk that popularity if need be. You hate Spain, but you have the vision to compromise if it is to the larger advantage. And as an old privateersman, you seem to me the ideal person to deal with those backsliders who may find the logwood trade dull. *Bon voyage*, Admiral. I would give much to be slipping down the river with you; out to those coloured islands that I shall never see. Spare a thought for me as you pass.'

Morgan spared more than a thought. His eyes lingered a long time on the misty grey palaces of the north bank as his boat dropped downstream to join the ship that was waiting for him in the Downs. It was a clammy January morning, and he was shivering; but his heart glowed. With that sword-tap on his shoulder the King had completed his rehabilitation.

They had been prepared to offer him up as a sacrifice to Spain, the jacks-in-office, the party men. And they had been not only defeated, they had been disowned. That tap on the shoulder had been England's answer to Spain.

There remained now only 'the malice of small persons', and about that he could do nothing. Wherever there was achievement, there was that: the rats nibbling at reputation. The lying stories would go from mouth to mouth, on into the years, smirching his name; but the truth would be there still for those who wanted it. And there always, beyond argument and denigration, would be the fact that his King had knighted him and found him worthy to administer a province.

He watched London stream past and away from him, grey and magnificent and misty, and remembering the 'coloured islands' that waited for him knew that he would never come back. He would never see Llanrhymny now. It would stay small and clear and faraway, like something in the wrong end of a telescope. His future was in the islands; the islands across which he had written his name.

Presently Modyford, too, would be back in Jamaica, and life would be sunlit again.

As they left Greenwich behind a pale English sun, doing its best, shot a gleam across the water like a blessing.

But Morgan did not see it.

He was planning how he could give Vaughan's transport the slip in the Channel and outsail her to Jamaica, so as to have the Council nicely in his pocket before his outmanoeuvred countryman arrived.

AUTHOR'S NOTE

To write fiction about historic fact is very nearly impermissible.

It is permissible only on two conditions:

(*a*) That neither the inevitable simplification of plot nor the invention of detail shall be allowed to falsify the general picture;
(*b*) That the writer shall state where the facts may be found, so that the reader may, if he cares, compare the invention with the truth.

The definitive biography of Henry Morgan is by Brigadier-General E. A. Cruikshank: *The Life of Henry Morgan*; which can be obtained from any public library. It is dispassionate, exhaustive, and accurate, and will prove an excellent corrective to both fictional biographies and biographical fictions.

It is, further, advisable when writing fiction about a period now 'historic' that no distortion should take place owing to the use of 'period' dialogue. If the characters in the story did not sound quaint to each other, then they have no right to sound quaint to us. What a young man may actually have said to his patron may be: 'I am vastly gratified by your condescension, sir, and very sensible of my obligation to you,' but that is not how the words sounded to his benefactor. What his benefactor understood him to say was: 'Thank you very much, sir. That is very kind of you.'

Arthur Hailey

The book that remained for over six months on the American bestseller list, now filmed with a star-studded cast—

HOTEL 5/-

Against the background of a great New Orleans hotel move the characters—tycoons of the hotel industry, guests, and staff; men and women, young and old, dedicated and amoral—sealing their own destinies in five days of dramatic change.

'Compulsively readable' DAILY EXPRESS

THE FINAL DIAGNOSIS 5/-

The engrossing story of a young pathologist and his efforts to restore the standards of a hospital controlled by an ageing, once brilliant doctor.
'Probably the best and most potentially popular medical novel since *Not as a Stranger*'.
NEW YORK TIMES BOOK REVIEW

Arthur Hailey and John Castle

FLIGHT INTO DANGER 3/6

High over Canada a crippling emergency strikes an airliner—on the ground, helpless observers wait and pray . . . A brilliant novel of suspense in the air that enthralled millions as a TV play.

Angélique

'The intrepid, passionate and always enchanting heroine of the most fantastically successful series of historical romances ever written.'
DAILY HERALD

ANGELIQUE I: The Marquise of the Angels
ANGELIQUE II: The Road to Versailles
ANGELIQUE AND THE KING
ANGELIQUE AND THE SULTAN
ANGELIQUE IN REVOLT
ANGELIQUE IN LOVE

These novels by SERGEANNE GOLON (5/- each) comprise a tremendous saga of 17th-century France, tracing Angélique's career from childhood through a series of strange marriages and amorous adventures, perils and excitements, unequalled in the field of historical fiction. Translated into most European languages, a sensational runaway success in France, Angélique is one of the world's most fabulous best-sellers.

The most ravishing — and surely the most ravished — heroine of all time.